Opal Plumstead is fiercely intelligent: a proud scholarship girl, with plans to go to university. Yet her dreams are shattered when her father is sent to prison, and fourteen-year-old Opal must abandon school and start work at the Fairy Glen sweet factory.

Opal struggles to get along with the other workers, who think her snobby and stuck-up. But Opal idolizes Mrs Roberts, the factory's beautiful, dignified owner, who introduces her to the legendary Emmeline Pankhurst and her fellow suffragettes. And when Opal meets Morgan – Mrs Roberts' handsome son, and the heir to Fairy Glen – she believes she has found her soulmate.

But the First World War is looming on the horizon, and will change Opal's life for ever.

www.**randomhousechildrens**.co.uk

ALSO AVAILABLE BY JACQUELINE WILSON

Published in Corgi Pups, for beginner readers:
THE DINOSAUR'S PACKED LUNCH
THE MONSTER STORY-TELLER

Published in Young Corgi, for newly confident readers:
LIZZIE ZIPMOUTH
SLEEPOVERS

Available from Doubleday / Corgi Yearling Books:
BAD GIRLS
THE BED AND BREAKFAST STAR
BEST FRIENDS
BIG DAY OUT
BURIED ALIVE!
THE BUTTERFLY CLUB
CANDYFLOSS
THE CAT MUMMY
CLEAN BREAK
CLIFFHANGER
COOKIE
THE DARE GAME
DIAMOND
THE DIAMOND GIRLS
DOUBLE ACT
DOUBLE ACT (PLAY EDITION)
EMERALD STAR
FOUR CHILDREN AND IT
GLUBBSLYME
HETTY FEATHER
THE ILLUSTRATED MUM
JACKY DAYDREAM
KATY
LILY ALONE
LITTLE DARLINGS
THE LONGEST WHALE SONG
THE LOTTIE PROJECT
MIDNIGHT
THE MUM-MINDER
MY SECRET DIARY
MY SISTER JODIE
OPAL PLUMSTEAD
PAWS AND WHISKERS
QUEENIE
SAPPHIRE BATTERSEA
SECRETS
STARRING TRACY BEAKER
THE STORY OF TRACY BEAKER
THE SUITCASE KID
VICKY ANGEL
THE WORRY WEBSITE
THE WORST THING ABOUT MY SISTER

Collections:
JACQUELINE WILSON'S FUNNY GIRLS
includes THE STORY OF TRACY BEAKER *and*
THE BED AND BREAKFAST STAR
JACQUELINE WILSON'S DOUBLE-DECKER
includes BAD GIRLS *and* DOUBLE ACT
JACQUELINE WILSON'S SUPERSTARS
includes THE SUITCASE KID *and* THE LOTTIE PROJECT
JACQUELINE WILSON'S BISCUIT BARREL
includes CLIFFHANGER *and* BURIED ALIVE!

Available from Doubleday / Corgi Books, for older readers:
DUSTBIN BABY
GIRLS IN LOVE
GIRLS UNDER PRESSURE
GIRLS OUT LATE
GIRLS IN TEARS
KISS
LOLA ROSE
LOVE LESSONS

Join the Jacqueline Wilson fan club at
www.jacquelinewilson.co.uk

Jacqueline Wilson

OPAL PLUMSTEAD

VOTES FOR WOMEN

Opal's life has turned sour. Can she make it sweet again?

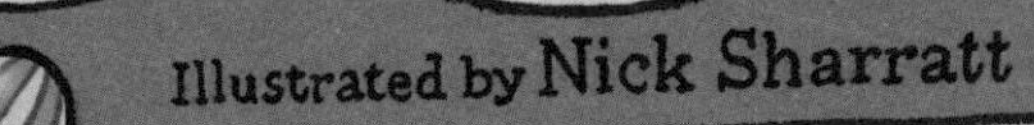

Illustrated by Nick Sharratt

CORGI

OPAL PLUMSTEAD
A CORGI BOOK 978 0 552 57401 3

First published in Great Britain by Doubleday,
an imprint of Random House Children's Publishers UK
A Penguin Random House Company

Doubleday edition published 2014
This edition published 2015

3 5 7 9 10 8 6 4

Printed and bound in Great Britain by Clays Ltd, St Ives plc

Set in New Century Schoolbook

Random House Children's Publishers UK,
61–63 Uxbridge Road, London W5 5SA

www.**randomhousechildrens**.co.uk
www.**totallyrandombooks**.co.uk
www.**randomhouse**.co.uk

Addresses for companies within The Random House Group Limited can be found at: www.**randomhouse**.co.uk/offices.htm

THE RANDOM HOUSE GROUP Limited Reg. No. 954009

A CIP catalogue record for this book is available from the British Library.

To dear Trish, who typed all thirty chapters for me.

1

'Do you believe in ghosts?' Olivia asked.

We were wandering through the graveyard, trying to find some privacy. Olivia had bought a pennyworth of Fairy Glen toffee chews and we were desperate to eat them. We had to be careful, though. Last week Miss Mountbank had caught us sucking sherbet on our way home from school. She'd pounced on us from a great height, her unfortunate nose more like a hawk's beak than ever, and had smacked us both on the back so violently that we choked. I spilled sherbet all down my school tunic. It was even worse for Olivia. She snorted in surprise and inhaled half her packet. She coughed uncontrollably, her eyes streaming, slime dripping out of both nostrils.

'How dare you eat in school uniform, you uncouth little guttersnipes!' Mounty shrieked.

She gave us detention the next day, shutting us in the classroom and making us write *I am disgustingly greedy and a disgrace to the whole school* in our best copperplate handwriting. She made Olivia write it out two hundred times. She gave *me* an extra fifty lines – 'Because you of all girls should know better, Opal Plumstead.'

I was top of the class. I couldn't seem to help it. It meant that some teachers liked me and made me their pet, while other teachers like Mounty seemed to resent me bitterly. I tried hard to make the other girls like me, but most of them despised me. They considered it shameful to be such a swot – though what else did they expect from a scholarship girl? I had been dreadfully lonely, but now I had Olivia and she was my best friend.

Olivia Brand came to St Margaret's last term and didn't quite fit into any of the little gangs of girls. She wasn't pretty enough to be popular – she was quite plump so that the pleats on her tunic were stretched out of place. She had a very prominent forehead. She looked as if someone were permanently pulling hard on her long frizzy plait. She wasn't from a desperately wealthy family. Her father was a buyer at Beade and Chambers, the big department store in town. This meant that Olivia was shunned by the lawyers' and doctors' daughters. She was very young for her age, liking to play little-girl games. When she was particularly happy, she would break into a lumbering skip. She was scornfully ignored by the sophisticated girls, who already had proper figures and pashes on boys.

For the first few days of term Olivia had blundered around by herself. She didn't make any overtures of friendship to me and I was too proud to. It was actually Mounty who brought us together. She paired us up in housecraft and had us sharing a worktop while we made rock cakes. We measured and mixed together, and I grinned sympathetically when Olivia couldn't resist having a sly nibble at our raisin allowance. We ended up with very bland rock cakes with scarcely any flavouring – but we'd become firm friends.

Now we went round arm in arm and wrote little notes to each other in class and walked home together every day. Olivia was given a weekly allowance. It was supposed to be for books and stationery and ribbons and stockings, but she spent most of it on sweets. She was a generous girl and shared them scrupulously with me, though I didn't get an allowance of any kind and couldn't reciprocate.

'Never mind – you're my best friend,' said Olivia. 'Of *course* we go even-stevens.'

She shook the bag of Fairy Glen toffees as if it were a tambourine until we skirted the church and threaded our way between the gravestones. I liked reading the quaint inscriptions and admired the stone angels, but Olivia seemed suddenly disconcerted.

'*Do* you believe in ghosts?' she repeated. She was peering around warily, staring at a broken sepulchre.

'Perhaps I do,' I said. 'Shush! Let's listen for them.'

'Ghosts don't *talk*,' said Olivia, giggling nervously.

'I think they might, if we're very receptive. Hush now, let's see.'

I made an elaborate show of putting my finger to my lips. Olivia clamped her hand over her mouth to stop herself spluttering. We waited.

A bird sang in the tree, repeating the same three trills again and again. Leaves rustled slightly in the breeze. There was a very distant rumble of traffic. Nothing else.

Then we heard a faint keening sound.

Olivia gasped and clutched me. 'Did you hear that?' she whispered.

'*Listen!*' I hissed.

Silence. Then it came again, soft, sad, yearning.

'Oh, there it is again. Quick, Opal, let's run. I don't like it,' Olivia cried.

Then she saw my face. 'It was *you*!' she said, and thumped me with her satchel.

'Of course it was me, idiot!' I said.

I hummed again, and Olivia put her hands over her ears.

'Stop it! It sounds so creepy. Stop, or I won't share my toffee chews.'

That shut me up effectively. I mimed buttoning my mouth and hitched myself up on a tomb, swinging my legs.

'All right, I've stopped now. Come on,' I said, patting the space beside me.

'I'm not sitting *there*, right on top of a dead person,' said Olivia.

'Well, they can't *do* anything, can they? Not if they're dead.' I looked again at the broken sepulchre, the stone lid crumbling away. 'Though perhaps I wouldn't sit on that one. They *might* just reach out a very bony hand and grab our toffee chews.'

'*Stop* it! I'm warning you, Opal Plumstead. I'll eat them all myself. Look!' Olivia sat down on the sandy pathway, undid a banana chew, and stuffed it into her mouth. She crammed in a raspberry chew as well, to emphasize her point.

'You're getting your tunic filthy – look,' I said.

'Don't care,' said Olivia indistinctly, her cheeks bulging.

'Let's sit on the grass,' I suggested.

'How do I know that the dead people haven't wriggled about a bit *under* the grass. The plots are so overgrown, you can't work out exactly where the graves are.' Olivia unwrapped another banana chew. They were my favourites. Sometimes there were only a couple in a whole bag.

'Pax!' I cried quickly, jumping off the tomb. I sat down beside her, not caring if I made my own tunic dirty, though I knew Mother would be angry.

Olivia ignored me, slowly unwrapping the banana chew, the tip of her tongue sticking out in anticipation. I edged closer to her, putting my hands up like paws and making beseeching panting noises.

'All right, you wicked greedy beast,' said Olivia, and she posted the banana chew into *my* mouth.

'Thank you!' I said, chewing vigorously, my whole mouth filled with the wonderful sweet banana flavour.

'You're such a tease. If you weren't my best friend, you'd be my worst enemy,' said Olivia. 'Just don't go on about g-h-o-s-t-s any more.'

'I don't believe in them, not really,' I said. 'I think when you're dead, that's it. You just moulder away in your coffin.' I pulled a silly corpse face, and Olivia shoved me again.

'What about angels?' she said, looking up at the stone figures around us, all standing on their white tiptoes, wings spread, as if about to fly away. 'I believe in angels. They're in Heaven.'

'I'm not sure I believe any of that any more,' I said. 'I think it's all just a trick to make us meek and good. Never mind if your life is awful now, if you have to toil away twelve hours a day in a factory and live on bread and dripping, you will be rewarded when you die and go to Heaven. Only what if Heaven doesn't exist?'

'Shush! You are dreadful. God could smite you down right this instant,' said Olivia. She looked up fearfully, as if she seriously thought a giant hand were about to punch its way through the clouds and pulverize me.

I swallowed the last of my banana toffee chew and looked at the bag hopefully.

'Another?' said Olivia.

'Oh, yes please!' I delved into the paper bag and found a strawberry chew this time. 'Well, you don't have to worry about Heaven, Olivia. If it *does* exist, you'll fly straight there, flippity-flap, because you're so good.'

'You will too,' said Olivia. 'You're ever so good. You always come top at school.'

'Yes, but that's just because I can do the lessons. That's nothing to do with being a good *person*. I'm not at all good at home. My mother says I'm a very bad girl.'

'Why, what do you do?' Olivia asked, looking very interested.

'It's not really what I do, it's what I *say*. I don't think the same way as Mother and Cassie,' I said. 'I'm always saying the wrong thing and vexing Mother. She fusses so over the slightest little thing – and yet she lets Cassie get away with murder. When I point this out, she says I'm just jealous of Cassie and I've got an unfortunate nature.'

Olivia sucked at her toffee chew. 'I wouldn't blame you if you were a bit jealous of Cassie,' she said. 'I mean, *I* would be if she were my sister.'

I had invited Olivia to tea after we'd vowed eternal friendship. She had clearly been expecting my sister Cassie to be another version of me, only slightly older – pinched and pale and plain, with mouse-coloured hair and little oval glasses. She was taken aback by Cassie, in all her irritating abundance: her long thick wavy fair hair, her big brown doe eyes, her round rosy cheeks, her extraordinary curves, her flamboyant gestures, her peals of laughter. Olivia sat opposite her at the tea table totally struck dumb; she could scarcely eat. She gazed at Cassie as if she were a turn at the music hall. I tried not to mind. I was used to Cassie having this effect on everyone. I found I *did* mind all the same. Rather a lot.

It hurt that even my very best friend was in awe of Cassie. She looked so dazzling that no one else seemed to notice how infuriating she was – the way she acted all the time, widening her eyes, licking her lips, winding a curl round and round her little finger. I saw her practising in the looking glass, peering at herself this way and that, her hand at her waist to emphasize the curves above and below.

No one else saw her first thing in the morning, scratching herself and yawning, sniffing at yesterday's stockings to see if they really needed washing, sticking her finger in the jam jar when Mother wasn't looking. No one else objected to the way she talked. She drivelled on and on about herself, debating what sort of shampoo she should use on her wretchedly abundant hair. She congratulated herself on having naturally pearly skin. She told us all about the fine gentlemen who winked at her admiringly on her way to and from Madame Alouette's. Mother encouraged her. She still brushed Cassie's hair for her, a hundred strokes every night, and made her little oatmeal messes to apply to her famous pearly skin. Mother tutted disapprovingly at the tales of winking gentlemen – but she seemed proud of their attention too.

'You've got the looks that will turn every man's head, Cassie,' she said, preening as if they were her looks too. 'But don't you go wasting yourself on the first Tom, Dick or Harry who comes along. You can aim much higher than any local lad. You just bide your time, my dear. No winking back, no giggling, no saucy remarks. You can't go getting a reputation now, or no one will want you, stunner or not. You need to act like a little lady at all times.'

'I'm not the slightest bit jealous of Cassie,' I told Olivia.

I was lying. I found Cassie incredibly irritating, and I didn't want to be like her, so lazy and vacant, never wanting to read a book or look at a painting. I certainly didn't envy her working at Madame Alouette's milliner's shop, stitching away at flimsy silks and satins and having to bob and curtsy to fancy ladies. I didn't want to be her in the slightest – but in my secret heart of hearts I had to admit I wanted to look like her. I didn't want the attention of all the silly young men. I didn't even want Mother fussing over me. But I did wish that Father would look at *me* with such helpless admiration in his eyes. He'd always seemed dazzled by Cassie too. But poor Father was so sad and self-absorbed now, he didn't look at any of us when he was at home. He kept his head bent and his eyes lowered and he hardly ever spoke.

'Cassie will make a lovely angel,' said Olivia. 'I can just see her in a long white dress with a halo above her gorgeous hair.'

'Cassie's no angel,' I said sourly, but the image was

in my head too. I rummaged in my school bag and found a notebook. I started sketching, showing Cassie with a devout expression, eyes wide, lips pursed, a halo attached to her hair like a little gold sunhat. I exaggerated her hair, letting it tumble all the way down to her bare feet, and I drew several young men prostrated before her, kissing her toes.

Olivia peered at my page and spluttered with laughter. 'Oh, Opal, you're such a hoot. That's *exactly* Cassie. You're so good at art.'

'Tell that to Miss Reed,' I said.

I loved to draw and paint, but art was my worst subject at school. I was used to getting ten out of ten in all my other lessons, but Miss Reed awarded me seven at best, and often gave me a disgraceful nought out of ten. She hated the way I drew.

'You've got the skills but you don't apply yourself seriously. Art isn't a *joke*, Opal Plumstead,' she said. She had some problem with her teeth and always unintentionally spat a little saliva at you if you stood face to face with her.

I *did* take art seriously, but I hated drawing the boring vases and boxes and leaf sprays she arranged as still-life compositions. I tried to sketch each object accurately, but my pencil had a will of its own. I executed the vase perfectly, but drew an exotic genie leaping out of it in a puff of smoke. I attempted the box and mastered its perspective, but then drew ropes of beads and gold coins spilling from its carefully shaded depths. I managed the leaf spray, noting every line on each separate leaf, then drew a miniature Jack climbing up the beanstalk I'd grown for him.

'I will *not* have you drawing this nonsense!' Miss Reed spluttered, and failed me each time. In fact, she sent me directly to Miss Laurel, the headmistress, when I drew the genie, because I'd pictured him in a loincloth and she felt this was obscene.

Miss Laurel lectured me at length, though the corners of her mouth had twitched when she saw my offensive drawing. 'You're a bright girl, Opal, and you generally work hard. Why do you have to be deliberately subordinate in your art lessons?' she asked.

I pondered. It was easy enough to do the work properly in all my other lessons. It was as if I set a little machine clicking away in my head. It solved the mathematical problem of the men digging holes in a field; it parsed the passage of English; it could trace the rivers and lakes in Africa without wavering. But somehow I couldn't *draw* mechanically. My mind took over and wanted its own way. I considered trying to say this to Miss Laurel but knew she wouldn't consider this an adequate explanation.

'I'm very sorry, Miss Laurel,' I said instead.

She shook her head at me. 'Then stop plaguing poor Miss Reed,' she said. 'And you're simply short-changing yourself, you silly girl. You need to get perfect marks in every subject if you want to matriculate. You seem like an ambitious girl. This is your chance to better yourself. You don't have to end up as a shop girl or a servant. If you really worked hard, you could even be a teacher at St Margaret's one day.'

A teacher like Miss Reed, Miss Mountbank, Miss Laurel herself! I didn't *want* to be a teacher, though everyone seemed to assume that this would be my ideal career, because I was good at lessons and had the knack of passing exams.

'What do you want to be when you grow up, Olivia?' I asked now.

She took another toffee chew and threw one to me. 'Mm, chocolate! I think I'll have my own sweet emporium. Imagine being able to munch and crunch all day long. No, I'll marry a man with a sweet shop, and then I won't have to stand on my feet and serve people. I'll just lounge on the sofa with a huge box of chocs and be the lady of the house. And I'll have two children, a boy and a girl, and we'll keep several servants to do all the work and it will be so jolly.'

'You'll be jolly *fat*, lying around all day stuffing yourself with sweeties,' I said, pulling her plait.

'Don't,' said Olivia, looking fussed. 'Do you think I'm fat now?'

'What?' I *did* think her fat, but I knew I couldn't

say so. 'Of course not, you loopy girl. You're just . . . comfortable.'

'Mother says I'm getting very tubby,' said Olivia. 'She's bought me this awful corset for Sundays. It's unbelievably uncomfortable. I can barely talk when I've got it on. It flattens my tum a bit, but I bulge out above and below it in a totally disgusting way. I couldn't even *move* after I'd tucked into my roast beef and Yorkshire pudding. Does your mother make you wear a corset for best, Opal?'

'I've got nothing to push up or push down,' I said, peering at my flat chest and sighing. '*My* mother keeps on berating me as if I'm being wilfully defiant in not growing bosoms, just because Cassie had a figure when *she* was fourteen.'

'Does Cassie wear a corset?' Olivia asked.

'Yes, but it's not one of those really *fierce* ones. It hasn't got proper bones.' I'd secretly tried it on, but it just looked ridiculous on me and I hated the cloying smell of Cassie on it, of powder and musk.

'Mother says I should be mindful of my figure now. She's stopped letting me have second helps of anything. She's so mean.'

'I'd swap her for my mother any day,' I said.

'Why do mothers have to be so difficult?' said Olivia. 'I shall be so lovely to *my* children. I shall let them eat their favourite meals every single day, always with second helps, and I'll buy my little girl an entire family of dolls and my boy will have a toy fort with a battalion of little lead soldiers. I will play with them all day long while the cook makes our meals in the kitchen and the maid does all the housework.'

'I hope you will let your servants have their favourite meals and give *them* second helps too,' I said.

I had been to tea with Olivia and observed her family's single servant, a skinny little mite with untidy hair tumbling out of her cap and dark circles like bruises under her eyes. I'd talked to her, asking her name and age and when she had left school as she served us lopsided sandwiches and little scones like stones. She had blinked nervously and mumbled her replies.

'I'm Jane, miss, and I'm thirteen years old, and I only went to school when I was small, miss, because I had to help Ma at home with the little ones.'

I was shocked to discover that Jane was younger than us. I wanted to find out more about her, but Olivia's mother was frowning at both of us. Poor Jane's hands started to tremble. She very nearly dropped a plate of bread and butter and poured half the tea onto the tablecloth. She murmured a desperate apology and fled the room.

'Oh dear,' said Olivia's mother. 'We've unsettled her.' She raised her eyebrows and said to me in a tone of gentle reproof, 'We don't usually ask personal questions of servants, Opal – at least, not when they're performing their duties.'

I felt my cheeks burn. I was terrified that Jane might be punished, all because of me. It seemed such a heartless rule. It was as if they weren't acknowledging that Jane was a girl, just like Olivia and me – and yet the whole family made a huge fuss of their two smelly spaniels, chatting to them in baby talk, rolling them over on their backs and petting them in a hugely embarrassing way.

Olivia had put her arm round me when we were ushered off to play cribbage in the parlour.

'Don't take too much notice of Mother – she can be very stuffy,' she whispered. 'And she's really very kind to Jane. She's training her carefully and she hardly ever gets cross when she makes mistakes.'

I wondered what it would feel like to be Jane. I knew I didn't want to be a teacher – but I certainly didn't want to be a servant, either.

'Oh Lordy, there are only three toffee chews left,' said Olivia now.

'You have them. They're your sweets, after all,' I said, though I hoped she wouldn't take me seriously.

'No, no, fair dos,' said Olivia. She gave me one – banana flavour! – and popped a strawberry chew in her own mouth. Then she bit hard into the remaining toffee.

'Careful! Mind your front teeth. You won't get that

husband of yours if you've got a great gap in your mouth,' I said. 'Here, let me.'

I had a go at severing the sticky toffee and was more successful than Olivia. We both chewed happily.

'What about *your* husband?' asked Olivia. 'What will he be like?'

'Oh, I don't think I want one,' I said.

'You have to have a husband!'

'No I don't. I don't think it would be congenial at all, having to flap around after a man. I'm not very keen on men, anyway,' I said airily, trying to sound sophisticated.

'Wait until you fall in love,' said Olivia, grinning.

'I don't believe in falling in love,' I told her. 'I don't believe in love itself. I think it's just a comfort story for adults. Children get to believe in fairies and Father Christmas – adults believe there's one true person out there. Your eyes meet, and that's it, you're in love.'

'But it's true. Of course you fall in love!' said Olivia. 'Look at Romeo and Juliet. See, even your boring old Shakespeare believed in true love.'

We were studying Shakespeare at school, but in the silly bowdlerized version considered suitable for young ladies. I'd taken a proper volume of Shakespeare's tragedies out of the library and had learned many passages by heart because I thought they were so beautiful. I'd chanted them at Olivia when I wanted to annoy her.

'Shakespeare was writing *poetically*. *Romeo and Juliet* is beautiful because of the words. It's ridiculous as a *plot*. It takes place over a matter of days – in which they're supposed to fall in love so passionately that they risk everything and then die for each other,' I said scornfully.

'You don't think it's like that for real people?' asked Olivia.

'No, I don't.'

'So why do so many people have sweethearts?'

'Because the young men *desire* the young women,' I said grandly, though I couldn't stop myself blushing.

I had very little clear idea what sweethearts did when that desire was consummated. Neither did Olivia. I knew that because we'd whispered and giggled over the conundrum many times. We both got the giggles now, choking over the last of our toffee chews.

'But there's more to love than that,' Olivia gasped at last. 'Haven't you ever felt all swoony over someone?'

'No!'

'Not Mr Andrews?' Olivia suggested slyly, smoothing out our sweet wrappers.

He was our music teacher, and he was tall and dark. He told us stories about all the tormented composers and played us extracts from their work on his Edison phonograph. I *did* like Mr Andrews very much.

'Go on! I bet you'd like to kiss Mr Andrews,' said Olivia.

That set us giggling again.

'Certainly not! Think how that moustache would tickle,' I said. 'Anyway, Mr Andrews has got a wife – I've seen her – and he seems very fond of her.'

'There! Husbands and wives love each other, silly,' said Olivia, twisting each toffee paper round her little finger, turning them into tiny glasses.

'They're fond at first – that's the passion. But it wears off. Think of our parents, Olivia – your mother and father and mine.'

We thought.

Olivia sighed, looking depressed. 'Well, I'll love my babies, even if I don't always love my husband,' she said. 'Let's drink to that.' She gave me a toffee-wrapper glass and we touched them together and pretended to drink. Then Olivia consulted her pocket watch. 'Cripes, look at the time! We're going to be in trouble.'

We stood up and ran helter-skelter out of the graveyard, all the way to our respective homes.

2

I lived in a house called Primrose Villa. It was a pretty name, but our home was small and stark, one of ninety-eight built in bright red brick in an ugly terrace. We didn't have any primroses in our garden – just a dusty privet hedge, a square of grass, and some puny rose bushes at the front. We had no garden at all at the back, just a bleak yard with a washing line and an outdoor WC. The word 'villa' implies a large, spacious house, but ours was the opposite. It had a meagre front parlour, a living room and kitchen downstairs, and two bedrooms and a box room upstairs.

Mother and Father had the bedroom at the front, Cassie had the room at the back, and I had the box room. It wasn't much bigger than a cupboard, but I didn't mind. It was *my* room, where I kept all my books and could nail my own choice of pictures on the walls. Mother favoured sentimental reproductions of children with fat cheeks and soulful expressions cuddling bug-eyed rabbits. I had reproductions of proper art in my room – soulful Madonnas in glorious cobalt blue cradling pale little Infants.

When I was nine or ten, I went through a fervently religious phase and decided I wanted to be a nun. I used to unhook the dark curtain from the parlour and parade around in my 'nun's habit', chanting psalms and doing my best to look holy. I had grown out of that phase now and tended to think religion a myth – though I still prayed when I felt despairing.

I longed for a proper desk in my room but it was too cramped. My bed and washstand and wardrobe nudged each other uncomfortably as it was. When I painted or did my homework, I had to sit bolt upright on my bed and balance a tray on my lap to make a flat surface. Once absorbed in my work I often relaxed, with disastrous consequences. The tray tilted and my water jar or inkpot spilled. Mother was furious.

She couldn't get the ink stains out, no matter how many times she laundered the sheets.

'Well, you'll just have to sleep in black sheets, you careless little missy. We can't afford to get you any new ones,' she hissed at me.

I didn't care. I'd have liked a black coverlet too, and maybe black wallpaper and a black painted ceiling. I liked the décor of deep mourning. Now that I was in my teens I'd developed a taste for Gothic literature and devoured *Dracula* and *Frankenstein*.

I sat down now, balancing the tray across my knees as best I could. I concentrated hard for an hour, doing two pages of algebra and an English comprehension. Then, for a second hour, I painted. I used sepia tones for extra effect, painting the graveyard. I drew the stone angels flying away from their plinths while skinny corpses crept out of their graves and gambolled in the grass.

I heard Mother calling for me intermittently but ignored her as long as possible.

'*Opal!*' she cried, bursting into my room. 'What's the *matter* with you?'

'Sorry, Mother, were you calling?' I said, trying to look innocent.

'You heard me, young lady!'

'I was engrossed in my painting.'

'What are you doing *painting*? What about your homework?'

'I've done it all – see,' I said, gesturing at my notebooks.

'Then you can come downstairs and help me make supper.'

'I don't think I want any supper today,' I said, truthfully enough, because the surfeit of toffee chews had made me feel a little queasy.

'Oh, that's so typical of you, only thinking of yourself. What about the rest of us? What sort of a daughter are you?'

'Can't Cassie peel the potatoes for once?'

'Poor Cassie's fingers are sore from stitching. *She's* done an honest day's work at Madame Alouette's.'

Cassie was an 'improver' at an expensive hat shop in town. It said it specialized in *the Finest Parisian Millinery* in curly writing on the shop sign – but none of the staff had ever set foot in Paris. Mother always pronounced Madame Alouette's name with proud emphasis, her tongue waggling, but Cassie told me that Madame only bothered to speak with a French accent in front of clients. Behind the scenes she was plain Alice Higgins from Walthamstow, though she was still as sharp as her own scissors if any of the staff gave her any cheek.

She was rarely sharp with Cassie, who was her favourite apprentice. She sometimes let her model new hats to show them off to clients.

When I stamped reluctantly downstairs to the

kitchen, Cassie was wearing silk flowers in her hair. They were deep purple with embroidered crimson centres and dark green leaves. They looked quite wonderful twined through her long red-gold hair.

'What do you think you are – a bridesmaid?' I said, pushing past her to the sink.

'Our Cassie will be a bride, not a bridesmaid,' said Mother. 'You look a picture, dear. Did Madame Alouette give you them?'

'They were left-over trimmings from some old dame's titfer,' said Cassie carelessly. 'Do you think they suit me, Opal?'

I rolled my eyes at her.

'I'll give you a couple if you like,' she said, smiling.

We both knew perfectly well that the flowers would look ridiculous stuck in my limp mousy locks.

'Oh yes, I'll twine them all round my specs. Then I'll look a picture too,' I said grimly, starting to peel the potatoes.

'Now now, no need to take that tone. Your sister's only trying to be kind,' said Mother. 'And watch those potatoes – you're peeling half the goodness away. Don't they teach you anything useful at that fancy school of yours? They fill your head with all sorts of silly ideas – they'd be far better training you up to be a decent little housewife.'

'I'm not going to *be* a housewife,' I said through gritted teeth.

'Well, you're certainly going to find it hard to catch a man with that sour look on your face,' said Mother. 'Don't you go filling your mind with daft daydreams, Opal. You don't want to end up like your father, do you?'

As if on cue, we heard Father's key in the lock of the front door. We listened to him shuffle into the hall, pause to hang his hat and coat on the hook, and then trail his way into the kitchen.

'Hello, my girls,' he said softly.

He looked exhausted, with dark circles under his bloodshot eyes, his face sickly pale. His economy paper collar had somehow come unbuttoned at the back and stuck out at a rakish angle. His old business suit was a size too big for him now, and drooped unbecomingly. He stood unfastening his boots, blinking in the gaslight.

'Hello, Father,' I said.

'Hey, Pa,' said Cassie.

Mother didn't greet him at all. She just tapped the large fat envelope on the corner of the kitchen dresser.

'Your post, Ernest,' she said, sniffing. 'Your chick's come home to roost again.'

I hated the way she said it. And I hated the way Father picked up the heavy envelope, held it to his chest for a moment, and then walked slowly out of the kitchen. We heard him trudge upstairs to the bedroom.

'Don't stay up there half the night brooding,' Mother called. 'Your supper will be on the table in half an hour.'

Mother and Cassie shook their heads at each other.

I glared at them. 'Why do you have to be so hateful to him?' I said fiercely.

'Now then, don't take that tone with me,' said Mother. 'Can't you show a little respect?'

'That's precisely my point. You're failing to show Father any respect whatsoever,' I said.

'I'll thank you to mind your own business,' said Mother. 'You think you know it all, Miss Clever-clogs, don't you?'

I felt I *did* know it all. I knew Father was a very clever man, much cleverer than me. He'd won a scholarship when he was a boy, taken his Higher Oxford exams and gone to the university. That was when he met Mother. Her parents owned a little stationer's supplying all the young gentleman scholars. She was only sixteen and I suppose she looked very fetching. It's difficult to imagine this, because now Mother is frankly stout, so tightly corseted she creaks when she moves, and her bright hair has faded to pepper and salt, scragged back into a tight bun that exposes the lines on her forehead. Even so, I can see that when she was a girl she might have had her fair share of Cassie's charm.

There was a courtship and then a hasty marriage, disapproved of by both sets of parents. Cassie and I had never met any of our grandparents. Father didn't get to finish his degree. He had to go and teach in an elementary school, which he hated. He had been a silent, scholarly child. He couldn't understand these rough rowdy pupils. He couldn't control them at all. It made him so ill that he had to stop work altogether for a while.

He started writing when he was lying in bed at home – first tortured confessional pieces, and then fiction, though this was frequently autobiographical. He also wrote children's stories for Cassie and me. They were melancholy moral tales about little children who misbehave once and consequently suffer terrible disasters and death. Cassie didn't like these tales and put her hands over her ears and chanted la-la-la so she couldn't hear. I couldn't get enough of them, and begged Father to tell me the tale of the boy who ran into the road and got trampled to death by horses, or the story of the little girl who went paddling in a stream and fell into deep water and drowned.

'Stop telling the children such morbid nonsense!' Mother said, whenever she overheard.

Perhaps she'd thought the world of Father once, when he was a varsity man and seemed to have prospects. She was full of resentment now. It seemed so unfair, because he was always the sweetest man with the mildest manner, even when she shouted at him. He tried very hard to sell his stories, but without any success so far.

He took a position as a clerk in a shipping office in London. He bent over his desk nine hours a day, entering information in a big ledger, to try to clear our debts. He wrote his stories in the evening after supper. He had a large callous on the middle finger of his right hand from all his penmanship, and developed a permanent headache, so that he often held a cold wet cloth to his temples.

I hated to see him so afflicted. At times I couldn't help wishing that he was an ordinary father, a bouncy red-cheeked shop man like Olivia's, who always had a chirpy quip and walked with such a spring in his step that his boots tapped out a tune on the pavement. Then I felt guilty and tried even harder to be a sympathetic daughter, though at times I wanted to seize him by the shoulders and give him a serious shaking.

When supper was ready (sweetbreads and onions and mashed potatoes, an unattractive meal that made me shudder), I said I'd fetch Father.

'That's right, ginger him up, Opal. And take that look off your face. I dare say you'd prefer a prime cut of steak, but beggars can't be choosers.'

'But why do we have to have *sweetbreads*, Ma?'

said Cassie, for once winking in sympathy with me. 'They're cow's innards, all slimy and disgusting! You chew and chew, and you still can't swallow them.'

'You girls should be grateful I stand sweet-talking the butcher so he'll save me the cheaper cuts,' said Mother indignantly. 'He's promised me a sheep's head for the weekend.'

Cassie and I made simultaneous vomiting noises and I ran upstairs to Father.

He was sitting on the side of his bed, his rejected manuscript on his knee. He had a dazed expression on his face.

'Please don't take on so, Father. All the publishers are fools. I think you're a brilliant writer,' I said earnestly.

He wasn't listening to me. He was reading a letter.

'Is that from the publishers?' I asked. Father didn't usually even get a letter, just a rejection slip.

He nodded. He started to speak, but his voice came out as a croak, and he had to begin again. 'From Major and Smithfield,' he whispered. He held the letter close, as if checking it. 'They *like* it, Opal! They truly like it!'

'But . . . but they've still returned it?'

'Only for a few trifling corrections. They suggest a different twist to the plot, and a more dynamic opening chapter. Yes, I understand – I can do that easily.'

'And then they say they'll *publish* it?'

'If I re-submit my manuscript, then they say they will reconsider it. It's very cautiously put, but that's what they mean! Oh, Opal, they truly like my novel.'

'I'm so happy for you, Father!' I threw my arms around his neck and hugged him tightly.

'If you only knew how much this means to me,' he murmured into my hair.

'I *do* know, Father. I'm so proud of you.'

'Wait till your mother hears!' said Father. He stood up, clasping my hand. 'Let's go and tell her.'

We clattered down the stairs, both of us wanting to be first in the kitchen, jokily pushing and shoving each other as if we were little children.

'Mother, Mother, guess what!' I shouted from the hall.

But Father gently elbowed me out of the way and reached the kitchen before me. 'It's astonishing news, Louisa!' he said. He hardly ever called Mother by her full name – she was always 'Lou', or 'my dear'.

'What?' said Mother, pausing in her serving of the sweetbreads.

'What what what indeed!' Father took the stewing saucepan out of her hand, placed it back on top of the range – and then picked her right up! He was a slight man and Mother was stout, but he seized her as if she were a sack of feathers and whirled her about the kitchen.

'Put me down, you fool!' Mother screamed. Her cheeks were bright pink, and half her hair came tumbling down so that she looked almost girlish again.

Cassie screamed too and clapped her hands at the extraordinary sight. 'What is it? What's happened to Father?' she cried.

'His novel's going to be published!' I shouted.

'Truly?' Mother gasped.

'I have to make a few minor alterations, but then, yes, truly! Your hopeless old Ernest has done it at last!' said Father, and he kissed her on the tip of her nose.

'How much are they going to pay you?' Mother asked.

'They don't specify a sum. I'm not sure what the going rate is,' said Father.

'Charles Dickens got paid a fortune,' I said.

'Yes, but I'm hardly Mr Dickens,' said Father. 'Perhaps I'll get . . . twenty-five guineas . . . Maybe fifty if they're really enthusiastic! And then there will be royalties if the book sells well.'

'Of course it will sell well!' said Mother, astonishing us all. 'Oh, Ernest, I'm so proud of you.'

Father set her down tenderly and gave her a proper kiss on the lips. He had tears in his eyes. Cassie and I exchanged glances, open-mouthed.

'We need to celebrate in style,' Father said, setting

Mother aside at last. 'I'll go out and buy a bottle of wine. I'll be back in two ticks.'

'Get champagne!' said Mother.

Father really did buy a whole bottle of champagne – and a great parcel of cooked fish and fried potatoes.

'But we have sweetbreads,' Mother protested faintly.

'We're not celebrating with cows' doo-dahs,' said Father, setting out the golden food upon four plates.

'Oh, Father, this is a meal fit for kings,' said Cassie.

'Fit for *literary* kings,' I said.

Father popped the cork of the champagne and poured the sparkly liquid into four crystal glasses. They were a wedding present, never yet used. It said they were sherry glasses on the presentation box – as if we cared.

'Here's to clever Father,' I said, holding my glass high.

We all drank to his success and devoured our splendid meal, while the sweetbreads stayed in their pan. None of us were used to drinking alcohol, so we started laughing uproariously at the silliest things, and planning in detail the life we would lead once Father became truly rich and famous.

'Now hold on, it hasn't happened yet,' he said.

'But it will, my dear, I know it will,' said Mother, reaching out and squeezing his hand. 'You'll be able to give up your position at the shipping office and live like a gentleman. You'll simply go to work each day in your study.'

'But Father doesn't have a study,' I said.

'He will, once we move. Oh, to think we've a chance to better ourselves at last! We'll rent a much bigger house – maybe one of those grand new villas overlooking the park,' said Mother dreamily.

'Hey, hey, not on fifty guineas' income,' said Father.

'But that's just this first novel to be published. You've written many more, haven't you? Maybe they'll publish them too. I'll say this for you, Ernest, you've persevered all these years with little encouragement. God bless you, my dear,' said Mother, sounding choked.

A tear slid down Father's cheek.

'God bless you too, dearest Lou. And Cass and Opal. I don't think we'll be moving out of Primrose Villa just yet, but we can certainly indulge in a few little luxuries at last. Once I get that cheque you shall all have a trip to the dressmaker's to order yourselves fine new outfits.'

'Oh *yes*, Father, and new boots too, and gloves – and maybe one of my own hats!' said Cassie.

'Blue silk,' Mother breathed, plucking at her brown worsted skirt.

'Can I have a new paintbox instead of a dress?' I begged. 'One with thirty-four paints in the palette, like the one I saw in Gamages last Christmas?'

'You can have all these, my girls,' said Father, spreading his arms wide.

3

Father set to work that very night, correcting and amending his manuscript. Mother tiptoed up the staircase every so often to see how the work was progressing. She refreshed his genius with cups of tea. She even prepared a cold flannel in case his forehead was burning. They were still toiling in their different ways long after Cassie and I went to bed.

I was too happy to go to sleep, and Cassie felt the same. After half an hour or so, she crept out of her room and into my cupboard.

'Budge over, Opie,' she said, clambering in beside me.

'There isn't enough room for me, let alone the two of us,' I said, but I put my arms around her as she squeezed under the sheets.

We hadn't cuddled up like this since we were little girls and it felt very cosy, though Cassie's abundant hair tickled my nose and her great curvy body was squashing me.

'Fancy our pa getting a book published!' Cassie murmured.

'I always knew he would,' I said, which was a total lie. I'd always *hoped* he would, but it had never seemed remotely likely.

'You can't seriously want a boring old paintbox instead of a new outfit,' said Cassie. 'Look, I'm sure Father will let you have both. So what colour and style of dress will you choose?'

'I don't want a new dress. I'm not interested in clothes,' I said.

This was a lie too. I was acutely aware of fashion. On rare train trips to London I stared at the young ladies trit-trotting elegantly about in their little heeled shoes, in their spotted silks, their lace-trimmed stripes. I marvelled at the colours of their costumes: subtle sage, soft violet, dusky blue. I was confined to my harsh schoolgirl navy. But it was the shape of modern costumes that unnerved me. They were soft and clinging, emphasizing the bust and clutching the small waists. I didn't see how I was ever going to acquire the right shape, whereas Cassie in her plain white nightgown showed it off effortlessly.

'Don't you want to look pretty, Opie?' said Cassie. She said it softly, but there was a tinge of smugness in her tone. She knew that all the fine dresses in the world would never make me pretty. Part of me wanted to kick her right out of bed – but it was so comfortable, the two of us curled up together.

'I don't want to look pretty, I want to look artistic,' I said. This gave me an idea. 'Perhaps I shall go to Liberty in Regent Street. I've seen their advertisements in the newspaper. They have long flowing dresses in beautiful fabrics.'

'No, you don't want one of *those* – you'll look weird,' said Cassie.

'Then I'll stick to my tunic.'

'Honestly! I don't know how you can bear still being at school – and St Margaret's is such a frightful school too, all lumpy girls and old-maid teachers. I wouldn't have gone there for all the tea in China.'

Cassie *couldn't* have gone there because she'd never have passed the scholarship examination, and Father wasn't rich enough to pay – well, until now.

'You don't want Father to pay for you to go back to school?' I said. 'Or you could go to a special girls' college and learn to cook and arrange flowers and how to dress.'

'What nonsense! I don't want to cook, I can make flowers and I know very well how I want to dress.'

'So you want to stay on at Madame Alouette's?'

'Not for ever.' Cassie stretched out in bed, nearly tipping me out. 'I'll meet some fine gentleman—'

'Rich, and foolish enough to be very indulgent, I suppose,' I said.

'Not foolish. I want someone who can master me,' said Cassie.

'You've been reading too many trashy romance novels,' I told her. 'Do you picture yourself lying on a tiger skin like Elinor Glyn?'

'Oh yes!' she said. 'That would be thrilling.'

'And your dark lover will thrust you upon his white stallion and ride off with you into the desert . . .'

'*Yes!* Oh, go on, Opal, this is good! Tell it like a story.'

I made up a whole load of nonsense, though it kept Cassie enthralled. I floundered a little when I came to describing actual embraces, but Cassie didn't know much more than me about the mysteries of the bedroom, for all she pretended to be so worldly wise. We ended up giggling helplessly and went to sleep with our arms around each other.

It was strange feeling close to Cassie when we usually fought like cat and dog. It was as if a spell had been cast over our whole family. Breakfast was usually a sullen, hasty affair, with Mother, still in her nightgown, nagging at us to get a move on. Poor Father would have trudged off to the railway station breakfast-less long before.

Breakfast the next morning was very different. Mother was neatly dressed but with her hair still down, which made her look strangely young and girlish. There were eggshells and toast crumbs and a tea-stained cup at Father's place, so she'd obviously got up early and made him a meal. She made Cassie and me breakfast too – just tea and bread and butter, but she sprinkled sugar on our slices too, which had always been a long-ago little-girl treat.

I set off for school with a new spring in my step. I usually made up stories in my head to entertain myself on the long walk through the town, blush-making fantasies of living in an alternative family where I was the prettiest and most popular sister, but I didn't feel the need to do that today. I was happy to daydream about my own family now.

In the playground I seized hold of Olivia and said excitedly, 'You'll never guess what! My father's going to be a published author! Yes, he really, really is. Imagine – in a matter of months we'll be able to go into a bookshop or a library and see his name on a book jacket!'

'How lovely,' said Olivia, but she sounded more polite than genuinely thrilled.

I suppose it was because she didn't set much store by books. I read avidly, racing through the latest E. Nesbit one day and then happily tackling Hardy or H. G. Wells the next. Olivia was reluctant to try any adult novels, and even found Girl's Own annuals hard work. I loved her dearly and was very grateful to have a best friend at last, but inside my head I sometimes couldn't help wishing I could find a true soul mate. I imagined discussing books and art and sharing ideas. I grew impatient with myself because I knew this was a silly dream, as ridiculous in its way as one of Cassie's desert romances.

The only people who knew more than me about books and art were the teachers who taught these subjects at school. The idea of discussing anything with Miss Reed was ludicrous. Perhaps she was knowledgeable, but I disagreed violently with her opinions. She particularly admired seventeenth-century landscape paintings, all muddy browns and dreary greens. She thought anything with colour and drama was vulgar.

Miss Peterson taught us English, mostly Shakespeare. I *liked* Shakespeare, though it was sometimes hard work unknotting his elaborate sentences to discover their full meaning. I felt a little thrill each time I deciphered a passage, and I loved the sound of the words, even when I had only a hazy understanding. Miss Peterson didn't just like

Shakespeare, she loved him with an embarrassing passion. She read poetic passages aloud in a throbbing, ardent manner, letting her voice swoop up and down as if she were singing scales, and threw her arms about in wild gestures as if conducting herself simultaneously. We always had to bite the insides of our cheeks and press our lips together to stop ourselves bursting out laughing. I couldn't possibly discuss Juliet or Miranda or Rosalind with her.

I found myself telling the *least* likely teacher about Father's success – Miss Mountbank. In housecraft, I hadn't been concentrating while preparing my dish of baked apple. I let the custard burn for lack of stirring and I forgot to cut round the skin of my apple before baking it. It exploded with extraordinary force, spattering the inside of the oven.

'You hopeless fool, Opal Plumstead! I *told* you to prepare the apple properly. Now look at the mess. What were you *thinking* of?'

'I'm so sorry, Miss Mountbank. I – I was thinking about my father, who has just received such exciting news. He's going to have a novel published!' I declared.

Miss Mountbank seemed even less impressed than Olivia. 'Is that so?' she said, handing me a cloth and scouring powder. 'Or are you telling stories again?'

'I don't tell lies, Miss Mountbank,' I said sharply.

'I dare say that's a lie in itself,' she said. 'I've never

known such an insubordinate girl. Come along – you can start scrubbing as soon as the oven cools down. Meanwhile you can clean all the work surfaces as a punishment. You can also write me two hundred lines after school: *I must not daydream*.'

I daydreamed intensely while writing out my two hundred lines, devising hideous tortures for Mounty. I beat her about the head with her ladle, I buttered her vigorously, I baked her in her own oven. I must have had a smile on my face thinking this, because Mounty suddenly rose from her desk and approached me.

'This isn't a laughing matter, Opal Plumstead,' she hissed. 'You will do another hundred lines.'

'Then it's a *crying* matter,' I muttered.

'What did you say?' she demanded.

'I was just talking to myself, Miss Mountbank.'

'You think you're so superior, you silly little girl. You'll get your come-uppance one day, just you wait and see.' She spoke with real venom, her little eyes black beads of hatred, her great nose as sharp as any beak. It was if she were some ancient crone of the dark arts, cursing me. I couldn't help shivering, even though I knew she was just awful old-maid Mounty, the worst teacher in the school.

I had a roaring feeling in my head and my eyes were stinging, almost as if I were about to burst into tears. I blinked hard, willing myself not to break down in front of her. She had no real power over me.

I might be singularly untalented when it came to housecraft, but what did that matter? I wasn't intending to become a cook when I grew up. It seemed doubtful that I'd ever be able to afford a cook myself, but I didn't care. I certainly wasn't going to spend my time stirring sweetbreads. I'd buy my hot food, fish and fried potatoes, with Fairy Glen sweets for dessert. I might grow so fat I'd burst right out of my corsets, but who cared? I didn't want to wear them anyway. I'd lumber around happily in a capacious artistic robe and all my large bits could lollop around within, totally untethered.

I cheered myself up enough to complete the extra set of lines and handed them to Miss Mountbank. She kept me a further five minutes, going through each and every line. Her eyes darted from side to side, desperate to find a 't' uncrossed or a 'y' without a proper tail so she could set me the task all over again, but my penmanship was perfect.

'Very well. Run away now. I dare say you have interesting duties at home now, putting new nibs in your father's pen and keeping him supplied with blotting paper, seeing as you say he's going to be a published author.' She spoke in tones of withering sarcasm.

'That's quite right, Miss Mountbank,' I said blithely, and then marched out of the room before she found an excuse to detain me further.

I was terribly touched to find Olivia playing a listless game of bouncy-ball-on-a-string in the playground.

'Oh, Olivia, you waited for me!' I said, hugging her. 'But I've been *ages*.'

'I know,' she said, rolling her eyes. 'It felt like twenty-four hours at least. Did the old bat give you extra lines?'

'A hundred more. She hates me.'

'Well, I love you, and you're my best friend ever, so let's go to the sweetie shop because I have more funds.'

We deliberated long and hard in Mr McAllister's sweet shop, debating the various merits of pear drops and aniseed balls, but I eventually steered Olivia in favour of lime drops, my particular favourite.

'Amy in *Little Women* got into trouble for sucking limes at school,' I said. 'But I think that was the real fruit.'

'I've never read that book,' said Olivia.

'Oh, you *must*. I'll lend you my copy.' I was always lending Olivia my few books, but she didn't always read them even then.

'What's your father's book about?'

I realized I wasn't quite sure which novel the publishers had taken. Was it the story about the impoverished student at university? The tome about the daily grind of factory workers? The modern fable about all the animals escaping from London Zoo? I'd read all Father's manuscripts. I gave Olivia a little précis of each book, trying to make them as dramatic as possible to hold her interest. I impersonated half a dozen stampeding wild animals when I came to the last story, which made Olivia laugh so much she swallowed her lime drop and I had to thump her hard on the back to stop her choking.

When I got home, there was a wonderful rich smell flooding the kitchen. Mother was making pastry, up to her elbows in flour. She even had a smudge of flour on her pink cheeks.

'I'm making a steak pie. It's your father's favourite,' she said.

'Steak!' I exclaimed.

'I don't have to settle with the butcher until next month, and then hopefully Father will have his cheque,' said Mother.

She'd clearly bought a lot of items on tick. There was a bottle of port wine and new crystal glasses on the table, a board of cheeses and a big bunch of purple grapes.

Cassie had spent even more of the money we hadn't yet got. She came home wearing an amazing green silk dress that set off her red-gold hair to perfection.

'Oh, Cassie, you look a picture!' said Mother.

'I've never seen you in such a fetching dress. But however much did it cost?'

'It's all right, Mother, don't fuss. I got it for a song. I just popped into Fashion Modes in my lunch break, and they were having a special sale of all their slightly shop-soiled dresses. It was half price, I swear,' said Cassie, swishing up and down the hot kitchen.

'But even so . . .' Mother said weakly.

'Madame Alouette herself said the dress might have been made specially for me. I'm paying it off weekly, don't worry, and I'm sure Father will help me out,' said Cassie, smiling at her reflection in the saucepan.

Father had been extravagant too. He came home with a positive armful of presents: a big bunch of roses for Mother, a fancy box of Fairy Glen fondants for us all to share and, bizarrely, a little blue budgerigar in a cage.

We all squealed at the bird. Cassie and I were thrilled, but Mother was clearly not so keen.

'What on earth is that creature doing in my kitchen?' she said, sounding like her old self again. 'You know I can't bear birds, Ernest.'

'I know you don't like pigeons, dear, or gulls, or starlings or sparrows – but this is a songbird, Lou. I saw it in the market on my way home, and when I heard what they'd taught it to sing, I knew I had to have it. Listen now. *Listen!*'

Father cocked his head towards to the cage, as if he fully expected the budgerigar to trill an operatic aria. The bird flapped its wings on its tiny perch, beak closed.

'Never mind, Father, it's still very pretty,' I said quickly.

'I'll teach it to sing,' said Cassie. 'Come on, little birdy. *The boy I love is up in the gallery . . .*

The bird hopped off its perch and looked around pointedly.

'I think it's tired and hungry,' I said. 'Let's give it something to eat and drink and let it rest.'

'Let *us* eat and drink, seeing as I spent the last two hours slaving in the kitchen to make your favourite supper,' said Mother, still a little irritated.

I fetched the bird some water in a little dish and Father brought out a packet of birdseed from his pocket. Cassie and I discussed names for the budgerigar. I fancied calling him something poetic, to suggest a creature with wings – Puck, Cobweb, Ariel, Peaseblossom.

Cassie spluttered derisively. 'He's Billy the budgie,' she said, and somehow that name stuck.

Billy settled down in his cage while Mother served her great steak pie. We were so distracted by its savoury splendour that we almost forgot the little bird, but while we were all eating fondant creams and grapes for pudding, Billy suddenly threw back his head and sang.

'*Happy days!*' he trilled, as clear as anything. '*Happy days, happy days, happy days.*'

'You see!' said Father, terrifically pleased. 'You see why I had to buy him, my girls. These are *our* happy days at last!'

We hugged Father, all three of us, while Billy chirruped his one little phrase relentlessly all evening, until Mother put the chenille tablecloth over his cage when it was time for us to go to bed.

4

They were truly happy days. Father settled himself to work on rewriting his novel about the lacklustre life of a shipping clerk straight after supper and carried on cheerfully halfway through the night. Mother stayed up with him, bringing him tea and lemonade and weak whisky, as if his talent needed constant watering. After several nights of feverish activity they both slept in. Cassie and I were late for work and school, and Father was spectacularly late for the shipping office.

Mother was agitated, especially when Father told her that evening that he'd been given an official warning.

'They told me if I'm ever as late again they will halve my wages – and a third time means instant dismissal,' he said.

'Oh, Ernest!'

'Don't look so anxious, Lou! I won't be needing the wretched position much longer, will I? I very nearly told them to stick their job then and there, but I just about managed to be prudent. But I reckon if the publishers accept one more novel, then I can stop the daily grind altogether and become a free man.'

'Of course, of course, but meanwhile it's best to be careful,' said Mother, though she had just treated herself to a fancy Japanese workbasket. It was fitted out with household tape, assorted pins and needles, a tiny pair of scissors with blades in the shape of a bird's beak, three skeins of darning wool and twenty coloured cottons. Mother didn't even like sewing, and put off darning our socks and stockings till we had great potato holes, but she couldn't resist the novelty Japanese basket. She especially liked the scissors, and sat opening and closing them with a little smile on her face, like a child with a new toy.

Cassie was rather put out. '*I'm* the seamstress of the family, Ma! I'm a professional! Why can't I have a workbasket like that?'

'You can have my old workbasket, dear,' said Mother.

Cassie wrinkled her nose, making it plain what she thought of that idea.

'You shall have a new workbasket too, Cassie,' said Father magnanimously. He dug into his pockets and brought out two ten-shilling notes. 'Here you are, girls – one each.'

'But Ernest—' Mother protested.

'Don't worry, Lou. I'll take out a little loan of cash to ease things along until I get my advance from the publishers.'

'But . . . is that wise?'

'Now then, dear, you must leave all money matters to me,' said Father.

He had a new authority in the family now. He even seemed to stand taller and walk more briskly, though he was still pale from lack of sleep, with dark circles under his eyes.

Cassie came home the next day with a beautiful Japanese lacquer haberdashery box. It had an intricate pattern of birds and flowers on the shiny black top, and a special fitted lift-out tray with little cotton-reels tucked neatly into place.

I liked sewing even less than Mother, but I felt ferociously envious of that glorious box, and it didn't help when Cassie produced a casket of otto violet soaps that she'd bought with the change. The soap for general use in our house was harsh red carbolic. The ugly smell lingered for hours after every wash.

'*My* personal soap,' said Cassie, sniffing her delicate pale purple tablets. She kept them in her dressing-table drawer, taking them backwards and forwards to the sink, because she didn't trust anyone else not to use them.

I longed for my own japanned box and fragrant soap, but I held true to my own vision. I waited until Saturday and dressed in my Sunday best frock, deep green with black buttons all the way down to the hem. It made me look very sallow and the long skirt was too tight for me to stride out comfortably, but I hoped it added a year or two to my age.

I told Mother I was going to spend the day at Olivia's house. I didn't go anywhere near my friend. I needed to make this expedition by myself. I'd decided to go all the way to London.

The journey was easy enough. I knew Father's route to work, and in the past we'd made several family trips to the West End to see the Christmas decorations. I took the local bus to Putney, changed to a number 14, and caught a number 81 at Piccadilly Circus, travelling at the front of the top deck with the wind blowing my hair. Little boys breathed down my neck, wanting to bag the front seat for themselves so that they could pretend to drive the bus, but I wouldn't budge. I stared round-eyed at all the sights, envying Father for taking this magical trip to London every day, though I knew he hated commuting. I had no clear idea of direction, and several times panicked a little, wondering if the bus was going the right way, but in Holborn I spotted the great Gamages department store at last, and shot down the steps.

I wandered aimlessly around the store for half an hour, seduced by all the wonderful things on display. The toy department was especially beguiling. I was too old for toys, of course, and I didn't particularly care for the French and German china dolls with their disconcerting haughty expressions, but I loved the soft toys, particularly the expensive stuffed animals – the monkey, the cat, the Welsh terrier and the wonderful jointed white polar bear. I couldn't help handling them each in turn. I set the monkey capering, I made the cat mew and the dog bark, and I took the polar bear for an amble along the glacier of the glass counter.

I loved the miniature worlds too – the grocer's shop with its jars and packets and tiny scales, and the farmyards with their finger-sized sheep and cows and goats. Most of all I loved the big Noah's Ark. I took off its red roof and saw all the animals stabled two by two in compartments, the fierce creatures with sharp teeth prudently separated from the small and the fluffy. I had always ached for a Noah's Ark as a child: I imagined carrying it to the park on a rainy day and setting it to sail on the duck pond. I looked at the price tag, but, alas, it was twenty-three shillings and sixpence, much more than I could afford. I mustn't get diverted anyway. I was here to buy a paintbox.

I went to look at the painting sets in the toy department, but they only had little tins of eight colours, the same as my one at home.

'Don't you have any bigger tins?' I asked the young male shop assistant.

'Of course, madam,' he said.

This nearly started me giggling like a fool, because it was the first time anyone had ever addressed me as 'madam'. I struggled to compose myself as he gave me instructions on how to get to the art department.

Oh, that art department! It was total heaven. I wouldn't have been surprised if I'd spotted great celestial beings with wings gliding about the easels and sketching pads and the huge boxes of paints.

I was tempted to try oil paints like a real artist, but I knew Mother would never stand the smell in our small house. I looked at water colours – glorious boxes of Landseer and Winsor & Newton. I fingered the japanned tins, but then I was distracted by gleaming mahogany boxes with brass clasps. They had *thirty-six* pans of paint, with fine brushes and a water glass and a fat tube of Chinese white. There was a nine-shilling box, the exact sum I had in my pocket bar the sixpence I needed in bus fares to get home.

It seemed like an omen. I *had* to have that paintbox.

Another assistant wrapped it carefully for me. 'It's quite heavy, madam. If you've other purchases to make today, you could always use our delivery service.'

'No thank you. I shall carry it easily,' I said.

I didn't want to be parted from my glorious paintbox for a second. I'd paid for it and it was truly mine.

I'd planned to do a little sightseeing while I was in London, but my skirt seemed to have got even tighter, hobbling my knees, and my best boots were a little small for me now so that my toes were crammed painfully against the leather. I was hungry and thirsty, but I didn't have enough money left for a cup of tea and a currant bun in an ABC. I needed to go to the lavatory too, but didn't even have a spare penny.

If I'm honest, I was also a little scared of wandering too far. I didn't have a map and I'd been to London only half a dozen times in my life. I was pretty certain I'd get lost if I set off on foot for Liberty's Eastern Bazaar or the National Gallery or the Zoological Gardens. So I caught the three buses back home, clutching my precious parcel to my chest, and arrived just after lunch time.

'I thought you were staying at Olivia's for the day?' said Mother. 'I hope you've had lunch, because there's hardly any cold meat left. I gave your father an extra slice because he's been working so hard, bless him. And what's that great big parcel you're lugging around? Have you gone and bought yourself a sewing box too?'

'It's a paintbox,' I said.

'A paintbox? But you've got a perfectly good paintbox already,' said Mother. 'What a waste of your father's money!'

'It's not at all a waste if it's what Opal wants,' said Father, sliding his slice of corned beef onto an extra plate and adding some beetroot and a tomato. 'Here, Opal, have a bite of this. Is it a good paintbox, dear?'

'It's the best,' I said. 'The very, very best. Oh, Father, thank you so much.'

'You're more than welcome. You enjoy your paintbox.'

I painted my first picture for Father in gratitude. I painted him on a splendid throne, dressing him in a crimson smoking jacket, Prussian blue trousers and viridian Turkish slippers. He had a pen in his hand and was writing in a magnificent manuscript book. Mother stood looking up at him on his high throne. Her hands were clasped in admiration, her eyes rolled upwards in ecstasy. I'd made her look a little ridiculous, so I clothed her in her coveted blue silk in compensation. I drew Cassie and me kneeling at each side, looking suitably awed. I painted flowers in Cassie's long hair and had her stitching busily at a preposterous hat on her lap. I painted my own new paintbox by my side, and myself painting on a sketching pad – a tiny version of the portrait of Father, with a pin-sized me painting a minute picture. I drew Billy the budgie flying over Father's head, like a cobalt-blue representation of the Holy Ghost. I put the title of the painting right at the top in scarlet lettering: *Happy Days*.

Cassie came banging in and peered at my painting. 'You're so weird, Opal,' she said. 'And you've got the hat all wrong. Ladies don't care for huge great hats all over flowers and fruit and feathers. Small is chic now, you silly girl.'

But when I shyly tapped at Father's bedroom door to show him my painting, he was delighted.

'Darling girl, it's a witty little masterpiece. You've got all the likenesses just so, and it's such a clever idea. You've got the most singular talent, Opal. I'm so proud of you.'

I felt as if I were growing blue feathers on my back like Billy's, ready to fly me up to the ceiling. When the painting was completely dry, Father took down one of Mother's insipid kitten lithographs, prised it out of its frame, and inserted my *Happy Days* painting under the glass.

He went to hang it above the mantelpiece in the living room.

'Are you sure, Ernest?' Mother asked.

'Of course! Our Opal's painted a little masterpiece,' he said.

'She *has* painted it very well, but I'm not at all sure about the composition. It looks a little like a copy of a holy picture,' Mother said, lowering her voice.

'Exactly!' said Father. 'That's the whole point.'

'But won't visitors think it blasphemous?'

'I should hope they'd appreciate its inventive homage.' Father carefully hooked the string at the back of the frame over the nail in the wall. 'There, in pride of place!' he said.

Mother still looked extremely doubtful, but she didn't like to argue with Father nowadays. It wasn't worth fussing about visitors' opinions because we very rarely *had* any visitors. Both Mother and Father had always kept themselves to themselves. Cassie had a whole gaggle of girlfriends, but she generally went to their houses or met them in the town after Sunday lunch. I just had my one friend, Olivia, and she liked my paintings.

Father went back to his work. He said he had finished the corrections and adaptations already, but he was copying out a new neat version to make it easier for the publishers to read. This took him many days. His wrists swelled painfully and his fingers were rubbed raw with the pressure of his pen, but he persisted industriously, and at long last finished it. He called us all to watch him write *The End* with a flourish. Then we all cheered and hugged him.

Mother took the precious manuscript to the post office in the morning and sent it off. 'I actually kissed the parcel for luck!' she said.

Then we started waiting. Waiting and waiting and waiting. We hoped Father might hear in a couple of days, a week at the very most. How long could it take to read a manuscript, after all? Another week went by, and then another.

'Oh Lord, do you think Pa's rewritten manuscript got lost in the post?' said Cassie.

'It couldn't have. I sent it by express delivery,' said Mother.

'You *did* put your address on it, Father?' I asked.

'Of course he did! Don't treat your father like a fool,' Mother snapped. 'Perhaps they're very busy at the publishers, dealing with hundreds of manuscripts. We simply have to be patient.'

'Unless . . .' said Father. He looked very pale. 'Unless they've decided they don't want to publish it after all.'

'Don't!' said Mother, putting her hands over his lips, as if she wanted to push the words back into his head. 'Don't you dare say that, Ernest. Of course that's not true. Oh Lordy, I couldn't bear the disappointment. We must be totally positive. Why, I'm sure the publishers' letter will arrive first thing tomorrow, with a wonderful cheque attached.'

But we still heard nothing. Father sat down the next night to write a letter of enquiry to the publishers. He laboured over it for hours, sipping the whisky and water that had become a habit.

'I have to get the tone right. I don't want to appear querulous and demanding,' he said. 'But on the other hand, I don't want to seem too meek and humble.'

He made half a dozen attempts but tore them all up. He drank another whisky and then thumped his fist on his knee. 'I'm not going to write. I'll go to their offices first thing tomorrow and ask, man to man.'

'Oh, Ernest!' said Mother. 'Do you really think that's wise? And how can you go to their offices during work hours? You don't want to get another warning.'

'I shall find a way,' said Father grandly. 'You told me to be positive, Lou.'

'Oh, Ernest!' Mother repeated, but there was more admiration than exasperation in her tone.

I didn't think Father would go through with it in the clear light of day when he was stone cold sober. He was late coming home from work. Very late.

Mother and Cassie and I sat and gawped at each other in the kitchen, glancing at the clock every now and then.

'Father's late,' Cassie said eventually, stating the obvious.

'Perhaps if he was late into the office this morning, he had to stay later this evening?' I suggested.

'He's not a naughty child doing detention at school,' said Mother. She didn't add *like you*, but it was clear that's what she meant. She went to turn down the oven as far as she could. The roast beef spat inside, filling the room with its rich smell.

'That beef's going to be dry as a bone if I leave it in much longer,' Mother moaned. 'And it cost a small fortune at the butcher's. I've run up such a bill lately. I don't see how we're going to pay it off if we don't get that cheque soon.'

'I've been offered another salon-soiled dress, the softest, subtlest shade of strawberry pink,' said Cassie. 'I know red-heads aren't supposed to wear pink, but Madame Eva says it looks pretty on me even so – and I do think she's right. She's a friend of Madame Alouette so she's offering me the dress at half price. It's a wonderful bargain, but I'm still paying off the green gown and—'

'Oh, Cassie, for goodness' sake, don't you ever think of anything but your wretched dresses?' I said sharply.

'Don't start an argy-bargy, girls – my nerves can't stand it,' said Mother. She poked at the cabbage and carrots boiling on top of the stove. 'These are being done to death too. Oh, I *did* want it to be a lovely meal. Your poor father has worked so hard. And he's looking so very pale. He needs some good beef to give him a little boost.' She looked at the clock again.

'He's never been this late before. Opal, run down the road and see if you can see any sign of him. Ask some of the gentlemen coming back from the City if there's been any trouble with the buses.'

I ran out into the street, right down to the bus stop. I waited ten minutes for the next bus, and then glared at the gentlemen alighting, willing each and every one to change into my dear pa.

'Please, sir, I'm waiting for my father and he's very late. Has there been an accident anywhere? Have any of the buses been diverted?'

They all shook their heads in unison, giving me no comfort. I waited for the next bus, and the next. Still no Father. I knew I should go home, but I couldn't bear the idea of being cooped up in the kitchen with Mother and Cassie again. I started marching up and down the streets just to give my legs something to do, walking all round the block in between each bus.

I walked past Victoria Park, where Father used to take Cassie and me to feed the ducks when we were little. I saw a man hunched on a bench beside the pond who looked a little like Father. I stopped, blinking hard. It was Father, sitting there all by himself, staring into space.

I felt my heart beating hard beneath my tunic. I hurried towards him. He must have heard my footsteps on the stony path, but he didn't look up.

I sat down beside him on the bench. He still stared straight ahead.

'Father?' I whispered.

He started and then turned towards me. 'Hello, Opal! What are you doing here?' he said. He looked paler than ever and his eyes were bloodshot.

'Oh, Father, we've been worried about you. It's so late!' I cried.

'Late?' Father pulled his pocket watch out of his waistcoat pocket. 'Oh my goodness, so it is! I expect your mother will be wondering where we are.'

'Yes, she has supper all ready.' I swallowed hard. 'So why are you sitting here? Why didn't you come straight home?'

'I just took a fancy to have a little stroll first. I've always loved this park. Remember when you and Cassie were children?'

'Yes, you always took us to feed the ducks with stale bread.'

'*Very* stale – but you would always have a little nibble on a crust too,' said Father. 'I used to call you my Jemima Puddleduck, remember?'

'And I'd go *quack, quack, quack*,' I said.

We both chuckled, but the laughter didn't sound right at all. I reached out and put my hand over Father's. It was a warm evening, but his hand was icy.

'You're so cold, Father! Have you been sitting here for ages?' I said.

'I suppose I have,' he said. He tried to squeeze my hand reassuringly. 'Don't look so worried, Opal. I'm perfectly fine.'

'Oh, Father, don't! Has something dreadful happened?' I couldn't hold back any longer. 'Did the publishers tell you they don't want your novel after all?' I felt the tears running down my cheeks because I was so sad for him.

'Hey, hey, you mustn't cry, little Opal,' said Father, gently dabbing at my tears with his cold fingertips. 'No, you've got hold of the wrong end of the stick. The publishers love my book. They think it's vastly improved now I've done all the corrections. They all clapped me on the back and called me an excellent chap.'

I stared at Father. He had tears in his own eyes but he was smiling determinedly.

'Is that really true, Father?' I whispered.

'Yes! Yes indeed.'

'Then why didn't you come rushing straight home to tell us?'

'Oh dear, you sound like a little Sherlock Holmes now! I suppose I just needed a bit of peace and quiet to let it all sink in. I couldn't concentrate properly at work. Oh Lord, what a day! The happiest day of my life. Our little Billy bird is so right. *Happy days, happy days.*'

I wanted to believe him, but he was acting so

strangely, and he looked so tired and shaken. Was he *really* happy?

'What about your work, Father? Were they very angry when you went in late again? Did you explain?'

'Oh, those cold-hearted slave-drivers are never interested in explanations,' he said. 'They gave me another warning. If I'm even one minute late starting work now, it means instant dismissal.'

'But that's so unfair! What if a bus breaks down? What if you're taken ill?'

'Don't be so concerned, dearie. I won't need the job soon, will I?'

'I – I suppose not.'

'That's right. There, dear girl.' Father reached round and hugged me close. 'Be happy now.' He cleared his throat and chirruped in a bad attempt at a budgie voice, '*Happy days, happy days*.'

'Oh, Father.' I was laughing and crying together.

'There now, my little girl,' said Father, patting my back. 'We'd better get along home now, hadn't we?'

We stood up and linked arms. I kept glancing anxiously at Father as we walked, trying to work out what was true and what wasn't. I didn't feel I could start questioning him again. No one wants to accuse their own father of lying.

There was a great clamour from Mother and Cassie the moment we got home, wanting to know where he'd been.

'I took a little walk to clear my head, my dears,' Father said. 'I must admit, I did stop off at the Black Lion to have a celebratory drink.'

'Celebratory?' said Mother.

'Yes, yes, Lou, they love my reworked novel. They couldn't be more pleased.'

'And did they give you a cheque?' Mother asked, clapping her hands.

'Yes, indeed they did.'

'Oh marvellous! Let's see it, dear.'

'I've already paid it into my bank account,' said Father.

'So we can go on a spending spree!' said Cassie. 'Can I have the money for a wonderful pink gown, Father? I know pink's a surprising colour for a red-head, but it truly suits me.'

'I'm sure it does, my darling, but wait a little while for the cheque to clear – just a few days and then we can all indulge ourselves.'

'Oh, you're the best father in the world,' said Cassie.

'And quite the best husband too,' said Mother. 'Now sit down, my dear, you must be famished. I'll whip up some gravy to moisten this poor old joint. I'm afraid the roast potatoes are past their best.'

'I love them crispy – they couldn't be better,' said Father.

He went over to the birdcage and made little

tutting noises to Billy. 'Sing for us, little birdie,' he said. '*Happy days, happy days!*'

Billy chirped obediently, and we all laughed.

I ate my meal and sipped wine-and-water and joined in all the celebrations that evening, but my tummy was churning all the time. I couldn't sleep for ages that night. I lay rigidly in my narrow bed in my cupboard room, feeling as if the walls were moving in on me, the ceiling pressing down on my head. I could hear Cassie snoring next door. It was always a surprise that such a lovely-looking girl could snort like a warthog at night. After a while I heard a door open and then the soft pad of bare feet along the landing.

I knew it was Father. I heard him rustling downstairs, then the soft clump of shoes being dropped on the carpet. Had he carried his clothes with him? Was he now getting dressed? I imagined him putting on his shabby suit, his white work shirt with the sad paper collar, the muffler to keep his thin neck warm. I had made him that muffler for his Christmas present last year. I wasn't nimble with my fingers like Cassie. The muffler was unevenly knitted, tightly stitched in some places and very slack in others so it wouldn't hang straight. I'd tried to be so careful, but there were several dropped stitches. It was a disgrace of a garment, though Father said he loved it and wore it proudly even on warm days.

Was he wearing the muffler now, putting on his hat and creeping to the front door? Was he planning to walk out on us?

I sat up in bed, suddenly terrified. I ran to my door and listened hard. I heard slight movements downstairs, slow and regular. It sounded as if Father were pacing the floor, trying to make up his mind.

I waited, ready to run to him if I heard the snap of the bolt, the creak of the front door opening. There was a long silence, and then at last I heard the stairs creaking again. The footsteps returned along the landing. The bedroom door closed.

I couldn't settle. I waited and waited, wondering if Father really was safely back in bed beside Mother. At last I crept along the landing myself and listened outside their door. I could hear Mother snoring, just like Cassie. I couldn't hear Father at all.

At last I seized the doorknob and edged the door open a crack or two. I peered in. The room was very dark, but I could distinguish two heads on the pillows.

I had a sudden ridiculous urge to run to that bed and climb in between them, as if I were a tot of two or three and not a great girl of fourteen. I resisted, of course, and trailed back to my own bed, shivering.

5

The next few days were very strange. Father went off to the office as usual and came home at his regular hour, but he didn't go up to his bedroom and write after supper. He sat in the parlour with us. I didn't feel I could steal away to my room as I usually did. I wanted to watch over Father.

Mother flicked through her ladies' magazines and Cassie fashioned little flibberty items for herself. I did my schoolwork and sketched. Mother wouldn't let me paint in the parlour in case I spilled water on the

Turkey carpet. It was our one and only carpet – we made do with plain linoleum in every other room. But now Mother had plans to refurbish the whole house. She started cutting out items in the magazines – bedding, lampshades, great Chesterfield sofas, and every kind of domestic appliance. Father would have to have fifty books published to fulfil all Mother's dreams.

Father let her show him pictures and rattle on, scarcely drawing breath. He nodded and murmured in all the right places, but it was clear to me that he wasn't listening properly. He was equally absentminded with Cassie when she described her dream outfits in suffocating detail.

'You'll look a picture, my dear,' he said several times, but I'm sure if Cassie had suggested she wear a sacking gown with a codfish on a plate for a hat he'd have mumbled the same response.

He gently cautioned both of them against making any purchases just yet. On the Friday he came home very late, but laden with gifts once more. He had another big box of Fairy Glen fondants, a huge bunch of brightly coloured asters and dahlias, a carton of fancy cakes, a great paper bag of strawberries, fresh cream and a bottle of port wine. Father had been drinking already, his face flushed almost as dark as the wine. All the presents were a little crushed: the Fairy Glen fondants tumbled about in their waxed containers, the flowers losing petals, the cakes colliding till their icing cracked, the strawberries bleeding through their paper bag, the cream dribbling out of its bottle.

Mother would once have berated him for carrying them so carelessly, but now she greeted him lovingly and rushed to redistribute the fondants, put the flowers in a vase, set the cakes on a fancy plate, put the strawberries in the best blue glass bowl, decant the cream into a jug, and pour Father a glass of port wine, all the while giving little oohs and aahs of admiration.

'Has the cheque been cleared now, my dearest?' she asked.

'Oh, Father, may I have the pink dress?' said Cassie.

'Yes, yes, my girls can have anything they want,' Father declared, opening his arms wide. His voice was a little slurred and his gestures unusually exuberant. It was as if a clever actor were impersonating him and fooling us.

I went to give Father a hug and looked straight into his eyes. 'Is it really, really all right, Father? You can tell me, truly,' I whispered.

'Of course everything is superbly all right,' he said. 'What are you going to have for a treat, my dear? Another even more splendid paintbox? How about a set of oil paints, with your own easel? Or a series of art lessons from a good teacher? And why should Cassie grab all the pretty dresses for herself? Wouldn't you like your share of silks and satins, Opal?'

'Father, stop it. I think *you* would look less ridiculous in fancy silks and satins than me. I am far too plain.'

'My little Jane Eyre!' said Father, tapping me gently on the nose.

'*Don't*, Father. I know there's something you're not telling us,' I whispered while Mother and Cassie were serving the supper. 'I'm scared – and I think you are too, deep down. There's something awful you're not telling. I can sense it.'

'Now *you're* playing at being Cassandra,' said Father. 'Little Opal foretelling the future. The voice of D-O-O-M.'

'Don't mock me, Father.'

'Well, try to cheer up a little. These are happy days, remember.' He began his ridiculous budgerigar imitation, capering around Billy's cage, trying to get him to join in too. He grabbed my hand and made me dance along beside him. '*Happy days!*' he said, as if it were a command.

'*Happy days*,' I echoed, giving up.

Saturday and Sunday *were* happy days. On Saturday we went on a delirious spending spree, buying all kinds of things we didn't really need – a buffalo-horn walking stick with a silver crook for Father, though he could walk very well without one; a tortoise-shell hairbrush for Mother, though she kept her hair scragged back into a bun; a pair of three-button white French kid gloves for Cassie, though she'd already got them covered in smuts on the train by the time we got home again; a set of fine camel-hair paintbrushes for me, though the ones in my new paintbox were perfectly adequate. But it was a good day out all the same, and we had luncheon in a proper restaurant rather than an ABC teashop. There was a waiter who called Father 'sir' and Mother 'madam'. He even 'madamed' Cassie and me, which made us giggle.

There was a set menu of four courses. We thought we were going to be royally stuffed, but the portions were actually on the small side. We had brown Windsor soup with a roll, a tiny portion of sole, then roast beef with horseradish sauce, roast potatoes and carrots and cabbage, with a trifle for pudding.

Father said the beef wasn't a patch on Mother's roasts, which was true enough, but we were all delighted by the trifle, which came in little silver goblets. Mother made us trifle for our birthdays, though it was a meagre affair – sponge and jelly, Bird's custard from a packet, a smear of cream and a glacé cherry. This trifle was a very rich relation. There were exotic fruits studding the sponge, the jelly was blackcurrant, a flavour we didn't even know existed, and the cream rose in high peaks, sprinkled with rainbow dust. We praised every mouthful.

I joined in enthusiastically. I'd been very aware of the other diners around us while we ate our way through the first three courses, worrying that they might be disapproving or mocking, but Father insisted I have a proper glass of the table wine, and now I felt relaxed and merry enough to enjoy myself properly. If Cassie had seized her trifle bowl and attempted to wear it like one of her hats, I think I would have simply laughed indulgently.

Cassie was certainly in the mood for foolishness as she'd had several glasses of wine, but she confined herself to eyeing up all the gentlemen in the room, including the waiters, who seemed very eager to flap about her. Mother was so jovial she seized Father's hand and brought it to her lips.

'You're the best husband in the whole world and I'm quite the luckiest wife,' she declared, making Father's face crumple, as if he were going to cry.

I didn't make any proclamations, but I raised my glass to Father. I drank it down to the dregs, consciously trying to drown all the doubt and fear coiled in my stomach.

When we reeled home, rather the worse for wear, Father and Mother went to their room to have a nap and Cassie starting trying on all her clothes, planning to discard most of them now that she had the promise of a whole new wardrobe.

I fetched my paintbox and tried experimenting with each of my new brushes. I composed a picture of our house, cut off down the front wall to resemble a doll's house. I drew us cowering in corners and Billy flapping in a panic in his cage, while the animal originals of our new purchases stampeded through the house. The buffalo violently butted the coat-rack in the hallway, the giant tortoise took possession of the sofa, the kid bleated on the kitchen table, lapping up spilled milk, and the camel kicked down my bedroom door in a fury.

I was rather pleased with the effect and showed it to Cassie, but she shook her head at me and said it was clear that the wine had addled my brain.

On the Sunday Father took us for a pleasure boat trip on the river Thames, all the way up to London. It was a great novelty at first, looking along the riverbank and seeing all these different little islands. It made Cassie and me remember our games of 'Island', when she was Queen Cassie and I was Princess Opal and we ruled over our own desert island kingdom. We used to play it on Mother and Father's big bed, pretending the dark lino all around was the sea.

Now, we started fantasizing about owning our own island, building a little house and rowing our boat to shore to collect provisions. We got so carried away it felt as if we were nine and seven again. Father and Mother seemed to have retreated into the past too, and were huddled up together holding hands like young sweethearts. But we had all underestimated just how long the boat journey would take, and how dreary the riverside became when dark warehouses took the place of weeping willows. Mother grew pink and fretful because she needed a ladies' room and didn't care to use the reeking little cupboard down below. Cassie got tired of playing games and waved at all the boatmen instead. She was delighted when they responded, until they became raucous.

We were all heartily sick of boats by the time we reached town, but Father had made the mistake of booking a return trip. We were supposed to stay in our seats, but Mother couldn't help wishing aloud that we could go to a decent restaurant where we could have a proper bite to eat and relieve ourselves in comfort.

'Very well, Lou. Hang the return trip. We'll catch the train back instead,' said Father grandly.

'Thank you, Ernest,' said Mother, not breathing a word about the expense of the wasted tickets.

We went to a restaurant and ate huge portions of steak-and-kidney pudding, and then jam roll and custard. I was glad I didn't wear corsets yet. Both Mother and Cassie squirmed uncomfortably afterwards.

'I'm sure I can't carry on eating like this. If I lose my figure, I won't be able to fit into any of my new dresses,' said Cassie.

We were all tired out by the time we got home at last. We weren't used to such hectic family outings, especially not two on the trot. We were all ready for bed, but Father insisted we stay up for a while 'to make the most of our lovely day'. He had us playing card games together, though we were too exhausted to think straight, and then he suggested a sing-song around the piano.

The piano was very old and battered and hadn't been properly tuned in many a year. It had been a long-ago impulsive purchase from a curiosity shop. Mother thought that it would make our humble parlour look genteel. She couldn't play a note and neither could Father, but Cassie and I had been forced to take piano lessons with a fierce old lady up the street. She put pennies on the backs of our hands, and poked us hard between the shoulder blades because she said we were slumping.

Cassie soon rebelled and refused to go any more. I stuck it out because I rather wanted to be able to play the piano. I attended weekly lessons for a couple of years and practised grimly most days. I became passably competent at playing a few tunes, but I was so hopelessly unmusical that Miss Bates would cover her ears and shudder.

'No, no, with *feeling*!' she'd protest. 'Not *plink-plink, plod-plod*. Where is the passion? Don't you have any *soul*, Opal?'

This upset me, because as I grew older I was starting to worry that I really *didn't* have any soul. I didn't seem to think the same way as anyone else. The girls at school became passionate about the silliest things. They screamed with joy if they scored a goal at hockey, they giggled and nudged each other in geography lessons because they all had a crush on the fair-haired master, and they vied with each other to run errands for Judith, the head girl. I detested hockey and couldn't see the point of knocking a ball into a net. I thought Mr Grimes, the geography master, was a silly, vain man who delighted in all the attention, and I didn't give a hoot for rosy-cheeked Judith and her favours.

I couldn't seem to let go and just *be*. I felt as if I were watching myself all the time, commenting slightly sourly on my actions. I couldn't really feel passionate about anything at all. I didn't believe in romantic love. I suppose I loved Father and Mother, and even Cassie, but in a reserved, embarrassed fashion.

I hated playing the piano now, horribly aware of my shortcomings, but I loved Father more than anyone else, so I did my best. I hadn't been taught any amusing singsong-in-the-parlour pieces. Miss Bates would wince at the very notion. The tunes I could play properly were either classical extracts or a selection of particularly melancholy hymns, which were completely unsuitable. So I tried very hard to play by ear, reproducing plonking versions of the music-hall numbers Mother used to sing when she was dusting, plus several silly novelty songs Olivia and the other girls sang at school. I frequently missed the right notes, but luckily Cassie knew all the songs and was word-perfect. I played badly and she sang loudly but off-key, yet somehow we sounded jolly enough to please Father. Mother joined in too, but Father didn't try to sing. He just sat in the soft lamplight, gazing at us intently, as if he were trying to commit every little detail to memory.

We didn't go to bed until nearly midnight, an unheard of event in our house. Not surprisingly, we all overslept in the morning.

I woke to hear Mother shrieking, 'Ernest, Ernest, get up! It's gone eight o'clock! Oh my Lord, you'll never be at work by nine, and you're on your last warning at the office.'

I expected poor Father to fling on his shabby business suit and bolt from the house within minutes, but when Cassie and I went down to breakfast, pulling on clothes and doing up laces as we staggered downstairs, Father was there in the kitchen, chewing on a triangle of toast and marmalade.

'Father! Why aren't you going to work?' I asked.

'I am going to work at home today,' said Father calmly.

We stared at him.

'Your father's not going to the office any more. He's going to concentrate on his writing,' said Mother. She said it proudly, but her voice was high-pitched and she kept giving Father worried little glances.

'You mean you've given in your notice, Father?' I asked.

He shrugged. 'I don't really need to,' he said.

'What about a reference?'

'I don't *need* a reference.'

'Do stop your silly questions, Opal,' said Mother. 'You can be very aggravating at times. Now, take a piece of buttered bread and get yourself off to school, sharpish. You quit gawping too, Cassie, and get to Madame Alouette's. Dear me, what a pair you are.'

So we had to leave the house. I dare say Cassie was late and got told off. I arrived at school a full ten minutes after the bell, and then Mounty screamed at me for a further ten minutes, which was a terrible bore.

I couldn't concentrate all day. I didn't even want to dawdle at the sweetshop with Olivia after school. I felt I had to get back home immediately to check on Father. He was acting so strangely now, I wouldn't have been surprised if I'd discovered him perching on the chimney stack pretending to be Father Christmas, or banging a drum in the parlour in his under-drawers. But when I got home, he was neatly dressed, writing decorously in the parlour. Mother had decided that being banished to the bedroom with a tea tray was ignominious. She had set him up at the parlour table. We only used it at Christmas time. It was generally shrouded with a fringed chenille cloth. Father was writing rapidly in his manuscript book. He paused to nod his head at me. 'Hello, my dear,' he said, and then carried on writing.

'May I join you, Father?' I asked. 'I could do my homework while you write.'

I knew Mother wouldn't trust me not to spill ink or somehow scratch the polished table, but she was busy preparing a rabbit stew in the kitchen so couldn't intervene. I settled down at the other side of the table with my schoolbooks. Father nodded again and smiled at me, hunched over his work. The table was a fair size and I couldn't read what he was writing, but I was impressed by the fluency of his hand.

Then Mother came tiptoeing in with a cup of tea and exclaimed crossly when she saw me. 'For goodness' sake, Opal, leave your father in peace. Gather your things and go on up to your bedroom.'

She patted Father's shoulder and set his tea down beside him. He had covered his page protectively, but when I squeezed past his chair, I dropped my ruler and he lifted his hand to retrieve it for me. In that split second I saw what he'd written: *Oh dear Lord, what am I going to do?* He'd written it over and over again, as if he were doing lines for Miss Mountbank.

6

I didn't say anything to Father. If only I'd had the courage to confront him! I might have been able to help in some way. I could have devised some desperate plan. At the very least I would have urged him to run away. But I said nothing because I was too worried and embarrassed. Perhaps I thought, like Father, that if I said nothing, then somehow it wouldn't become real.

We both tried to act as if everything was normal that long evening, while Mother and Cassie prattled away, making plans for a grand holiday for the four of us. When we all went to bed, I put my arms around Father and hugged him hard instead of just brushing his cheek with my usual quick kiss. He hugged me back too, his hands icy cold on my back through my school tunic. I'm so glad we had that last close embrace.

We were all late again in the morning. Mother didn't have the same incentive to get Cassie and me out on time now that Father was choosing not to go to work. I was in more trouble with Miss Mountbank. She was outraged that I dared be late two days in a row. She said I was an idle, lazy girl who couldn't drag herself out of bed in the morning, and I must write five hundred lines in detention: *Procrastination is the thief of all time*.

'Poor poor you, Opie. And what on earth does pro-whatsit mean, and how do you spell it anyway?' said Olivia.

'Don't know and don't care,' I said. I couldn't be bothered to explain.

'It'll take you *hours* to write all that. But don't worry, I'll still wait for you.'

'You needn't, Olivia.'

'That's what friends are for. And you're my absolute best friend, Opal. I was thinking – we should start our own select club. We could call ourselves the two "O"s, after our names. We could make badges with two "O"s intertwined. It would look *ultra* select.'

I wasn't so sure. It was the sort of thing that little girls did, not great girls already in their teens. But I was very fond of Olivia, so I went along with this idea, furtively designing a heraldic sign for us during geometry, and at break time I scrupulously split my Fairy Glen fondants with her – my share from the box Father had bought.

It was lucky we filled up on fondants, because school lunch was particularly atrocious that day: fatty grey mince with lumpy mashed potato, and then frogspawn tapioca, which would make anyone heave. I was messing about with mine, stirring it with my spoon, imagining little tadpoles squirming in the milky depths, when Miss Mountbank came through the canteen door and called my name.

'Oh no, not *more* lines,' I muttered to Olivia.

Miss Mountbank pointed at me and then beckoned. I had to climb off my bench and go right up to her while the whole school craned their necks to see my disgrace.

I thought she would jab her beaky nose at me and maybe tap me about the head with a spoon. But she simply said, 'Go to the headmistress immediately, Opal Plumstead.'

I stared at her. You were only sent to Miss Laurel if you were in the most terrible trouble. I hadn't been *that* bad, for goodness' sake. I had been late for school and I had fooled about with my lunch. Surely these were relatively trivial crimes?

'But, Miss Mountbank!' I protested.

Her eyes were very small and beady. 'Go to Miss Laurel *now*.'

I glanced back at Olivia, who was red in the face with shame and sympathy, and then walked out of the canteen with every single girl staring at me.

I tried to tell myself that this was just silly old school and they couldn't really punish me properly. I wasn't going to be beaten or locked in a dark cupboard, but even so, I felt pretty scared. Miss Laurel could be a most formidable woman, with intricate coiled plaits pinned all over her head, like a coiffured Medusa. Last year she had awarded me a prize at Speech Day – a copy of *Little Women*, which I already owned and had read at least a hundred times, but I treasured it all the same, especially as it had my name in fancy italic writing and the words *Form Prize* embossed in gold ink.

I knew from Miss Mountbank's tone and the gleam in her tiny eyes that Miss Laurel didn't want to see me to give me another prize. I knocked timidly at her door.

'Come in, come in,' she called in her very deep voice.

I slipped into the room and stood before her, my fists clenched.

I expected her to start berating me, but she stood up, came round her desk, and patted me on the shoulder.

'There's been a message from home, Opal. You're needed there. You must go at once,' she said.

'Why?' I said, totally unnerved.

'Why, Miss Laurel?' she corrected, but gently. 'I don't know the details, my dear. I just know that your mother is unwell and needs you now.'

'My mother? Not my father . . . Miss Laurel?'

'I'm simply passing on the message. I do hope this is just a temporary crisis. Now run along.'

I ran. I ran nearly all the way home, the mince and tapioca slopping uneasily in my stomach, so that I wondered if I might have to stop and be sick in the street. Mother unwell? What on earth had happened? Mother was always in the rudest of health. She rarely had coughs or colds and I'd never known her take to her bed, ever. Father was the parent who got influenza every winter, had to inhale a steaming bowl of Friars' Balsam, and endure goose grease rubbed into his chest.

Why on earth would Mother call for *me*? Why me and not Cassie? She was the eldest and Mother's favourite. I couldn't help feeling a flicker of pride that Mother had asked for *me*.

I was exhausted by the time I got home, my shirt sticking to my back, a hole worn in my stocking so my toe poked out uncomfortably. I let myself in the front door, calling, 'Mother, Mother, it's me, Opal, I'm home.'

Mrs Liversedge from two doors along was lurking in our hallway. Mother couldn't stand Mrs Liversedge, a large blousy woman known to be a terrible gossip. She was flushed with excitement now.

'Thank goodness, Opal! I've taken the liberty of putting your mother to bed, she's in such a state,' she said. 'I had to give her smelling salts to calm her down. Go up to her now, dear, and see if you can quiet her.'

I ran up the stairs. I heard the most tremendous sobbing, a wild keening sound that seemed near demented. I ran into Mother's room, and there she was writhing on the bed, the collar of her dress undone and her boots unbuttoned, but otherwise fully dressed. She was clutching a lace handkerchief but totally failing to mop her face. Tears were streaming rapidly down her cheeks and her nose was dripping too.

'Mother? Oh, Mother, what's happened?' I looked around wildly. 'Where's Father? Is it Father? Oh Lord, what's happened to Father?'

Mother heaved herself up, gasping. 'Your wretched father!' she cried. 'Trust you to be more concerned about your father! God rot his soul – I wish I'd never set eyes on him,' she declared, so caught up with emotion she continued to let her eyes and nose stream freely.

I heard footsteps and saw the dreadful Mrs Liversedge standing in the bedroom doorway, arms folded, watching avidly.

'Mother, please. Stop it! You don't know what you're saying,' I said. I took her lace handkerchief and tried to dab her damp face.

'Oh, she knows all right,' said Mrs Liversedge, making tutting noises with her large horsy teeth. 'Poor soul, this has hit her hard. Your ma's always considered herself a cut above us ordinary folk in the street, I know that. I'm not blaming her – it's natural to want to better yourself, especially when you've got a husband with a fancy Oxford degree who goes off to the City every day in his serge suit, with his bowler at a jaunty angle. Oh, it's always that type what lets you down in the end, never your decent working bloke who does his share of honest toil.'

I wanted to scream at her. How dare she talk to us like this? Why didn't Mother shut her up?

'Thank you, Mrs Liversedge,' I said as coldly as I could, as if I were a mistress dismissing an impertinent servant. 'You've been very kind looking after Mother, but we don't need you any more.'

'Ooh, Miss High and Mighty!' said Mrs Liversedge. 'You're going to come down to earth with a bump when you find out what's happened to your precious father. No more toff City job for him.'

'If you must know, my father has decided to concentrate on his novel writing,' I said, trembling with rage. 'He has retired from City life.'

This set her off in such a spiteful cackling fit that I couldn't bear it any longer.

'Please get out of our house this instant,' I said. I looked to Mother to back me up, but she was lying there moaning, tears still seeping out of her shut eyes.

'All right, then, I'll go. There's the thanks I get for bringing your poor mother round from a fainting fit after her terrible shock. I was all prepared to be a good neighbour and tried to help as best I could in these dreadful circumstances, but now I don't see why I should lift a finger.' She was so indignant that little beads of spittle gathered at the corners of her mouth. I wondered if she might actually spit straight at me and I took a quick step backwards.

'You're a stuck-up little nobody,' she said, nodding her head emphatically, and then she marched out of the room.

Mother moaned, hiding her face in her hands.

'Mother! Oh, Mother, please tell me what's happened,' I said, trying to prise her hands away.

I heard the door banging downstairs. 'There, she's gone! Why ever did you let her in? She'll be rushing down the street spreading terrible gossip about us now. Look, you must tell me – where's Father?'

'Your father's under arrest,' Mother said, shaking her head from side to side as if trying to deny her own words.

'*What?*'

'Two policemen came this morning and took him away. The whole street saw. Oh, the shame of it!' said Mother, and she sobbed even harder.

'But why did they arrest him? There must be some terrible mistake. Father isn't a criminal!'

'Oh, but he *is*,' said Mother. She heaved herself upright, looking straight into my eyes. 'He stole money from the office – wrote himself a cheque. It was all so obvious and pathetic, the police worked it out straight away. How could he think he wouldn't get caught? How could he do this to me?'

'Oh, poor, poor Father!'

'He's not *poor* Father, he's disgraced us all. It turns out the publishers changed their mind about his wretched book. They didn't want it after all. He wasn't man enough to admit to it so he stole the money to deceive us,' Mother sobbed bitterly.

'He wanted to treat us, Mother. He wanted us all to be happy. Oh, it's so *sad*.' I was crying too at the thought of poor, silly, valiant Father trying so hard to convince us all that these were happy days. I'd *known* something wasn't right. I should have made him confide in me. He must have been in such secret agony – and how must he be feeling now?

'Will Father be at the police station? I'll go to him,' I said urgently.

'No! No, don't leave me,' said Mother, clinging to me.

'Look, I'll go and fetch Cassie home. She will look after you.'

'I absolutely forbid you to call for Cassie! If Madame Alouette finds out, then Cassie will be disgraced too, and unable to continue her apprenticeship,' said Mother.

I felt a pang. So that was why Mother had sent for me and not Cassie, though if the teachers found out at school, then I would also be disgraced. How Miss Mountbank would glory in my humiliation! I felt ill at the thought, but I couldn't dwell on that now. Father was my first priority. I had to go and find him.

'Listen, Mother, I have to go to Father. He has to be supported. If he is to be charged and taken to trial, then he will need a lawyer.'

'A lawyer! How are we going to pay a lawyer – with buttons?' Mother said bitterly. 'Don't you realize we are ruined now? Without your father's income we can't even pay the rent, let alone feed and clothe ourselves. You think you're so clever, but you didn't realize that, did you?' she went on, seeing the shock on my face.

I knew it, of course I did. I just hadn't let the full realization wash over me. I felt like bursting into tears and weeping like a baby, but I knew that one of us had to stay in control.

'We will work something out. We can't be the first family to be in such circumstances,' I said, trying to sound calm.

'I dare say there are many such families. *In the workhouse*,' said Mother, still weeping.

I knew I should feel sorry for her in her terrible distress, but her monstrous selfishness made me almost hate her. She was lying there howling, without an ounce of pity for poor Father and his far more dreadful situation. Mother looked so awful too, her face purple with rage and grief, her nose still smeared, her mouth puckering hideously as she moaned. She smelled strongly of perspiration and sal volatile, an unpleasant combination.

I was ashamed to feel such revulsion for my own mother. I dumped a cloth in the cold water of her basin, squeezed it out, and put it on her forehead.

'There now, Mother, this will help,' I said. I went to her dressing table and sprinkled some of her lavender water around to try and clear the air.

'What in God's name are you doing? Don't waste my precious scent!' Mother cried.

'I'm simply trying— Oh, never mind. Now, Mother, you lie here quietly, and I'll go and find out the situation at the police station. I'll see if I can be of some service to Father. You try and sleep a little. I'll be back as soon as I can,' I said quickly.

I rushed out of the room, though Mother protested

bitterly. I tore down the stairs and out of the front door, while she called after me. For ever afterwards she declared I'd abandoned her when she was taken so ill. Perhaps this is true, but even so, I'm glad my first concern was for Father.

I knew where the police station was – the tall four-storey building at the end of the high street. When I was very little and fretful, Mother used to say she'd fetch a policeman to take me away. On trips into town I'd stared fearfully at the bleak brick building, wondering where they'd keep me locked up. I could scarcely believe that my own father was actually imprisoned inside. I hurried up the stone steps, took a deep breath, and then pushed open the sturdy door.

I found myself standing in an ordinary little vestibule, with wooden benches against the wall and a polished parquet floor. I'd been imagining stone cells with prisoners in leg-irons. A policeman behind a counter gave me a cheery smile. 'Yes, missy? You look a little distressed. How can I help you?' he asked.

'Oh please, I think you've arrested my father!' I blurted, and then, like a fool, burst into tears.

The policeman was astonishingly kind. He vaulted over the counter into the vestibule, offered me his own large handkerchief and patted me on the shoulder. He looked serious when I gave him Father's name.

'Oh dear, yes. We do have that gentleman in our cells.'

'A cell?' I sobbed.

'Rest assured we're looking after him. We've served him lunch, and he's got a bed and a blanket, though of course it's not quite home comforts.'

'How long will he have to stay there?'

'We'll take him to court in the morning when we've done all the paperwork, and then—'

'Then he can come home?' I interrupted.

'Afraid not, my dear. He'll very likely be sent to a remand prison until his trial – and seeing as he's confessed everything, as far as I'm aware, it's an open and shut case. He *could* be sent for a five-year-stretch, but as he's been very cooperative and behaved like a proper gentleman, I think we're more likely looking at one year maximum.'

'A year . . .' I whispered. 'A whole year in prison.'

'Don't look so shocked, my dear. It won't be so bad. I dare say they'll be quite soft with him. They'll find him a nice little job in the library, say, as he's got lots of book learning.'

'But he'll hate being in prison!'

'Well, he shouldn't have broken the law, then, should he?'

'He did it for all of us. He just wanted us to be happy,' I said. 'Oh please, could I see him now?'

'I'm sorry, dear. Prisoners in our cells aren't

allowed any visitors – especially not little girls.'

'Then can I go to court tomorrow and see him?'

'No children allowed in court. I dare say your mother might be able to sit in the visitors' gallery, though.'

'But *I* can't – even if I dress to look grown up? I look especially young in this silly school tunic.'

'You can dress in all the finery you care for, but you'll still look like a young girl. How old are you, missy? Twelve, is it?'

'I'm fourteen,' I said indignantly, but I knew I looked fearfully young for my age. 'Then will I be able to visit my father when he's . . . in prison?'

'I doubt it, my dear. It's not a suitable place for the likes of a young girl like you.'

'Then I won't be able to see him for a whole year?' I said, and I started crying in earnest. 'I have to tell him how much I still love him. I don't think any the worse of him even if he has committed this crime. I need to let him know I'll be thinking of him every single day.'

'I dare say they'll let you write to him, dear. Don't take on so. Please don't cry,' said the policeman, dabbing at my face with his handkerchief.

His kindness made me weep even more, till I was almost as hysterical as Mother.

The policeman tutted sympathetically. 'Dear, dear, dearie me,' he murmured. He consulted his pocket watch. 'Ah! My boss the sergeant is having a late lunch break with some of his chums from the Chamber of Commerce. I'm pretty sure he won't be back at the station till three or even later. So if we were to say you needed to bathe your poor face with cold water – which would be a very good thing because your pretty eyes are looking very red and sore – then I'd have to escort you to the tap in the kitchen. That means we would pass right by the cells. If we were to pause for a minute – and I mean just a minute, mind – you might be able to say a word to your pa.'

'Oh, *please*!' I said.

So he took me gently by the arm and opened up the counter for me to walk through. He escorted me down some narrow stone steps, and there were the cells, but the doors were all closed and bolted so I couldn't see inside.

'Oh please, could you open the door for me,' I begged.

'Now, dear, I can't go that far. That would be truly scuppering all chances of promotion if it were ever found out. You mustn't ask it of me. But put your eye to the peephole and you'll see him. And if you speak loud, he'll hear what you have to say.'

I put my eye to the peephole, having to stand on tiptoe to do so. I could only see a bleak cell at first, with writing scratched all over the walls, but then my eyes swivelled and I saw Father sitting on the edge of a very narrow bed. His head was down, his chin right on his chest, and his arms were folded very tightly, as if he were literally trying to hold himself together.

'Oh, Father!' I called, and he looked up, terribly startled. 'Father, it's me, Opal.'

Father covered his eyes and started to sob.

'Oh, Father. Please don't! I can't bear it. I know it's all so very dreadful, but we'll get through it somehow. The policeman here says they will be kind to you in prison. He thinks you'll get a light sentence. It will be terrible even so, I know, but I'm sure you'll be very brave and bear it.'

Father was shaking his head. 'I'm so sorry,' he murmured. 'I don't know what possessed me. I've disgraced you all. Whatever must you think of me.'

'I think you're the finest father in the whole world,' I said stoutly.

'I feel so utterly dreadful to have inflicted this on you. We'll never be able to hold our heads up high again.'

'Look at *my* head, Father! My neck is positively stretched. Just remember how much I love you. They say I'm not allowed to visit you, but I'll write to you every week. Maybe the time will pass quicker than we think – and then you'll come back home and we'll have happy days again, just you wait and see.'

7

I kept my head stretched unnaturally high all the way home. I glared at everyone I passed, though they couldn't possibly know what had happened – not yet, anyway. Mrs Liversedge would do her best to inform the whole street by sundown. I suddenly realized that local reporters might well be at the courtroom tomorrow. I saw a crude headline – GENTLEMAN EMBEZZLER ON MAD SPENDING SPREE – as clearly as if the words were inked in the air in front of my eyes.

Poor dear Father had risked everything just to keep the love and respect of his wife and daughters, even though he must have known he would be found out soon enough. It hadn't been a mad spending spree at all – a dress, a few accessories, a paintbox, wine, chocolates, flowers and a talking budgerigar in a cage. They were all luxuries to us, but relatively modest purchases for many folk.

I didn't want to go back home to Mother. I found my footsteps slowing as I got nearer. I was positively creeping by the time I turned into our street. I found myself playing the childhood game of not stepping on the cracks in the pavement. If I placed my feet carefully enough, I might wake up any minute and find myself safe in bed, hearing Father pottering about downstairs, making us an early morning cup of tea. I opened my eyes so wide they watered, but I couldn't wake from this nightmare world.

The moment I opened the front door I heard Mother moaning. I felt a wave of revulsion. It was mostly because of Mother that Father had stolen the money. Mother had belittled him for as long as I could remember. He had gone on steadfastly loving her, meekly accepting every slight and insult. She'd never valued his writing, but she'd been cock-a-hoop when she thought he was going to be a published author and make our fortunes. She'd suddenly made him feel totally loved and cherished. The past few weeks had been wonderful, even though I'd felt uneasy. Now that the very worst of my half-aware suspicions had come true, Mother seemed to have changed her mind about Father yet again.

I trudged dutifully upstairs. She started even before I opened the bedroom door:

'How dare you leave me on my own for *hours*? Here I am, lying here helpless, scarcely able to move, my head turned to jelly with all the shame and worry. Where have you *been*?'

'Surely you know where I've been, Mother,' I said. 'I've been to see poor Father at the police station.'

Mother gave a great shriek, and then started huffing and puffing like a steam train. 'How *dare* you go there! The *disgrace*! Your father has ruined our lives.'

'You mustn't take on so,' I said coldly. 'Don't act as if it's the worst tragedy in the world. We've got the easy part. I dare say Mrs Liversedge will gossip, but do we really care so much what the neighbours think? We shall simply hold our heads up high and get on with our lives. The police think that Father will be sentenced to a whole year in prison. All we have to do is wait. But Father has to *serve* that year, locked up with thieves and robbers and murderers. His is the far greater ordeal. All right, he's committed a crime – but is it so very dreadful? He didn't steal money from a person. He stole a paltry amount from an enormously rich company which paid him a pittance and never gave a thought to his welfare or comfort. And I keep *telling* you, Mother – he stole it for us. He felt so worried when he couldn't make our fortune with his writing. You treated him like a king when you thought he was successful. How can you turn against him now?'

My words came tumbling out in an angry torrent. I'd never spoken in such a way to my own mother before. It was terribly exciting to berate her properly. I felt my whole face flushing, though I'd also started to tremble. When I paused for breath at last, the room was unnaturally quiet. The ticking of the grandfather clock on the landing seemed to beat right inside my head.

Mother heaved herself upright, leaning on her elbow. 'Have you finished?' she gasped, her voice hoarse from all her howling.

'I – I think so, for the moment.' I took a deep breath. 'I'm sorry, Mother. I know I've been a little outspoken. It's only because I'm so upset.'

'You think yourself so superior, Opal Plumstead. Your very name's a total foolishness, just because your father said your eyes flashed blue and green like an opal. He insisted on the name for your christening. If I'd had my way you'd have been plain Jane – and a plain Jane you are, with your pinched face and hair as straight as a poker. How you're so full of yourself when you look such a fright I don't know at all.'

I was shaking from head to toe as she spoke the words. I knew that Mother had always found me difficult, but did she actually *detest* me?

'Well, you're going to come down to earth with a bump now,' she went on. 'You think you're so clever and yet you haven't the brains of a blancmange. Look up, girl. Look *up*!'

I looked up, wondering if she had gone demented.

'What do you see?' Mother demanded.

'The . . . the ceiling,' I said.

'And above that? The roof, you fool, the roof. How are we going to keep a roof over our heads now, hmm? It's been hard enough to pay the rent on your father's salary all these years. Well, it's going to be even harder now. And how are we going to pay the bills? Oh my Lord, we owe such a lot now too. How are we going to feed ourselves without any income whatsoever?'

I blinked at her.

'We're going to end up in the workhouse, that's what,' said Mother. She burst out crying again. 'That's what your precious father's brought us to. The workhouse!'

I struggled to collect myself. 'Of course we're not going to end up in the workhouse,' I said calmly enough, though my head was whirling. Mother was right. I was a total fool. I hadn't even thought about our financial situation. How *were* we going to manage? Was it remotely possible that we really *would* end up in the workhouse?

It was an ugly stone building at the edge of the town. There were no windows on the ground floor so you couldn't peep inside. I had no clear idea what happened to the poor inmates. I wasn't even sure what kind of work happened in this grim house. I had vaguely heard of people picking oakum. I had no idea what oakum was, or how you picked it. I had a vivid imagination, but it was hard to picture Mother, Cassie and me sitting in rags and picking this oakum all day long. I had a sudden urge to paint a picture of us, surrounded by little Oliver Twists all begging for more gruel, but I could hardly leave Mother again to closet myself in my room and paint.

I made a pot of tea instead, and we both sipped at it, looking wary. We had both said too much, and now we didn't know how to engage with each other. Mother's long sobbing fit had stopped now, though her breath still came in little gasps and she kept clutching her chest dramatically, as if she had a pain in her heart.

It seemed like the longest afternoon of my life. Mother and I talked in a desultory manner of this and that, neither of us able to face discussing our circumstances again. I could tell that Mother was in internal agony, though. She didn't just clutch her chest, she started giving sharp little moans, as if someone were intermittently stabbing her.

I sat thinking of Father, hunched in the prison cell. I couldn't help thinking of myself too, wondering what was going to happen to me. It still seemed impossible that we might really end up in the workhouse. It was an institution for the destitute, not families like us.

I tried to make coherent plans. I had to think of some way of raising money. Perhaps I could do a little babysitting? I knew a girl in my class at school who regularly babysat in the evenings for her sister and brother-in-law, and they paid her half a crown a time. But they were family. I didn't have any infant nephews or nieces. I didn't know anyone with babies. There were several women in the street who had young children. Could I approach them and offer my services? But I didn't know anything about children. What if they cried? What would I feed them? And – oh Lord – what if they needed their napkins changing?

I couldn't possibly be a babysitter. Maybe I could try to help elderly folk? I was good at reading aloud and could just about manage little domestic tasks, so perhaps I could be a part-time paid companion after school and at weekends. But when would I do my homework? And I wouldn't be able to spend precious hours dawdling with Olivia and stuffing my face with sweets.

At ten past four there was a *rat-a-tat-tat* on our front door – Olivia's signature knock.

'Oh dear God, who's that? Is it that Liversedge woman come back to gloat?' said Mother.

'No, Mother, it's Olivia, come to see why I was called away from school,' I said, leaping up.

'What? You mustn't let her in! You mustn't say anything to her. Oh, how that whole family will crow if they find out. They've always acted as if we're not good enough. That girl's mother looks down her nose at me,' my own mother hissed.

'I can't *ignore* her. She's my friend,' I said.

I was suddenly desperate to see dear old Olivia. Before Mother could stop me, I ran into the hall and had the front door open in a trice. Olivia stood there scuffing her boots on the doormat, her plaits unravelling, her mouth open anxiously.

'Oh, Olivia!' I said, and I threw my arms round her.

'Opal?' She hugged me back warmly. 'Opal, what's happened? Why did they call you away? I was so worried!'

I heard Mother shouting, telling me to send Olivia away this instant.

Olivia couldn't help hearing too and screwed up her face. 'Gosh, what's up with your mother? What have *I* done?'

'Nothing!' I took hold of her and led her back onto

the garden path, out of Mother's earshot. 'Mother's just hysterical. That's why I had to go home. She's gone off her head because . . .' I suddenly faltered, wondering if I could really tell Olivia the truth.

'Because what?' she asked.

'Look, do you swear you won't tell anyone? Anyone at all?' I whispered.

'Cross my heart and may I die if I tell a lie,' Olivia murmured solemnly, crossing her chest and miming cutting her own throat.

'Father's been arrested,' I whispered right into her ear.

'*What?*'

'Shush! Oh, Olivia, it's so dreadful. He's going to court in the morning, and then he'll be locked away, and the policeman thinks he'll be in prison for at least a year.'

'Prison!' said Olivia, her eyes enormous.

'You won't tell, will you?'

'No, I won't – but golly, what has your pa *done*? Surely it's all a terrible mistake?'

'I wish it was, but I think he really did take some money from his firm.'

'Oh my goodness!' Olivia looked so shocked that my stomach lurched.

'It's not such a very bad crime, is it? I mean, he didn't harm anyone – and it wasn't money to spend on himself, it was for the family. He wanted us to think he'd earned it from his writing. You can understand, can't you?' My voice wavered.

Olivia didn't look as if she understood at all. She kept staring at me as if she couldn't quite believe I'd said it.

'Opal!' Mother was at the door, dishevelled and furious. 'Opal, come inside this instant!'

I pressed Olivia's hand urgently and then obeyed. Mother slammed the door shut, then slapped me hard across the cheek.

'How dare you!' she cried.

'How dare *you*,' I said, holding my stinging face.

Mother used to slap Cassie and me regularly when we were little, but she hadn't done it for years.

'I am your mother! I shall treat you severely until you learn to do as you're told. *I* am head of the family now,' she said.

'Father hasn't *died*,' I protested.

'If only he *had*! Then we could go about our normal lives with dignity,' said Mother.

'You can't really mean that. You love Father. You've been so specially nice to him recently.'

'Well, more fool me, letting myself believe he'd at last achieved something, acted like a real man.' Mother's voice wavered, but she didn't cry again. She pressed on her eyes with the backs of her hands, as if literally stopping the tears. 'I suppose I'd better start preparing supper. Cassie will be home soon.

Oh, poor dear Cassie, how I dread breaking this to her.'

Cassie was singing as she came through the front door. She had a large paper package in her arms, cuddling it as if it were a baby.

'Hello, Mother, hello, sis. Wait till you see my new gown! It's heliotrope – oh, so sophisticated! Wait till I put it on. It's perhaps a little too décolleté, but I can always fashion a piece of lace to act as a modesty panel – though do you know what? Madame Alouette herself said I had a beautiful figure and I should be proud to show it off.' Cassie giggled coyly, and then at last took in our expressions.

'What is it? Why are you looking at me like that? Why *can't* I have lovely clothes now that we have money. Where's Father? I'm sure he'll let me keep the new gown.'

'You must take it back tomorrow and say you're not allowed to have it,' said Mother. 'God knows how we're going to pay for the other dresses. Oh, Cassie!' This time she couldn't keep back her tears.

'*What's happened?*' said Cassie. 'Aren't Father's publishers going to cough up after all?'

'He was pretending all the time. Lord knows why I believed him. I knew his writing nonsense was a waste of time. If only he'd been man enough to admit it! But what does he do? *What does he do?*' Mother repeated histrionically, gulping for breath. 'Tell her!' she gasped, pointing at me.

'Father stole from the shipping office. I think he made out a cheque to himself and paid it into his own bank,' I said.

'Father did?' said Cassie. 'Our father *stole*?' She suddenly burst out laughing. 'Father!' she repeated. 'Who would ever have thought it! *Father!*'

'It's no laughing matter, you little fool,' said Mother.

Cassie was shocked into seriousness. Mother had never spoken to her so harshly in all her life.

'Your father's been arrested. He didn't even have the sense to make a good job of it. He's got no defence whatsoever. He's admitted everything. He'll go to prison.'

'But what will we do?' said Cassie, tears brimming now. 'What will become of us? How will I ever find a decent man if I have a jailbird for a father?'

Suddenly I'd had enough. Cassie could be responsible for Mother now. I ran up to my room and actually barricaded myself in, with my heavy washstand tight against the door, determined that they wouldn't get at me. Cassie came and knocked a while later, telling me that supper was on the table, but I said I didn't want any. Then Mother herself came knocking, telling me to stop this childish sulking and come down at once.

'I've gone to bed, Mother,' I lied. 'I have a sick headache with the shock.'

They both left me alone. I lay fully clothed on top of my bedclothes and tried desperately to send thought messages to Father, telling him I loved him and wished I could be with him to comfort him. Then I cried until I really *did* give myself a headache.

I fell asleep at some point, and then woke in the middle of the night, my heart pounding, scarcely able to breathe. My clothes were all tight and twisted about me, but even when I'd torn them off and put on my nightgown, I still felt constricted.

Father, Father, Father! I thought, through the rest of that terrible long night.

8

Mother didn't get up to make breakfast the next morning. She lay on her bed. Cassie stayed in her room and I stayed in mine, though I could tell from the rustle of bedclothes and creakings of the beds that we were all awake.

Cassie gave in first. She knocked on my door until I pushed the washstand aside. She came trailing into my room in her nightgown, yawning and rubbing her eyes.

'Come on, you. It doesn't look as if Mother's going

to stir. Oh Lordy, what a palaver.' She sat down on my bed. I stayed curled in a tight ball. 'Try not to worry, sis,' she said softly, patting my shoulder, her long hair tickling my face.

I struggled up and we gave each other a quick fierce hug. Then Cassie padded off to get dressed. I put on my ugly school uniform – but when Cassie had trailed off to work, sadly clutching the heliotrope dress, I went back to my own room and undressed down to my drawers.

I was sure that Mother was still awake, although she'd refused to respond to our knocking and had ignored the cup of tea Cassie had brought her. I tiptoed into Cassie's room. It smelled just like her – of rose soap and Parma violet powder and soft girl body. I wanted to curl up in her warm bed and lull myself to sleep, but instead I looked through the clothes hanging on a rail behind a flowery curtain. Cassie was an untidy girl by nature and she'd gone out without making her bed and left her dressing table smeared with powder, but her clothes were in immaculate order, each dress sponged at the armpits, every hem sewn neatly into place.

I selected the smallest dress, sage green with a little beige lace trimming at the neck, and a tight skirt. It still hung loosely on me, though my knees were uncomfortably hobbled. The dress gaped at the bust line and drooped at the waist, but I covered it with a large scarf that I tried to arrange in an artful manner. It wouldn't tie neatly, and I looked like a clumsily wrapped parcel. Still, I wasn't trying to look stylish, only several years older.

I wound up my hair into a perilous knot on top of my head, and then stuck one of Cassie's fancy hats over it, securing it with six or seven long pins. I didn't dare move my head too much, fearful that the pins would scrape my head. Even though I looked a fearful scarecrow, I didn't seem like a schoolgirl any more, and that was all that mattered.

I crept out of the house and set off for the court. I was there before the big wooden doors were opened. I sat on the wall outside, and gradually more people joined me. I had no idea whether they were family too, come to support their loved ones, or the idly curious. One sly-faced man in a trilby hat clutched a notebook, which made me suspect that he was a reporter. I glared at him ferociously.

Then, just before ten, a series of grim covered carriages drew up, and pairs of policemen emerged, each dragging a prisoner between them. I gazed in horror at all these pale bound men. I couldn't see Father at first – and then I realized that he was the last man, looking so old and frail I scarcely recognized him.

'Good luck, Father! Take heart!' I called.

I'm not sure if he heard me. He didn't look round,

though the rest of the crowd stared dreadfully. I felt myself flushing, but I stood as tall as I could, as if I couldn't be prouder of my dear father.

The prisoners were all escorted to a door at the side of the court, which presumably led to the prison cells. Then the main doors were opened by a solemn lackey dressed all in black, and we all marched forward.

I tried to keep close to two other women, so that we might enter in a bunch, not individually observed. But my plans were all in vain. As soon as I started up the steps, the man in black frowned at me, and when I tried to go through the doors he took hold of my arm.

'You can't go through,' he said gruffly.

'Let me go, if you please,' I said. 'I need to attend the court proceedings. It is a matter of great importance.'

'No children allowed in the courts,' he said.

'I am not a child,' I said, pretending outrage.

'No silly young ladies playing games, either. Run along home now.'

'You are very impertinent,' I said, trying to keep my dignity. 'I may be petite, but I am eighteen years old.'

'Yes, and I'm the cat's grandmother,' he said. 'Off these steps or I'll fetch a policeman.'

I had to do as I was told. I couldn't go home, though. I stayed perched on the wall, keeping a lonely vigil. I was cold without a proper coat, and very hungry. I hadn't stopped for breakfast, which was a big mistake. After an hour or so a gentleman came back through the wooden doors, a document case under his arm.

I jumped up. 'Please, sir, can you tell me if the case of Ernest Plumstead has already been heard?' I begged.

'Ernest who? I don't know. I'm not the clerk of the court.'

'Could you possibly go and ask for me, sir? They won't let me in and I so badly need to know,' I said. I tried to make my voice soft and I opened my eyes wide to gaze at him imploringly. If I'd been Cassie, I'm sure he'd have gone to enquire like a shot, but I was only me, dressed up like a scarecrow. He backed away from me, shaking his head.

I pleaded, but he walked off, almost running in his haste to get away from me. I sat on and on. When I was cramped with sitting, I walked the length of the wall and back, pacing like a caged tiger. I thought of Father and wondered how he would cope with being locked in a cell, perhaps alongside fellow prisoners. He already looked a broken man after just one night in a police station. A prison sentence would surely kill him.

I prayed for a miracle to happen. Perhaps the people in the court would see that Father was a gentleman and a scholar and decide to let him off with a warning, provided he paid the money back. *I* would certainly do such a thing. Surely they might have equal compassion . . . They must realize that Father wasn't a true criminal, even though he had committed a criminal act. He hadn't been thinking straight. He was exhausted and despairing, simply trying to make his family happy. He probably wrote the wretched cheque in a moment's madness, scarcely realizing what he was doing.

I was acting like my father's defence lawyer as I paced the pavement, convincing myself until I was ready to declare Father entirely innocent. Indeed, I found myself muttering, '*Innocent, innocent, innocent*,' so that passers-by glanced at me nervously and hurried on. Then, suddenly, a hand grasped my shoulder, and a voice gasped, 'Cassie! Oh, Cassie!'

It was Mother, dressed in her Sunday best, though her old fox-fur stole was thrown on askew. The sad little fox's head nudged her neck as if about to take a tentative bite.

I stared at her and she stared at me, her face contorting. 'Opal?' she said. 'What are you doing here – and in your sister's clothes?'

'I wanted to see Father in court, but they won't let me in,' I said.

'They'll let *me* in,' said Mother.

'Oh yes, please go!' I said. 'Oh, Mother, I'm so glad you came.'

'Of course I had to come,' she said. 'I have to find out what's going to happen.' She reached out and squeezed my hand. 'Let us both take courage.'

Then she went up the steps to the doors, and I saw that in her haste she was still wearing her old felt slippers with worn-down heels. Yet somehow she still managed to cut a dignified figure, draggled fox fur and all.

Mother was inside all morning. At one o'clock she came out with a little group of people, and I seized hold of her to hear the news.

'The court is adjourned for lunch. Your father's case hasn't even been heard yet,' she said.

She took me to a little eating house round the corner, and with the few coins in her purse bought us cups of tea and a meat pie to share. I was starving hungry, but as soon as I took a mouthful of hot fatty meat I felt my stomach turn over. I had to beg the woman behind the counter for permission to use her facilities. I rushed out the back to an unpleasant privy and was very sick. I returned so white and shaky that the woman took pity on me, and gave me another cup of tea and a slice of dry toast on the house. I managed to keep the toast down, and Mother spooned several sugars into my tea to give me extra energy.

'You should go home now, Opal. There's no point hanging about outside the court. I'll come straight back when I have news,' she said.

But I couldn't go home. I kept my lonely vigil by the wall all afternoon. At last Mother came out, looking very pale.

'They didn't let him go?' I asked desperately.

'No, he's been remanded. I asked the policeman where they were taking him, and it's at Whitechurch – miles and miles away,' she said.

'How long will he be there?'

'It could be months,' Mother said hopelessly. 'And he hasn't a chance of getting off because he's still pleading guilty. And another thing – all the money in his account is being frozen. I checked at the bank before coming here. We are destitute, Opal. I have been driving myself demented all day long, trying to work out what to do.' She looked at me, and a little of her animosity crept back. 'You think you're so clever, Opal. Do *you* have any suggestions?'

I shook my head, so worn out and despairing that I couldn't stop the tears trickling down my cheeks.

'Now, now, aren't we both done with crying?' Mother said, and we trailed home together.

I'd have sooner trekked through the darkest Congo jungle than walk down our street. There were faces at windows, people pointing, children sniggering – worse than any poisonous snake or snarling lion. Mrs Liversedge had been very busy. When we passed her door, she came rushing out all a-quiver, her long nose twitching.

'How did it go in court, dears?' she said, her voice oily with false sympathy. 'Did he get sent down for long, then? How are you going to manage, eh?'

Mother's hand tightened on my arm. 'Take no notice of her,' she muttered to me.

I squeezed her back and we walked faster, but Mrs Liversedge's voice followed us all the way to our front door. We could even hear her faintly when we were inside. Mother leaned against the wall for a moment. Then she took a deep breath. 'I'll put the kettle on. Go and take off your sister's clothes. Hang them up neatly now, or you'll be in trouble.'

Cassie came home more than an hour early, breathless from running.

'I told Madame Alouette I had a sick headache – which is true enough, I've felt really seedy all day long. Tell me about Father! Oh please, tell me they let him off or gave him a suspended sentence? *Please* tell me,' she begged.

We told her the grim truth and she wept. Mother and I wept a little too as we huddled together on the sofa, trying not to look at Father's empty chair.

Mother hadn't bought any meat for supper. She did not even have the wherewithal to buy three chops or a neck of lamb. We had a strangely comforting nursery tea instead: hot baked potatoes, then bread and milk mushed up into a porridge. We went to bed early, Mother making us Horlicks malted milk. I was sure I wouldn't be able to get any rest, but within minutes I was sound asleep. I had dreadfully sad dreams about Father. When I woke in the night, I thought for a moment that the past few days were simply part of my nightmare. Then I realized it was all true and wondered how I should bear it.

Mother was up early the next morning, washed and neatly dressed, though her hands were shaking as she cut us slices of bread for breakfast.

Cassie noticed too. 'I'll stay home with you today,' she said.

'No, *I'll* stay home,' I said quickly.

Mother shook her head. 'You'll neither of you stay home. You must go to Madame Alouette's, Cassie, and you must go to school, Opal.' She said it so firmly there was no arguing.

I set off in my familiar bunchy tunic, my straw hat jammed uncomfortably on my head. It was a relief to smell the chalk-dust and rubber plimsolls, hear the jangling bell and the chatter of a hundred girls. I was back in my own safe school world. Nobody knew about Father – nobody but Olivia.

She stared at me anxiously, wringing her hands. 'Oh, Opal!' she said, so tragically that half a dozen girls looked up curiously.

'Be *quiet*,' I hissed.

Olivia blinked, looking desperately hurt.

'I'm sorry I snapped at you,' I said, when we were alone together at break time. 'It's just, you *mustn't* talk about it. And you must stop looking so sorry for me.'

'But I *am*,' she said. 'Opal, it *is* true, isn't it? This isn't one of your big teases?'

'I wish it was.'

'But . . . your pa will get off, won't he? I mean, this is all a ghastly mistake, isn't it? He's really absolutely innocent, like the father in *The Railway Children* . . . That was such a ripping story – it always makes me cry at the end.'

'This isn't a story,' I said. 'I wish it was.' My voice wobbled.

'Oh, Opal, you poor, poor thing!' Olivia threw her arms round me and hugged me tight.

I put my head on her plump shoulder and cried all over her blouse sleeve.

'There now,' said Olivia, rocking me like a baby. 'Well, don't you worry, Opal. I'm still going to be your friend for ever and ever, no matter what.'

'You're the best friend in all the world,' I said.

'Here – these are for you. I bought them yesterday.' Olivia fumbled down the front of her tunic and brought out a very crumpled bag of toffee chews. There was less than an ounce in the bag, and they were all bitten in half.

'I checked – these are all banana flavour. I saved them for you,' she said.

'Oh, you are kind,' I said. 'But we must share them out equally.'

We saved one each for lesson time, because it made the toffee even more enjoyable when it was sucked illicitly, though we had to try very hard not to move our mouths to avoid detection. We had a little competition to see which of us could make her toffee last the longest during mathematics. We opened our mouths at each other whenever Miss Marcus turned to chalk another sum on the board. I won, managing to keep a tiny sliver of toffee on the end of my tongue throughout the entire lesson.

'I don't want to eat lunch because it will take away the flavour,' I said as we queued in the canteen.

'We'll buy more after school,' said Olivia comfortingly.

Her pocket money seemed to last for ever. It seemed likely that she had more money to spend on sweets than Mother did for all our meals. I wondered if I could ask Olivia to spare me a shilling or two on a weekly basis. I knew she'd be generous enough to give it to me, but thinking about it made me blush with shame.

I forced myself to eat double helpings of the dubious steak pie. We always called it 'rat pie', and wouldn't have been surprised to discover a little claw or piece of tail peeping out of the soggy pastry. I ate my watery cabbage and lumpy mash too. I even chewed my way through the jam coconut tart for pudding. This dish was always called 'blood and dandruff pie', which didn't help the digestion. I felt sick by the time I'd finished, but at least I was full, if all we had to eat for supper was bread and milk. I could even nobly offer my portion to Mother.

After lunch we had the terrible hawk-nosed Mounty for a double housecraft lesson. I hoped to be able to snaffle a handful of raisins or a spoon or two of sugar, but Mounty decided to devote the two lessons to a long and dreary lecture on household matters. She gave us timetables for running a decent household, with set hours for every task – mostly ridiculous matters such as sorting through sheets in the linen cupboard and checking for dust swept under the carpet.

'Old Mounty takes it for granted that we'll all have servant girls like your Jane to wash the sheets and do the sweeping,' I whispered to Olivia.

I wasn't quite whispery enough. Mounty did one of her hawk pounces, flying through the desks and alighting right in front of me.

'I beg your pardon, Miss Plumstead?' she said, affecting deafness, even cupping her hand behind her ear in a pantomime gesture. 'I couldn't quite catch your contribution to my lecture. Please repeat it and enlighten all of us.'

'I – I was simply remarking that you are assuming we'll all have servants, Miss Mountbank,' I said.

'Indeed,' she replied. 'St Margaret's just happens to be a school for the daughters of gentlemen. It is the general assumption that most of our pupils will go on to *marry* gentlemen and achieve a respectable standard of living. Of course, we cannot guarantee this, especially in the case of scholarship girls.' She sprayed my face with saliva as she spat out the word 'scholarship'.

There was a little gasp. It was clear that she was deliberately insulting me. I thought for a moment of her triumph if she should happen to find out about poor dear Father. *Oh please God*, I prayed, *don't let it be in the papers*.

'Ah, that's obviously struck home,' said Mounty. 'But take heart. If you buckle down and learn how to behave like a young lady, then maybe you too will became a proper lady one day, with your own staff.'

I wasn't going to let her patronize me like that.

'I very much doubt it, Miss Mountbank,' I said. 'But even if I happen to marry an extremely rich gentleman, I shall keep a liberal house, with no servants whatsoever.'

'So you will do all the heavy work yourself, in your modern establishment?' said Miss Mountbank.

'I think we'll probably *share* any menial work,' I said boldly. 'And we will both pursue our careers and not mind terribly about clean sheets and dust.'

'How very Bohemian,' said Miss Mountbank, sneering. 'Well, if you're deliberating choosing a future life of makeshift grime, my lecture is probably wasted on you, but I'll thank you to keep quiet so that the *other* young ladies can benefit from my words of wisdom. And if you comment or contradict further, I will give you two hundred lines in detention.'

I kept my mouth shut for the rest of the lesson. It was a huge relief when it was over at last. One more lesson to go – music with Mr Andrews. He was as calm and quiet and dignified as ever, talking to us seriously as if we were equals, never using the heavily sarcastic tone of all the other teachers.

Then he started playing us a Bach violin concerto. It was simply beautiful, and I slumped at my desk, chin on my chest, giving myself over to the music. But then the music became so searingly sweet I could hardly bear it. I was filled with such profound sadness that I couldn't stop myself sobbing. I tried desperately hard to control myself. I pressed my lips together and clenched every muscle in my face, hiding behind my hands, but I still couldn't stop my shoulders shaking. I started making terrible snorting sounds. I heard giggling behind me. I knew everyone was staring at me. I felt myself flushing purple with shame.

The music ended just as the bell went for the end of school.

'Class dismiss,' said Mr Andrews. I felt his cool hand on my shoulder. 'Stay where you are, Opal,' he murmured.

I kept my face covered while everyone else clattered out. Then there was a little silence. I felt a large cotton handkerchief being pressed into my hands.

'There now,' he said as I mopped myself as best I could.

'I'm sorry. I feel such a fool,' I mumbled.

'No, you should feel proud to be so sensitive. *I* feel proud that the music has such a wonderful effect on you. My goodness, Bach himself would feel proud. You're what every music teacher longs for – someone who can listen properly and be stirred to her very soul,' said Mr Andrews.

I started blushing all over again. I felt such a fraud. I wasn't really crying because of the music. I was crying because my poor father was in prison and I felt so sorry for him. I felt even sorrier for myself, because I didn't know what on earth was going to happen next.

9

Mother was out when I got home. The house seemed horribly still and silent. For once I couldn't settle to my homework. I didn't even want to paint. I just wandered miserably through each room. I couldn't stop myself going into my parents' bedroom, opening up Father's wardrobe, and breathing in the smell of his clothes. I even slipped his old dressing gown round my shoulders, pretending he was standing there in person, hugging me.

I wondered how on earth he was managing in prison without any nightclothes, any washing things, any of his own possessions. As the years went by, Father had been unable to avoid looking a little shabby, his suits very tired, his collars beastly paper, but he always kept his down-at-heel shoes brightly polished. He was very particular about his person, shaving with a cut-throat razor every morning, putting pomade on his hair, clipping his nails. Did prisoners really wear those awful coarse suits with the arrow design? Surely all those men were awful and coarse themselves, not quietly spoken, scholarly gentlemen like Father? Would they mock him and make his life even more miserable?

When Cassie came home from Madame Alouette's, she found me weeping, sitting right inside Father's wardrobe, perched uncomfortably upon his shoes.

'Opal! Oh, come out, you fool! I didn't know where you were. And where's *Mother*?'

'I don't know. There was no sign of her when I got in,' I said, snivelling, having to wipe my face on Father's dressing-gown sleeve.

'But she's always here when we come home. Do you think she's gone to visit Father in . . . you know.' I'd heard Cassie mutter all sorts of naughty words but she couldn't seem to cope with saying the word 'prison'.

'Whitechurch is too far away and she hasn't enough money for the journey,' I said.

'Then where on earth is she?'

'I don't know. She's probably just gone for a walk to clear her head,' I said, though this seemed extremely unlikely.

We went downstairs together and made a pot of tea. There were still a few potatoes left, so we scrubbed these and put them in the oven to bake.

'I'm starving *now*,' said Cassie mournfully, peering into the larder. The only thing she could find was half a slab of Madeira cake, so stale it was like a solid brick, but we broke off little chunks and nibbled them cautiously.

'It tastes all right if you suck at it a little,' said Cassie. 'Here, let's go halves.'

'You can have it. I had a big school dinner,' I said.

'I never thought I'd say this, but I actually miss those vile school dinners. Madame Alouette brings all us girls what she calls our "déjeuner", but it's just little fancy rolls that you gobble up in one mouthful. The others don't mind because they're all set on reducing their figures, the silly things,' said Cassie, giving her own ample curves an approving glance.

'You'd better watch out, though, or you won't be able to squeeze yourself into any of your fancy frocks,' I said.

'Don't! It was so *awful* taking the heliotrope gown back. I had to pretend that Pa had put his foot down – and then I felt so mean, because he's never stopped me doing anything.' Cassie started chewing on her thumb, something I hadn't seen her do for years. 'Opal, do you think he'll be all right?'

'I don't know,' I said helplessly.

'Still, it's his own wretched fault,' Cassie said.

'It isn't! Well, he shouldn't have taken the money from the office, obviously, but it was just to please us and make us all happy,' I said.

Cassie looked at me. 'You're meant to have such a sharp mind, Opal, but your moral sense is very blurry. I love Pa just as much as you, but at least I'll admit that he's done a very bad thing. A *stupid* thing, because now look at us all. How can any of us ever be happy again?'

Billy had been drooping on his perch, but now he lifted his head and fluttered his wings. '*Happy days, happy days, happy days*,' he chirruped merrily.

'Oh shut up, for goodness' sake,' said Cassie, and gave him some birdseed to distract him.

The room was silent again, except for the tiny sound of his beak among the seeds, and the relentless ticking of the clock.

'Where *is* Mother?' said Cassie. 'You don't think something has happened to her . . .'

It was what we were both thinking. Mother had been so distraught. What if she'd decided she really couldn't bear it? What if she'd hurled herself under a bus or over the railway bridge? I thought of all the bad things I'd said to her and started to tremble.

But Cassie's head went up. She was listening hard. Then we both heard Mother's key in the front door. We ran and hugged her, nearly knocking her off her feet.

'Careful, girls, mind the shopping,' said Mother. 'There are fresh eggs in that bag, and tomatoes too! Let me get my coat off and I'll start on the supper.'

'Oh, Mother, we've been so worried about you,' said Cassie.

I carried Mother's shopping bag into the kitchen. I unpacked it for her. There was a bottle of milk, half a pound of bacon, a bag of mushrooms, a stick of best butter and an enormous crusty loaf. I stared at them, trying to work out how much they'd cost. Whatever the sum was, it was far more than Mother had had in her purse this morning.

She saw me staring. 'You can take that look off your face. I didn't steal them! I went to the pawn shop by the market and pawned my engagement ring and my pearl brooch and that fancy sewing basket your father bought me,' said Mother.

'Oh, Mother, how brave of you,' I said. My heart started thumping. Should I offer to pawn my paintbox? It was expensive, made of real mahogany, but I wanted to keep it so badly. I saw the expression on Cassie's face and I knew she was thinking of her green dress.

I took a deep breath. 'Do you think we ought to pawn our special things too, Mother?' I asked.

'I don't see much point. They'd only raise a couple of bob and keep us going for a day or two. The rent's due at the end of the month. No, we've got to find a more sensible solution,' said Mother. 'Look, let's get a meal on the table first, and then we'll discuss it.'

We had the most glorious fry-up: eggs, bacon, tomatoes, mushrooms and fried bread, all so good that we didn't talk at all, simply bolted our food. Cassie cut herself another slice of bread and used it to wipe up all the little crispy bits left on her plate. Mother would never have allowed this before, but now she just shook her head mildly and let Cassie continue.

She cleared the dishes and made a fresh pot of tea. 'Now, girls,' she said. 'I have been out looking for work today.'

We stared at her.

'But, Mother, you're still a married lady!' said Cassie.

Mother had always drummed it into us that no respectable lady should ever carry on working after she got married. She should devote herself to her household duties and rear her children. The only married women who worked were poverty stricken, with feckless husbands who couldn't support their families. It was a shock realizing that this was now our own situation.

I knew just how hard it must have been for Mother to go out seeking work. I reached out and took hold of her hand. 'Well done, Mother,' I whispered.

'No, it is not well done,' she said, pulling away from me. 'I've been unsuccessful. I've been to Beade and Chambers department store, Evelyn's the draper's, Maxwell's the toyshop, Henley's china emporium, practically every wretched shop in town, but without success. No one wants to take on a middle-aged lady with scarcely any experience. I even went to the Fairy Glen factory and asked for light work there, but they're only taking on young girls.'

'As if you could ever work in a factory, Mother,' said Cassie fiercely, but Mother glared at her too.

'We can't take that attitude now, girls. We have to do what we can. So I'm going to be working at home making novelty rabbits for Porter's toy factory. They'll be delivering all the pieces on Monday. I'm to make three dozen a day.'

'Three dozen?'

'Apparently they have some women who manage up to a hundred, but even then I don't think I'll earn enough to pay the rent,' said Mother, and a tear rolled down her cheek.

'Don't, Mother, I can't bear it,' said Cassie. 'Look, *I'll* get a job. Hang it, I'll even work at Fairy Glen.'

I stared at my sister, amazed at her heroism.

'No, Cassie, I won't hear of it,' said Mother. 'You're

halfway through your apprenticeship. You'll start earning next year. It would be madness to throw up your position now.'

Cassie slumped with relief.

'But . . . what are we going to do?' I said.

Mother bent her head, not looking at me. She stirred her tea, though it had gone lukewarm.

'I think *you'll* have to start at the factory, Opal,' she said.

I was so shocked I could scarcely breathe.

'*Opal?*' gasped Cassie.

'She's fourteen. There's many a lass of fourteen who goes to work,' said Mother, still staring down at her teacup.

'But I've got my scholarship!' I said. 'I'm going to stay on at school and take my exams. Father says I might even go to university.'

'Yes, well, your father has no say in things now. And I can't quite see the point of all that schooling – it doesn't teach you anything useful. It's time you started work, Opal. You can always catch up with your book learning later.'

'Not at Fairy Glen, though!' said Cassie. 'Can't Opal start an apprenticeship like me?'

'No she can't,' Mother snapped. 'She needs to start earning money.'

'What about one of the shops in town?'

'I've *told* you, there are no positions anywhere.

The only place needing girls is the factory. So that's where she's going. Starting Monday,' said Mother. 'I've fixed it.'

'But she'll *hate* it. Opal will be so different from all the other girls,' said Cassie.

'It's time she learned to fit in. Stop looking at me like that, both of you. I don't want her to have to leave school. I tried to get a job at the factory myself, I keep telling you. There isn't any other option. You'll have to like it or lump it.' Mother stirred her tea so violently that the cup tipped and spilled all over the green chenille cloth. She and Cassie mopped and wrung the cloth and dabbed at the wooden table underneath. I sat in a daze, tea all over my blouse and tunic.

'Opal! Shift yourself! You're sopping wet. It's going to be the devil of a job to get those tea-stains out if you don't soak those clothes immediately,' Mother told me.

'I don't care. It doesn't matter anyway. I'm not going to be wearing them again, am I?' I said, and then I burst into tears.

I went up to my room, took off my uniform, and lay on my bed in my underwear, howling. How *could* Mother say I had to leave school? If Father knew, he'd be horrified. He'd been so proud of me when I won my scholarship. I'd worked hard. I might wind up old Mounty sometimes, but I was still top of the class in every subject except art – and that was simply my pride, because I wouldn't work Miss Reed's boring way. I was *clever*. I was going to go on and come top in every exam and go to university. Intelligence was my only asset. I was small and plain and prickly, with lank hair, weak eyes and a sharp tongue. I was nothing without my scholarship. I couldn't give it all up! Especially not to work at the Fairy Glen factory!

It was at the south end of town, near the railway station, where the houses were terraced and tumble-down. The streets were so narrow the mothers slung their washing on lines across the cobbles and their children dodged in and out of the wet sheets, patterning them with sooty handprints. The women were big and blousy, with great swollen stomachs. The men wore cloth caps and shirts without collars and were drunk every night. I'd never *seen* them drunk of course, but Mother had given us dark warnings, especially about the young men. The young women were the most frightening – bold girls who wandered around with linked arms and whistled and shouted and swore. I *had* seen these girls. Once, when I was fetching shoes from the cobbler's at the railway station, three brassy girls had mocked my accent and laughed at me. I'd done my best to ignore them, but I'd blushed furiously, and this had made them laugh even more.

Now Mother wanted me to work in the factory alongside awful girls like that!

'I won't, I won't, I won't!' I muttered. 'I hate

Mother. I hate Father, because it's all his stupid fault. I *hate* them.'

But that made me feel so bad I hated myself even more. I wanted to be good, to be mature and silently long-suffering. Perhaps I should go to the factory and earn enough to feed my family without complaint. I tried to stop crying and calm myself. I rehearsed it inside my head: I'd go downstairs, kiss Mother, and tell her not to worry any more. I knew it couldn't be helped so I'd start earning my living and work hard. I'd be a dutiful daughter.

I couldn't make myself do it. I lay there sobbing instead, though I was hurting my eyes and giving myself a thumping headache. After a long while Cassie came in and sat down on the edge of my bed.

'You poor old thing,' she said, and she put her cool hand on my burning forehead. 'I've been arguing with Mother, you know. It really isn't fair on you. It would be better for *me* to go to Fairy Glen, seeing as I've left school already, but she won't hear of it. I mean, I quite like it at Madame Alouette's. She's not a bad old stick, and it's fun being in the fashion world and I'm actually getting quite good at making all the hats – but it's not as if I'm going to be doing it for the rest of my life. Catch me ending up a fussy old spinster like Madame herself. As soon as the right man comes along I'll be off like a shot. But it's different for you, Opie.'

'So I'm clearly destined to be a fussy old spinster . . .' I said, blowing my nose.

'No, I didn't mean that! But you want to be one of these new independent women who work and campaign and all that other boring stuff. You're a brainy bluestocking already. It's hateful that you have to throw away all your chances. How are you going to cope at Fairy Glen? Those girls will make mincemeat of you.'

'Shut up, Cass,' I said, but I gave her a big hug all the same.

I couldn't come down and make my peace with Mother. When I eventually got to sleep, I had nightmares, dreaming of a vast rattling machine in a bleak factory. I was seized by a crowd of raucous girls and stuffed right inside it. I felt the machine crunching my bones, mangling me flat. I fought wildly and woke with my bed sheets tangled around my arms and legs.

I spent most of the weekend in my room, painting pictures of dark satanic mills with towering chimneys, though I knew perfectly well that the Fairy Glen factory was a squat, white-walled building with no Gothic features whatsoever.

I tried to read too, but for once I couldn't concentrate on storybooks. My own life seemed to be veering outlandishly into melodrama, so that the troubled lives of the young David Copperfield and Jane Eyre seemed prosaic by comparison.

I wasn't used to having so much free time. I usually spent several hours studying. I'd been set a great deal of homework, but what was the point of doing it now? My schoolbooks stayed in my satchel. It was the oddest feeling knowing that I never needed to get them out again.

I thought of all the girls and how they'd gossip about me when they discovered I'd left school so abruptly and started work in a factory. I tried to pretend I didn't care what any of them thought, but I did, dreadfully. I thought of Miss Laurel and all the teachers tutting and shaking their heads. Mounty and Miss Reed would cluck triumphantly, insisting that they'd always known I would get my come-uppance. I thought of Olivia, and at last this galvanized me into action.

I went downstairs and took my coat from the hall stand.

'So you've stopped sulking at last,' said Mother.

'I wasn't sulking. I was painting,' I said.

'I can see that. You've got brown paint all over your hands. Whatever does it look like, Opal!'

'Oh stop fussing, Mother,' I said, and I went to the front door.

'Where are you going?'

'I'm going to see my *friend*,' I said, and slammed out of the house.

I ran most of the way to Olivia's, suddenly desperate to see her. She was my dear, funny best friend, and she'd been so kind and comforting to me when I'd told her about Father. I wanted her to hold me and rock me again. She'd be devastated when I told her I had to leave school. How would she manage without me? We sat together, we ate lunch together, we walked home together. Olivia wasn't very good at managing by herself. She often needed my whispered help in lessons, and I frequently did her homework.

I started to feel almost as sorry for Olivia as I did for myself. When I got to her house, I banged eagerly on the door. I had to knock several times. Then the young servant girl, Jane, opened it, her cap crooked, a coal smear all down her apron.

'Hello, Jane,' I said, starting to go in, but she gave a little squeal and put out her hand to stop me.

'Sorry, miss, I have to ask the missus,' she blurted out.

'What? But I've not come to see your missus, I've come to see Olivia.'

'I'm not sure it's allowed, miss,' said Jane, looking terribly flustered.

Then Mrs Brand herself came into the hallway. She was holding a newspaper. She actually shook it at me. 'You've got a nerve coming here, Opal Plumstead,' she said.

'I'm sorry, I – I don't know what you mean,'

I stammered, though the sight of the newspaper filled me with dread.

'Of course you know! It's written here in black and white,' she said, stabbing at the newsprint. 'Your father's total disgrace!'

I swallowed, feeling dizzy. 'I'm sorry,' I mumbled. 'Could I – could I just see Olivia please?'

'No you could not!'

'But I need to explain, to tell her that I can't come back to school,' I said.

'Of course you can't! St Margaret's is for the daughters of *gentlemen*.'

'My father might be a thief, but he is still a gentleman,' I said.

I heard a scuffle on the stairs and got a glimpse of Olivia hanging over the banisters, looking stricken.

'Please come down, Olivia – I must talk to you,' I called desperately. But she scuttled back across the landing into her bedroom.

'Olivia isn't allowed to talk to you any more,' said Mrs Brand. 'Now go home at once. Shut the door on her, Jane.'

Jane started to close the door, her white face creased with misery. 'I'm sorry, miss,' she whispered, and then she slammed the door shut.

10

On Monday morning I walked to the Fairy Glen factory, so frightened I could barely put one foot in front of the other. As I got near, I became part of a milling throng of jostling girls, burly men walking three or four abreast, and larky boys dashing about, laughing and joking. I felt like a hopeless alien in a foreign country. When I got to the tall factory gates, I stopped in my tracks, grasping the railings, not sure I could go through with it.

Then the factory clock struck eight. There was a

last surge of workers, and I got swept along with them, across the yard and in through a dark doorway. They rushed off purposefully in different directions. I stood dithering, not having a clue where to go or what to do. It was far worse than my first day at school. I had to struggle not to dissolve into tears like a five-year-old.

'Can I help you, missy?' A plump man in a white coat came out of his office and looked at me kindly.

'Oh please!' I said. 'I'm new and I don't know where to go.'

'You're coming to work here? We don't take on little girls! How old are you? Ten? Twelve?'

I wasn't sure whether he was serious. 'I'm fourteen,' I said, trying to sound dignified.

'Oh I say, quite the little lady,' he said. 'What's your name, dear?'

'Opal Plumstead.'

'My goodness, that's a name and a half. Well, Opal Plumstead, we'd better get you kitted out and then I'll give you a grand tour of the factory. I'm Mr Beeston. I'm the floor manager. Your boss. So mind your "p"s and "q"s when you're talking to me, and give me a curtsy to show you know your place.' His eyes were twinkling. I was pretty sure he was teasing me, but I bobbed him a curtsy all the same.

He shook his head at me, chuckling. 'You're a caution, Opal Plumstead. Right, first we have to get you a cap and overall. I'll have to ask you to pin that pretty pigtail out of sight. We're very hygiene conscious at Fairy Glen.' He took me to a storeroom and gave me a floppy white cap and a starched white overall and showed me the door of the ladies' cloakroom.

There was a girl standing at the mirror, brushing her long black hair in a leisurely way, as if she were in her own bedroom. She saw me staring at her and stuck out her tongue.

I didn't know whether to stick mine out at her, or not. I turned away and struggled into the overall. It was far too big for me, the hem brushing the floor, the cuffs reaching to my fingertips.

The girl burst out laughing. 'Well, you look a right guy!' she said, expertly twisting her hair up into a thick knot on top of her head. She crammed her cap on over it and sauntered off.

I struggled hard to force my own limp hair into a knot, but I didn't have a brush or enough pins so it kept collapsing. I pulled the cap on as low as possible so that it contained all the loose ends. I looked ridiculous with it resting on my eyebrows, but it couldn't be helped.

'That's a good lass,' said Mr Beeston when I crept out again. He looked me up and down. 'Bit tight on you, seeing as you're such a big girl!'

I stared and then gave a timid snigger at his joke.

'That's right, girly. Have a little laugh. You don't want to walk about as if you've got the collywobbles. Now come with me and I'll show you around. It's a sight for sore eyes, I'm telling you!'

He led me down a corridor and then opened a heavy door. Immediately there was an extraordinary jammy, sugary smell, so strong that it made my head swim.

'Mmm, yes – delicious, isn't it?' he said. 'Follow me, then, little Opal Plumstead.'

We entered the vast hot room. Workers in white overalls were toiling at great copper pans. Mr Beeston took me by the elbow to stand beside a large burly man who was tending a huge copper cradle, rocking it like a baby and stirring the contents with intense concentration.

'What is he cooking?' I whispered.

'Take a peep,' said Mr Beeston.

I peered in cautiously and saw that he was stirring almonds, gently browning them.

'Ready now! Sharp with the syrup, young Davey,' called the burly man.

'Young' Davey was a thin, wizened man in his fifties, but his sinewy arms were strong enough to lift a two-handled copper pan full of sugar syrup. He propped the pan on an iron frame by the cradle, taking over the rocking, while the burly man dipped a big ladle into the thick syrup and then flung it over the hot almonds. I watched carefully as a glaze formed around each one.

'Oh my goodness. So . . . are these sugared almonds?' I said.

'Well done, Opal Plumstead. Ten out of ten for you. No, nine out of ten, for they're not sugared almonds just yet. The first coating has to dry – then what do you think will happen?'

'He'll pour another ladleful in?' I said.

Mr Beeston nodded. 'The whole process is repeated for an hour or more until each almond has several coats. Next time you bite into one, missy, see how they crackle into little layers, thin as paper. Try counting how many layers each one has. Then you'll know how many ladlefuls have gone into the whole process. Magical, isn't it?'

'Yes it is! Can I take a turn with the ladle?' I said, wanting to show willing.

'Not for a long while, lass,' said the burly man. 'It's skilled work. We can't trust a peck or two of Jordan almonds to a little kid still wet behind the ears.'

Mr Beeston smiled at me. 'Still, we like 'em keen. Here's another process you'll want to try your hand at, missy, but you'll have to get trained up for this one too.'

He steered me down aisles to where another man was boiling up more syrup in a great copper kettle. 'This is Alfred. Alfred the Great,' he told me.

‘Is that sugar you’re boiling, Mr Alfred?’ I asked timidly.

‘Sugar and water. We make all sorts of sweets that way, with different shapes and flavours,’ said Alfred.

We watched him pick up a basin of cold water.

‘Aha! You look carefully, missy,’ said Mr Beeston.

The man chilled his hand in the water for a few seconds, and then, astonishingly, thrust it into the boiling syrup, scooped some out, then plunged it back into the cold water. It was caked all over with light yellow flakes of brittle sugar.

‘It’s just like a magic trick!’ I exclaimed.

‘No, no, *this* is the magic part,’ said Mr Beeston as Alfred buttered a large marble slab. He tested the syrup again with his extraordinary hand-and-cold-water trial, and then poured the contents onto the marble. It spread rapidly, but then cooled so quickly that it was easily contained within little iron bars.

I stared at the great golden mass, fascinated. Alfred took a phial, pulled open a lump of the golden glory and sprinkled a few drops here and there, kneading them in quickly to distribute the flavour.

‘What is he making?’ asked Mr Beeston.

I sniffed. ‘Lemon drops!’ I exclaimed. ‘Oh, he’s going to make hundreds of lemon drops.’

‘No, our Alfred isn’t a one-trick pony, dear. We pride ourselves on our variety of sweets at Fairy Glen,’ said Mr Beeston. ‘Let’s see what he tackles next.’

Alfred cut off another lump of sugar dough and sprinkled it with a different phial.

I sniffed again. 'Peppermint!'

Alfred kneaded the new piece of dough thoroughly, turning it time after time and slapping it about on the slab.

'It must be quite cool now,' I said.

'Only on the surface,' said Mr Beeston. 'You try sticking your little finger right inside the sugar dough, Opal Plumstead.'

I did as he suggested and gave a little squeal. It was still boiling hot. I had to suck my finger hard. Mr Beeston and Alfred laughed at me.

Alfred seemed to have hands made of cast iron, because he continued working the dough without flinching. Then he suddenly seized it and flung it over a great hook set in a post. I stared, open-mouthed, as he pulled the sugar into a great shining strand, then threw it over the hook again and again and again, his rhythm as regular as a metronome. As he worked, the yellow syrup turned pure white before my eyes.

'It *is* magic,' I said.

I watched Alfred make several skeins of peppermint, then carry them to another corner to lay them in front of a row of gas jets. He went backwards and forwards making more pliable candy, keeping it warm once it was successfully pulled.

He now coloured one of the skeins bright pink.

‘To make raspberry drops?’ I asked.

‘To make pink-and-white kisses,’ said Mr Beeston.

‘Kisses!’ Olivia and I had often bought these lovely little pink-and-white sweets, giggling as we popped each one in our mouths, comparing it to an imaginary kiss.

‘Kisses are pink *and* white,’ I said. ‘How do they get mixed up together?’

‘Look, look!’

Alfred snipped off another lump of white, pulled it together with the pink, then folded them firmly. He fed them into a little machine, placing the pink and white mixture between the rollers, like Mother passing shirts through our mangle. There was a grinding noise as a young lad turned the crank of the machine. The dough came out the other side, a long strip of pink and white marked into small squares.

‘See to it, Freddy,’ said Mr Beeston. The young lad beat it firmly, and it divided into familiar little kisses.

Mr Beeston consulted his pocket watch and speeded up our tour. I watched sugar syrup being mixed with gum and turned into a paste spread out on a marble table. It was punched out into little lozenges with a tin tube. I saw the syrup boiled extra vigorously until it turned brown, and was then sprinkled with slices of coconut to make dark coconut candy, cut into slabs when cold. I saw sugar mixed with great slabs of butter over the flames, the smell so sweet and rich my mouth watered.

'It's toffee!' I said, and watched as my favourite toffee chews were concocted, a toffee layer poured on the slab and left to cool a little, then a layer of flavoured soft sugar dough, and then another layer of toffee. It seemed so strange to me now that when I'd popped one in my mouth I'd never wondered how each toffee chew had been constructed.

'Where will I work, Mr Beeston?' I asked, wondering if I could turn the handle of the kiss machine, or cut the slabs into little squares.

'You'll be upstairs, missy, with the other young girls,' he told me. 'Come with me. And pick up those skirts, I can't have you taking a tumble.'

I clutched handfuls of my unwieldy overall and made my way up the rickety spiral staircase at the end of the vast hot room. I was clearly showing too much leg because Freddy, the young lad on the factory floor, gave a loud whistle. I blushed scarlet, my shirt sticking to me under the starched overall.

'Careful now,' said Mr Beeston as we got to the iron landing. He opened a door and I stepped into a strange new room with a stifling atmosphere. Mr Beeston had said that young girls worked upstairs, but at first glance the room seemed full of grey-haired old grannies. I wiped my steamed-up glasses on the sleeve of my overall and peered again. No, they were girls – girls with pale grey hair and pale grey skin and pale grey overalls.

'What's happened to them?' I whispered in alarm.

'These are my ghost girls,' said Mr Beeston. 'I lock 'em up here for months if they give me any cheek and they go grey when they don't see the sunlight.'

I stared at him.

He nearly split his sides laughing at me. 'You believed me! Just for a moment you believed me!' he spluttered.

I hadn't seriously believed him, but I smiled foolishly to be obliging.

'It's starch, Opal Plumstead. Don't look so worried – it soon washes off,' said Mr Beeston. 'Here, Patty, let me demonstrate to our little new girl.'

He gestured to the black-haired girl who had called me a guy. She was stooping over a large shallow box, and rolled her eyes, but came and stood before us, grey hands on hips.

I knew she'd been as pink and white as a candy kiss half an hour ago. Mr Beeston took a white handkerchief from his overall, licked the corner with his big pink tongue, and then wiped it on her cheek. The handkerchief was smudged with grey, while she was left with a pink stripe on her face.

'Have you had your bit of fun now, Mr Beeston?' Patty said.

'Yes indeedy, Miss Pattacake. Back to your work

now. Do you see what the girls are doing, Opal? They're making starch moulds – all different shapes, see.' He opened a drawer and showed me a selection of sticks with a dozen little plaster balls like halves of marbles fastened to each one. He went over to Patty's box of starch powder and pressed it down lightly. It left a row of little hollow shapes.

I thought hard. 'Fondants!' I said.

'Fondants indeed. These are the standard moulds, but we've got rosettes, bows, little fish, flowers, all sorts for our seasonal novelties. Come with me.' He steered me towards the corner, where two men in protective aprons hunched over another big copper pan.

'Here's my burly twosome, George and Geoff,' said Mr Beeston. He patted their rolled-up shirt sleeves. 'See the muscles! It's a wonder they don't join the circus as strongmen.'

The older man, George, took the vast copper pan and lifted it off the flames as easily as a teacup. He poured some of the fondant mixture into a smaller pan with a little spout. Then young Geoff delicately poured his mixture into each of the holes in the starch powder in the box.

'They go off to the drying room over there and will be left until tomorrow. Then they are given their special finish – look, over here,' said Mr Beeston. He took me over to another girl, who was standing in front of shallow pans and yet more boxes. She poured sugar syrup over the hardened fondants. We waited a little, and then watched the sugar crystallize on the shapes. She drained the syrup off to be used again and showed off the finished fondants, shining like precious jewels.

'Here, sample the wares,' said Mr Beeston, and he picked out a gleaming fondant and popped it in my mouth. I pressed my tongue against it, my whole mouth filling with sweetness. It was the taste of *Happy Days*, and I didn't know whether to laugh or cry.

'There now, Opal Plumstead. Isn't it sweet to work at the Fairy Glen sweet factory?' said Mr Beeston.

'Yes, sir,' I replied uncertainly.

'So we'll set you to work straight away,' he went on. 'Patty, you're in charge of this little lass.'

My heart sank as the dark girl looked up again, her eyebrows raised quizzically.

'Keep an eye on her, show her what to do, and generally be kind to little Opal Plumstead,' said Mr Beeston.

'Yes, sir,' said Patty. 'As if I'd be anything else,' she added with emphasis.

All the other girls in the room tittered ominously.

11

They started the moment Mr Beeston left the room. All the girls crowded round me, leaving their work. George and Geoff watched impassively.

'Opal Plumstead? What kind of a name is that?' asked Patty. 'Is that really your name or is old Beeston fooling about? Hey, I'm talking to you.' She gave me a poke in the chest.

'Stop it!' I said, my voice sounding high and strange. 'Don't you dare poke me!'

'Well, tell us your name, then,' said Patty.

'It's Opal Plumstead, as you very well know.'

'Opal Plum-in-the-mouth Plumstead!' she said in a ridiculous approximation of my accent. 'Oh-pal? Well, you're no pal of mine, little squirt.'

'What you come to work here for, girl? You're not a factory lass,' said one of the other girls.

'She doesn't look like *any* kind of lass. Look at her chest. Flat as a pancake!' said another.

I felt myself blushing painfully. I glanced at George and Geoff, horrified that they might have heard.

'Yes, why have you come slumming it here, Opal Plum? I bet you're the swotty type, wearing them stupid specs. Did you blot your copy book and get chucked out of school, then?' Patty demanded.

'No I didn't! I was going to stay on. I had a scholarship!' I declared.

This was a big mistake. They all went 'Ooooh!' and then squealed with laughter. I wanted to slap their silly faces, but they outnumbered me twenty to one, and they all towered above me too.

'A scholarship girl! Oh, swipe me, are we fit to be in your presence?' Patty said. 'Maybe we should all curtsy to the superior brain in your noddle. Or maybe we'll just knock it about a bit, teach it that life isn't all sums and grammar and silly rules. Knock-knock, Plumbrain.' She hit my head twice with her knuckled fist, sending my cap even further down my face.

They all roared with laughter at that.

'You're the one without any brain at all, treating me so horribly. Mr Beeston told you to be kind to me!' I shouted.

'Oh, temper temper! What are you going to do, then? Go running to old Beeswax?' said Patty.

I hesitated. I wasn't a total fool. I knew how girls reacted if you told tales to a teacher. I felt a wave of longing for St Margaret's, where I'd been important, and I'd had Olivia for a friend. It was fatal thinking about her. I felt the tears pricking my eyes.

'Oh look, I do believe she's going to cry!' said one of the girls.

I struggled desperately. 'I am *not* crying,' I said fiercely. 'I'm here to work. Now, will you please show me what to do?'

'If you're so clever, you can work it out for yourself, Plumbrain,' said Patty, and she turned her back on me.

'Very well,' I said. I went to the drawer of moulds and selected a stick. I moved to a pile of starch boxes. I set about making shapes with my stick and its half-marbles. I felt I was doing a reasonable job, but then Patty came and peered.

'Let's see . . .' She took hold of the box and shook it deliberately, so that all the shapes were sifted over with loose starch. 'Whoops!' she said. 'Better start again.'

This time I couldn't stop my tears dripping down into the powder.

'Here now.' It was Geoff, the younger man with rosy cheeks. 'Yes, that's coming along fine. We have a set number to do of each pattern. You stick with the rose design and work your way through all the boxes. Then, when we've filled them up with our sugar mixture, they all go in the drying room and you start all over again with a fresh box.'

I sniffed inelegantly. 'Is that all I do? I don't do anything else?' I thought perhaps he was teasing me, but he shook his head solemnly.

'Nothing else. It's a nice easy job, ain't it?' He leaned nearer and whispered in my ear, 'Don't let the other girls get you down. It's just their silly way. They'll ease off soon enough.'

I looked up at him gratefully, but this was a mistake too.

'Would you believe it! She's making sheep's eyes at Geoff already, the little minx!' said Patty. 'You watch out, Geoff, or I'll tell your missus.'

'Less of your cheek, Miss Pattacake,' said Geoff, and he gave her a pat on the bottom.

Patty squealed. There was a little whirlwind chase around the room until she blundered into a box and sent it flying, starch going everywhere, making us all choke.

The older man, George, shook his head. 'Now then,

simmer down, you lot,' he said. 'Especially you, Patty, or I'll throw you in my pot and boil you into syrup.'

He spoke lightly, but even so the girls settled down, and Patty swept up the spilled starch and applied herself to her own boxes. I hunched over mine. My back started aching terribly. I couldn't believe we were required to stand all day long. I took a pride in moulding neatly for a while, but long before an hour was up I was finding the work incredibly tedious. I was used to the variety of school, with a different lesson every forty minutes. It was so hard to keep doing the same simple repetitive thing. I felt like an infant in a sandpit, making mould after mould after mould.

Patty and the other girls chattered away together. They were ignoring me now, thank goodness, but it was hard to be deliberately left out of all the conversation. I couldn't have joined in anyway. They were saying the most unspeakable things about their sweethearts. I kept blushing for them, wondering how they could say such things aloud, let alone in front of Geoff and George. Mercifully the two men didn't seem to be listening. They talked to each other, debating the qualities of different brown ales, so I couldn't join in that conversation, either.

I wondered what my prim teachers would think of my listening to these factory folk. I would tell Mother, and then surely she wouldn't insist that I work here.

What would *Father* say? But perhaps he was having to suffer worse treatment in prison. I began composing a painting in my mind: Father and me as martyrs with uplifted eyes and soulful expressions, being terribly tortured by prisoners and factory girls. I decided to portray Patty as a certain lady of Babylon.

Mr Beeston looked in halfway through the desperately long morning. He watched over me for a few minutes. My hands started shaking and I grew clumsy with my stick, but he didn't seem to notice. 'Excellent, excellent!' he said. 'You've taught her very well, Patty.'

Patty smirked, but her eyes flicked to me warily. I held my tongue and stalked over to the drying room with my completed tray.

Mr Beeston poked my cheeks when I came out. 'How many dried fondants have you popped in your mouth in secret, eh, Opal Plumstead?'

'None, Mr Beeston!' I said indignantly.

The temptation had been great but I wasn't a fool. You couldn't pilfer a fondant out of a finished box without leaving an obvious gap.

'Not the slightest bit peckish?' he said, sounding surprised. 'Don't you care for our fine Fairy Glen fondants, Opal Plumstead? You ate one readily enough earlier.'

'I love them, Mr Beeston, of course I do,' I said.

'Then you must claim your new girl's perks, little

silly! Didn't Patty explain? Here!' Mr Beeston strode into the drying room and returned with a big box of finished fondants.

'Here we are – for your delectation and delight,' he said, laying the box beside me with a flourish.

'What do you mean?' I said uncertainly.

'Gobble as many as you want, my dear. Make the most of it. You won't ever get the chance again.'

'Are you teasing me, sir?' I asked.

'Me? I'm the most deadly serious chappie in Christendom.' He tweaked my nose and then went off, leaving the full box beside me.

I looked at the glowing fondants. It was a select assortment: vanilla, rose, lemon, pale peppermint green, and apricot. Could I *really* eat them? Patty was watching me, hands on her hips. She made no attempt to snatch one for herself. That made me even more suspicious. Perhaps it was a dummy box, though the fondants certainly looked and smelled delicious. If I put one in my mouth, maybe I'd discover it was made of cardboard. Then they'd all burst out laughing.

I ignored the fondants determinedly and got on with my moulding.

Geoff came over and peered at my work. 'You're very neat,' he said politely.

'Thank you,' I said. I didn't dare look up at him in case Patty started cat-calling again.

'You're not eating your fondants!' he said, sounding surprised.

'Well, I'm not sure they're real,' I mumbled.

'Of course they are!'

'But am I really *allowed*?'

'You get cracking, girl. I ate my way through three whole boxfuls my first day,' said Geoff.

'Would you like one now?' I asked.

'No fear,' said Geoff. 'Can't stand 'em now. That's the whole point, see. First day you eat as many as you want. You get so sick you can't bear the thought of eating them ever again. So there's no pilfering on the job. Go on, help yourself.'

So I reached out and took a rose fondant. It was even more delicious than the one Mr Beeston had given me. I savoured it slowly as I moulded, and then tried an apricot. It was even better, its slight tanginess blending beautifully with the sugar coating. I sampled a lemon, and a peppermint, then a vanilla – and then I started all over again.

Eating them was so soothing, it helped take my mind off my boring task. I could quite easily see how Geoff could get through three boxes. I'd do that too – maybe even manage more! I'd eat fondants all day long and never sicken. They didn't realize what a sweet tooth I had. I finished the entire box, but now I wasn't so sure about starting another. My teeth felt furry with sugar and my whole throat seemed coated with soft, slimy fondant cream. The smell of sugar crept right up my nostrils. The sweets I'd already eaten started churning in my stomach. I was scared I might disgrace myself and be sick. I thought of the ladies' room, so far away – down all the stairs and right through the factory. Would I be able to make it that far? But I couldn't be sick *here*, in front of everyone. I felt the sweat start out on my forehead.

'Watch out, she's going to chuck any minute!' said Patty.

I took a deep breath. 'No I'm not. I'm perfectly fine,' I said, willing this to be true.

Then a bell suddenly clanged loudly and all the girls stopped moulding and practically ran out of the room.

'Oh goodness, is it a fire alarm?' I asked.

George and Geoff shook their heads at me as they took the great copper pan off the flames and stood it on a large rack.

'It's dinner time,' said Geoff. 'Follow us – we'll show you where to go.'

'I – I'm not sure I want any dinner,' I said.

'Course you do, silly girl. It'll settle those fondants.'

Geoff was very kind, but I wished he wouldn't call me silly. It was so humiliating not knowing the simplest thing. I wasn't sure he knew the state of my stomach better than I did, but I let him take me by the elbow and lead me downstairs. George started to take an interest in me too, telling me several times to 'Perk up, little lass.'

The dining hall was in another building altogether. A rich savoury smell was seeping through its doors. For a moment my stomach lurched alarmingly and I thought I might have to make a run for it, but then I breathed deeper, hoping that the meat and vegetables might counteract the cloying sweetness inside me.

I followed Geoff and George into the dining hall and looked at the milling crowd in alarm. There were unruly queues at the serving hatches, some wanting soup, some meat, some pudding, some content with a cup of tea and a bun. There was an even longer queue at a desk, where people balanced trays. People ate at long tables, but I saw that the men all sat on one side, the women on the other. I'd hoped to nestle near Geoff and George, but it looked as though I'd have to chance my luck with the girls. I resolved to sit as far away from Patty as I could.

I went to join the meat queue, surprisingly hungry now. It looked better than school dinners: boiled beef and carrots and mounds of fluffy mashed potato. I waited politely in the queue, furious when several girls with pointy elbows squeezed past me.

'There is a *queue*,' I said.

'Oh Lordy, there's a queue, is there! Well, swipe me pink,' said one girl.

'A queue, indeed! And there's me thinking it was a free-for-all,' said another.

They both stayed exactly where they were. I tried to ignore them, but they started making fun of me now, commenting on my ill-fitting overalls and ridiculous cap. So it wasn't just Patty. *All* the girls were coarse and unkind. This factory was even worse than I'd feared. I wondered about running out of the dining hall and hiding in the ladies' room. Oh dear, if only I'd done so! But I stuck it out and waited until I was at the front at last. I received my plate of meat and veg and was then directed over to the desk. I couldn't understand why we had to queue all over again, our food cooling on our trays. Then I realized what the folk ahead of me were doing. There was a woman with a cash register at the desk. The people were *paying* for their meals. A sign above the desk swam into focus.

THREE-COURSE MEAL	3*d*.
MEAT AND VEGETABLES	2*d*.
PUDDING OR BUN	1*d*.

It was just like a restaurant. I'd been a fool to think the meal was provided for free. I didn't have tuppence for my meat and veg. I didn't even have a penny for a bun. I had no money at all.

I felt the shame of it wash over me. I stood

dithering, peering around for Geoff or even Mr Beeston, wondering if I could possibly pluck up the courage to ask them to lend me the money, but I couldn't spot either of them now. I waited until I was at the head of the queue.

'Tuppence please,' said the woman. She was so fat she oozed out on either side of her seat and hid it totally, so it looked as if she were squatting in thin air. Perhaps she ate the thrupenny, tuppenny and penny choices all day long.

'Please, I'm terribly sorry – I'm new, you see. I didn't realize we had to pay for our meals. I haven't got any money on me,' I whispered to the fat woman. 'Could you possibly see your way to giving me credit just for today?'

'What?' she said, frowning at me, her chins wobbling indignantly. 'We don't give credit here. We're not a bleeding charity institution. You pays your money and you has your meal. No money – no meal.'

'But what am I going to do with it if I can't pay,' I said, staring at my meal in despair.

'Take it back! Now. Before it gets any colder. And don't try and play this trick again, girl, it ain't funny.'

I had to carry my wretched tray of food back to the hatch. Some fool thought I was pushing in, returning for a second helping, and objected bitterly. The woman behind the hatch was most put out when I thrust my loaded tray back at her.

'Make up your mind, miss! Don't you go messing me about again,' she said.

I was sure I'd never ever dare return to the dining room. I fled from the hall, across the deserted factory floor, back to the ladies' room. The fondants were churning around again. I reached a cubicle just in time and was horribly sick. I stayed shuddering and crying behind the locked door for a while and then emerged shakily to wash my face.

I got another shock when I saw myself in the mirror above the washbasins. I was pale grey. The morning working in the fondant room had done its work. I set about washing it off determinedly. I managed to scrub my face and hands pink again, but my cap and overall were still covered in starch. At least the ridiculous cap was preventing my hair turning grey too.

I wondered what I should do now. I was still feeling weak from vomiting. The rare times I'd been taken ill at school I was sent to the sick room and encouraged to lie down on the bed with a glass of water and a bowl beside me. I very much doubted that the factory had a similar refuge. Should I just ask to go home because I wasn't feeling well? I had such an urgent longing to be back in my bedroom with my books and my paintings that I doubled up, moaning.

'Oh my goodness! What's the matter, child?' A woman was standing in the doorway, peering at me anxiously. Her cap and overall were snowy white and fitted her perfectly. She had extraordinary blue eyes with dark lashes, and a fine complexion. She stood beautifully, with a ramrod-straight back. If she weren't obviously a factory worker, I'd have thought her a true lady. Her voice sounded like a lady's too, quiet and melodious.

I straightened up, feeling incredibly foolish.

'Are you ill, dear?' she asked.

'No. Well, yes, I've just been sick,' I said.

'Oh dear.' But the lady looked faintly amused. 'Is it by any chance your first day here at Fairy Glen?'

'Yes, it is.'

'So perhaps you spent the morning eating rather a lot of sweets?'

'Fondants, miss. It *is* allowed, isn't it?'

'Oh yes indeed, but it often has rather unfortunate consequences,' she said. 'Shall I fetch one of the girls from the fondant room to look after you?'

'*No!* I mean, no thank you, miss. I'd sooner be quiet by myself,' I said.

'It's not very pleasant in here,' said the lady. 'Perhaps you'd like to walk outside in the yard for a while and get some fresh air? You'll hear the bell when it's time to go back to work.'

'Yes, I should like that,' I said.

'Come here.' She took several pins from her own hair and deftly adjusted my cap, securing it at a much more sensible angle. 'That looks a bit better, doesn't it?'

'Oh yes, miss!'

'You *are* fourteen, aren't you? You look so young to be working. But at least you'll be properly looked after here. There's a lovely family feel to the Fairy Glen factory, don't you find?'

I stared at her. What kind of warped family were Patty and all the other girls? But perhaps Geoff was like a kindly big brother, and Mr Beeston was certainly the jolly uncle type.

I shrugged my shoulders.

The lady looked perplexed. 'You don't look very happy. You do *want* to work here, don't you?'

This was too much.

'No, of course I don't want to work here! It's absolutely awful. I'd give anything in the whole world to be back at school,' I said. Then I ran out of the ladies' room, along the passageway and out into the yard.

It was very tempting to keep on running. I wanted to go home so much, but we had no money. I *had* to work, even if it was just until the end of the week. We got our wages on Friday lunch time.

I walked round and round the yard by myself, taking in great gulps of air. It was a sullen, grey day, and there was a faint sour smell from the tannery on the other side of the railway station, but even so the air felt clear and pure after the stifling fondant room. I could still feel little prickles of starch up my nose and in my ears. I could still smell and taste the fondants and I prayed I wouldn't be ill again.

When the bell clanged, I clenched my fists and made myself march back inside. I started moulding, my head bent over my boxes, taking no notice when Patty began goading me again.

'What's the problem, Plumbrain? Why're you ignoring me? Can't you hear me? Ain't you got any ears? Let's look.' She snatched at my cap, pulling out the lady's hairpins. 'Oh yes, here we are – two sticky-out little lugs.' She put her mouth close to one of my ears. 'Hello hello hello!' she bellowed.

'Stop it! I can hear you perfectly. You just don't say anything of consequence so I don't bother to listen,' I said fiercely.

'Oooh!' said Patty. 'Little Lady Muck. Anyfink of consequence, eh! What a blooming cheek. Who do you think you are, talking to me like that?'

'*I* am Opal Plumstead. And *you* are a great big uncouth bully,' I declared.

'That's it, little Opal, you tell her,' said Geoff.

'No more joking now. Get on with your work, girls,' said George.

Patty pulled a face at him but stopped tormenting me. The other girls started chatting amongst themselves. I moulded on and on in silence, taking each completed box to the drying room. I made rose after rose after rose. I was really hungry now, but I wasn't tempted to try to eat the sweets again, though Geoff offered me another box. I thought longingly of my supper at home.

I wondered what sort of lunch they'd given Father in prison. Would it be the bare minimum – a plate of watery gruel, a hunk of butterless bread? Father was so thin already. I wondered if he would actually survive such harsh treatment. Perhaps I would never see him again.

This thought sent me dangerously close to tears again. I started frantically reciting in my head to distract myself – Tennyson and Christina Rossetti, and long passages from *Romeo and Juliet* and *A Midsummer Night's Dream*. When I couldn't think of any more poetry, I silently sang every hymn I could remember, and then regressed to infant nursery rhymes. I moulded in time to 'One, two, buckle my shoe' and marched to the drying room to 'Seesaw, Margery Daw'.

I had to start the whole process all over again, but at long, long last, at six o'clock, the bell went.

'Home time!' said Geoff cheerily. 'Well done, lass, you've worked hard.'

'Yes, you'll do well here, so long as you try to fit in,' added George.

Try to fit in! I would never ever fit in at Fairy Glen.

I hated all these awful girls and they hated me too.

I wasn't quick enough putting my moulds away and depositing my last box in the drying room. Geoff and George went out of the door, and before I could follow them, two girls seized hold of me.

'Now you're for it, Plumbrain,' said Patty. She snatched off my cap, picked up a full box of starch, and emptied it over my head.

They all screamed with laughter as I gasped and choked, then ran out of the room, leaving me to clear up the terrible mess.

12

I felt terrible walking home. I'd tried to wash off as much starch as I could in the ladies' room, but there was nothing I could do about my hair. I felt as if everyone were staring at me, pointing behind my back. It was so dreadful, so shameful. I resolved never ever to go back, no matter what.

I got home at quarter past seven feeling desperately tired and wretched. I'd had no idea factory hours were so long. I thought Mother and Cassie would be terribly worried about me, but when

I got home they were absorbed in other things. I found Cassie stirring minced meat on the stove while Mother sat at the table, assembling little grey rabbits – each one to be cut out of felt, stitched together, stuffed with sawdust, and given bead eyes and an embroidered smile. Fifteen or twenty were lying on the floor with their stiff paws in the air, as if a farmer had been out shooting with his gun.

'Oh, Mother,' I said. I sat down beside her. She barely glanced at me, stitching rapidly, her eyes screwed up to see properly in the dim gaslight. She didn't even take in my stiff grey hair.

'How did you get on, dear?' she asked.

'It was *awful*,' I said. I was about to launch into my woeful tale when I saw her dab quickly at her thumb with an old cloth. It was spotted with red marks. 'Mother, is that blood?'

'It's nothing,' she said.

I caught hold of her fingers and smoothed them out. The tips were so raw that several were bleeding, and there were great blisters on the two fingers and thumbs in contact with the needle. All her fingers were swollen, especially round the joints.

'Mother, stop sewing! Oh my goodness, you can't possibly carry on with your hands in such a state. Look, *I'll* finish this one.' I suddenly had a wonderful thought. 'In fact, you don't have to do any more. I'll make the little rabbits. My fingers are strong and nimble. I won't need to go to the factory any more. I can just stay home and stitch.' The idea of sewing rabbits all day long instead of going to school would have appalled me last week, but now it seemed a blissful idea.

'Don't be silly, Opal,' said Mother, starting stitching again. 'Piecework is far too poorly paid. I'm getting paid six shillings for twenty-four dozen wretched rabbits. I've been stitching as fast as I can with no break whatsoever, and yet I haven't managed *half* my quota for the day. You're getting *eleven* shillings a week, with a bonus after six months. There's no comparison, child. You have to stay there, even if you do find it awful. Why was it so bad? Could you not get the hang of the work?'

'*Look*,' I said, crouching beside the lamp.

Mother groaned, and Cassie screamed and came running.

'Opal – your *hair*! What's happened to it? Oh Lord, how will you bear it? It's *grey*. You've turned into an old woman!' she cried.

'It'll wash out,' said Mother. 'Oh dear, is it the starch? I hoped they wouldn't put you in that room. Don't they provide you with caps?'

'Yes, but a hateful girl snatched it off and shook a whole boxful of starch all over me,' I said.

'What?' said Cassie. 'Well, I hope you tipped a box over her and banged it hard on her head for good measure.'

'I couldn't. She's much bigger than me. All the other girls take her side,' I said, trembling.

'Didn't you tell the supervisor?' said Mother.

'She can't do that. They'll all hate her if she does, and get at her more than ever,' said Cassie. 'You must learn to fight back, Opie! Don't let them get away with it. They'll always pick on a new girl unless you stand up for yourself.'

'You don't know what it's like,' I protested.

'I do so! When I started at Madame Alouette's, the other girls didn't like me, especially Rosa, because she always used to be Madame's pet. She hated it when I was praised. Once Madame told the other girls to watch me making satin rosettes, because I was so good at it, but when I got back from running an errand to the dressmaker's, I found them all snipped into little pieces. I knew that Rosa had done it, so I bided my time, and then, when she had her back to me, engrossed in her sewing, I snipped off a lock of her hair!'

'Cassie!' said Mother wearily. 'I thought Rosa was your friend.'

'She is *now* – we're thick as thieves – but she knows not to mess with me. It was only a little lock of hair anyway,' said Cassie. She ran her fingers through *my* hair. 'Poor Opie. I'll wash it for you after supper. Oh lawks, the mince!'

We ate burned mince, lumpy potatoes and watery

cabbage. Cassie might be wonderful at making satin rosettes, but she was a hopeless cook. Then we cleared the dishes, gathered as close as we could to the lamp, and set about sewing those wretched rabbits. I could see why Mother's hands had got into such a state. Cassie was good at sewing, of course, but even she struggled to get the stitches small and tight enough for the four paws, and then it was the devil's job to push the sawdust in. We worked till gone ten, and then had to give up, still a dozen rabbits short of the suggested daily quota.

Cassie washed my hair at the kitchen sink, using up a great deal of her Rainbow Silk shampoo, and giving it three rinses to get it squeaky clean.

Mother was so tired and her hands so sore she couldn't even undress properly for bed. Cassie and I had to unbutton her and help her into her nightdress.

'You're like two wounded soldiers,' said Cassie. 'I feel so bad that I'm not suffering too. Perhaps I really should leave Madame Alouette's and work at Fairy Glen like Opal. Then we'd have twenty-two shillings a week. We could live like three queens on that.'

I couldn't help selfishly hoping that Mother would agree to this suggestion. If I had Cassie working alongside me, it wouldn't be nearly as lonely and she'd help me get the better of Patty and her friends. It wouldn't be so desperately boring moulding all day if I had Cassie to talk to. We could play pretend games again. It had been such fun playing Islands on our river trip.

But Mother wouldn't hear of it. 'You must finish your training, dear,' she said, giving Cassie a hug.

'What about *my* training?' I said shakily. 'What about my scholarship?'

'Oh, Opal, don't start!' Mother sighed wearily. 'I'm too tired for arguments. I'm sorry you don't like it at Fairy Glen. We'll keep looking for another job for you. There might be a suitable position in one of the shops, especially just before Christmas.'

'I don't want to work in a shop! I don't want to work in a horrible factory. I don't want to work at all.'

'And what good's that going to do you?' said Mother. 'It will just give you even more airs and graces and turn you into a frump of a bluestocking. And what would you *do* if you stayed on at that silly school till you're a great girl of eighteen?'

'I – I could manage to go on to university. Go to Oxford, like Father,' I said.

'And what good has a varsity education done him,' said Mother bitterly. 'Now get to bed and wrap that wet hair up in a towel or you'll catch a terrible chill.'

I decided I *wanted* to get a chill. I hoped I'd wake up so ill and feverish I couldn't go to work. I lay on my bed feeling wretched, crying into my damp pillow.

'Opie?' It was Cassie, creeping up to my bed. 'Don't cry! I'm so sorry you have to go to that factory.

Look, I'll start making eyes at every passable rich man I come across. If I make a good marriage, I'll be able to keep us all in style.'

Cassie's kindness only made me feel worse. She was doing her best to help out. And although I was angry with Mother, I had to concede that *she* was trying her hardest to help out too. I knew I should be brave and suffer silently like a martyr, but all I could do was grind my teeth and mutter, 'It's not fair, it's not *fair*.'

Father was the only one who would understand, but he wasn't here. I ached to talk to him. I woke up in the middle of the night, missing him dreadfully, terrified of going back to the factory in the morning. I had so lost my senses I had a desperate urge to call for Father. I even found myself moaning his name aloud, as if by sheer need alone I could summon him through his prison bars all the long way back home.

I sat up in bed, lit a stump of candle and found my sketching pad. I tried to draw a portrait of Father but couldn't get the likeness right, though I made four or five attempts. It was as if I'd already forgotten what he looked like, though I'd seen him only last week.

I tore the crude sketches into shreds and started writing a letter to him instead. I wrote a blow-by-blow account of yesterday's events, recalling every slur and insult from Patty and the girls. I told Father about the desperate tedium of moulding all day long, the stifling smells of warm sugar and dense starch, the heat, the harsh conditions. My legs were cramped and aching, my shoulders and neck so stiff I could barely move, from standing up hour after hour. I exaggerated my physical woes and wrote paragraph after paragraph about my psychological misery.

Father was the only member of my family who had taken pride in my scholarship. I knew he'd hoped for a great future for me. Maybe I *could* have gone to Oxford or Cambridge. I couldn't take a degree like the gentleman undergraduates, but women were now allowed to study alongside them. I thought of learning Latin and Greek, such strange, magical languages. I hungered after all those wondrous volumes in vast college libraries. I yearned for inspirational lectures. I saw myself walking across grass lawns in medieval colleges, talking to my fellow students.

But now I had no chance of learning a single phrase of Latin, opening just one of those books, hearing even a sentence of a lecture. I would never tread on one blade of that grass. My only future was the Fairy Glen factory – day after day, week after week, month after month, year after year. *My* prison sentence was even worse than Father's because I was now trapped for life. I ranted on for several closely written pages, long after my candle flickered and went out. Even after my pad and my pencil fell to the floor I still wrote on in my head.

I went to sleep and dreamed of the factory. It was staffed by a thousand terrifying Pattys. They prodded and pushed me until I tumbled right into a huge vat of simmering sugar, then they stirred me with great wooden paddles and I felt myself dissolving into sticky syrup.

'I'm me, I have to stay *me*!' I screamed, and woke myself up.

In the dawn light I looked at the long letter I'd written to Father. The last two pages were completely incoherent, the lines swerving up and down and crisscrossing at random. I read it through as far as I could, blushing at my rambling self-pitying rant. What was I thinking of? How could I seriously send such a letter to Father? He would only blame himself for my misery.

I tore up all the pages in shame and wrote a short, loving note instead:

Dearest Father

I'm missing you so much already. I wish I could see you! It must be so sad and lonely and worrying for you. You must be fretting terribly, especially with the thought of your trial before you. Perhaps the judge will be kind and compassionate and understand that you're not a wicked man at all and let you off lightly. You only wanted to make us all happy. If only the publishers hadn't let you down over your book!

Perhaps you can write another while you are away from us?

We all love you very much – especially
Your loving daughter,

Opal

P.S. You mustn't worry about us. We're all coping splendidly. I go out to work now and it makes me feel very grown up.

I didn't feel very grown up going to work. I felt incredibly little, like a tiny mouse scuttling along the gutter on the way to Fairy Glen. I had been nervous enough yesterday, but today was five times worse because I knew what it would be like.

Mr Beeston was in his office, and when he saw me through the window, he gave me a cheery wave. I managed to wave back, though my arm felt like lead. He beckoned me in.

'Good morning, Miss Opal Plumstead.'

'Good morning, Mr Beeston,' I replied.

'Lovely manners! What a girl you are. So, how was your first day?'

I hesitated. If I told him everything, perhaps he'd move me downstairs. Maybe I could even try rolling out the sugar jellies? I would sooner work anywhere than in the fondant room. I'd even prefer to scrub the water closets all day.

'Speak up, little Opal. You don't seem like a girl who's usually lost for words,' said Mr Beeston.

My words were sticking in my mouth. If I told him that Patty and her friends had tormented me all day long and then tipped an entire box of starch over my head, he would surely be sympathetic. But what would he say to Patty? I didn't care if she got into trouble. I wanted that to happen. But what would she do to me afterwards? What would all the others do? I had enough experience of school to know that everyone hates a telltale.

I cleared my throat. 'My first day was rather as I'd expected,' I said carefully.

Mr Beeston raised his eyebrows. 'Mmm! Excellent answer! Off you go, then. See if the second day is the same.'

I collected a clean overall and cap and went into the ladies' room warily, fearful of Patty. She wasn't there – but several of the girls from the fondant room were larking about, discussing the men on the factory floor.

'What do you reckon to that Paul – you know, the one with the curly hair? I think he's a real looker.'

'Listen to her! Sounds like she'll be down the alley with him at dinner time.'

'He's a bit too girlish for my taste. I like 'em strong and beefy, like Bill. Oooh, what I'd like to do with him!'

'He's courting Lizzie Seymour. You know – does the candy twists.'

'Her! He's wasted on her, she's so niminy-piminy. I reckon if I could just cosy up to Bill, he'd realize he'd be much better off with me.'

'Watch out you don't cosy too close. Some say it was that Bill got Jenny Moore in the family way.'

'Think I don't know how to look after myself? Catch me being landed with a baby.'

'Well, teach us, then, because my Sandy's getting very overheated on a Saturday night and I'm scared I'm going to land in trouble. But I just can't help myself when he starts. The things he does!' She squirmed and they all giggled.

She saw me staring at her. 'Watch out, the new girl's all ears,' she said. 'Look, her specs are steaming up!'

'Clear off, small fry. You're not old enough for this sort of talk.'

'I don't want to be!' I declared. 'I think you should all wash your mouths out with soap.'

I marched out while they all screamed with laughter. I stalked across the factory floor, scarcely able to look at all the men, especially when they started calling and whistling at some of the other girls. I blushed at the comments, feeling as prim as Miss Mountbank. If Mother knew the way folk talked, she'd surely sooner we all starved than leave me working here.

'Hey, little 'un! Got your mother's overall on? Watch out you don't trip!'

I scuttled up the iron staircase to the fondant room. Geoff and George were already at work heating up the copper vats.

Geoff gave me a nod. 'All right?' he asked.

'Yes, thank you,' I said.

I glanced around fearfully for Patty. She didn't seem to be there yet, but some of her friends were frowning at me. A large girl with strands of red hair escaping from her cap came over to me.

'Saw you having a chat with old Beeswax this morning,' she muttered.

'That's right,' I said.

'Telling on us, were you?'

'No, I was simply exchanging pleasantries,' I said.

'What? Talk proper! You sound like a blooming schoolmarm,' she said.

'I was just passing the time of day with Mr Beeston,' I said, spacing out my words and pronouncing them with emphasis.

'No need for that tone, you stuck up little ninny,' said the red-haired girl.

'Did she grass on us, Nora?' asked another.

'I'll bet she did,' said Nora. 'I hate telltales. Wait till I let Patty know!'

'I thought you hated telltales,' I said, and dodged round her to the cupboard where the moulds were kept. 'Excuse me, I want to get on with my work.'

'You little whatsit!' said Nora.

The girls muttered together while I started working. I tried not to take any notice, but my hand was trembling so badly I couldn't make precise moulds.

Patty sauntered in five minutes later. She seemed to be trying to assert her authority by arriving as late as she dared. She walked past me, deliberately barging into my back, so that my whole box shook and the starch scattered everywhere.

'Patty!' said Geoff.

'Whoops!' she said. 'So sorry, Opal Plumbrain. Did I accidentally knock you?'

'Can't you leave her alone today? You've had your fun,' said Geoff.

'Have we?' said Patty, wide-eyed.

'We think she grassed on us to Beeswax,' said Nora.

'What?'

'Serve you right if she did,' said Geoff.

'But I *didn't*,' I said. 'I wouldn't do that, even though I had just cause.'

'Don't believe her, Patty. I *saw* her nattering away to him in his office,' said Nora.

'Well, see if I care if she did,' said Patty, shrugging. 'She can't prove anything, can she? It'd be her word against ours, right?'

They all agreed.

'There, *see*!' said Nora, giving me a shove.

'For heaven's sake, you're like nasty little children at elementary school.' I struggled to sound superior, though my heart was thumping hard.

They all made ridiculous 'Oo-ooo' sounds, mocking me. I struggled to ignore them all, resolutely moulding, though I jumped whenever one of them came near me.

Halfway through the long morning Mr Beeston strolled into the room. I saw Patty stare at him and then look at me. *All* the girls were looking. Several were fearful, but Patty put her chin up and squared her shoulders.

'How do, Mr Beeston,' she said boldly. 'Come to keep an eye on me and my girls?'

'As if I need to do that, Miss Pattacake,' said Mr Beeston. 'I know you little lasses are all as good as gold. No, I've come to chivvy these two work-shy rascals here – the saucy lads.' He patted Geoff and George on the back, while everyone laughed uneasily. Geoff and George were the steadiest, most hard-working men in the entire factory, and everyone knew it.

Mr Beeston had a stir of the syrup in the big copper vat, nodding approvingly at the texture. He stepped into the drying room to count the boxes.

The girls whispered to each other while he was in there:

'She *did* tell. He's come to tick us off!'

'He's just playing with us. He'll suddenly turn nasty – you wait.'

'Do you think he'll dock our wages?'

'That hateful tattletale Plumbrain!'

But Mr Beeston came back smiling. 'Well done, ladies and gentlemen. Don't stand there staring at me now. On with the good work!'

He patted me on the head, squashing my cap. 'Mould on, little Opal Plumstead!' he said, and then he walked out of the room.

The girls all breathed out heavily.

'So Plumbrain *didn't* tell,' said one.

'She did, I saw her,' Nora insisted.

'*Did* you tell, Plumbrain?' Patty asked menacingly.

'Can't you girls give it a *rest*? You're making my head ache,' said Geoff.

'Oh, gallant Sir Geoff, all a-quiver to protect little Plumbrain,' said Patty unpleasantly.

'What did you girls do to her yesterday, then? It's clear you did something if you're all so scared of Mr Beeston finding out. Leave her alone, can't you!' he said.

'All right, then, we *will* leave her alone,' said Patty.

They stopped speaking to me altogether. They turned their backs, and whispered and giggled as they worked. I heard my name and knew they were cracking stupid jokes about me. I tried to tell myself I didn't care. I wanted to be left in peace, didn't I? I could work quietly, free to think my own thoughts. But though these were the last girls in the world I wanted to be friends with, it was still horrible to be totally left out of their conversation. I felt lonelier than ever. When I next went into the drying room, I had a little weep.

Geoff followed me in. 'There now,' he said softly when he saw me snivelling.

'Why do they hate me so?' I whispered.

'They don't hate you, silly. It's just a spot of teasing. It's because you're a new girl. They'll get used to you soon enough. Try to laugh along with them. They'll only get worse if they see you're upset,' he told me.

'I'm not really a laughing sort of girl,' I said mournfully.

'Yes, you're a solemn little lass. It's like you've got all the cares of the world heaped on your shoulders.'

'That's what it feels like,' I said, sighing. This sounded such a self-pitying statement that I blushed and giggled in embarrassment.

'That's better,' said Geoff. 'You cheer up now, dearie.'

'I'll try,' I said, but I didn't think that was possible.

13

I knew how much dinner cost now, but Mother could only spare me a penny a day until I got my wages at the end of the week. The oxtail soup and meat and potato pie smelled wonderful, especially now that I wasn't feeling sick from eating fondants, but I resolutely joined the tea and bun queue.

There was a whole bunch of women standing in a cluster and I hung back, not quite sure where the end of the queue was. I worried that they'd start abusing me if I stood too close.

Another couple of women lined up after me.

'Budge up, little darling,' said one.

'Yes, tell that lot of old natterers to sort themselves out. We're hungry, aren't we.'

They spoke in such a friendly manner that I could have hugged them.

'You *are* a little 'un, aren't you. Didn't think they were employing infants at Fairy Glen! Where have they put you, then?'

'I'm in the fondant room,' I said.

'Oooh, with all the saucy girls. Are you going to sit with them now?'

'No!'

'Well, come and sit with us. What's your name? I'm Jess, lovey, and this is Maggie.'

They were about twenty-five, I reckoned, both plump and rosy-cheeked. At first it was hard to distinguish one from the other in their identical caps and overalls, but by the end of the meal I realized that Jess's plumpness was mostly because she was going to have a baby – and when Maggie took off her cap to scratch her head, I saw that her hair was pure white.

She noticed me staring. 'It went that way when I was nineteen and had my first baby. Weird, ain't it? Still, my hubby likes it, would you believe. He calls me his little Snow White – though in *my* fairy-tale book she's got black hair, but never mind.'

'You have a baby too?' I said.

'I've got four, dear – two boys, two girls – couldn't be better.'

'Whereas I've got three girls, and if this little beggar isn't a boy I'm going to give it a serious ticking off,' said Jess.

'Are you allowed to keep working when you're . . . ?' I paused delicately.

'Oh yes, Mrs Roberts is very understanding,' said Maggie.

'Who's she? I thought Mr Beeston was in charge.'

'He's the manager, dear, but Mrs Roberts *owns* the whole bang-shoot. Well, it used to be *Mr* Roberts, but he died of pleurisy years ago, and so Mrs Roberts took over. There's a son, but he's still away at school somewhere. He'll take over the firm in time, but meanwhile Mrs Roberts is a fair boss, especially to us women. She's very keen on women's concerns. She's one of them suffragettes, wanting women to have the vote.'

'How splendid!' I said.

'Don't you think all them women make fools of themselves, throwing bricks through windows and yelling in Parliament?' asked Jess.

'But it's for a very important cause,' I said. 'If we had the vote, then there would be fairer laws and happier times for all women, especially in the workplace.'

'Bless you, dear! We're happy enough as we are, ain't we, Maggie? We like our workplace. Mrs Roberts runs a special nursery for our babies, so we don't have to leave them with some old crone who won't mind them properly. You wait till you find a fellow and start having babies, dear. You'll thank your lucky stars you can carry on working here, earning a good wage,' Jess said earnestly.

'I don't think I want a fellow,' I told her.

'Oh, don't worry, sweetheart, your time will come,' said Maggie, misunderstanding. 'I reckon you'll grow taller, blossom a bit, turn into a true dazzler and have all the fellows giving you the glad eye.'

'I don't think so – but even if I did, I wouldn't give *them* the glad eye.'

'Nonsense! You wait till some lad takes your fancy.'

'I don't believe in romantic love. I think it's just a myth to make us procreate,' I said grandly.

Olivia had listened to my theory and had been impressed. Jess and Maggie simply doubled up with laughter.

'Oh, you're a one!'

'Just you wait, you funny little thing!'

'Proper little caution, you are.'

'Absolutely priceless. Ooh, stop me laughing or I'll wet myself!'

I didn't like them laughing at me, but I knew there was no malice in their cackles. We walked back onto the factory floor together. The same gawky lad whistled at me.

'Oh, there you are, Opal. Young Freddy's fallen for you already!' said Maggie, and Jess made silly kissing noises.

'Well, I'm not falling for him!' I hissed, going pink with indignation.

Freddy had hair stuck flat to his forehead with cheap pomade, and he'd clearly grown recently and rapidly, because his sleeves stopped several inches from his bony wrists and there was a similar gap between his trousers and his boots.

'Is he not good enough for you?' said Maggie, with a slight edge to her voice.

'Oh no, I don't mean that at all,' I said – though that was precisely what I felt.

'Don't worry, dear. You're obviously bright as a button and you speak lovely, like a little lady,' said Jess.

'So what are you doing here, eh?' asked Maggie.

'Well, I . . .' I swallowed hard. 'My family need the money.'

It was a painful admission. The girls at school would have been shocked and embarrassed by such a confession, but Jess and Maggie sighed and smiled at me.

'Down on your luck, dear? Well, good for you to help out.'

'Yes, well done, pet. Your parents must be proud of you.'

I wished they were. I had no real idea what Father was thinking. Mother was too distracted and miserable to feel anything very much. When I got home after the desperately long afternoon, Cassie was taking a turn making the wretched little rabbits, while Mother was stirring a thick vegetable soup on the stove. Both her hands were bandaged and she winced when she stopped stirring to cut chunks of bread.

'Did you have a better day today, dear?' she asked wearily.

'Let's have a look at your hair! Did they give you another starch shampoo?' asked Cassie.

'I didn't give them the chance. I shot out of there the very second the bell rang,' I said.

'Good for you,' she said. 'Oh Lordy, these rabbits are all staring at me with their beady little eyes. Horrid things.'

'Shall I help too?' I offered reluctantly, though I was so weary I just wanted to fling myself down on the sofa and sleep.

'Well, we've got at least a dozen more to do tonight – so yes, come here. You stuff this little beggar while I cut out the next,' said Cassie.

I sat down and started stuffing. My fingers ached after moulding all day. I couldn't get the sawdust to fill the spindly limbs properly. It went up my nails and hurt, and when I started sewing the limbs to the body, I managed to dig the needle into the soft pad of my thumb while struggling to pull it through the felt. No wonder Mother was wearing bandages.

Just as she served the soup there was a knock on the door.

'Oh no, our soup will get cold!' said Cassie. 'Don't answer it, Mother!'

'I'm not going to, don't worry,' she replied. 'It'll only be that terrible Liversedge woman again.'

'But what if it's someone important? Oh Lord, what if it's someone with news of Father?' I said, feeling sick.

I imagined a policeman standing there, pale under his helmet. I imagined his voice saying, 'So sorry, miss, but is Ernest Harold Plumstead your father? The gentleman who is currently in Whitechurch remand prison? Well, I'm very sorry to tell you that there's been a sad accident – a matter of rope in his cell. I'm afraid he's gone and hanged himself.' The voice echoed in my head as plain as anything, though I was still sitting at our kitchen table, stuffing a little rabbit so hard its leg swelled as if it had dropsy.

Mother and Cassie looked at me.

'How could there be news of Father?' said Cassie shakily.

'I'd better go and see.' Mother scrabbled at her apron with bandaged hands. She went out of the kitchen and Cassie suddenly clasped me tightly.

'You don't half smell of sugary sweets,' she said.

We both strained our ears. We could hear a voice saying something and Mother murmuring, but we couldn't gauge the tone. Then Mother said something else and we heard heavy footsteps in the hall.

'Oh God, I think it *is* a policeman,' I blurted. 'I can't bear it.'

I put my hands over my ears, not wanting to hear any further terrible news. But it wasn't a policeman at all. Mr Andrews, my music teacher from school, came into our kitchen! I stared at him, open-mouthed. Cassie must have been even more bewildered, but he was a reasonably handsome man, so she tossed her hair about and stood up straight.

'Good evening, sir,' she said. 'I'm Cassie and this is my sister, Opal. How can we help you?'

'Shush, Cassie! It's my schoolteacher,' I hissed.

'Indeed,' said Mr Andrews apologetically.

Mother followed him into the room, in a fluster because of the state of the kitchen. 'Please let us go in the parlour!' she implored.

'No, no! Oh dear, I see you're about to have supper,' said Mr Andrews. 'I'm so sorry to come at such an inconvenient time. I promise I'll only be a minute or two. I just want a quick word with Opal.'

'Take him in the *parlour*, Opal,' Mother insisted, sweeping the pile of rabbits off the table, her face on fire. 'I'm making a few toys for my nieces and nephews,' she lied, though it was obvious that the rabbits were factory piecework. She was very aware that no respectable middle-class married woman went out to work, let alone did piecework in her own home. She glared at me ferociously to make me do as I was told.

'Please follow me, Mr Andrews,' I said, and led him into the parlour. It was dark and stuffy in there, and almost too neat. The chairs and table had a melancholy look, because they were so rarely used.

'I'm sorry, Opal. I just wanted to come and see if you were all right,' said Mr Andrews, standing uncomfortably, making his soft hat slowly circle in his hands.

'Please, do sit down,' I mumbled. 'I'm perfectly fine, Mr Andrews. At least, I'm not ill.' I waited. 'The reason I haven't been to school is . . .' It was no use. I couldn't say any more in case I burst into tears.

'I do know the reason,' said Mr Andrews, very gently. 'I read about your father in the newspaper.'

'Oh,' I said hopelessly.

'I'm so sorry, Opal.'

'Does everyone at St Margaret's know, then?'

'I – I believe a few people saw the newspaper,' said Mr Andrews.

It was clear that the news had spread like wildfire. I thought of Miss Mountbank, Miss Reed and Miss Laurel whispering amongst themselves. I thought of all the girls gasping and giggling, their eyes bright with the scandal, and I burned.

'I can entirely understand why you stayed away. Stay away a few days more, if you like, but I'm here to ask you to come back.'

'Surely I wouldn't be allowed?'

'Of course you are. I've had a word with Miss Laurel. You yourself have done nothing wrong. You still have your scholarship. You're one of the brightest girls I've ever taught, Opal.'

'Really?' I said, thrilled in spite of everything.

'Really,' said Mr Andrews. 'So you must be a brave girl and come back to school and finish your education.'

'I can't,' I said sadly.

'I know it will be embarrassing for you. There might be a little gossip for a few days. Girls can be very silly. But things will settle down quickly enough. You're a steely girl with a lot of spirit. You'll manage.'

'Thank you, Mr Andrews. I wish I *could* come back. It means so much to me that you've come here to tell me this – but I can't, because I have to start earning a living to help support my family,' I said in a rush.

'You have to work? Don't you have any savings at all? Then surely your mother . . . or your sister . . .?'

'Mother's tried to get a position, but can only find piecework to do at home – those rabbits. Cassie goes out to work already, but she has an apprenticeship and doesn't get paid till her third year. So I have to work. I started at the Fairy Glen factory on Monday.'

I couldn't help enjoying the look of shock on his face.

'Surely you could find more congenial work in an office, Opal. You could be a junior clerk, maybe learn to use a typewriter.'

'Would that earn me eleven shillings a week?'

'Probably not,' said Mr Andrews, sighing.

'I think I have to stay at the factory for now.'

'Are they kind to you there?'

'No. They're hateful!' I said. Then I thought of Mr Beeston, Geoff, Maggie and Jess, the well-spoken woman in the ladies' room . . . 'Well, some people are quite kind, I suppose.'

'You're being very brave,' said Mr Andrews.

I felt myself glowing. Fancy Mr Andrews paying me such a compliment! *Oh, wait till I tell Olivia,* I thought. Then I felt such a pang because she wasn't my friend any more.

'How is Olivia, Mr Andrews?' I asked.

'It's plain she's missing you enormously, Opal. It's very sad to see her trudging around by herself, so cast down. I'm sure she's been in touch with you.'

'No, I don't think she's allowed to, not now. Her mother said I wasn't ever to see her again.'

'Oh dear, oh dear. That's very sad for both of you. What a wretched state of affairs. I wish there was some way I could help.' Mr Andrews looked truly upset.

'I don't think there is, but I'm very glad you came to see me all the same,' I said.

We sat there for a minute or two, neither of us knowing what to say next.

'I'd better be going. You're missing your supper,' said Mr Andrews.

He stood up. I stood up too.

'Well, good luck, Opal,' he said, and he held out his hand.

I shook it shyly, worried that my own palms were clammy with emotion. I went with him to the front door and we said our goodbyes.

'Don't lose heart,' he said. 'Listen to classical music, keep reading, keep learning, even if you have to teach yourself.'

'I will,' I promised.

I went back to Mother and Cassie, feeling uplifted. Mr Andrews truly cared about me. He thought I was really clever. He was appalled that I had to work in the factory. He thought I was very brave, very valiant. Surely Mother and Cassie would be impressed.

'Your soup's cold,' Mother said. 'For goodness' sake, why did he have to come round? The nerve!'

'He cares about me,' I said.

'It was *me* he was staring at,' said Cassie.

'Oh be quiet, both of you. Do you have to spoil

everything?' I declared, and stamped up to my room supperless.

I still felt inspired by Mr Andrews' visit. I took him seriously. I couldn't listen to music because we didn't own a phonograph, but I got out all my schoolbooks and piled up all the serious works of literature I could find. I put aside *Little Women* and *What Katy Did* and *A Little Princess*, though reading them by candlelight had been such a comfort. I borrowed from Father's small library of second-hand books: Gibbons' *Decline and Fall of the Roman Empire*, the Romantic poets, George Eliot's *Middlemarch*, Henry James . . . I handled each dusty book reverently, feeling as if I was sharing them with Father. *See, Mr Andrews*, I thought as I opened each one. *I've taken what you said to heart. I* am *teaching myself.*

In spite of all these resolutions, my eyes glazed in the flickering candlelight, my head nodded, and I didn't manage more than half a page before falling asleep. And as I worked on, day after day, week after week, moulding an entire garden full of fondant roses, my mind seemed set in a starch mould too. I had totally free Saturdays and Sundays, but I couldn't seem to concentrate enough to read difficult books. Well, I could *read* a page or two, but none of it made any kind of sense. I started to find even Dickens and Hardy too hard.

I found I was too listless to paint. Ever since I was

a tiny tot I'd been drawing pictures with a packet of chalks, but now I seemed to have no inspiration, no inclination. My beautiful paintbox might just as well have been reclaimed because I scarcely used it.

The only time I truly applied myself was when I wrote to Father. I covered page after page, but most of these letters were never sent.

'He's only allowed one letter per week,' Mother said. 'You mustn't be so selfish, Opal. You must let Cassie have a turn.'

I dare say Cassie loved Father, maybe almost as much as I did, but she wrote him very cursory letters.

Dear Father,

I hope you are well. I am very well and all the girls at Madame Alouette's say I look very fine in my green dress.

From your loving daughter,

Cassandra

Sometimes she wrote no words at all, but simply attached a silk rose to a piece of card or snipped a lock of her beautiful hair and sent it in a twist of tissue. I felt painfully jealous then, because I couldn't compete. I knew Father probably treasured these hasty little gifts far more than my long letters.

Mother did not write or send him little treasures.

Even Cassie felt this was strange. 'Maybe you could box up one of your stuffed rabbits and send it,' she said.

She was joking, but Mother looked at her sourly, her mouth set. She'd discarded her bandages now and her fingers no longer bled, but her hands still clearly pained her. Every night, when at last she stopped sewing, she filled a stone bottle with hot water and then sat holding it in her hands, trying to soothe the stiffness. There was a stiffness in her soul too. Sometimes she clutched her chest as if in pain, sometimes she winced if we touched in passing, sometimes she walked in such a rigid way she looked as if she were wearing iron corsets. I remembered her gay girlishness during the *Happy Days* time. It didn't seem possible that Mother could ever be that woman again.

Poor Billy the budgerigar seemed to have absorbed the dour family atmosphere. He gave a chirrup or two when I fed him and occasionally sharpened his beak on a piece of cuttlebone, but spent most of his days drooping silently on his perch. Cassie tried to teach him new little phrases: 'Pretty girl', 'Lovely dress', 'Brush your hair' – repeating them over and over again. Billy watched her with his beady little eyes but couldn't seem to get the hang of it.

'*Try*, you silly little thing!' said Cassie. 'Dear me. You're nothing but a painted sparrow!'

'Don't say horrid things to him. He can't help it. He dislikes being cooped up,' I said.

I couldn't bear the thought of anything being in captivity now. One Saturday, when Mother and Cassie were out, I opened the cage door. 'There you are, Billy! Have a little fly about the room and stretch your wings,' I said encouragingly.

Billy didn't seem at all interested at first. His clawed feet stayed clutching his perch, his wings tucked into his sides.

'Look, Billy, fly!' I gently moved the little door in his cage. 'See – it's open. You can get out. Quick.'

I had to give him several little prods before he realized that this was his one chance of freedom. He suddenly hopped to the door, blundered out into thin air, and then his wings worked by instinct and he flew up to the ceiling. He circled madly three or four times and then perched on the picture rail to get his breath.

'There! Did you like that? It was good, wasn't it? Well, go on, make the most of it. Explore the room!'

I'd taken the precaution of shutting the window and closing the door so it seemed quite safe. Billy flew another few circuits and then landed on my head. It was the most curious sensation feeling his claws clinging to my hair.

'Better not try this with Cassie or you'll get in a terrible tangle,' I said. 'Are you going to talk to me now? Say *Happy days* just once for me, Billy. They *were* happy days, weren't they? Do you think we'll ever be happy again? Say it for me so I can believe it.'

Billy stayed resolutely silent, but he took off again and seemed to be enjoying himself flying all over the parlour. I was a little alarmed when he lifted his tail and sent a jet of white onto Father's chair. It mostly went on the antimacassar and hardly showed, but I thought I'd better give it a good scrub before Mother came back.

I sidled out of the door to get the washing cloth and yellow soap from the kitchen. When I got back I opened the door cautiously again, but Billy must have been waiting, hovering in mid-air. As soon as the door opened a crack, he was out, soaring into the hall.

'Oh help! Come back, Billy! Please, come back!' I entreated him.

He took no notice of me. He flew all the way upstairs. I ran after him, pleading uselessly.

Billy flew through the open door into Mother and Father's room.

'Oh, I think you're looking for Father! How I wish he were here. But you can play with all his things. See, here's his wardrobe. His clothes still smell of him.'

Billy didn't pay them any attention. He flew past the dressing table to the open window behind the net curtains.

'No! Billy, don't! Please don't!' I screamed.

Billy aimed his little blue body like an arrow. He flew straight through the gap in the curtains, out into the air.

'Come back!' I called.

Billy flew away, so fast that I lost sight of him in seconds.

I threw myself down on Father's side of the bed and cried.

14

We had to wait a whole month, but then we received a letter from Father.

My dearest Lou, Cassie and Opal,

I worry about you every minute of the day. I am so horribly aware that I have inflicted hardship and humiliation upon you. I will do everything in my power to make it up to you in the future.

Until then, please remember that I am your very loving husband and father,

Ernest

The writing was shaky and sloped crookedly down the page. The letter seemed pitifully short for a man who had filled so many manuscript books with his stories. He didn't tell us anything at all about his health or his circumstances. He didn't answer a single one of my questions or give so much as a hint about his daily routine in prison or his diet or his companions. There was no personal message for me, though I was the only one who had written to him at length. As far as I knew, Mother hadn't written to him at all, and yet Father had addressed her as, 'My dearest Lou'. I was simply 'and Opal'.

I hadn't told Father very much about working at Fairy Glen, so I couldn't expect him to write extra sympathetically to me, but surely he must be aware that my whole life had changed now? Had he forgotten? Did he think I was still at school and that somehow good fairies paid the rent and made the food appear in the larder by magic?

I took pride in my weekly salary, handed to me in a buff envelope every Friday morning – a ten-shilling note and a shiny shilling coin. A few weeks ago this would have seemed a fortune: enough for a storybook, a sketchpad and a tin of crayons, and several bags of Fairy Glen sweets. Now this sum seemed piteously small. After the rent money was put aside, we didn't have much left for food. We chose day-old bread because it was a penny cheaper, fatty mince and scrag-end of lamb, streaky bacon and dubious market eggs. We ate endless mounds of potato because it was cheap and filling. It was fattening too. Cassie squealed in shock when she found she could barely do up the buttons on her beautiful green dress.

'I shall starve myself for an entire week. I cannot bear being stout,' she declared dramatically.

She refused her Sunday roast lunch, the one good meal in the week, but became so hungry she ate five slices of bread and dripping at bed time.

'I don't suppose it matters,' she said mournfully, her mouth full. 'There won't be any occasion for me to wear my wretched dress now. I'd better resign myself to being a fat old maid for the rest of my life.'

But the very next day, when I trailed home from the factory, I found Cassie all of a twinkle, dancing around the kitchen.

'Oh, Opal, *such* a lovely gentleman came to Madame Alouette's today. Quite old, I suppose – at least thirty, but, oh so handsome – dark, with thick wavy hair, a little long, and the most wonderful warm brown eyes. You know the way some men can look at you and you simply *melt*!' she said, whirling about.

'No I don't,' I said.

'He was dressed so exquisitely too, with a purple scarf and a velvet jacket cut in the most gloriously artistic way, but not at all foppish. Mr Evandale's a truly manly man,' said Cassie.

'Why is a truly manly man frequenting a milliner's shop?' I said sourly.

'Because he's choosing a special hat for his younger sister, as a surprise. He persuaded me to model for him, as he said I was a very similar size and colouring. Well . . .' Cassie went a proud pink. 'He said I was a little prettier, but I'm sure he just said that to be congenial.'

'Now, Cassie, you mustn't let a gentleman like that turn your head,' said Mother. 'If he's thirty he must be married – or a very bad sort. He definitely shouldn't be flirting with a young girl like you.'

'He behaved with complete propriety,' Cassie said, but there were little dimples in her cheeks and she couldn't stop smiling.

'Now, now, aren't there any nice *young* gentlemen around? Did you not say that Madame Alouette's nephew was currently visiting?'

'Philip. Or Phil*ippe*, as silly old Madame calls him. Now he *is* a fop. I've never known such a vain young man, peering in all the shop mirrors and asking me earnestly for advice about the cut of his new coat,' Cassie said scornfully.

'There! If he's asking your advice, he's clearly interested in you,' said Mother.

'But *I'm* not interested in *him*. He's so pale and slender. He can't even stand up straight without wilting. If we were ever to embrace, I'm sure I'd knock him over. Whereas Mr Evandale . . .' Cassie was clearly imagining an embrace with this Mr Evandale, her twinkles and dimples even more in evidence.

'You watch yourself, madam.'

Although I had no interest in men whatsoever, it was a little galling to note that Mother did not feel it necessary to give me lectures about men, suitable or otherwise. She thought me far too plain to attract anyone at all. Strangely, she was wrong.

I was becoming quite friendly with Geoff, but in the most platonic, big brother–younger sister way. He was very comforting, especially when Patty and Nora were especially tormenting.

'They're silly girls but they're not *bad*. Try laughing along with them,' he kept suggesting.

'Why should I laugh when they're being so horrid?' I asked. 'And *why* do they keep picking on me?'

'It's because you're new – and you're little,' said Geoff. 'It's not nice, but it's human nature. My little girl, Jenny, is barely two, but she's desperate to play out in the alley with the big children. She frets and screams and kicks at the door until her mother gives in and takes her outside. She'll only get five minutes' peace, because there's screams all over again. And when she goes running, she finds our Jenny tipped over in the gutter and the other children nowhere in sight.'

'But that's awful when she's only a baby,' I said.

'It's just the way of things. They don't mean her any real harm. They'll get used to her and let her in on their games soon enough. And then, when she's bigger and there's a new little 'un sent out to play, I dare say she'll tip it over and run away laughing with all the others,' said Geoff. 'Human nature, see?'

'I don't *want* to see, because it's thoroughly depressing,' I said. 'I don't *like* human beings.'

But I did like Geoff and his gentle ways and his cheerful acceptance of his lot in life.

I liked Mr Beeston too, once I got used to his dry sense of humour. He seemed popular with most of the factory folk, which was most unusual, according to Maggie and Jess.

'Most factory managers are hated because they have such power over you – they can send you packing on a whim. But old Beeswax is a fair man, kindly even, though he can be firm too, and sharp. You wouldn't want to cross him. But if you work hard, he'll act like he's right proud of you,' they said.

So I liked Mr Beeston and I liked Geoff. I *didn't* like Freddy, the lad on the factory floor who whistled at me, but he certainly seemed to like me. He did that dreadful whistle every day without fail. It was shrill and high-pitched. After a week of cringing I went up to him and said, 'Please don't whistle at me like that, it embarrasses me.'

He seemed embarrassed himself, his pale face

flushing tomato red. He was usually colourless, his lank hair so blond it was almost white, and the fluffy whiskers growing above his lip white too. I felt mean for considering him a bit of a freak. I knew I was certainly no top-notcher. My hair and face and hands were grey by mid-morning, and even freshly scrubbed, I was lamentably plain – small and scrawny, with spectacles to boot. But Freddy seemed as moon-dazzled as Titania lusting over Bottom. 'I whistle because I like you,' he said, touching his red cheeks as if startled by their heat. 'All the lads do it to the girls they fancy. There's no harm in it.'

'I know, but I still don't like it. And I'm too *young*. I'm only fourteen,' I protested.

'That's only five years younger than me,' said Freddy. 'Will you walk out with me at the weekend?'

'No I will not!' I said.

'Why? Have you got a sweetheart already?' he asked anxiously.

'No. I *said*, I'm too young.'

'If you're old enough to go out to work, you're old enough for sweethearts. You tell your father that if he's objecting,' said Freddy.

That shut me up. I felt my chin wobbling. I had to shut my eyes to stop the tears spurting.

'Opal?' When I managed to look at him, I saw that he was terribly concerned. 'Oh dear, I didn't mean to upset you. Have you – have you lost your father?'

I knew he was asking if he were dead, but I felt I'd truly lost my dear father for the moment, so I nodded solemnly.

'Oh dear, I'm so sorry. I didn't mean to be so tactless. Of course, that's why a clever girl like you has come here to work. I'll bet you passed all your exams at school.'

'I had a scholarship,' I said, unable to stop myself.

Patty would have made vulgar noises of disgust at such showing off, but Freddy seemed extremely impressed.

'Oh my, a scholarship! Fancy me having a scholarship girl for a sweetheart!'

'I'm *not* your sweetheart,' I said.

It was ridiculous. We didn't even know each other. But Freddy seemed firmly convinced that we were courting. He started giving me little gifts: a piece of Fairy Glen candy fashioned into a heart, a pink ribbon, a coverless book of poetry bought off a penny stall. These were touching presents. I tried to behave graciously, though I kept telling Freddy he mustn't give me any more.

'But I want to,' he said plaintively.

Patty noticed that he was courting me and was merciless in her ridicule. She started up a silly story about Freddy and me, making out that we were doing the most obscene things. She generally muttered it to the other girls, but occasionally her voice got louder so that Geoff and George could hear.

'Hey, Patty, wash your mouth out with soap,' said Geoff.

Patty took no notice until George stumped over to her, shaking his head.

'You look such a pretty lass but you've got a mind like a sewer,' he said. 'Stop torturing that little girl or I'll put you over my knee and spank you.'

'It's not a crime to chat to my friends, is it?' said Patty, but George was still frowning, so she quietened down after that.

The next Monday Mr Beeston ushered a new girl into the fondant room. She was almost as young as me. Her hair was still in plaits and she had a large, guileless face and an anxious smile that showed too much of her bad teeth.

'This is little Edith Catchpole,' Mr Beeston announced. 'It's her first day at Fairy Glen. Say hello to Edith, girls and boys.'

I said hello with extra warmth. I saw Patty and Nora looking at each other, eyes bright. It looked as if they were going to start on Edith now. Maybe I was expected to join in too. Well, I wasn't going to! I didn't want to hurt poor Edith, who looked a little simple. She blinked at everybody, her mouth still open.

I would protect Edith! I would take her under my wing and show her what to do. I'd warn her to keep right out of the way of Patty and Co. I'd guard her like a little dog and walk her to the canteen and back, *and* the ladies' room, so she need never be vulnerable and alone.

I'd make Edith my friend. She didn't look anywhere near as much fun as Olivia, but perhaps we would become really close. Then life in the fondant room might actually become bearable. Let Patty and the other girls cat-call and say dreadful things – Edith and I would work quietly together, talking of this and that. She didn't look as if she'd had much schooling. Perhaps I could teach her a little, tell her stories, talk her through history, instruct her in how to count and say how-do-you-do in French. My imagination knew no bounds. I saw us conversing rapidly in French (though this was a task beyond me too, scholarship or not), able to insult Patty for all we were worth in the Gallic tongue.

Patty started her nasty teasing the minute Mr Beeston had departed.

'*What* did he say your name was? Edith Catch-a-cold?'

'No, it's Edith *Catchpole*,' said Edith, thinking she'd simply made a mistake.

'Yes, Catch-a-cold. A-tishoo, a-tishoo, a-tishoo,' said Patty, pretending to sneeze violently. Edith looked completely blank for a moment, and then her face crumpled.

'Leave her *alone*,' I said fiercely, assuming that Patty had made her cry already.

But Edith was *laughing*, doubled up, helpless. 'A-tishoo!' she spluttered weakly. 'Catch-a-cold a-tishoo! You're so funny!'

Geoff didn't need to give Edith brotherly advice. She couldn't *help* laughing along with the other girls.

They still teased her a little, not showing her how to mould properly. Patty insisted she should use the mould upside down. I tried to put Edith right, but she shook her head at me.

'No, Patty says do it this way,' she insisted, making pointless patterns in the starch.

George had to gently put her right in the end, but even when she knew they'd played a trick on her, Edith seemed pleased.

'That was a good joke!' she said appreciatively. 'I'm such a fool, I always fall for things.'

At the end of the day I told Edith to run for it, because they might well tip a box of starch over her.

'They'll tip it all over me?' she said, eyes round, as if it were a great treat.

They didn't, as it happened. They simply flicked a little starch at her – and she flicked some back, laughing hysterically.

Edith followed Patty around like a little pet dog after that, quivering with delight whenever she paid her any attention at all. She seemed proud to be re-named Catch-a-cold, and laughed every single time any of the girls said 'A-tishoo'. She was soon the treasured baby of the fondant room.

'You see?' said Geoff, when we were together in the drying room.

I did see, but I was far too proud to fawn over Patty and the others. It was too late now anyway. They cordially hated me – and I them.

I found it so depressing and lonely working there day after day. If only I could make candy kisses alongside Maggie and Jess! It would be more interesting rolling the hot sugar paste, and they were so much more accepting of me. I ate with them every day in the canteen. Now I had enough money from my earnings to afford a tuppenny hot dinner. I could even have managed a thrupenny three-courser, and I certainly had the appetite for it, but Maggie and Jess were penny-bun women, so I was too. As fully experienced factory hands, they earned more than me, but saved every spare penny for their families.

I thought things over carefully and resolved on a plan of action. I rehearsed a little speech inside my head, and then went to confront Mr Beeston in his office.

'Ah, little Opal Plumstead, I do believe,' he said. 'How can I help you?'

I took a deep breath. 'It's more a matter of how I can help *you*, Mr Beeston. I don't think you're getting your eleven shillings' worth at the moment,' I said, trying to sound very grown up, which was not easy with a cap clamped about my eyebrows and an overall trailing on the ground.

'Is that right?' said Mr Beeston, looking amused. 'Elucidate!'

Luckily I knew what he meant. I prided myself on my vocabulary.

'I think it's time you upgraded me, now that I'm an experienced fondant maker,' I said.

'Experienced! You've only been here a few weeks!'

'Moulding isn't skilled work, Mr Beeston. I'm sure I could learn all kinds of confectionery skills if you give me the chance. I am very good at learning quickly. If you could find me a position on the factory floor – making the candy kisses perhaps – then I would work deftly and prove my worth. You would be getting a bargain. Because I'd still be happy to be paid my eleven shillings a week until I'm a little older,' I said.

Mr Beeston looked at me thoughtfully. 'Why are you so keen to work on the factory floor, Opal? Aha! Is it so you can work alongside young Freddy? Is that the idea?'

'Absolutely not!' I said indignantly.

'A little bird told me you and he were sweethearts,' said Mr Beeston.

'Well, it was a very confused and silly little bird,

because I don't have any sweetheart at all, especially not Freddy,' I said.

'Oh dearie me, there's poor Freddy's hopes dashed to dust! So *why* are you so keen to change your work if it's not for more money?'

'I want to extend myself, Mr Beeston,' I said loftily.

He roared with laughter. 'Well, you're certainly a little titch, so I can see you're in need of extending.'

'I think you're deliberately misunderstanding me, Mr Beeston,' I said.

'On the contrary, I understand you very well, but I think you're in too much of a hurry, Miss Plumstead. You'll be putting yourself forward for my job in a matter of months, and taking over from Mrs Roberts herself by the end of the year. That would put us all in a perfect pickle, though I dare say you'd be happy enough. Now run along, dearie, back to your moulding. I'm keeping you there for a while yet, unless there's a specific reason why you'd like me to move you, other than ambition?'

He looked at me directly. I fidgeted inside my overall. Yes, yes, yes, there *was* a specific reason. It was called Patty Meacham, and she was continuing to make my life a misery. I'd held my tongue before, but was now the time to tell him? It couldn't make Patty and the other girls hate me more than they already did. If Mr Beeston would only free me from the fondant room, I'd be out of their clutches. Jess and

Maggie would stand up for me if they trailed after me, cat-calling.

'Well, as a matter of fact, Mr Beeston . . .' I began.

He waited patiently, his head cocked to one side. He was still smiling jovially, but he'd opened his eyes a little wider as if in warning. 'Well?'

'No, I simply fancied a change,' I said.

Mr Beeston nodded at me approvingly. 'Very understandable. You're a bright young girl and I see you are indeed a quick learner. Off you hop now.'

As I trudged back across the factory floor, Freddy spotted me. I saw him taking a deep breath and knew he was about to whistle piercingly.

'*Don't* whistle,' I hissed as I approached his bench.

He swallowed convulsively, his pale blue eyes swivelling. I remembered Cassie saying her Mr Evandale made her melt every time he looked at her. Poor Freddy made me simply itch with irritation. I was certain this uncomfortable feeling wasn't love or attraction, but I was feeling so low that I felt in need of his attention.

'Hello, Freddy,' I said, as affably as I could. I disliked his very name. 'Is your full name Frederick?' I asked hopefully.

'No, I'm just Freddy,' he said. 'Though some of the lads here call me Lanky, or Big Lugs if they're jeering at me, just in good humour.'

'That's nothing to what some of the girls call me,' I said.

It didn't matter unburdening myself to Freddy because he was as powerless as I was.

'It sounds like it gets you down, Opal. Don't take it to heart. I promise *I'll* never call you names. I won't whistle again, not if you don't like it, though it's meant as a compliment.' Freddy beamed at me earnestly, his face glowing pink.

He was such a good-hearted fellow. I wished for once that I was more like a normal girl.

'You're a kind friend, Freddy.'

I meant him to understand that was simply how I saw him, but he reacted as though I'd made a declaration of love.

'Oh, Opal,' he said. He always pronounced my name strangely – *Oh-pal*. I couldn't help feeling irritated by that too, but I tried not to let it show.

'Haven't you two young lovebirds got any work to do?' said big Alfred, Freddy's gaffer. 'Come on, young Freddy, the sugar is sticking to the pan.'

'Sorry, big Alfred. Just having a little dally with my sweetheart.' Freddy grinned.

'I'm *not* your sweetheart,' I insisted, my irritation coming to the fore all over again. Perhaps I had better ignore Freddy altogether in future.

15

Cassie certainly wasn't ignoring her Mr Evandale. He'd made another visit to Madame Alouette's to see how the hat he'd ordered was progressing.

'Madame Alouette came rushing to attend to him personally. She's particularly fond of Mr Evandale, but you'll never guess what!' Cassie said triumphantly over supper.

'Mr Evandale asked if he could be served by little Miss Plumstead,' I said.

'Yes!' said Cassie. 'He asked for me. He

remembered my name. And then he had me show him veiling and feathers and silk rosettes. He even asked if I'd make a rosette for him right there on the spot because he was so fascinated by the process.'

'Or fascinated by *you*,' I said, chewing my way through a mouthful of plaice and potato.

Mother put down her knife and fork. 'Now I've told you, Cassie, you mustn't go encouraging a much older man like that, especially one buying frou-frous in a ladies' hat shop,' she said firmly.

'Oh, Mother. He's not *that* old, and I told you, he's buying a hat for his sister's birthday,' said Cassie, laughing.

'Some men call all sorts of women their "sisters",' Mother sniffed. 'You let Madame Alouette deal with the likes of him or you'll get a reputation, and then no decent young man will want you. You listen to me, Cassie Plumstead.'

'Oh, Mother, how you do go on! You don't understand,' said Cassie, shaking her head. She laughed – which wasn't wise.

Mother was nearly always in a bad mood nowadays because she was so tired. She'd had to give up making the stuffed rabbits. She simply couldn't manage the weekly quota, even if Cassie and I helped her in the evening. She tried looking for a proper job again, and actually got taken on as an assistant in a butcher's shop. We ate steak for a week, which was wonderful, and Mother cured her sore hands by rubbing them in mutton fat, but the constant smell of meat and the unsanitary blood and guts out the back turned her stomach, and she was unfortunate enough to be sick in the shop.

Cassie and I squealed when she told us, and for some terrible reason found ourselves shrieking with laughter, though we knew it wasn't remotely funny.

Mother was furious with us. 'That's it, laugh at me, you stupid, heartless girls! Well, let's hope you can carry on laughing when there's no food on your plates,' she cried bitterly.

The butcher had sacked Mother on the spot. He didn't believe she had a weak stomach. He accused her of drinking alcohol. Mother was mortally offended and now refused to set foot in his shop. His was the only butcher's within walking distance, so unless Mother caught a bus to the next town, we had to be content with fish or cheese.

She started taking in washing, though she found this terribly demeaning, especially when Mrs Liversedge got wind of it and came knocking at the door with a basket of her soiled linen. It meant that every day was washing day now, with water boiling constantly, the smell of suds tickling the nose, and yesterday's garments dripping on a rack overhead if it was too wet to string them in the back yard. Mother's hands were now permanently deep red, as if she boiled them along with the babies' napkins, and her temper was frequently at boiling point too.

She'd slapped me several times for my attitude, and now she slapped Cassie. Cassie burst into noisy tears. Mother put her head in her sore hands and wept too. I sat there, my own cheeks burning, but Cassie was a warmer girl than me and went flying to Mother, putting her arms round her and hugging her hard.

'Don't take on so, Mother. You mustn't worry about me. I'm a good girl really. I don't mean any harm.'

'I know, I know, but I *do* worry,' Mother sobbed. 'I don't know how we're going to manage. I'm scared you girls will go to rack and ruin, and I'm so tired all the time – and look at the state of my hands. I used to be so proud of my soft white hands – real lady's hands – and now they're so rough and red and sore.' She wrung them piteously. Her fingers were so swollen her gold wedding ring bit into her flesh. She twisted it desperately, unable to ease it.

'Oh, Mother, don't, you'll make it worse.' Cassie held her hands, stroking them gently. 'There now. How could I have been so heartless as to laugh at you, dear brave Mother. Come, let me help you up to bed – you're tired out. Opal and I will do the dishes and clear up, and we'll make a start on the ironing so it is easier for you in the morning.'

She really *was* a good daughter, better than me,

because I couldn't force myself to make such a fuss of Mother. I washed our plates instead and set the iron to heat, though I was tired out myself and longed to escape to my own bed to read a little by candlelight.

Cassie was a while with Mother, so I got started on the ironing. I didn't care for ironing my own clothes, but it was especially tiresome ironing other people's. They were scrubbed clean, of course, but the camisoles and drawers and combinations were still so personal. It felt far too intimate ironing into every crease and corner.

My neck and shoulders and back ached fiercely after a day spent bending over boxes of starch. I tried singing softly to keep my spirits up, but the only songs I knew by heart were the hymns we sang at school. After one verse of 'He Who Would Valiant Be' I was in tears. I thought of Olivia and Mr Andrews. I was in such a state I almost felt nostalgic for hawk-nosed Mounty.

'Oh Lordy, don't you cry too,' said Cassie, coming back into the kitchen at last.

'I'm sorry,' I said, knuckling my eyes. 'I just feel so fed up.'

'Here, let me take over while you make us both a cup of tea,' said Cassie. She flapped an enormous pair of drawers. 'Dear Lord, look at these! Imagine having a rear that huge.' She held them up against herself, shaking her head. 'Look, they go round me twice, and we could fit at least six of you inside. You're skinnier than ever, Opie.'

I put my arms round myself defensively. 'I can't help it,' I said.

'Oh, don't look like that. I didn't mean to be horrid. Come on, give me a smile.' Cassie put down the iron and came over to me. She tickled me under my chin.

'Stop it!' I said, squirming, but I couldn't help giggling.

'There, that's better. Let's see, do you have dimples when you smile? Mr Evandale says all kinds of silly things to see my dimples.'

'Oh, you and Mr Evandale! You do rattle on and on about him. He's just a customer,' I said irritably.

'Well, he might be a bit more than that,' said Cassie. She put her arm round me. 'Swear not to tell Mother? He waited for me outside Madame Alouette's tonight and walked down the road with me, and then he took me to the Royal Hotel!'

'Cassie!'

'Don't look so shocked. It was all very proper. We had a late afternoon tea in their lounge. Oh, it was so grand. The tea was served in the most delicate white china with a gold rim, and there were little almond biscuits on a plate and white linen napkins in case we made crumbs. A waiter served us and he called Mr Evandale "sir", and me "madam".'

'Does Mr Evandale want you to be his sweetheart?'

'Oh, I do hope so!' said Cassie.

'But he's an old man!'

'No he's not. He's thirty-seven – he told me.'

'Cassie, that's *old*. More than twice your age.'

'No it's not!' said Cassie. She'd never been any good at mental arithmetic.

'It is so. He's practically as old as Father.'

'Well, so what?' said Cassie. 'I *like* older men. They've got so much more style than silly tongue-tied boys. Mr Evandale knows exactly what to say, what to do. It's marvellous.'

I thought of Freddy and reluctantly understood.

'But if he's so marvellous, why do you think he's never got married?'

'I don't know,' said Cassie airily, but she looked furtive. She could never fool me.

'Cassie! Oh Lord, *is* he married?' I hissed.

'He might have been once. He assured me that he's not any more. He's not a liar, Opie, he's a real gentleman.'

'Are you completely demented? Look, Father is a gentleman, and yet even he tells lies. So what did he say? How did his wife die?'

'She didn't die. She's still alive and he pays an allowance for her and the children.'

'Children!'

'Do stop shrieking, it's getting on my nerves. And what's that funny smell?' Then Cassie screamed.

'Oh my Lord, the iron!' She dashed over and raised it high, leaving a large brown triangle on the fat lady bloomers. 'Oh gracious, what will Mother say! Do you think it will wash out?'

'No, scorch marks are permanent. Oh, Cassie!'

'It's just as much your fault as mine. You would have me tell you all my secrets. Oh dear, *look* at this mark. Well, this customer will never come back to Mother!'

'Perhaps we could patch it? Cut it out altogether and then sew in another piece of material? Would the fat lady notice?' I wondered.

'Yes, she would, unless she's an idiot – but I know, look, I could cut down the seam, snip off the entire length of material and then sew it up again. Then there won't be anything to show. The bloomers will be tighter, but she'll just think she's got even fatter. Yes!'

So I took over the ironing while Cassie cut and stitched and sewed. She made a very neat job of it too. If the owner ever suspected any jiggery-pokery, she certainly didn't complain to Mother.

Cassie confided more details about Mr Evandale as she stitched, though I had to question her hard.

'So is Mr Evandale . . . divorced?'

'Apparently so. Don't look so shocked. Lots of rich folk get divorced nowadays. I for one think it's sensible. Why should you have to stay with someone for ever if you discover you no longer love them.'

'Oh, you're so sentimental about love. You be careful, Cassie. Mother would have a fit if she knew you were taking tea with an old man with a wife and family.'

'He's *not* old. I'll stick this needle in you if you say it one more time.'

'And you think he's rich?'

'Quite rich, certainly. I think he has some sort of private family income.'

'Goodness! He doesn't work, then?'

'Oh, he works ferociously hard. He says he sometimes stays up all night working.'

'What on earth does he do?' I asked, suspecting the worst.

'He's an artist,' said Cassie proudly, taking the wind out of my sails.

'An artist?' I repeated dully.

I couldn't believe our Cassie was on afternoon-tea terms with a real artist. I thought of all my heroes – Fra Angelico and Piero di Cosimo, Raphael and Titian, Rossetti and Burne-Jones. One of these godly beings was canoodling with my own *sister*?

'A *real* artist?' I asked.

'Yes, he's exhibited at some Academy place, and various people buy his work,' Cassie said proudly. 'And you'll never guess, Opie – you'll never, ever guess!'

Of course I could guess. 'He wants to paint you.'

'Yes! Isn't that amazing!'

'He doesn't want to paint you naked, does he?'

'No! Well, I dare say he might *want* to, but I'm not that foolish. I shall wear my green dress, of course. Oh, Opie, imagine – an artist painting my portrait.'

'Will you tell Mother?'

'She wouldn't understand. And she seems to have set herself against Mr Evandale without even meeting him. No, it would be kinder not to tell her as she'd only worry. I'm to go to his studio on Sunday, so I'll make out I've been invited to Madame Alouette's for the day. I'll say it's to do with the dreary nephew. That'll keep her happy.'

'Where is his studio, then?'

'Oh, it's somewhere near the park. He's drawn me a little map. I shall find it easily enough.'

'Cassie, are you *sure* he's a gentleman?' I asked.

'Oh yes. His voice is wonderful and his clothes are beautifully made.'

'I didn't mean that! I meant, can you *trust* him? You're going to be all alone with him in this studio. What if he attacks you?'

Cassie giggled. 'You make him sound like a tiger! Don't fuss so, Opie. You're worse than Mother. He's simply going to paint my portrait. If by any chance he starts to behave alarmingly, I can simply walk away, can't I?'

'I'm sure Father wouldn't like you going to an artist's studio to pose,' I said.

'Well, Father isn't here to tell me what to do, is he?' she replied.

'No, but I wish he was.' I bent my head over the shirt I was ironing. A tear splashed on the hot iron, making a little hiss.

'I do too, silly – you know I do. But he's not, and we have to make the best of things the way they are,' said Cassie.

She lied very smoothly to Mother on Sunday when she appeared at breakfast in all her green finery.

'Oh, Cassie, Madame Alouette must be very fond of you,' said Mother. 'I'm sure that nephew hopes to enjoy your company too. I'm so happy for you, dear. You run along, then.'

Cassie went upstairs to brush her teeth and rearrange her hair. I followed her up.

'Oh, Opie, do I look all right?' she asked, turning this way and that to see herself in the old spotted looking glass.

'You look a picture – you always do,' I said.

Cassie took my hand and put it on her chest. 'Feel my heart! Oh Lord, it's beating fit to burst! Do you think I should let a few curls loose to tumble around my ears? Would that be more artistic?'

'Your hair's lovely whichever way you wear it,' I said.

'And my dress – do you think it makes me look a little stout? Please be absolutely honest.'

'You look stunning. You know you do, so stop flapping.'

'I can't help it. I'm so excited. Lord knows how I'll manage to stay still to pose.' Cassie gave me a squeeze. 'You won't tell on me to Mother, will you?'

'Of course not. But do take care, Cass. Do be good.'

'I'll be very, very good, I promise,' she said. 'I'll be back this afternoon – certainly by supper time. Now don't worry.'

I couldn't help worrying about her. It was hard talking to Mother, who burbled on and on about Madame Alouette and the wretched nephew. But at last she finished the rest of her ironing and packed all the laundry into separate piles to return (mercifully folding the giant lady's drawers without noticing they were ever so slightly diminished). She set out to deliver them, and I helped her, carrying my share.

It was hot, heavy work and I found myself perspiring inside my old blouse and tunic, though it was a cool day. I'd worn my old school clothes for ease and comfort, but I soon regretted it bitterly. The last of Mother's clients lived at the better, northern end of town. Her servant's mother lived in our street and had told her about the new washerwoman. When we knocked at the back door of their large red villa, I saw the daughter of the house in the basement kitchen, chatting to the cook. She was about my age and looked horribly familiar. It was Lucy-Ellen Wharton!

She'd been in my class at school. Lucy-Ellen, who couldn't grasp mathematics; Lucy-Ellen, who cried if Mounty told her off; Lucy-Ellen, who once tore her bloomers over-exerting herself in gymnastics. Lucy-Ellen, the girl I'd rather despised.

She noticed me, though I was trying to hide behind Mother. If I hadn't been wearing the distinctive St Margaret's uniform, she would never have focused on me. But she did. I saw the shock of recognition in her eyes. She gave me such a look, a mixture of pity and contempt. So all the school must know now.

I forced myself to stand up straight and stared hard at Lucy-Ellen until she looked away in confusion. As Mother and I trudged back home, I had to fight back tears of sheer humiliation. I imagined Lucy-Ellen rushing into school on Monday morning – 'Hey, girls, you'll never guess who brought our washing back on Sunday. Opal Plumstead – you know, the one whose father is in prison. And now her mother's our washerwoman, would you believe!'

We ate bread and cheese for lunch, Mother all the time wondering what Cassie would be eating.

'I should imagine it'll be French cuisine at Madame Alouette's,' she said excitedly.

'Mother, she's not really French – she just pretends to make her shop seem more impressive.'

'I'm sure she has French relations. Doesn't Philip usually live in Paris? I'm sure Cassie's invitation is his doing. She's always been Madame Alouette's pet, I know that, but she's never asked her for the day before. Oh, Opal, I wonder how she's getting on.'

I was wondering too – and worrying. After lunch Mother went for a nap and I went to my room. I got out my precious paintbox, stroking its beautiful wood, admiring all its pristine paint pans, gently tickling my cheeks with the brushes. Then I started sketching. I drew Cassie posing in her green dress, her hair tumbled past her shoulders, her dress unbuttoned, showing her impressive bosom. I caught her expression, her stance. When I started colouring her, she became almost too real. It was as if I were actually spying on her.

I drew Mr Evandale. I knew he had warm brown eyes and longish hair and bohemian clothes, though obviously I couldn't attempt a true likeness as I'd never seen him. I drew him smiling as he painted Cassie's portrait, his teeth large and prominent. I gave him a very long nose like a snout. I didn't just give him long hair, I made him hairy all over so that the skin emerging from his white silk shirt was like a fur pelt.

I expected Cassie to come back at supper time, but she didn't. She stayed out half the evening, until I was in agony.

'She said she'd be back for supper,' I wailed, unable to eat my own fish pie for fretting.

'Don't take on so, Opal. Madame Alouette's obviously invited her to dine with them. It's a real compliment. They must be very taken with her,' said Mother, unperturbed.

I couldn't explain why I was so worried. I kept having terrible visions of a wolf-like Evandale attacking Cassie. I didn't even know exactly where he lived, so I couldn't go in search of her. I was reduced to pacing the parlour, watching the clock tick on and on relentlessly.

At ten, when Cassie still wasn't home, Mother started to get a little anxious herself.

'Of course, they may have invited her to stay the night,' she said doubtfully. 'But she hasn't any night things with her – and she'd surely send word to us?'

'Oh, Mother, I do hope she's all right,' I said.

'Of course she is, silly girl,' said Mother, but she'd started to watch the clock too.

When we heard the sound of the key in the door at ten to eleven, we both ran into the hall. There was Cassie, rosy cheeked in the gaslight, beautiful in her green dress.

'Cassie darling! At last! Did you have a good time?' Mother asked eagerly.

'Oh yes, I had a splendid time,' said Cassie, picking up her skirts and twirling up and down the black and white tiles.

'I can see that! I assume Philip was there. I doubt

whether Madame Alouette herself could put such a sparkle in your eyes,' said Mother.

'Philip?'

'Don't try to bluff, dear. You can't fool your mother.'

'Oh, Philip!' said Cassie. 'Yes, of course, he was there.'

'I'll make us some cocoa and you must tell us all about it,' said Mother.

She hurried into the kitchen while Cassie unpinned her hat and hung her little cape on the hatstand.

'Are you all right?' I whispered urgently.

'Oh yes!' breathed Cassie. 'Wait till we're in bed. I have so much to tell you!'

'You haven't been good, have you?' I said.

'Shush! No, I've been a little bit bad – and it's been marvellous,' Cassie said, giggling.

Mother called us into the kitchen. 'Don't start telling Opal. I want to hear too,' she said.

Cassie sat at the table sipping cocoa, and told Mother a long elaborate tale of a day with Madame Alouette. She said the house was very elegant – French style, of course, with striped wallpaper and a lot of gilt and china cherubs. The garden was large, with a beautifully manicured lawn where they all played croquet after luncheon. Cassie said yes, Philip was there, with a sister and several of his old school chums. It had all been delightfully jolly. Cassie said she'd tried to go home at five but they wouldn't hear of it. 'Philip positively insisted I stay for supper. I didn't want to worry you, Mother, but it would have seemed so rude to refuse,' she said.

'I wasn't worried at all, dearie. I knew you'd be having a good time.'

'Madame Alouette made me feel so welcome. She's always kind to me at the shop, but she's a different person when she's at home. She was treating me almost like a daughter. She even hinted that one day she saw me taking over. Think of it – Madame Cassandra!'

I stared at Cassie, astonished. She was so incredibly convincing that I started to wonder if it were really true. Perhaps she'd run away from Mr Evandale and sought refuge at Madame Alouette's. And the nephew really *had* been there and taken an interest in her, because now she was telling us all about his schooldays and his boxing tournaments and studying in Paris, and his determination to take Cassie there one day to show her all the sights.

Mother kept giving little oohs and ahhs, drinking in every word as if it were champagne. At last she grew tired, yawning and rubbing her feet, which were troubling her after our long tramp around the town.

'Come on, Mother, let us put you to bed,' said Cassie.

'I shall never sleep, darling. I'm so excited! All my

dreams have come true. I *knew* you'd meet a wonderful young man one day, but I never thought it would be Madame Alouette's nephew. It couldn't be more perfect.'

'Now don't go making plans, Mother. It's early days yet,' said Cassie. 'Perhaps Philip has his eye on any number of Madame's protégées.'

'I know none of them could hold a candle to my girl,' said Mother, kissing Cassie's flushed cheek.

We all went up to bed, and for all her protestations Mother was snoring hard five minutes after we'd tucked her up.

'Right, Cassie,' I whispered, pulling her into my cupboard. 'Tell all.'

'Oh Lordy, I don't know where to start. And I'm tired out, spouting all that rubbish for Mother's sake. Did it sound too ridiculous?'

'It sounded amazing. I was starting to believe you.'

'It *is* amazing if you could only see the nephew. I very much doubt he's interested in girls at all, and he certainly looked down his nose at me,' said Cassie. 'Luckily Daniel is totally enchanted.'

'Daniel?'

'Daniel Evandale. Do you know what he said? He said I was a young English rose just coming into bloom.' Cassie giggled affectedly. 'He said I even smelled like a rose, and my skin was as soft and velvety as a rose petal.'

'You're making it up. You've read too many silly romantic novels.'

'No, this time I swear I'm speaking God's honest truth. If you think that's romantic, you should hear some of the other things he said. He loves my hair and said I was like that girl in the fairy tale who let down her hair. What's she called again?'

'Rapunzel. Cassie, you took down your *hair*?'

'It was for the portrait. Daniel said I looked far too stiff and formal with my hair up. He didn't want to paint me like some stuffy society lady.'

'So how *did* he portray you? Like a young *Eve*?'

'No! I was fully dressed – though not in my actual dress. He had this beautiful white frock he wanted me to wear, perhaps a little décolleté, but totally decent, I promise you, Miss Prim. It showed off my figure to perfection, even if I say so myself.'

'You changed your dress in front of him?' I squealed.

'Shush! You'll wake Mother. No, I went behind a Japanese screen. This is how artists work with their models. It's all very proper and accepted, I assure you.'

'You don't know that. It's just what he's told you.'

'Well, all right, then, I don't know and I don't care. All I know is that Daniel is the most heavenly man I've ever met and he's totally smitten with me, Opie. He thinks I'm—'

'A wretched English rose just coming into bloom – you've already told me,' I said. 'So he painted you all day long and half the evening too?'

'Well, he painted me a lot of the time, but we had to have little breaks, of course. You've no idea how tiring it is, keeping the same pose all the time, though Daniel played us music. Some of the time it was shouty opera, but he made it quite interesting by telling me all the stories. Opera's very sad, you know. They don't seem to like happy endings. But then he played me some music-hall songs, and they were terribly comical. Daniel knew all the words and sang along. Do you know, if he wasn't an artist I do believe he could go on the stage. He was astonished when I said I'd never been to a music hall. He said we should remedy that as soon as possible, which sounds very hopeful, doesn't it?'

'But Mother hates music halls. They're very vulgar and the wrong sort of people go there.' I was only parroting what Mother said, but I blushed to hear myself speak. I sounded so prim and disapproving. I didn't really have any strong feelings about music halls. The strongest feeling I was experiencing now was envy.

'Mother won't know. I'll make out I'm going somewhere else – with Philip,' said Cassie.

'You can't keep this up for ever,' I protested.

'I can so – at least until Daniel proposes, and then

Mother will be so thrilled she won't mind that he's a little older than me.'

'Cassie, you're living in cloud-cuckoo-land. He might well propose something to you, but it won't be marriage. You'll end up ruined, with a baby.' I tried to make myself sound worldly wise, though I still only had a hazy idea of how this would happen. I'd gleaned a little information from books. *Tess of the d'Urbervilles* had been quite educational, but there hadn't been any detailed descriptions.

'Oh, you're such a gloomy old fusspot, Opie. I'll be fine, you'll see. And one day – hopefully one day quite soon – there'll be a ring on this finger.' She rubbed the significant finger on her left hand as if she could magic a ring there by sheer willpower alone.

16

Cassie spent every Sunday with Daniel Evandale. She said he often met her after work and took her off to tea as well. One evening he took her to the bar of the hotel and gave her champagne!

'Champagne!' I echoed. 'Oh, what does it taste like, Cassie?'

'Marvellous.'

'Yes, but what *kind* of marvellous?'

'It's very bubbly and it tickles your nose.'

'Like ginger beer?'

'Well, a little, but much better. And we ate oysters.'

'But you hate shellfish,' I said. Cassie had screamed in disgust when Father once bought us a bag of whelks on a trip to the seaside.

'I must admit they *look* disgusting, but Daniel showed me how to tip them down my throat and they were marvellous too,' said Cassie.

'If Daniel showed you how to tip a wriggly worm down your throat, you'd say it was marvellous,' I said. 'How is your portrait in the white dress progressing?'

'Oh, that's more or less finished. He works on all the background when I'm not there. He's started another painting of me now.'

'In another white dress?'

'Without a dress this time.' Cassie went into peals of laughter when she saw my face.

'Naked?'

'Not exactly.'

'What does that mean?'

'I'm wearing my stockings and my hat.'

'Nothing in between?'

'It's a very artistic pose,' said Cassie.

'You really take all your clothes off? *Your corset and your drawers?*'

'I *said* it's artistic. Goodness, you've seen all those pictures in art books.'

'I could no more take my clothes off in front of a man than fly!' I declared. I imagined undressing in front of Freddy or Geoff, or Mr Beeston or dear Mr Andrews, and blushed at the very thought. Cassie seemed to have stepped onto an entirely different planet. It was bizarre thinking of her being so grown up and daring when she was still my own sister, scratching herself and humming maddeningly and yelping like a hyena if anything amused her. 'Don't you feel dreadful standing there with him staring at you?'

'Well, to be truthful, I felt terribly anxious the first time I took off my dress and all my other things. I wouldn't come out from behind the screen for ages and ages. Daniel had to coax me out, and then, when I did, I blushed all over. It was so embarrassing. But Daniel said such lovely things. He was so gentle and reassuring, and admiring too, that I soon calmed down. I don't turn a hair now.'

Cassie managed to give an entirely fictional account of her Sunday activities to Mother, elaborating endlessly on life at Madame Alouette's. Mother was extremely inquisitive, listening attentively, her mouth slightly open like a child hearing a bedtime story. She and Cassie grew closer than ever. I felt terribly left out.

I wrote to Father – long letters in which I bared my soul and told him everything. I fretted over Cassie's secret trysting and fumed over my wretched lot at Fairy Glen. I didn't *send* these letters, of course.

I folded them up into tiny squares and hid them in my fondant fancy treasure box. I wrote him conventional real letters, submitting them for Mother's approval, and he sent one in return. It was very short and uninformative. I was still simply addressed as 'and Opal'.

But then we received another letter, brief and to the point.

My dearest Lou, Cassie and Opal,

I have been told my trial is at Kingtown Assizes on 5th December. Pray God they will be lenient with me.

Your own loving husband and father,

Ernest

Mother read the letter through, and then collapsed in tears. It was as though she'd been able to put Father right out of her mind while she was concentrating on Cassie's fictional social success with Madame Alouette's family. Now she seemed steeped in despair all over again.

'Oh, Mother, you will go to the trial, won't you? It's so important that Father sees you there,' I said.

'I don't know whether I can bear it,' she sobbed.

'What about *Father*? We must think of him. Well, *I* shall go. I look much older now I'm out at work,' I said determinedly.

'Don't wash the starch out of your hair – that'll help!' said Cassie.

'How can you joke at a time like this? Oh Lord, I shall die if it's all over the papers again,' said Mother. 'What if any of my customers see? And – oh, horrors – what about Madame Alouette? She'll never want her nephew consorting with the daughter of a convicted prisoner.'

'He's not convicted yet, Mother. He might still be let off with some kind of penalty or fine,' I said, though I did not really think it was possible.

'Madame Alouette only reads the fashion journals,' said Cassie.

'But what about Philip?' Mother wailed.

'Oh, bother Philip,' said Cassie, forgetting herself. 'Listen, I'm coming to the trial too. I'll make out to Madame that I've had hideous toothache or some such thing.'

'You mustn't! I can't have either of you girls jeopardizing your jobs,' said Mother, but she was no match for the two of us together.

I hugged Cassie when we were on our own. 'I'm so glad you're coming too,' I said.

'I feel so bad that I didn't come to the magistrate's court, but this time we'll go together.'

'Perhaps you can help me dress up a little? I looked like a clown when I tried last time.'

'Of course I'll help, silly. Oh dear, why ever did

I start this Philip nonsense? The wretched man's getting on my nerves and I don't even know him!'

'Cass, what about Mr Evandale? What will you do if he reads about Father in the newspaper?' I said.

'He already knows about Father,' said Cassie.

'Oh my goodness, how did he find out?'

'I told him, silly.'

'And he didn't *mind*?' I thought of Olivia and the pain of never being able to see her again.

'He found it intriguing. I wasn't going to breathe a word, but he was teasing me about being – what was it? – a bourgeois little girl from the suburbs. It was because I was so shy about taking my clothes off. It annoyed me, and so I declared I wasn't at *all* bourgeois – how could I be with a father in prison? Then he got frightfully interested. He's one of those chaps who loves to mix with what he calls "low life", but I don't think he knows any real criminals. *Now* he knows a criminal's daughter,' said Cassie.

'Don't! Father isn't a real true criminal. Maybe the judge will realize that,' I said.

'Opal, he's pleading guilty.'

'Yes, but that shows he's really *honest*,' I said desperately.

'You're not using your famous intellect now. But I suppose it's understandable. You do love Father so,' said Cassie.

'Don't *you* love him?'

'Of course I do, but I could shake him for being such a fool.'

'He just wanted to please us, to please Mother.'

'I know, you keep saying that. But that's not the way to do it. He should have stood up to Mother more, been a little more manly. That's the way to please a woman,' said Cassie, as if she'd suddenly become a world expert on affairs of the heart.

We were all up very early on the fifth of December. We couldn't face any breakfast, apart from strong cups of tea, but we spent a long time getting ready. I submitted to Cassie's ministrations. She swept my hair up in an elaborate style, marshalling it determinedly into place with a whole army of steel pins. My face looked very stark and exposed and my spectacles very prominent.

'Oh dear, I look like a schoolmarm,' I said in dismay.

'Well, that's good, isn't it? Schoolmarms are old,' Cassie pointed out. 'Now, let's see . . . What shall you wear?' She searched in her wardrobe and produced the old grey suit Mother had bought her when she first went to work at Madame Alouette's. Cassie had always hated it and called it 'the elephant' because she said it was so wrinkled and plain.

'Do *I* have to wear the elephant?' I said.

'Try it. I think it will be tremendously ageing,' said Cassie.

'It's tremendously *enormous*,' I said, struggling into the voluminous skirt.

'You can wear my high-necked white blouse underneath the jacket. That will have to hang loose, but we'll pin the skirt here and there.' Cassie pinched the sagging waistband and pinned it into place. When she'd finished, she made me peer into the looking glass.

'There!' she said proudly.

I didn't know whether to laugh or cry. All I had to do was grow my nose and I'd be a dead ringer for Miss Mountbank. But I certainly looked older, and that was really all that mattered today, so I gave Cassie a kiss. She looked splendid herself, though a little more subdued than usual, in her black velvet two-piece. She normally wore it with a pink blouse, a pink silk rosette pinned on the jacket, and a pink ribbon threaded through her hair – 'But I don't want to look too frivolous today,' she said.

Mother wore black too: her best winter coat with a black and grey striped skirt. Cassie needed to pin this at the waist too, because she'd lost a lot of weight since Father was arrested.

We looked as if we were going to a funeral. Certainly that was the way it felt. When we set out to get the bus, everyone in the street stared at us curiously. Some might simply have been wondering where we going looking so smart and sombre, but others nudged each other and whispered, and it was clear they knew our destination. The terrible Mrs Liversedge came rushing out of her house, calling loudly, 'Off to court, dears? Well, I wish you luck. Maybe he'll get a light sentence.'

We ignored her and hurried on down the road.

'Or maybe he'll be locked up for life,' she called after us.

Mother gave a little gasp.

'Take no notice. She's being ridiculous. You don't get locked up for life for embezzlement,' I said fiercely.

It took longer than we'd expected to get to the courthouse where the quarter sessions were heard. It was gone ten o'clock when we arrived. We stared up at the forbidding building and clasped hands.

'In we go,' said Cassie. 'You stay in the middle, Opie, so you don't stick out too much.'

The clerk at the door was so taken up with looking at Cassie and giving her instructions on how to reach the public gallery that he didn't give Mother a second look, let alone me. I scurried past all the same and led the way up the stairs to the gallery. Because of its name I thought it would be teeming with members of the public, out for a spot of salacious entertainment, but it was half empty. Little clumps of people sat here and there with pale, anxious faces, clearly relatives as wound up and worried as we were.

We stared down at the man in the dock, but it

wasn't Father. It was a poor cringing soul with a purple birth mark over half his face. We listened to a policeman in the witness box reading from his notebook. He'd seen the poor wretch run to the middle of the bridge over the Thames, haul himself up onto the parapet and then jump. The policeman had then dashed to the riverbank, removed his jacket and boots, and dived in to save him.

'I didn't *want* to be saved. I wanted to end it all,' said the man in the dock, but the judge shouted, 'Silence!' and wouldn't let him explain further.

'Poor man!' I whispered indignantly.

'Shush!' Mother hissed. 'We're not allowed to talk.'

It was difficult to keep quiet, especially when the man was sentenced for the 'crime' of trying to commit suicide, but at least the judge was merciful and gave him just one week's imprisonment.

Perhaps Father might be sentenced to just one week too. Oh, how wonderful that would be!

The next trial was a complicated robbery case, with a man and a woman in the dock. I tried to concentrate, but there were too many confusing stories, and too many witnesses giving conflicting evidence. I peered at the jury, wondering if they could seriously follow all the ins and outs of the case. At lunch time it still wasn't anywhere near finished.

'What if it goes on all day long?' Cassie wondered

as we sipped a bowl of soup in the small café across the road.

'I can't stomach this waiting,' said Mother, laying down her spoon.

'Well, imagine what it's like for Father, locked up in some dingy cell,' I said.

'Eat, Mother. You need to keep your strength up,' said Cassie. 'And you watch that soup, Opie. I don't want you slurping it all down my white blouse.'

We carried on bickering throughout our hasty meal. The people in the café seemed to be watching us. I suppose it was easy to guess from our general demeanour that we had a loved one due to appear in court. We couldn't stand their stares and left without finishing our soup.

The robbery case continued for more than an hour, and then the jury deliberated, but they reached a verdict quickly and the judge sentenced the woman to a year's penal servitude and the man to two years' hard labour.

'Hard labour?' Cassie whispered. 'What does that mean? It sounds horrible.'

'I don't know,' I admitted. 'Perhaps he has to do hard labour because he's a hardened criminal. I suppose it's working very hard with pickaxes.'

Mother gave a little moan.

'It's all right, Mother. They won't give Father hard labour – he's a gentleman,' I said, praying that this was true. 'The robbery man knocked someone over and beat him unconscious. Father hasn't hurt anyone. He just wrote out a cheque, for goodness' sake. It's a total travesty of justice that he's had to spend all these weeks in prison. I'm sure the judge will see this and let him off with a caution.' I thought if I said it firmly enough, over and over again, it might just possibly come true.

Then, at last, Father's case was announced and he was led into the courtroom. I thought at first they'd made a mistake and brought out the wrong prisoner. This was surely a very old man, a good decade older than Father, and his hair was all wrong – my father had a fine head of silky brown hair. This poor prisoner had white hair, and it was cut brutally short, almost to the scalp.

'That's not Father!' I declared.

I was immediately shushed by the clerk upstairs. 'You!' he hissed, pointing at me. 'Silence, or I will have you evicted.'

'It *is* Father,' Cassie whispered in my ear. Tears were running down her cheeks. 'Poor dear Father, what have they done to him?'

Mother had her hands clasped and was rocking to and fro on her hard seat, her eyes shut.

Another clerk was reading out the charge against Father. He spoke for a long time. I couldn't understand what was happening. Father had simply written out one cheque, but now they seemed to be saying that he had done far more. They were talking about false entries in record books going back years, accusing him of serious long-term embezzlement, saying he'd pocketed vast sums.

'No! Not Father!' I said aloud, but quietly enough for the clerk upstairs to ignore me.

'How do you plead?'

Father scarcely seemed to be listening. He was peering around the court in a dazed fashion, perhaps wondering where he was and how he had got there. He had to be asked a second time.

He jerked to attention. 'Guilty!' he said.

'No! No, no, no – he's just guilty of writing one cheque,' I whispered desperately. I ran over to the clerk. 'Please, there's been a terrible mistake. My father *isn't* guilty, not to all those charges. You must stop the trial and explain this to the judge.'

The clerk held me by the arms. 'Stop this nonsense. You cannot interrupt a trial. Now sit down and be quiet or I shall remove you from this courthouse.'

There was nothing more I could do. I had to listen in silent agony while the head of Father's shipping office and various weaselly-looking clerks gave evidence. It became horribly clear what was happening. When Father's naïve attempt at embezzlement was discovered, the accountant had gone through the company's books and discovered many more fraudulent entries. These were nothing to do with Father. Some dated back to long before he was even employed at the wretched firm.

I willed Father to sit up and take notice and argue the point, but he still seemed in a stupor, clearly fuddled and ill. I ached to go and comfort him. Cassie held my hand tightly. Mother rocked to and fro, eyes still shut, fists clenched, whispering to herself. Perhaps she was praying – but Father now seemed beyond heavenly help.

The shipping clerks continued to give evidence, insisting that Father was the only man who had access to all the account books and declaring on oath that the false entries were in his hand.

When at last Father himself was cross-examined, he could not give a proper account of himself.

'I was hoping to pay it back. I simply wanted happy days for my family,' he kept repeating, not even listening to the questions properly.

He looked baffled when the prosecution lawyer insisted he had engaged in long-term embezzlement.

'I don't think so. I wrote the cheque, that is all. I don't understand what you mean,' Father said.

'Oh, I think you understand all too well. You have systematically used your mathematical skills to produce plausible accounts, while stealing vast amounts from your trusting employers over many years,' said the lawyer.

'Not vast amounts,' said Father, at last concentrating properly. 'One cheque, that is all. There must be some mistake.'

'You made the mistake, my good sir. You grew careless because you'd been undetected for so long and did not even take the trouble to cover your tracks writing out the latest cheque. You wilfully stole from your employers, year after year – admit it now.'

'I'm guilty of writing the one cheque, I've said that all along, but nothing else, I swear it,' said Father.

'Then how do you account for the vast financial losses over the years, the fraudulent entries in your own hand, sir?'

'We all use copperplate. My hand is indistinguishable from any other clerk's.'

'Are you implying that one of these other good hard-working men is equally corrupt?'

'Yes, yes, yes!' I breathed.

But Father tried hard to be fair. 'I cannot imply anything, for I have no proof,' he said quietly.

They had no real proof against Father, either. It did not seem to matter, even though this was a court of justice. The judge kept consulting his pocket watch, clearly keen for the proceedings to be over. I stared at this wizened little man in his ridiculous robes and wig. It seemed ludicrous that he had the right to sentence my poor father. He didn't even know him. He wasn't concerned with the ins and outs of the case. He ordered no further investigation of the other clerks, no re-examination of the fraudulent entries. Surely it should be clear to everyone in the court that my father was telling the truth. He was a weak man who, in a moment of desperation, had made one botched attempt at embezzlement. He wasn't a long-term cool-headed thief. He was an *honest* man who had admitted his guilt immediately.

It did not matter. The jury did not believe him.

'Ernest Horace Plumstead, I sentence you to one year's hard labour,' said the judge. 'Court dismissed.'

17

I couldn't sleep at all that night. The words 'hard labour' echoed on and on in my head. I thought of Father, already looking so old and frail, trying to heave a pickaxe. I remembered pictures in old books of prisoners chained together, manacled at the ankles, being beaten by a cruel overseer. Did that still happen? My poor father would be dead within days. And all on a trumped-up charge. He had written one wretched cheque, that was all. He was bearing the burden of someone else's wickedness.

In the middle of the night I went into Mother's room. She was lying on her front, weeping into her pillow. When I put my head on it next to hers, I found it was wet with her tears.

'Don't cry so, Mother. I've been planning what to do in my head. We must go to a lawyer tomorrow, a new one. The one supposedly defending Father was worse than useless. We will appeal. I'm sure you can do that. We will make them reconsider Father's case. It was a total travesty of justice. We will make another judge understand, and they will trap whoever the real embezzler is, and then they will let Father go. He's already served enough time for the little crime he's committed. We'll have him returned home to us in no time.'

'Oh, Opal, I know you mean to be helpful, but you're talking nonsense,' said Mother, crushing me.

'I'm not, Mother. I've thought it all out so carefully,' I said.

'Well, you haven't thought it out quite carefully enough,' she said. 'How are we going to pay for this new lawyer? Answer me that. Do you think your wages from Fairy Glen and my wretched washerwoman's pittance will foot his bill?'

I hadn't even thought about payment. I blushed with shame, but I still wouldn't give up.

'Then we will press for an appeal without a lawyer. We'll argue our own case. I am sure there are law books in the public library. I shall read them all. I'll make myself understand. I'll look up all the hard words in a dictionary and learn how to use them properly. I'm good at it, you know I am. We'll go to court and defend Father.' I saw myself making an impassioned speech, quoting former legal cases while the judge listened open-mouthed at my erudition and the jurors wept in pity.

'Don't be such a little fool, Opal,' said Mother. 'You're not even allowed in court – you're still a child. Now go back to bed. There's nothing we can do to help Father now.'

'Don't you even care?' I said. 'What sort of a wife are you?'

'How dare you!' Mother rose up in bed. 'How dare you say such a thing to me?' she shrieked, and she tried to slap my face.

She couldn't see properly in the dark and she was clumsy with exhaustion anyway, so her hand hit my shoulder instead. It didn't really hurt but it set me screaming.

'For goodness' sake, what are you two doing?' Cassie cried, rushing into the room.

'Mother hit me,' I wailed.

'I simply gave her a slap,' said Mother. 'And she deserved it too.'

'I'm just trying to find ways of helping Father. Mother won't even *listen*,' I said.

'Stop it, both of you,' said Cassie. 'Don't cry, Mother. Here.' She caught hold of both of us and held us tight. 'Stop fighting.'

We all ended up huddled together in Mother's bed. I still bitterly resented Mother's rejection, but in the morning I could see that my grandiose legal plans were nonsense. Instead, I wrote a long letter to the judge, explaining that my father was innocent of almost all the crimes mentioned in court. I begged the judge to reduce his sentence at the very least, because penal servitude would kill such a frail gentleman. I posted the letter – but never got any response.

I looked so dreadful in the morning that I was utterly convincing when I told Mr Beeston that I'd been ill the previous day.

'Yes, you still look a bit peaky, you poor little tuppenny,' he said. 'Perhaps you ought to trot straight back to bed?'

I didn't want to be at Fairy Glen, but I didn't want to be at home, either, not with Mother weeping into her washing. Besides, I didn't get paid if I wasn't at work.

'I think I can manage a day moulding, Mr Beeston,' I said.

'Well, that's the spirit, missy. I wish all my girls had your attitude. You're an example to them all, Opal Plumstead.'

I hoped very much that he wouldn't come into the

fondant room later and extol my virtues. It would make the other girls hate me more than ever.

I put on my cap and overall and trudged across the factory floor.

'Hey, sweetheart, why the long face?' said Freddy.

'I'm *not* your sweetheart, Freddy. I'm your friend,' I told him wearily.

'You and I were meant for each other, whatever you say.' He reached out and touched the corners of my mouth.

'Don't!'

'I'm just trying to make you smile. You don't look like my pretty girl with that frowning face,' said Freddy.

I made an effort to smile but it was too much of a struggle.

'Hey, is something really wrong?' he said more seriously. 'Where were you yesterday? I didn't see you.'

I hesitated. He was so kind that, for a second or two, I considered telling him everything. Perhaps he wouldn't be horrified. Perhaps he'd pat me on the back and tell me he was sure my father was innocent too. Perhaps.

The moment passed.

'I'm not very well. I think it's just a cold,' I said. 'I'd better get to work.' I hurried away up the narrow staircase.

'Hello, Opal,' said Geoff. 'We missed you yesterday. Were you ill, then, dear?'

I nodded. I must have looked pale and wan because he patted me gently on the shoulder.

'You take it easy today. I can see you're still feeling dicky.'

I found my moulding stick and starting working on a starch box. The other girls ignored me. They generally didn't initiate the goading. They left that to Patty, and she was her customary ten minutes late. She usually arrived at Fairy Glen spot on time, but she'd spend ten minutes in the ladies' room titivating and then come sauntering up to the fondant room when she chose.

Today she was even later than usual. She came into the fondant room holding the *Daily News*, reading as she walked.

'Watch out, Pattacake, you'll barge straight into the boxes,' said Geoff.

'Yes, look where you're going, girl,' added George.

'I'm too engrossed,' said Patty, and she glanced up at me. I saw the gleam in her eye.

Oh Lord, was there something about Father's trial in the national newspapers? I'd been dreading the local paper at the end of the week, but I'd never dreamed that his sad case would be written up for all to see from John o' Groats to Land's End. And the worst person in the whole of Britain was reading about it right before my eyes.

'It's so bizarre,' said Patty. 'We don't often see Kingtown in the newspapers. My pa pointed it out to me. He reads the newspaper from cover to cover. This column here is all about someone called Plumstead. Now there's a familiar name!'

'Our Opal Plumbrain?' said Nora. 'Tell, Patty!' She laughed, thinking Patty was about to invent some outlandish story.

'Stop your nonsense now, Pattacake,' said Geoff.

'It's not nonsense, Geoff. It's all here in black and white – see: page seven, column three. All about this Ernest Plumstead chap. Oh, what a bad boy he's been. Cooking the books at his office for years, but now he's been nicked. He was up for trial yesterday and he's got his come-uppance. A year's hard labour!'

'Stop it,' I said. My throat was so dry my voice cracked.

'Who is this Ernest Plumbrain? He has to be some swanky relation of yours. A cousin? Maybe an uncle?'

'He's my *father*,' I said hoarsely.

'Your father?' For a moment Patty looked surprised, and then she burst out laughing.

It was enough. I ran across the room, snatched the newspaper and pushed her violently in the chest. She gasped and then slapped me. I sprang at her and we both fell to the floor, screaming and punching and kicking, knocking over a whole pile of starch boxes.

All the girls yelled, and Geoff and George shouted and tried to drag us apart, but nothing could stop me now. Patty was bigger and stronger than me, but I was filled with such fury that I couldn't stop hitting her, even when she took hold of my head and banged it on the floorboards. I scratched her face and pulled her hair free of her cap and tugged it as hard as I could. I was suddenly aware that the yelling all around us had stopped. There was an ominous silence in the room.

Patty suddenly gasped and let me go. She scrambled to her feet. 'Sorry, missus,' she mumbled, tucking her hair back under her cap.

I leaned up on one elbow and peered blearily through the clouds of starch. A woman was standing in the doorway. She was tall and dignified, wearing her white overall with an air of authority. She was the beautifully spoken woman I'd once met in the ladies' room.

'What on earth is going on here?' she said.

'Beg pardon, Mrs Roberts,' said George. 'Just a bit of a scrap between the girls.'

Mrs Roberts? Oh my Lord, the Mrs Roberts who owned Fairy Glen?

'I can't have this sort of behaviour in my factory,' she said. She looked at Patty. 'How dare you attack a little girl half your size?'

'I didn't, missus,' said Patty.

'I saw you with my own eyes beating her head on the floor.'

'Yes, but Opal hit her first!' said Nora – and half the other girls echoed her.

Mrs Roberts shook her head.

'I reckon it was six of one and half a dozen of the other. Young Opal might have started the rough play, but she was severely provoked,' said Geoff.

'*Did* you start the fight, Opal?' asked Mrs Roberts.

'Yes I did!' I stood up, rubbing my eyes. My hair had tumbled down, my overall was torn, and my nose was bleeding. 'I hit her and I'm not one bit ashamed of it. I'd like to hit her again and again and again.'

'That's enough,' said Mrs Roberts. 'You two girls, tidy yourselves. I'll see you in my office in five minutes.' She turned and walked off, briskly brushing starch from her overall.

'Well, you've really been and gone and done it now, young Opal,' said Geoff. 'Whatever's got into you?'

'Why did you have to goad her, Patty?' said George. He picked up the pieces of the tattered newspaper and tore them to shreds with his big hands.

'I didn't twig it was her *father*,' said Patty. She was gingerly feeling her face. 'I didn't think she'd go for me like a wildcat.'

'You've got a scratch this long, Pats! She wants locking up, that one,' said Nora.

'Poor Patty,' said Edith, offering her own rather grubby handkerchief.

Beeston came rushing in, his hat at a slant, out of breath from flying up the stairs. 'What's happened? I've just seen Mrs Roberts. Who was fighting?' He looked around. It was easy to see it was Patty and me.

'I can't believe it. You two of all people! You're my senior girl, Patty Meacham, with all the privileges – and you're supposed to be the bright quick learner, Opal Plumstead. I had high expectations of both of you. How dare you let me down like this! And to have the stupidity to pick a day when Mrs Roberts is doing an inspection. I'll never live it down. Well, don't just stand there gawping at me, you pair of ninnies. Get yourselves to her office, pronto.' He shook his head so hard he nearly dislodged his hat.

I didn't know where Mrs Roberts' office was. I had to follow Patty down the stairs and across the factory floor. The men and women downstairs stared at us. They'd obviously heard all the shouting and thumping. Freddy was white-faced and stricken.

'Oh, Opal, you're not going to get the sack, are you?' he wailed.

I shrugged at him, trying not to cry. It was all very well feeling triumphant that I'd held my own against hateful Patty. What if I *did* lose my job? I couldn't stand it at Fairy Glen, but I knew enough to realize that it was the biggest and best factory for miles, with the fairest conditions and the highest rates of pay. If I got dismissed without a reference, I'd be totally stuck. We needed my wages to survive.

I followed Patty off the main factory floor, along the corridor, then down to a door at the end. She turned to face me. She was biting her lips, her eyes desperate. Perhaps she was terrified of losing her job too. She was very white, so the scratch on her face stood out lividly. I wiped my nose, which was still bleeding. Look at the pair of us! How could she *not* dismiss us?

Patty took a deep breath and then knocked on the door.

'Come in,' Mrs Roberts called. Her voice was severe. This was far worse than being sent in disgrace to the headmistress.

Patty opened the door. I started to follow, but Mrs Roberts stopped me.

'One at a time,' she said. 'You wait outside.'

I had to stand by myself in the corridor, waiting. I leaned against the wall, my head throbbing, my whole body sore and hurting. I had to keep sniffing fiercely to stop my nose dribbling. Eventually I used my overall cuff, and it came away smeared with blood.

I couldn't believe how my whole life had changed in just a few short months. I hadn't realized how happy I'd been back at school with Olivia. I had often wasted time feeling miserable or restless when I actually had everything: my scholarship, my dear best friend, my own family of four. *Oh, Father*, I thought wretchedly. I couldn't bear it that he was in the national newspapers. The *Daily News* was ripped to shreds now, but perhaps I ought to buy another, just to see how his case was reported. Then I would tear that up too. I'd buy all the newspapers in the shop and destroy them. I had a sudden mad vision of rushing from shop to shop all over the country, tearing up newspapers until my hands bled.

Patty was in with Mrs Roberts a long, long time. I tried creeping right up to the door and putting my ear against it, but I couldn't hear properly. There was just a low murmur and then a sound of sobbing. *Patty* sobbing? Then Mrs Roberts must have dismissed her!

I loathed Patty. But even so my stomach lurched. Patty was hateful to me, but she was tolerably good at her job. She took care to come in late as a matter of pride, but she could mould faster and more neatly than most, and she kept her eye on the other girls and made sure their work was up to scratch. She was a spiteful bully and yet they all looked up to her. I'd heard them talking about her family. She was the eldest of eight and had an invalid father, so her wages were vital. How would they manage now that Patty had lost her job?

She came out at last, her face blotchy, her eyes red.

She didn't even glance at me. She ran down the corridor towards the ladies' room.

'Patty?' I called, but she ignored me.

I knocked on Mrs Roberts' door.

'Come in.'

I walked in – and was utterly taken aback. I'd expected an office like Mr Beeston's – brown paint, lino, practical desk, files and books on a shelf, work rotas pinned on the wall. Mrs Roberts' room was like a lady's drawing room. It was wallpapered in an intricate leaf and flower design in subtle creams and greens. A Persian rug lay on the floor. Her desk was small and stylish, with carved handles, and a brass lion paperweight crouched on top of a neat pile of letters. She had a proper bookshelf with various manuals on sweet making, and blue-and-white-patterned vases artistically arranged here and there on the shelving.

Mrs Roberts herself sat in an easy chair, though her back was straight and her head erect. She had taken off her cap and overall. She was wearing a crisp white blouse with a cameo at the throat, and a beautifully cut deep purple skirt with a green belt around her narrow waist. I felt smaller and scruffier than ever as I crept towards her.

'Sit down, Opal,' she said, indicating the wooden chair in front of her.

I sat, and couldn't contain myself any longer.

'Please, Mrs Roberts, don't dismiss Patty,' I blurted. 'It wasn't really all her fault. I did push her first. And I hit her and hit her.'

'I dare say you did. You both behaved disgracefully. I won't have my girls brawling like hooligans.'

'I know. But you don't understand,' I said wretchedly.

'I understand that you've been very unhappy here at Fairy Glen,' said Mrs Roberts. 'I remember our conversation in the ladies' room on your very first day here.'

'I'm sorry. I didn't know who you were then.'

'Obviously. I hoped that after a few days you'd get used to things and settle in, but it's clear that hasn't happened.'

'So are you going to dismiss me too?'

Mrs Roberts sighed heavily. 'Not necessarily. I'm not that sort of employer. I want you to work hard and be happy here, though that doesn't seem possible in your case, Opal Plumstead.'

'I will be even more unhappy if you dismiss Patty and not me, because all the girls will detest me. And I will detest myself because I think Patty is the chief breadwinner in her family – without her wages they may very well end up in the workhouse, living on bread and gruel, even the little ones,' I said, trying to make it sound as graphic as possible to arouse Mrs Roberts' sympathy.

She raised one eyebrow. 'I'm impressed by your concern, seeing as you seemed intent on beating the living daylights out of Patty half an hour ago. You need not be fearful on her behalf. Patty will always have employment at Fairy Glen. Her father used to work here – when the employees' safety and employment weren't necessarily the concern of the owner. There was an accident with a vat of boiling sugar and Mr Meacham's hands were badly burned. He cannot work now, but members of his family will always be given a good position here at Fairy Glen – as long as they don't abuse it. I've had a few words with Patty. I think she's rather taken advantage of the situation and has not always been kind to her fellow workers.'

'Meaning me?' I said.

'Yes, I do mean you. You're very direct, Opal. It's a little disconcerting.'

'I'm sorry. I don't mean to be. The words seem to come out of my mouth before I can stop them, and then I upset people. I do it at home and I used to do it at school too. I know it irritated the teachers.'

'So you disliked school too?'

'On the contrary, I positively adored St Margaret's. I had a scholarship,' I said, unable to resist boasting.

'So why did you decide to come to Fairy Glen?'

'I didn't have any choice,' I said.

Mrs Roberts leaned forward enquiringly.

'I – I don't really want to talk about it,' I said.

'I can see that it's difficult, but if I'm to understand you properly, Opal, I think I need to know,' said Mrs Roberts.

I wanted to retort that it was none of her business, but I pressed my lips together, knowing that this would be going too far. I waited. Mrs Roberts waited too. At last I managed to say, 'My father is . . . away. We are in straitened circumstances. It wasn't possible for me to stay on at school. I have to earn money now.'

'Do you know when your father will be coming back?' Mrs Roberts asked gently. 'There's no question of your going back to school?'

'No chance at all. My father will be away for a year. I wouldn't be able to catch up on my schooling. I've tried to read my textbooks in the evenings but I'm too tired to concentrate.'

'Because I work you too hard here?' said Mrs Roberts, looking concerned.

'No, because the work is so *tedious*. You would surely hate to mould for ten hours a day, wouldn't you, Mrs Roberts?' I put my hand over my mouth. 'I'm being too direct again, aren't I?'

'Yes, you are. I don't know what to do with you, Opal. My girls generally enjoy their time in the fondant room where they can chatter together.'

'Couldn't I be put to sugar rolling, or twisting or

stirring? That would be so much more interesting,' I said.

'Those are all skilled jobs. You might think yourself equal to anything, Opal, but you are sadly mistaken. I don't want any more accidents on my factory floor. But I can see that moulding isn't necessarily a fulfilling occupation for you. Perhaps I would find it tedious too, as you suggest. Let me think a little . . .' Mrs Roberts sat very still, her blue eyes gazing into the distance. She was perhaps as old as Mother, maybe even older, but she still looked extremely beautiful.

'You were a scholarship girl. Were you good at all subjects?'

'I came top of everything,' I said eagerly. 'Well, except art.'

'Oh dear – I take it you're not good at art?' She looked disappointed.

'My art teacher didn't care for the way I work. But I am passionate about art. I love to paint,' I said. 'I don't want to boast, but other people seem impressed by my artwork, though they think I have unusual ideas.'

'Yes, you are a very unusual girl, Opal Plumstead. You're also a very bad girl to start a fight in my factory. I want you to return to the fondant room, make your peace with Patty, and work quietly and diligently without further outburst. I won't dismiss you – I won't even dock your wages, because that will make your family suffer. I'll expect you to work particularly hard for the next few days to make up for the spilled moulding boxes. I shall ask George to keep an eye on you. But if you show willing, I might find another outlet for you – one that may prove more congenial.'

'Thank you, Mrs Roberts,' I said. I seemed to be dismissed, so I stood up.

'Opal . . . I can see you're having a very hard time, dear. But take heart. A year seems a lifetime now, but it will pass eventually.'

'You don't understand,' I said, my face crumpling.

'Oh, I think I do. I have been in prison myself.'

I stared at her, dumbfounded. 'That can't be true!'

'Oh, indeed it is. I have been in prison three times for my political beliefs. I am an ardent supporter of the suffrage movement. I've taken part in many demonstrations and am proud to say I have been imprisoned as a consequence.'

'Is it very hard in prison?'

'Yes, it is. I won't pretend otherwise. But it's bearable.'

'You had your political beliefs to sustain you. My poor father is there because he made one wretched mistake, and now they insist he's committed long-term embezzlement, when he hasn't, he absolutely hasn't,' I said, starting to cry. 'And I am so worried that he will lose the will to live now.'

'How could he possibly do that when he has his family to think of – especially such a fine, spirited daughter,' said Mrs Roberts. 'Now dry your eyes and hold your head up high. He is still your father, in or out of prison.'

'How did you *know* about Father?'

'Let's just say it was a shrewd guess.'

'You're very clever, Mrs Roberts.'

'Well, I was once a scholarship girl myself,' she said.

18

I thought Patty would hate me even more. We worked in silence at opposite ends of the fondant room. Geoff and George and Nora and all the other girls watched us warily, but we didn't even look at each other. I ate my bun and drank my tea with Maggie and Jess at lunch time. They were astonished by my battle. The whole factory knew of the fight in the fondant room.

'You really took on Patty Meacham, a little scrap like you!' said Maggie.

'I've seen the scratch all down her face. You must have fought like a little wildcat,' said Jess.

'What on earth did she *say* to you to get you going like that?' Maggie asked.

Mrs Roberts had told me to hold my head up high and be proud, but I still didn't want to talk about it to Maggie and Jess. If they hadn't read the *Daily News*, then I didn't want to enlighten them.

'I'm sure you know what she's like. She is very provoking,' I said.

'Well, I'll take care not to provoke you myself, little Plum!' said Maggie.

'Though don't fly off the handle like that again, dear,' said Jess. 'Mrs Roberts might have let you off once, but she's firm as well as fair. She won't take any further nonsense from either of you.'

After lunch I had to go back to the ladies' room to bathe my sore nose as it was still bleeding intermittently. I was splashing cold water on it when the door opened and Patty came in. The two other girls at the looking glass gave a gasp and rushed out, clearly scared they would be caught up in another fight. I was anxious about this too. I carried on attending to my nose, but I was starting to tremble.

Patty came right up to me. She peered in the looking glass too. She winced when she saw her scratches.

'Look what you've done to me!' she said.

'Look what you've done to *me*!' I retaliated, cupping my poor swollen nose in my hand.

'Where did you learn to fight like that, a swotty little milksop like you?'

'I was angry.'

'Listen, I didn't know it was your *pa* in the paper. I knew it had to be some relation, but not someone you were really close to.'

'I love my father more than anyone in the world, even though he's in prison,' I declared.

'I love my pa too, though since his accident he's got a right temper when you cross him,' said Patty. She paused. 'You've got a right temper too!'

'Mrs Roberts isn't going to dismiss us, though,' I said.

'I know. She's a good sort really, though she can make you feel bad,' said Patty. 'Very bad.' She suddenly stuck out her arm. I jumped, thinking she was going to strike me again. But then I realized she wanted to shake hands.

I stuck my own arm out, still a little warily. We shook hands awkwardly and then sprang apart again, blushing. Patty gave a little nod and then disappeared into a cubicle. I ran out of the room and back onto the factory floor.

Freddy collared me anxiously. 'Oh, Opal, my Lord, look at your nose!' he said. 'I'll slap that Patty from here to next week for doing that to you.'

Poor gangling Freddy was never going to be a match for sturdy Patty, and perhaps even he knew that, but I smiled warmly at him.

'You don't need to do that, Freddy. We've sorted it out now. Anyway, I hit her too. And scratched her face.'

'My goodness, you're quite a girl. *My* girl.'

'Your friend, Freddy, your *friend*,' I said.

I wondered if he'd still want to be my friend if he read the *Daily News* himself. I thought perhaps he would. He was a sweet lad. In many ways I wished I *could* care for him.

Work was more peaceful now. I still found moulding incredibly tedious, but I worked diligently all the same. I wanted George to give a good report of me to Mrs Roberts. Patty left me alone now. Maybe she was worried about Mrs Roberts too, but she seemed less hostile. Perhaps it was because I'd stood up to her at last. Maybe she even felt a little sorry for me. Whatever it was, we could work in the same room without any tension now. We weren't exactly friends, but we weren't bitter enemies, either.

The other girls followed her lead and became a little friendlier. Nora still made a few snide remarks from time to time, but she was easy to ignore. I longed to find just one girl who might become a proper friend. I was still missing Olivia badly. In fact, I'd written to her once, a long letter reminding her of all the fun we'd had together, reminiscing about our favourite jokes, our special games, our solemn secrets. I finished it as follows:

I know your mother has forbidden you to see me – but couldn't you sneak out and meet me at the graveyard? No one would ever spot us there. I don't finish work till six, but I could be there by quarter past if I run all the way. I know that might be a bit late, so what about Saturday or Sunday instead? You could pretend you were going out to tea with some other girl from school. I won't be able to manage to give you a proper grand tea myself, but I can give you Fairy Glen sweets – lots of them!

Please please please be a sport and show me we're still close in spite of everything and that you still feel affection for

Your loving friend,

Opal

I didn't send it to Olivia's house because I was sure her mother would be suspicious, open it herself and confiscate it. I sent it sealed in another letter to Mr Andrews at school. This meant I had to write to him too.

Dear Mr Andrews,

It was so good of you to visit me. I remember your kind words every day. I wish I could say I've taken your advice to heart, but if I'm strictly truthful I have to admit I've been a lazy girl and done little private studying so far. However, I have *been working hard at the factory and seem to be making progress, though there has been one little altercation. Quite a big one actually, but Mrs Roberts has dealt with me very fairly (unlike Miss Mountbank!).*

I dare say you will have seen that there has been a travesty of justice. My poor father has been sentenced to a year's hard labour.

I am sorry the writing is a little blurred above. When I wrote the last paragraph, I could not help crying and a few of my tears splashed onto my writing paper.

I am hoping that Olivia might still be my friend, so I wonder if you would be very, very kind and give the enclosed letter to her. I know I shouldn't ask it of you, but these are exceptional circumstances, and I hope you still feel kindly towards

Your sincere former pupil,

Opal

I am sure Mr Andrews passed on my letter immediately, but I had to wait more than a week for Olivia to reply. Her response was horribly brief.

Dear Opal,

I can't. Be your friend, I mean. I just don't dare.

I'm so sorry. I do still care about you tremendously, though, and wish things were the way they used to be.

Love from Olivia

I cried again when I received the letter.

'For goodness' sake, Opal, what's the matter now?' said Mother.

'Olivia won't be my friend any more,' I wailed. 'Her mother won't allow it.'

'Well, I can't say that I blame her. If Olivia's father was in prison, I wouldn't want you to play with her,' said Mother.

'Yes, but I wouldn't let that stop me being her friend,' I replied.

'That's because you've always been a contrary, disobedient girl.' Mother sighed as she looked at me. Then she smiled at Cassie, as if to say, You've *never given me any trouble*.

If only she knew. Cassie was still secretly seeing Mr Evandale while spinning Mother endless tales of trysting with Philip Alouette.

'You can't carry on like this, Cass,' I whispered that night when Mother was asleep.

'Yes I can,' she said serenely.

'But Mother's bound to find out. I'm amazed she hasn't insisted that you invite this Philip back to our house for tea.'

'She won't do that, not now she's so hideously

embarrassed about our circumstances. She'd be worried about scaring Philip away. He can be wretchedly disdainful, you know.'

'Cassie, he's not real!'

'He's become real to me – and I find him a complete bore. How Mother can believe I'd be interested in such a pompous-sounding idiot, I don't know.'

'Just be jolly glad she does,' I said. 'She'll be expecting an engagement soon, and then she'll *have* to meet him,' I said.

'Well, maybe I'm engaged in real life already,' said Cassie.

'*What?*'

'Shush! You'll wake Mother.'

'You are pretending, aren't you?'

'Look.' Cassie crouched by the candle in my room and reached down inside her nightgown. She drew out a length of black silk ribbon with a ring dangling on the end.

'Oh my goodness!' I peered at the ring. It was a gold signet ring set with a square black onyx, a seed-pearl rampant lion embedded in the stone.

'It's Daniel's ring. He's had it all his life,' said Cassie. 'But he's given it to me. It's a little big for me and he says he'll have it altered, but I don't want to risk spoiling it as it's so perfect. I can't wear it anyway, not yet.'

'But is it a real engagement ring? He's asked you to marry him?'

Cassie fidgeted a little. 'He's asked me to be his love,' she said.

'That's not the same thing.'

'It's *better*,' said Cassie. 'Oh, Opie, he really does love me, and I love him with all my heart. You've no idea how wonderful it is. You don't understand. You're too young.'

'You're young too – much too young to be seeing a middle-aged man,' I said. 'Especially when all your meetings are so – so *clandestine*.' I wasn't even sure what the word meant, but it sounded sophisticated and superior. I was struggling to hold my own, my feelings in a turmoil.

'If you don't watch out, he'll have his wicked way with you,' I said. It was a phrase frequently used in Cassie's trashy romantic novels.

'Maybe he's done that already,' she murmured.

'I know you're simply teasing me,' I said.

Cassie giggled.

'You *are* teasing, aren't you?' I said.

'Of course I am,' she said – but I couldn't be sure.

I lay awake worrying long after Cassie had crept back to her own room. I couldn't tell Mother. She would be heart-broken, and Cassie would never, ever forgive me. I had a mad fantasy of confronting this Mr Evandale and telling him not to toy with my sister, but I was sure he would only laugh at me. I imagined him as a pantomime villain with a twirly moustache and a furtive manner, and shuddered at the thought. I told myself that Cassie was a fool to be taken in by such a man. I thought of all the Pre-Raphaelite paintings of fallen women – their stricken faces, their wretched attitude. How could my sister be so stupid? Yet she seemed so happy, positively rapturous. Perhaps I was jealous of her as well as concerned.

I was feeling so bereft, I became ridiculously jealous of Mother's babies too. She had abandoned her washing business. It was too hard on her sore hands, she hadn't had enough customers to make a proper living and, worst of all, a frightening woman with a fierce face and arms like a navvy came knocking on the door one night demanding to see her. It turned out that she was a washerwoman too and lived only three streets away. She insisted that Mother was stealing customers from her, and she'd better stop or she'd boil Mother's head along with the sheets and put her through her own mangle for good measure.

Mother decided she had better look for different employment. She tried doing the rounds of shops and factories all over again, with a humiliating lack of success. Then she ran into a young woman on the same job-seeking mission, carrying an infant in her arms because she had yet to find a reliable babyminder.

'I've brought up two fine girls. I'm very good with babies,' Mother found herself saying. 'I'll mind your child for you.'

It wasn't long before she found herself minding four infants – two babes in arms, a determined little creature who crawled everywhere and had to be kept on a lead like a dog, and a docile little girl of three who loved playing with the bright scraps of silk and satin that Cassie brought home from work. Mother doted on the babies, making them soft little mashes to eat, crooning to them while they drank, and playing peekaboo games when they were awake. She didn't even blink when she changed their reeking napkins.

I wondered if Mother had once been so doting and demonstrative towards Cassie and me. I had no memories of being sung to or rocked to sleep, but of course I would have been too little to remember. I was certain that she had never held me close or played with me when I was as old as four or five, though I could clearly remember her smacking me hard for climbing into the kitchen cupboard and 'cooking' with some flour and a few pots and pans. I also remember her forever wiping my face with a damp rag, twitching my skirts into place and buttoning my boots.

I *did* have the fondest memories of Father

dandling me on his knee and reading aloud to me from *The Blue Fairy Book*. In fact, I rescued the battered old copy from Father's bookshelf and wept all over it. I fingered the embossed gold illustration of a witch on the blue cover, remembering how I'd once shivered in delicious fear at the sight of her. I read all my favourite stories about Sleeping Beauty and Cinderella and Rumpelstiltskin. As I read, I could hear an echo of Father's gentle voice as he turned page after page, patiently amusing me.

I wished they'd allow families to send books to prison. I'd tried to pack up a parcel of all Father's favourite reading as a Christmas present, but Mother said I was being foolish.

'Prisoners are not allowed Christmas parcels from home. I've already enquired,' she told me.

It was so dreadful thinking of Father on Christmas Day, with no loved ones, no festive meal, no presents. Our own Christmas was bleak, but at least Mother and Cassie and I had each other. Poor Father must be desperately lonely.

'Why don't we all visit Father?' I asked now. 'I must come too. Cassie can dress me up again. I could leave the starch from the factory in my hair.'

Mother said I was talking nonsense and she very much doubted the prison authorities would allow Cassie inside, let alone me. I wrote eagerly to Father all the same, telling him to take heart, his family were thinking of him all the time and would visit him as soon as we'd saved the rail fare.

I was totally dashed when Father responded as follows:

Dearest Lou, Cassie and Opal,

Please do not put yourselves to the trouble and expense of visiting me. I don't think I could bear to let you see me in my current situation. It would only be distressing, most of all to me. Far better that you put me out of your minds altogether, until I can return home and be

Your loving husband and father,

Ernest

'Perhaps he doesn't really mean it,' I faltered.

'He's made it plain enough, Opal,' said Mother.

'I think we should go anyway,' I said.

'It would be foolish to go all that way and spend so much money if your father refuses to see us. We must respect his feelings. He's ashamed.'

'But he shouldn't feel ashamed. Mrs Roberts has been in prison and she acts as if she's proud of it.'

'What? The Mrs Roberts who owns Fairy Glen? She's been in prison?'

'She's a suffragette and she's been arrested at demonstrations,' I said.

'Then she's a total fool,' said Mother. 'I don't hold

with these hysterical women throwing bricks at windows and behaving like hoydens. They've no business interfering in politics. They should leave it to the men who know best.'

'I think women should be educated until they know just as much as men,' I said. 'Mrs Roberts is utterly splendid. I think I shall become a suffragette when I'm older.'

'Then you'll end up in prison too, and God help us,' said Mother. 'I don't want to hear any more of this nonsense. And anyway, it's different when you go to prison for a political cause. I'll bet she had an easy time of it because she's a high-born lady. She won't be doing hard labour like your father.'

'It's so wicked that he's been given such a hard sentence. We know he didn't embezzle all that other money,' I said passionately.

'We can't positively *know*, Opal,' said Mother. 'And we *do* know he wrote out a cheque to himself. That's a crime in anyone's book. When I was a girl, I knew an old man who was so hungry he dug up some potatoes in a farmer's field – just four or five potatoes. He was caught and sentenced to *five* years' hard labour.'

'But that doesn't make Father's case any less unfair,' I said.

'Opal, you're making my head spin. You can be so aggravating at times. Why can't you be more like your sister?' Mother nodded at Cassie. She was sitting demurely in her chair, making herself a new petticoat, embroidering daisies all around the hem.

Yes, and I dare say she'll be showing off those daisies to her darling Mr Evandale, I shouted – but only inside my head.

I stomped up to my room and read *The Blue Fairy Book*. When was my fairy godmother going to appear and wave her magic wand?

When I trudged into the factory the next morning, Mr Beeston beckoned to me.

'Hold your horses, Opal Plumstead. Mrs Roberts wants to see you this morning,' he said.

My throat went dry. What had I done now? I hadn't been in any more fights. I had moulded obediently, hour after hour. I completed more boxes than any of the other girls because I had a steady hand and I didn't waste time gossiping.

'Don't look so stricken,' said Mr Beeston. He reached out and snatched at my nose with his fingers. Then he made a fist of his hand with the thumb poking through, like a little nose. 'Dear, oh dear, what am I doing, stealing your funny little button nose. Shall I give it you back?' He dabbed at my forehead. 'There! Back in place. No – whoops! Doesn't it go *under* your eyes?'

'Mr Beeston, I'm not a child.'

'No? What are you, then, an ancient old woman? Well, child or crone, trot along to see Mrs Roberts, quick sharp.'

'She's not going to dismiss me after all, is she?' I said fearfully.

'There's only one way of finding out,' said Mr Beeston, flapping his hand in the air. 'Off you go.'

I went along the corridor, smoothing my hair and checking the buttons on my dress. It was one of Cassie's cast-offs, a tartan worsted for the winter. Although she'd turned up the hem and taken it in a great deal at the chest and waist, it was still far too roomy. I looked like a little girl dressing up in her mother's clothes.

I knocked on Mrs Roberts' door, wishing I didn't feel so nervous. It had been chilly on the way to work, yet now the tartan dress stuck to my back and my hands were clammy on the doorknob.

'Come in!'

I went in, and even though I knew what the room was like now, its splendour still took me by surprise. There was a beautiful new arrangement of bulrushes in one of the tall Japanese vases, and a willow-pattern bowl of dried rosebuds on the desk filled the whole room with their sweet musky smell. In spite of my anxiety, I resolved at once to have bulrushes and rosebuds in my bedroom at home.

Mrs Roberts was looking especially splendid too, in

a white silk blouse with lace trimming and a jade-green skirt with a purple cashmere shawl delicately arranged around her shoulders.

'Good morning, Opal,' she said. 'Oh my, your tartan dress looks very delightfully Scottish.'

'It was my sister's. It suited her a lot more than it suits me,' I said. I wondered if she would think it too direct if I complimented her on her own apparel.

'I love your own outfit, Mrs Roberts. I think green and purple must be your favourite colours,' I said.

'And white. Do you know why?'

'Because they go stylishly together.'

'Well, I hope they do, but that's not the reason. They're the colours of the suffrage movement. White for purity, green for hope, and purple for dignity.'

'Oh, I like that! I think it's wonderful that you're a suffragette, Mrs Roberts. I shall be one myself when I'm older,' I said.

'I like your spirit, Opal. You might try coming along to meetings now.' Mrs Roberts felt in her desk drawer. 'Here's a leaflet about our local gatherings.'

'Thank you!' I was certain Mother would forbid it if she knew about it – but she didn't have to know, did she!

'Now, let's talk about work,' said Mrs Roberts, looking serious.

'Oh, Mrs Roberts, I have tried to be very good and diligent and I haven't fought Patty again, I promise,' I said.

'I'm glad to hear it,' she said. 'I know you're speaking the truth too, because I've had a chat with George. So I think that, as you've kept your side of our bargain, I might keep mine. As from Monday you will work in another part of Fairy Glen altogether.'

'Oh, really!' I had to clench my fists to stop myself clapping my hands. 'Can I try rolling out the sugar paste now?'

'No, you're not going to work on the factory floor. Come with me.'

Mrs Roberts stood up and led me out of the room. She took me further down the corridor to another room. On the door was one word, written in fancy looping lettering: *Design*.

My heart started thudding. Mrs Roberts smiled and opened the door. It was almost as if she had that magic wand in her hand. The design room was quite wonderful: a large cream-painted studio with big windows and astonishingly bright electric lights. There were desks up and down the room in neat rows, reminding me of school. Women sat there, each wearing a delightful green pinafore instead of white overalls. The desks were set out with paintboxes even larger than my cherished box at home, china water jars and a selection of fine paintbrushes. Each woman was diligently painting onto a large padded satin box lid. I recognized the designs from the Fairy Glen deluxe gift range for fondants, toffee chews and candy kisses: flowers for the fondants, a meadow scene for the toffees, and butterflies for the candies. I sucked in my breath when I saw the flower box for the fondants. It brought back such sweetly painful memories.

'I have decided to try you in the design department, Opal. It's a decision that might well surprise that art teacher of yours. You will find it's a very exacting job, but a little more varied than moulding. My ladies work on all three designs. They're allowed two extra fifteen-minute breaks to rest their hands and eyes.'

'Oh, Mrs Roberts! If I can work here, I won't need any break whatsoever, I shall be so extremely happy,' I declared.

'I'm not saying this is a permanent position, Opal. I'm simply giving you a week's trial. You might not be competent enough artistically. Don't get too excited.'

I tried to calm down, but I couldn't help feeling thrilled. I wanted to fling my arms round Mrs Roberts and thank her for the opportunity, but I knew this would horrify her, especially in front of all the other women. I contented myself with taking her hand and shaking it earnestly for a very long time.

'I will be an exemplary artist, Mrs Roberts, just you wait and see,' I promised.

19

I wasn't quite exemplary. It was more difficult than I'd realized, painting straight onto satin. The women kept little scraps of rag to dab and absorb any mistakes, but you had to be very quick and deft because the satin was unforgiving. We didn't paint freehand, doing our own variations on flowers, meadows and butterflies. We worked to special templates, the design very faintly pencilled onto the satin pad. We were given colour charts so that each petal, each wing, each blade of grass was the correct shade of chrome yellow, cobalt blue or emerald green. I didn't always feel that the colours were exactly right. They could be a little harsh and bright, but I understood that they needed to be eye-catching to tempt folk to buy the boxes.

They weren't always true to nature, either. The meadow was dotted with yellow primroses and red poppies, which looked very decorative, but surely they flowered months apart? The butterflies were painted with dazzling designs of green and purple and rich crimson, not a combination ever seen on our shores. I knew that even the exotic Red Admiral wasn't truly crimson. The flowers for the fondant box were all an astounding flamingo pink against a gold background. I was encouraged by this imaginative approach.

'Perhaps we could try a variation – maybe blue roses against silver?' I suggested to Miss Lily.

I wasn't sure if 'Lily' was her surname or her Christian name. Everyone used it with a special reverent tone, as if she were a Mother Superior. She had joined Fairy Glen as a designer when Mrs Roberts' father-in-law first opened the factory, and had been a stalwart member of the team since she was a young girl. She was now a very old woman, with a little monkey face and a stooped back, but her hands were rock steady and she was still the finest painter in the design room.

She had a gentle, encouraging nature and took

infinite pains with me, setting me to practise my brushstrokes on sugar paper day after day before letting me start on a satin box lid. She showed me various techniques for brush control and the smooth application of paint. When at last she considered me ready to work on a lid, she watched closely, telling me where to start. She showed me how to apply the background, how to add a drop of dew to a rose petal, a glint in the meadow stream, and sunlight on a butterfly wing – to glorious effect. She seemed to like me, and gave little claps of approval from time to time. 'That's the ticket, dear,' she'd murmur.

I relaxed a little under her benign care, but when I suggested blue roses for a change, she quivered in horror.

'We never do blue roses, dear. That would be far too fanciful. Our roses are always pink – but we do have a blue butterfly in the right-hand corner of the candy kisses box, see. Once you've practised enough with roses and mastered the meadow stream, then you can try the butterflies. Is blue perhaps your favourite colour, dear?'

'Not especially. I just thought it might be an idea to add a little variety,' I said.

'Oh no. No, no, no. Fairy Glen gift boxes never vary,' Miss Lily said firmly. 'This is the way we've always done them. This is the way we will always produce them. *Always*,' she added, in case I hadn't quite understood.

I didn't want to upset her, so I didn't pursue my idea any further. Every time I finished a box lid, Miss Lily picked it up and took it to the window to examine it in daylight. She peered at it minutely, looking for any tiny variant, clearly not quite trusting me.

I wasn't a fool. I was so happy working in the design room I didn't want to risk being sent back to the fondant room in disgrace. I almost forgot that the rest of the factory existed now. We didn't eat in the canteen at lunch time. Miss Lily's girls all brought their own lunches – daintily cut squares of bread with a sliver of cheese or slice of ham. When they saw that I had no lunch with me on my first day there, they all contributed a morsel until I had a generous meal. A woman from the canteen brought in cups of tea and penny buns on a trolley mid-morning, and more tea and a slice of plain cake in the afternoon. Mrs Roberts herself often joined us for our tea breaks and chatted amicably, mostly to Miss Lily, but she took the trouble to say a word or two to all the girls, including me.

'Are you a little happier now, Opal?' she asked.

'Utterly, blissfully so,' I said. 'Can I take it I've passed my week's trial, Mrs Roberts?'

'You can indeed, Opal,' she said.

It was so wonderful to be free of the fondant room. I missed Geoff a little because he had been kind to me, but I didn't miss Patty or the other girls in the slightest. I hardly saw Maggie and Jess now that I ate my lunch in the design room. It started to be a little uncomfortable when I bumped into them before or after work.

'Oh, you're one of the bottles now, are you?' said Maggie.

The rest of the factory called the design women this because of their bottle-green pinafores.

'Like it in design, do you?' said Jess. 'Yes, it's more your kind of place, young Opal.'

They were both perfectly pleasant, but it was clear they no longer thought of me as their little pet. Even Freddy changed his attitude after a while.

At first he acted as if he were heart-broken. He waited for me outside the factory and walked all the way home with me, though he lived in the other direction.

'I can't stand it that you've become a bottle,' he said. 'I don't ever get to see you now. It's not the same at all. Why did you have to go and leave me?'

'Oh, Freddy, stop it. You know I hated it in that awful fondant room. I'm so much happier now. Don't you want me to be happy?' I said.

'But I want to be happy too. I need to see my girl.'

'Freddy, for pity's sake, I'm not your girl. We're friends, that's all. And we can still be friends, if that's what you want.'

'You know that's not at all what I want,' said Freddy. 'Why won't you walk out with me on a Sunday?'

I struggled to find some response that wouldn't be too unkind. I couldn't tell him the simple truth: that I wanted to spend my precious weekends painting and reading. The last thing I wanted to do was walk stiffly around the town with Freddy from Fairy Glen, and I definitely didn't want to end up canoodling with him in back alleys on Sunday evenings. I'd grown fond of him in a rather exasperated kind of way, but when I imagined his long spidery arms wrapped around me, his big lips on mine, I couldn't help shuddering. Heaven knows what Cassie got up to with Mr Evandale. I knew with a certainty that I wanted no part in that sort of behaviour.

I kept trying to make Freddy go home, but he insisted on following me right up to my front door. He seemed relieved that I lived in a modest terraced house. He peered eagerly at the peeling paint on the front door, the broken boot scraper, the crumbling plaster on the window frames. Father had never been any good at house maintenance, and Mother and Cassie and I had no time or inclination for such things now.

'You need a man about the place,' said Freddy. 'I could fix things for you, Opal.'

He was notoriously ham-fisted on the factory floor,

and frequently tripped over his own boot laces and sent everything flying with his flailing arms.

'It's very kind of you to offer, but I couldn't possibly accept,' I said quickly. 'I must go now, Freddy.'

'Aren't you going to invite me in? It's about time I met your folks,' he persisted.

'Not tonight, Freddy,' I said – meaning *not ever*.

But Mother must have heard our voices at the door. She opened it and stared at us. She had a grizzling baby on her hip. When it saw us, it stared comically too, forgetting to whine.

'Opal?' Mother said. She peered at Freddy in the dark. 'Who's this?'

He stood up straight, practically clicking his boots together like a soldier, and stuck out his hand.

'How do you do, Mrs Plumstead. It's an honour to meet Opal's ma. I'm Freddy Browning, Opal's sweetheart,' he declared.

'No you're not. Don't take any notice of him, Mother. He's just a daft boy from the factory. Go *home*, Freddy.'

'Opal! Don't treat the poor lad so dreadfully,' Mother reprimanded me. 'Come in and have a cup of tea, lad. Opal's kept you very quiet.'

'Because there's nothing to tell. Please go home, Freddy,' I wailed, but it was no use.

Mother practically seized Freddy's wrist and pulled him inside. She insisted on taking him into the parlour and lit a fire for him. We only sat in there on Sundays, spending every other evening huddled in the kitchen.

Mother went bustling away with the baby while Freddy and I sat in the parlour. I tried to feed the fire with rolled-up newspaper. When it still wouldn't catch properly, I held a whole sheet of paper in front of the fireplace to help the draught.

'Careful! You'll set yourself on fire doing that. Here, let me.' Freddy elbowed me out of the way with his long arms and made a great to-do of feeding the fire himself.

He had less skill than me and made it smoke dreadfully, but at last a log started burning properly.

'There!' he said, a satisfied grin on his face.

'Thank you, Freddy,' I said, though it was a struggle to sound grateful.

Mother came into the parlour with a tea tray, the baby crawling behind her. Cassie followed. She'd only had five minutes, but I saw she'd brushed out her hair, unrolled the sleeves of her blouse and taken off her work pinafore. She had a good stare at Freddy, her eyes bright. He looked astonished.

'This is my sister, Cassandra,' I said. 'And this is Freddy. He's just a friend.'

'Hello, Freddy. How lovely to meet you.' Cassie was all smiles and dimples, though she could hardly take a shine to poor plain Freddy, especially when he started slurping his tea noisily.

Mother was preoccupied with the baby, trying to stop it from grabbing the few ornaments in the parlour. It took hold of an antimacassar from the chair instead, crumpling it up and crooning to it as if it were a dolly.

'Is she a little sister?' Freddy said.

'She's a friend's child,' Mother said quickly, not wanting to admit to being a babyminder, though Freddy was clearly no higher up the social scale than we were.

'She's a bonny little thing.'

'She's rather a pest,' said Cassie, picking up the baby. She wasn't any keener on the babies than I was, but she couldn't help playing peekaboo with the child and the antimacassar, knowing it set off her curves and soft arms delightfully.

Freddy chuckled at them both. I glared at them. I didn't want his attention, but I hated to see him enchanted with Cassie, like every other male in the world. Cassie certainly didn't want Freddy, but she cooed and giggled with him and asked him endless questions about his job at Fairy Glen. She wasn't truly interested – she was barely listening – but Freddy explained in immense and tedious detail the whole process of sweet-making.

He accepted a second cup of tea and several slices

of bread and jam – we didn't have any cake to offer him. Mother cut the crusts off the bread and arranged it in red triangles to make it look fancy. Freddy ate it enthusiastically, managing to get a smear of jam across his chin.

'Freddy!' I hissed, tapping my own chin.

He felt in vain in his pockets for a handkerchief, and used his sleeve instead. I blushed for him and longed for him to depart. When he finally did, a full hour and a half later, I expected Mother and Cassie to mock terribly.

'Well well well, Opie! You never said you had a young man,' said Cassie, bored of the baby now and wedging it into a corner of the sofa. (Its mother was on a late shift and wouldn't be fetching it until gone nine.)

'He's not my young man. As if I'd want someone like him,' I protested, though I felt mean saying so.

'I don't know – he seems a reasonably polite young man, though his manners are a bit rough and ready,' said Mother.

I stared at her.

'We've come down in the world, Opal. It's no use having big ideas any more,' she said. She clearly meant *I* shouldn't have any big ideas. 'You can't necessarily expect to be as lucky as Cassie with her Philip.'

Cassie smiled smugly and I could have slapped her.

'Perhaps you'd like to invite Philip round to tea, Cassie,' Mother went on. 'If you give me enough warning, I could put on a bit of a show. We could always skimp on a few meals to make sure it's a really slap-up tea. Won't you consider it, dear?'

'I don't think it's a good idea, Mother,' said Cassie smoothly. 'He might start asking awkward questions, and I'm afraid our home is very humble compared with the Alouettes'.'

Mother winced at the word 'humble'. She stopped trying to persuade Cassie, and took the infant off to change its napkin.

'You are so crafty, Cassie,' I said irritably.

'You're the crafty one! I tell you everything about my Daniel – well, practically everything – yet you've never said a word about your factory sweetheart.'

'He is not, not, *not* my sweetheart!'

'He seems very sweet on you.'

'Nonsense. He couldn't keep his eyes off *you* while he was here,' I said.

'So why does that put you all in a flounce if you don't care a jot about him?' said Cassie, silencing me.

Freddy was waiting for me after work the next day, eager to walk me home again. I couldn't stand a repeat performance.

'No, Freddy. Do leave me alone. I don't want company tonight,' I said. 'In fact, I don't want your company at all. I don't seem to be like other girls. I don't want to walk out with anyone.'

I expected Freddy to be cast down, but he didn't look too wounded.

'Perhaps you're simply a little too young, Opal,' he said, in an infuriatingly patronizing tone. 'Tell me, how old is your sister? And is she walking out with anyone?'

'Yes, she *is*,' I said, and I pushed past him and ran swiftly home.

I was horrified by his fickleness. He had declared that I was his sweetheart, the only girl for him, yet now he seemed more than ready to transfer his attentions to my sister. And not only Cassie, it turned out. A week or so later, coming out of the factory, I spotted Freddy walking arm in arm with little Edith from the fondant room. He hardly gave me a second glance.

It confirmed everything I'd ever assumed about romantic love. I admired the poetry of *Romeo and Juliet*, but I couldn't believe in the passion. Romeo declares himself deeply in love with Rosalind at first, and then immediately falls for Juliet instead, and within days is ready to die without her. How could one take this kind of passion seriously? How dare Freddy say I was simply too young! I resolved never to speak to him again.

All the same I was angry with Cassie for stealing his affection. I was curt with her for days. When she came home one Sunday, bursting with excitement, desperate to confide the latest instalment in the Cassie-and-Daniel romance, I put my hands over my ears and refused to listen.

I felt lonelier than ever. It seemed I had no friends at all now. I'd had high hopes of making a congenial friend in the design room, but it didn't happen. Everyone was perfectly polite, but they already had their own friends. It was hard to get to know anyone properly because gossiping was frowned on by Miss Lily while we were painting, and when we were having our lunch she generally had me sit beside her while she gave me advice on painting techniques. It was kind of her, and I learned a lot, but I couldn't really count withered old Miss Lily as a friend.

I wondered if Father felt the same incarcerated in prison, unable to build up any rapport with his fellow prisoners, maybe having to make do with a few words here and there from a kind warder.

I was at a loss on Saturdays too, because Mother minded two babies for shop girls and it was therefore impossible to get any peace at home. I'd tried to barricade myself into my bedroom, but little hands would scrabble at the doorknob, little feet would kick at the paint, little voices would wail until I let them in. Then they'd rampage around, pulling my beautiful books off the shelf and crumpling the pages, even prising my precious paintbox open and stabbing their little fingers into each palette. I'd try to be gentle with them, but I found them so irritating that eventually I'd snap and shout at them, and then they'd go sobbing to Mother.

'For goodness' sake, Opal, can't you play nicely with them for ten minutes while I set the house to rights?' she complained.

'I'm trying to *study*. You're the babyminder, not me,' I said.

'You're the most intolerably selfish girl. What sort of a daughter are you? If only Cassie could stay home on Saturday.'

'Well, she doesn't make much effort to be here on Sundays, either, does she,' I said.

'Yes, because she's out with her young man. I dare say that's why you're being so sulky, because *your* young man didn't come to anything.'

I was so infuriated by this statement that I grabbed my coat and stormed out of the house altogether. I was determined not to return until dark, when the babies were reclaimed. I had nowhere to go, though, and no spare money to take myself up to London to see the grand shops and galleries. So I decided to go to a suffrage meeting.

20

It was held at ten thirty in the St Joan of Arc church hall in Ledbury Street, across town. It would take me forty minutes to walk there so I'd be late for the start, but I thought I'd be able to slip in at the back. It felt good to walk at first, though I couldn't stride out in Cassie's narrow skirts. At least I was out of the gloomy little house. The only exercise I got nowadays was walking to and from Fairy Glen. I loved my new job in design, but it was taxing sitting cramped in one position all day long. I'd been suffering from all sorts of aches in my neck and shoulders and back, but now I found myself stretching comfortably.

I started to get nervous as I turned into Ledbury Street. I wasn't sure what I was letting myself in for. I didn't know what happened at these meetings. I didn't really know what suffragettes were like. Mother said they were a disgrace, shrill and unwomanly, and couldn't see why they made such a fuss about a silly thing like a vote. Cassie said they were man-haters and looked a sight. I had quite naturally taken the opposite point of view. I found their ideas liberating, but I tended to think of these women as warriors, almost mythical, like Boadicea and Joan of Arc herself.

Mrs Roberts wasn't shrill – she looked quite beautiful, and I couldn't imagine her battling with police and politicians. If the Joan of Arc hall was full of ladies like Mrs Roberts, I would feel very shy, but find the assembly inspirational.

I reached the hall at last, hot from my brisk walk, though it was a chilly day and I had mittens, and a muffler wound round my neck. I fumbled with these, taking them off and stuffing them in my pockets. Then I took a deep breath and crept in through the front door.

I stood in the vestibule for a few seconds, hearing someone giving an impassioned speech, though I couldn't distinguish the words. Then I pushed the inner doors open and edged inside.

The hall was crowded, everyone straining forward to listen to the lady on the platform. Several women craned round to stare at the intruder. One put her fingers to her lips, another shook her head at me, and a third gestured to an empty chair at the end of her row. I tiptoed as silently as I could, though I was painfully aware of the creaking of my old boots. I sat down, feeling hot all over now, peering around at everyone in the audience.

I couldn't see Mrs Roberts herself, but there were many women who looked similar to her, quietly dignified and ultra-respectable. Some at the front were even grander than Mrs Roberts, judging by their elaborate, fancy hats. I wondered if Cassie had made any of them! But there were many other kinds of women there too – some in clothes far shabbier than mine, some in old borrowed men's coats, some with just a shawl over a thin dress. Some were quite young, almost as young as me, and some were surprisingly old, wrinkled and white haired. Some were fine-looking women with beautiful profiles. Some were alarmingly fierce. One had a nose just like a hawk's beak. Oh my Lord – it was Miss Mountbank!

I shrank back in my seat, my heart thudding. I certainly didn't want an encounter with old Mounty, of all people. For a moment I wondered if I'd better creep out again, but I didn't dare make another disturbance, so I sat still. After a while I actually started to listen. The lady on the platform was elegantly dressed in furs and a very fine hat. She was small and delicate, but her voice was clearly audible even at the back of the hall. She spoke very fluently, though she had no notes at all, and stood in one spot all the time, gesturing gracefully with her arms. She was addressing hundreds, yet she seemed to be talking just to me.

She spoke of the injustice of a world where we were all born equal in the sight of God, yet it was always the lot of women to come second. She addressed the argument that women should not have the vote because they were uninformed and could not make coherent decisions. She said that it should be every girl's right to be properly educated, that further education should be available to everyone, that women should be granted a proper degree if they fought their way through a university course. She said that women should be able to pursue proper careers if that was their wish.

Of course it was a woman's right to marry and have a family, but she needed liberation within the marital home too. As the law stood, even the most inadequate father had the final say in the upbringing of his children. He could remove them from the care of a loving mother, and quite legally cast her out into the streets and deny her access to them. The law needed to be changed. The only way this could be achieved was to give the vote to all adult Englishwomen. Then they could vote for decent, right-thinking men to represent them in Parliament. Indeed, they could vote for women to become Members of Parliament. One day there might even be a woman prime minister leading the country.

'We will work shoulder to shoulder, ladies, and achieve votes for women in our lifetime,' she said. 'But I've been speaking long enough. Remember our slogan, my friends: *Deeds, not words*.'

There was a great burst of applause. I clapped too. I felt like standing up on my chair and cheering. I'd never heard such stirring words in all my life.

Another woman got up to speak, and then another. I dare say they all made their points perfectly well, but they seemed weak and disappointing compared to the first woman. Their speeches were dull and prosaic, whereas she had spoken like an inspired leader, her voice soaring, her eyes flashing.

I found myself yawning and fidgeting. It was an enormous relief when the last of the women finished. Then everyone sang a very stirring song, rather like a hymn. The woman next to me gave me a sheet of paper with the words written down. By the time they reached the last verse I knew the tune and could sing out with the others.

'Life, strife, these two are one,
Naught can ye win but by faith and daring;
On, on, that ye have done
But for the work of today preparing.
Firm in reliance, laugh a defiance,
(Laugh in hope, for sure is the end).
March, march, many as one,
Shoulder to shoulder and friend to friend.'

We were told that light refreshments were now available. I nudged the woman next to me.

'Excuse me, but could you tell me who that lady was – the first one, with the furs?'

She looked at me as if I were simple. 'That was Mrs Pankhurst,' she said. 'Have you never heard her talk before? She's wonderful, isn't she?'

'Yes, quite wonderful,' I said.

I rather hoped she'd stay and talk to me, but she went off towards the tea-urn with a friend. Nearly all the women seemed to know each other and were talking earnestly. I did not know anyone in the room apart from Miss Mountbank, and I certainly wasn't going to start chatting to *her*.

She was deep in conversation with some other schoolmarmy lady in a severe suit and tie, but she suddenly looked across the room and seemed startled when she spotted me. I decided to make a run for it before she could approach. I elbowed my way through the huddle of ladies waiting for their tea and biscuits – and walked straight into Mrs Roberts.

'Oh my goodness, it's little Opal!' she said. She looked more distinguished than ever, in a beautifully cut purple and black two-piece, with green glass beads at her neck, and a white satin sash worn over her bosom like a queen.

I bobbed my head at her shyly.

'What on earth are you doing here?' she said.

I stared at her. 'You invited me, didn't you? You gave me the literature.'

'Yes, I did. I give leaflets to all the likely girls at Fairy Glen, but you're the first one to attend a meeting. Well done, Opal! I'm proud of you. Did you find it inspirational? Weren't there some wonderful speakers!'

She was standing with one of the later speakers, a particularly droning one who had nearly sent me to sleep, so I couldn't be truthful in case this woman was a friend of Mrs Roberts.

'I especially liked listening to Mrs Pankhurst,' I said.

It was clearly the right thing to say, because all the women smiled, the droning one most of all.

'Isn't she quite marvellous!' said Mrs Roberts. 'We always feel so honoured when she attends one of our branch meetings. I know her slightly. Would you like me to introduce you?'

'I think she's going straight to luncheon with Lady Rendlesham,' said the droning woman.

'Then I shall have to be quick,' said Mrs Roberts, taking my hand.

She hurried me through the crowd of women towards the platform, where Mrs Pankhurst was surrounded by the rich ladies in fancy hats.

'Excuse me, I wonder if . . .? I don't like to interrupt, but . . .' said Mrs Roberts tentatively.

They took no notice. Oh my goodness – fancy ignoring *Mrs Roberts*. They must be very grand indeed to snub her. But Mrs Pankhurst herself wasn't grand at all. She turned, and when she saw Mrs Roberts there, rather pink in the face, she smiled delightfully.

'Hello, my dear. It's Mrs Roberts, isn't it?'

I felt Mrs Roberts squeeze my hand, thrilled that she had been remembered.

'I thought your speech was excellent today, Mrs Pankhurst – very stirring. Young Opal here was particularly impressed. She is our newest and youngest member and a very ardent supporter,' she said, pushing me forward.

'Dear heavens, she's just a little girl,' said one of the fine ladies dismissively, and another couple tittered. They were almost as bad as Patty and her friends, for all they were so well-to-do. My own cheeks burned. But Mrs Pankhurst herself was a true lady.

'Welcome to the Women's Social and Political Union, Opal,' she said, solemnly shaking my hand. 'I'm so proud and happy that young women like you are joining us. You will be our fighters for the future.'

'I shall fight very fiercely for the cause,' I said seriously.

She did smile a little at that, but very sweetly. 'What is your full name?'

'Opal Plumstead.'

'A distinctive name. You are a very distinctive girl,' said Mrs Pankhurst. She looked as if she wanted to stay chatting to Mrs Roberts and me, but the Lady Rendlesham woman interrupted rudely.

'My car is waiting at the front, Mrs Pankhurst. Allow me to assist you through the crowd.'

Mrs Pankhurst sighed. 'Ah well, it seems I must go. But I hope to see you again, Opal Plumstead. I shall look out for you at future meetings,' she said. 'Goodbye, dear. Goodbye, Mrs Roberts. Thank you for bringing her.'

Mrs Roberts and I were left staring after her, both of us star-struck.

'Oh, she's quite wonderful,' I said.

'Isn't she just,' Mrs Roberts agreed. 'I'm so glad you came, Opal. When you're an old, old lady, you'll be able to tell your great-grandchildren that you once met Mrs Pankhurst.'

'I'm not going to have any great-grandchildren,

Mrs Roberts. I shall stay single and fight for women's rights,' I said grandly.

She smiled at me. 'Well, I suppose we'd better both go home for lunch.'

'Yes.' I nodded, though I couldn't bear the thought of going back home just yet. I surreptitiously fingered the few coins in my pocket, wondering if I had enough for a bowl of soup in an ABC teashop.

I think Mrs Roberts saw me do this. She suddenly said, 'Tell you what – why don't you come home and have lunch with me?'

I was as astonished as if it were an invitation to Buckingham Palace. 'Really?' I said stupidly.

'Really!' said Mrs Roberts. 'Come along, then.' She put her hand lightly on my shoulder and steered me towards the door.

'Oh my goodness, Opal Plumstead!' Miss Mountbank stood in front of me. 'Whatever are *you* doing here?'

'Good afternoon, Miss Mountbank,' I said. 'I could ask the same of you.'

She looked outraged. It was so wonderful to realize that she had no power over me now. She could order me to do a thousand lines and I didn't need to write a single word of them.

'How dare you be so impertinent!' said Miss Mountbank. She looked at Mrs Roberts. 'This girl is incorrigible. She comes from a bad family.'

'I disagree entirely,' said Mrs Roberts. 'Opal is my protégée. Excuse us, please.' She led me out of the door.

I grinned at her in triumph. 'Oh, Mrs Roberts, that was splendid of you. I can't bear Miss Mountbank. She can't bear me, either, as is obvious! She's a teacher at my old school.'

'I had similar teachers at *my* old school,' said Mrs Roberts. 'Still, she's a sister supporter of the cause.'

'I'm not sure I'd want to march shoulder to shoulder with Miss Mountbank,' I said. 'And she's certainly not my friend.'

'You've picked up our terminology already, Opal. Well done! You're a bright girl, even though you were obviously the bane of Miss Mountbank's life.'

'I won't be the bane of your life, Mrs Roberts, I promise. You've been wondrously fair to me,' I said as we went outside.

There were several chauffeurs standing beside motor cars, waiting attentively. To my intense joy, one of these men came hurrying up to Mrs Roberts. 'This way, madam. The car is just up here.'

I'd never been for a ride in a motor car before. Oh, wait till Cassie heard! Even her precious Mr Evandale didn't own a car.

It was the most glorious fun to sit beside Mrs Roberts and drive off through the town. We went so fast too. I hadn't secured my hat with enough pins, so

I had to hang onto it with one hand, while clinging to the leather upholstery with the other to stop myself sliding into Mrs Roberts. Most of my hair escaped and flapped in my face, and my eyes watered in the wind so that I could hardly see where I was going. Mrs Roberts had a special veil that acted as a shield. She stayed immaculate throughout the journey.

I was very curious to see where her house was. I thought it might be one of the grander ones overlooking the park. I was taken aback when the chauffeur drove right through the town, up a hill, and then down a little wooded lane, practically in the countryside. We went along this lane more slowly, pebbles rattling under the wheels, until we came to a pair of great ornamental gates. The chauffeur jumped out and unlocked them with a flourish, then drove along a narrow sandy path surrounded on either side by dark green bushes.

'My rhododendrons,' said Mrs Roberts. 'They are an absolute picture in spring – such splendid pinks and purples and crimsons.'

'It's as if you live in a real fairy glen,' I said.

The house was certainly like an enchanted palace. It even had turrets and a round tower.

'A medieval castle!' I breathed, knowing nothing of architecture.

'Hardly,' said Mrs Roberts. 'It's Victorian Gothic,

built for my father-in-law. I married his only son, so now it's mine.'

'Do you live here all alone, Mrs Roberts?'

'I have my dear son, but he is away at school during term time. He is in his last year and will go up to Oxford for the Michaelmas term.'

'My father went to Oxford,' I said eagerly. 'He always hoped I might go there too.'

'Would you like to, Opal?'

'I used to think so. But my circumstances are very different now, as you know,' I said. 'I was very cast down, but now that I can paint all day, I am happy.'

It was becoming a little tedious painting the same designs day after day. I'd had more than enough of butterflies, meadows and roses. When I closed my eyes at night, butterflies fluttered about the room, the lino turned into meadow grass and roses bloomed around my pillow. But I didn't want to tell Mrs Roberts this in case she thought me ungrateful. I knew she'd given me a remarkable opportunity. Miss Lily had impressed upon me that she'd never promoted any other girls from the factory floor to the design room.

The chauffeur opened the car door for us. I jumped out and gazed up the stone steps. The name of the house was engraved in the stone of the porch – *Fairy Glen*, just like the factory. The sea-green front door had a brass serpent knocker.

'I love your door-knocker! Can I give it a big rap?' I asked.

'Feel free,' said Mrs Roberts.

I thumped hard. After a little while the door opened and a servant stood there, looking surprised. She was a middle-aged woman, not a little girl like Jane – a stout grey-haired person in a black dress and an old-fashioned crisp white hat and apron. She looked very smart, apart from the strange greyish carpet slippers on her feet. I learned later that she had trouble with her bunions, and Mrs Roberts was happy to let her walk around in comfort.

'Hello, Mrs Evans. You were urgently summoned because I have an eager young guest,' said Mrs Roberts.

Mrs Evans shook her head at me, but still managed to look welcoming. 'In you come, miss,' she said, opening the door wide.

'Welcome to another Fairy Glen,' said Mrs Roberts, leading me inside.

The hallway was extraordinarily light because of a high atrium, with sunlight streaming downwards. There were palms in great brass pots and paintings beautifully displayed on both walls, just like an art gallery: pale maidens drifting in drapery, lounging beside pools or wanly embracing lovers.

'Very Pre-Raphaelite,' I said, showing off.

'Indeed,' said Mrs Roberts, amused. 'In fact, the

one over there, the moonlit girl, is a Burne-Jones.'

'Oh my goodness, a *real* one!' I said, gazing at it in awe. I knew that Mrs Roberts was wealthy, but hadn't realized she was rich enough to own proper art.

I wanted to linger in the hall, poring over every painting, but Mrs Evans took my hat and coat and then ushered me into another lovely light room with a crackling log fire in the peacock-tiled fireplace.

'Let's get warm,' said Mrs Roberts, sitting in a velvet chair and holding her hands in front of the fire. 'Mrs Evans, perhaps you could be an angel and fix us a kind of picnic lunch so we could have it here in comfort rather than in the chilly dining room?'

'Certainly, madam,' she said. 'I'll rustle up a few savouries – and would the young lady fancy cake, or a fruit pie?'

'I think perhaps both,' said Mrs Roberts.

I sat down on the chair beside her, but I couldn't stop my head swivelling round to take in the rest of the room. It was all so light and airy and elegant. It made me realize how cramped and poky our own parlour was. Even the chairs and chaise longue had style, sleek and simple in subtle shades of soft blue and dove grey, compared with our over-stuffed crimson sofas. There was a large black Japanese screen in one corner, with gold cranes flying across it. On one wall I saw Japanese embroidered silks showing strange mountains and streams, with more cranes standing on one leg as if taking part in a dance.

In pride of place in an alcove lit with a beautiful purple, green and white lamp was an illuminated scroll with three angels at the top.

'What's that?' I asked.

'I was presented with the scroll when I came out of prison. I'd been on hunger strike and had to endure the horrors of force-feeding.'

'Oh goodness,' I said.

I had seen illustrations in the papers of women being held down while terrible tubes were forced down their throats. The depiction of the process had always made me shudder. I'd no idea that Mrs Roberts had been quite so militant and so extremely brave.

'You may go and look at it properly if you like,' she said.

I went to examine it, awed. But then I became distracted by a quartet of smaller paintings in gold frames. I couldn't work out the subject matter, but they were very brightly coloured and intriguing.

I peered closer and saw that they were the most enchanting fairy paintings. The first was of a fairy wedding, with a diminutive bride and groom, and robin, blue-tit and butterfly guests. The second was a fairy school, with small elfin creatures sitting at toadstool desks. The third was a fairy nursery, with babes hanging in walnut-shell cradles from lavender spikes. The fourth was a fairy race, with little jockeys on saddled grasshoppers.

'They're wonderful!' I said, gazing at each one.

'They were my wedding present when I came to live at Fairy Glen,' said Mrs Roberts. 'I've always thought them a little whimsical, but Morgan adores them. He used to play the most elaborate fairy games when he was little. He fashioned his own fairies out of pipe cleaners and scraps of silk and made fairy houses out of boxes. He took such pains. He lined them with moss and picked fresh flowers for them every day.'

'Morgan?'

'My son.' Mrs Roberts pointed to a portrait above the fireplace.

It was of a solemn little boy in a sailor suit, with big brown eyes and a mop of fair curls like the boy in the 'Bubbles' advertisement.

'He's lovely too,' I said.

'Yes, he is,' said Mrs Roberts. 'I miss him terribly when he's away. When he finishes university, he will take over the running of the factory.'

I considered the luxury of being born Morgan Roberts, able to go to Oxford and then run his own factory!

Then I was diverted by Mrs Evans' picnic. When Cassie and I had picnics, we ate bread and dripping, then bread and jam, and a slice of seed cake if we were lucky. Mrs Evans brought us truly fairy food: little mushroom tartlets, oyster patties, miniature veal-and-ham pies, a sliced tomato and carrot salad, a purple plum pie with a large jug of cream, and a marmalade sponge cake with crystallized oranges on top. We had home-made sweetened lemonade to drink in glorious glass goblets.

I ate and drank with immense gusto while Mrs Roberts nibbled and sipped. When I was finished at last, she told me to put my coat on again because she wanted to take me on a tour of her garden before I went home.

I was rather disappointed. I wanted to stay much longer. In fact, I never ever wanted to leave this amazing house. I'd seen the garden, hadn't I? – two very formal flowerbeds with ornate ankle-high hedges forming a crisscross design.

But she led me further down the hallway, through the dining room and out through the French windows into what suddenly seemed like fairyland itself. Mrs Roberts' back garden was bigger than a whole park, but it wasn't laid out formally. It meandered up and down as far as the eye could see, with more rhododendron bushes and azaleas and magnolias, and many other trees and shrubs I didn't recognize. A stream trickled through all the greenery, crossed in several places by little bridges like the ones on willow-pattern plates. When we'd walked the entire length of the garden, I saw a small Japanese summerhouse decorated with orange lanterns.

'Oh, it's so beautiful!'

'It is, especially in spring and summer.'

'How wonderful to have inherited such a garden.'

'I didn't. Well, I inherited the land, but it wasn't a garden at all. There were flowerbeds and a lawn at the back of the house, but this was mostly meadow land when I came here as a young bride. I cultivated it all myself. It's taken many years to get to this stage.'

'You made it all? You planted all the trees and bushes?' I said, gazing at slender Mrs Roberts and her smooth white hands.

'I *did* plant a lot of the bushes, but I had a little troop of gardeners to do the really heavy digging. Three are still with me now. We've all matured together, along with the garden. I have to leave its care to them now, because I must run the factory too, but I try to have a stroll in my garden every day, winter as well as summer.'

'You are a truly inspirational lady, Mrs Roberts,' I said fervently.

21

I proudly told Mother all about my splendid day. I thought she'd be incredibly impressed. She always seemed delighted when Cassie was invited to Madame Alouette's (though of course this was pure invention). But although Mrs Roberts was a far grander lady, Mother seemed determined to be unenthusiastic.

'You met her at a women's suffrage meeting?' she said. 'How could you go to such a thing, associating with all those dreadful women? As if we're not in enough trouble with your father! If you get arrested too, then we'll really be in queer street.'

'I'm not going to get arrested, Mother – don't be so silly. They're not dreadful women at all, they're quite splendid. Mrs Pankhurst herself gave a speech, and she was wonderful. I was actually introduced to her by Mrs Roberts.'

'Terrible man-hating harridans, the lot of them!' Mother declared. 'That Mrs Roberts had no business luring you there and getting you involved. Just because you work at her wretched factory it doesn't mean you have to do what she says at the weekend.'

'She didn't lure me. She didn't even know I was coming. You're being ridiculous, Mother.'

'Don't you use that tone with me, young lady. I think this Mrs Roberts is a very bad influence – you say she's even been to prison herself!'

'They *tortured* her there, forcing tubes up her nose and down her throat. She's just the most incredibly brave woman in the world.'

'She sounds a right hussy. Why does her husband let her get up to such mischief?'

'She hasn't got a husband any more.'

'I'm not surprised!'

'She's a *widow*. She lives in this most amazing house. Oh, you should see the furnishings. It's all so elegant and beautiful, with so many paintings – a real Burne-Jones, imagine!'

'I don't know who Burne-Jones is, and I don't care. You shouldn't accept invitations from that kind of woman. She'll lead you into all sorts of trouble,' Mother said obstinately. 'You're not to go again, do you hear me?'

'Yes, Mother,' I said, just to stop her ranting, though I knew I would jump at the chance of returning to Fairy Glen.

Cassie was a more receptive audience that night, but I sensed she wasn't really concentrating on me.

'Cassie! Don't go to sleep!' I said sharply as I crouched on the end of her bed. She'd given a little snore when I'd been in the middle of a detailed description of the Fairy Glen garden.

'I *am* listening. Yes, it all sounds lovely,' she murmured.

'Aren't you just a little bit impressed that such a wonderful woman has taken me under her wing? She actually told Mrs Pankhurst that I was her little protégée,' I declared.

'Oh, Opie, you're such a scream,' Cassie said, turning over and snuggling into her pillow.

'I am *not* a scream,' I said stiffly.

'Yes you are. You're getting so het up about this Mrs Roberts of yours. I could never imagine having a pash on an old woman,' said Cassie.

'She's not old and I haven't got a "pash",' I said furiously, blushing. 'I just happen to think she's marvellous because she's so brave and intelligent and unusual and elegant.'

Cassie snorted. 'You're besotted!'

I gave her a thump. 'I'd sooner be besotted with a fantastically inspirational woman who runs an entire factory single-handed and fights for political causes and creates a beautiful garden out of a wilderness than with some lecherous old artist, so-called,' I said.

'He's not "so-called". Daniel's a really wonderful artist. His paintings are shown at the Royal Academy,' said Cassie, waking up properly.

'Well, I've never heard of him and I know much more about art than you do. I bet the only reason he paints your portrait is to see as much of you without clothes on as he possibly can,' I said. 'You watch out, Cassie Plumstead. You're spoiling your chances of ever getting a decent man.'

'You sound worse than Mother, you silly little prude. And he is decent. He's fantastically intelligent and he comes from a very well-to-do family,' Cassie protested.

'Have you met any of them?' I asked.

Cassie was silent.

'There!' I said triumphantly.

'Oh, shut your mouth.' She pushed me right off her bed so that I landed on my bottom with a bump. I struggled up, took hold of a handful of her long hair and tugged hard. We ended up scrapping on the floor until Mother heard and came running.

'For heaven's sake, what are you two great girls doing, brawling like hooligans!' she said, slapping at both of us.

I flounced off to my room, still furious with Cassie. I had so wanted her to be impressed by my new friendship with Mrs Roberts. I hadn't expected her to mock me.

I tried to stop feeling so hurt and ruffled. I lay in bed going through my whole day, remembering Mrs Pankhurst's stirring speech, savouring the car ride with Mrs Roberts, conjuring up as much detail as I could of Fairy Glen and its magical garden.

When I fell asleep at last, I dreamed of fairies – little creatures who flew through the garden in dresses made of flower petals. They perched decoratively on the branches, they skimmed the water in the stream, they gathered in a fluttering flock on the roof of the Japanese summerhouse. When I woke the next morning, they still seemed trapped behind my eyelids, flitting back and forth in a rainbow sparkle. I spent most of Sunday painting my own fairy scenes, suddenly inspired.

Cassie came to my room to make up with me that evening. She seemed taken aback by the ten watercolours tacked up on all four walls.

'My goodness, did you copy them, Opie?'

'No, I made them all up. They're totally original.

Well, I suppose I got the idea from the fairy paintings in Mrs Roberts' sitting room.'

'You and your Mrs Roberts,' said Cassie, but then she checked herself. 'Sorry, I won't tease you any more. I can see you really think she's splendid. I'm sure she is.' She paused, looking at me.

'I suppose your Mr Evandale is splendid too,' I said reluctantly. I didn't think it at all, but I wanted to be friends with Cassie again. She could be an infuriating sister, though it was horrid when we weren't speaking.

I dreamed of fairies that night too. I went into work the next morning feeling tremendously excited about a new idea. I wondered whether to discuss it with Miss Lily, but I was sure she would be very doubtful initially. I thought of approaching Mrs Roberts directly. After all, we were true friends now. But somehow things seemed a little different in the work environment. I saw her going into her room as I walked along the passageway to the design room. I gave her a great beaming smile, but she just gave me an abstracted nod and didn't say anything. Perhaps we could only conduct our friendship away from the factory . . .

I decided to proceed without further ado. After all, I had to remember the suffrage slogan: *Deeds, not words*.

It was my turn to paint a rose scene on a box lid.

I painted each rose with immense care, making sure I used the exact shades of blush cream and candy pink and deep crimson. Then I selected my finest brush and fashioned a tiny fairy peeping out between the petals, rubbing her eyes as if she'd only just woken up. I gave her a companion swinging on a stalk and a third flying high in the sky. They weren't noticeable at first glance. Miss Lily looked and nodded and started praising me for the bloom on a petal. Then she stopped abruptly. She took her spectacles off, rubbed them on her overall, and replaced them. She looked again, holding the lid up to the light.

The other girls were all peering now, sensing that something was wrong.

'Whatever are you playing at, Opal?' asked Miss Lily. 'You've painted little creatures – here and here and here!'

'They're fairies,' I said.

The girls heard me and giggled nervously.

'Fairies?' said Miss Lily. 'Opal, you know very well there are no fairies in our rose-in-bloom design.'

'Yes, but I thought it would be such a good idea if we included a few. After all, this is the *Fairy* Glen factory.'

'Don't be facetious,' said Miss Lily, 'I won't have this nonsense. You have wasted an entire morning with this foolery. The box lid will have to be scrapped. You're a very stupid, tiresome girl. You're employed to do serious designs, not fool around like a fanciful schoolgirl.'

'I'm not fooling. I seriously think the fairies improve the design,' I said.

'I created that design more than twenty years ago.' Miss Lily was trembling, clutching her lace handkerchief in one of her small fists. 'It's been one of our most popular designs. How dare you rework it in such a ludicrous manner! Who do you think you are, Opal Plumstead?' She was nearly in tears.

'I'm sorry. I didn't mean to upset you, Miss Lily,' I said.

I was starting to feel as if I'd done something terrible now. I had hoped Miss Lily would like my fairies once she saw them for herself. I had tried so hard, experimenting all day Sunday until I perfected each one. I thought she'd praise me, show the other girls, insist that my improved design be the future template for everyone.

Maybe I would have given up then and there, apologized profusely, taken some kind of punishment and never tried anything innovative ever again. Maybe, maybe not. But fate was on my side. At that very moment Mrs Roberts came through the door. She was taking one of her customary tours of the factory to make sure that everything was running smoothly. She could see straight away that something was seriously wrong with Miss Lily.

'Miss Lily?' She looked at her closely. Miss Lily was still shaking, little beads of sweat standing out on her lined forehead. 'Miss Lily, sit down. You don't look very well,' Mrs Roberts said, clearly concerned. 'Opal, run and fetch Miss Lily a glass of water.'

I did as I was told, terrified. Miss Lily was clutching her flat old-lady chest. Oh God, had the shock of dealing with me given her a heart attack? Had I literally killed Miss Lily? I started to cry. The other girls gawped at me as if I were truly a murderess.

'Opal, bring that glass!' Mrs Roberts said sharply.

I brought it, spilling some on the way. Mrs Roberts sat Miss Lily down, held the glass to her lips and made her drink.

'There now,' she said. 'Calm yourself, Miss Lily. When you're a little recovered we'll go into my office and you can tell me why you're upset.'

Miss Lily nodded, trying to drink. She waved one small hand in the air, her forefinger pointing in my direction.

'I thought as much,' said Mrs Roberts.

'Should I come too, Mrs Roberts?' I quavered.

She flashed me a terrifying look, a mixture of disappointment and contempt. 'You stay where you are, Miss Plumstead,' she said. Then she added, 'For the moment.'

Oh goodness, she hated me now for upsetting Miss

Lily, the treasure of the design room. What exactly did 'for the moment' mean? Was she going to dismiss me from the factory forthwith?

We were supposed to get on with our work, but this was impossible. The other girls murmured together. I was too proud to say anything, but I thrust my fairy lid into the waste-paper basket, unable to look at it now.

I waited for nearly an hour. Then at last Mrs Roberts returned, alone.

'Come with me,' she said. She looked at the box lid on my desk. I'd only been able to work up one rose, and I'd botched that because my hand was shaking so much.

'Is this the lid that offended Miss Lily?' she asked.

'No, no.'

'Then where is it?'

'I threw it in the waste-paper basket,' I said, shame-faced.

'Then retrieve it and bring it with you,' said Mrs Roberts. 'Girls, Miss Lily has been taken unwell and won't be returning today. Alice, I shall leave you temporarily in charge. Go to Mr Beeston if there are any further problems. Please continue your excellent work.'

I took my poor fairies out of the waste-paper basket. I'd thrust them in with such despair that the lid had crumpled. I hated the very sight of it now.

I carried it at arm's length like a banner of shame, and followed Mrs Roberts to her room.

I usually found it an oasis of style and loveliness, but now it seemed cool and alien, making me feel very grubby and guilty. I saw a little lace handkerchief in a soggy ball on the Persian rug.

'Oh, it's Miss Lily's,' I said. 'Is she really ill, Mrs Roberts?'

'She's very upset. I felt it kindest to send her home in my car,' said Mrs Roberts.

'Upset because of me?'

'Yes indeed. Oh dear, Opal, what am I going to do with you? I gave you the benefit of the doubt when you came to blows with Patty in the fondant room – but I simply won't have you upsetting poor Miss Lily.'

'I would never ever hit Miss Lily!' I said.

Mrs Roberts shook her head at me. 'Don't be tiresome, Opal. Though you might just as well have punched the poor lady in the solar plexus. She was doubled up with pain.' She saw my face. 'Mental distress. I don't think she was in actual physical pain, but I thought it wisest to send her home all the same. I very much value Miss Lily. She's been with the firm for so many years. Her designs are vital to the company. How could you have deliberately scribbled some nonsense on the box lid?'

'I didn't think it was . . . nonsense,' I said.

'But it wasn't the design,' said Mrs Roberts.

'I *embellished* the design,' I protested.

'Let me see.' Mrs Roberts held out her hand.

I gave her the box lid. She stared at it. I waited for her outcry, but she didn't say a word. She reached for a magnifying glass on her desk and examined my fairies.

'Fairies!' she said, peering at them.

'I saw your beautiful fairy paintings, you see, Mrs Roberts, and I started to think about our designs. They have the name Fairy Glen on every box, so why not incorporate a few fairies on the picture as a novelty? So many people have a special gift box of Fairy Glen fondants or toffees or candy kisses. They keep them as treasure boxes for their letters or handkerchiefs or jewellery. I have one in my own bedroom. Perhaps some people go on and collect all three designs. But there's no incentive to buy further gift boxes if they're all identical. You might just as well be saving our time and using transfers. But if we had *different* fairies on every box, think how girls would love to set up a grand collection. I'm not suggesting a whole host of fairies because that would be too time-consuming, but several in different costumes and attitudes each time would still be a delightful feature. Well, I thought it would. I thought Miss Lily would *like* my idea once she saw it.'

'You didn't think to consult her first?'

'I did wonder, but then I thought *Deeds, not words* would be more persuasive.'

Mrs Roberts gave me a sharp look, and then snorted with laughter. She actually threw back her head and roared. 'Opal Plumstead, you are the most extraordinary girl,' she said. She picked up my box lid and examined it again. 'I can see why Miss Lily was so upset. The purity of her design is jeopardized. Yet I rather like your little fairies, and I like your sales pitch even more. I can see you have a good business head on your shoulders as well as an inventive mind. Let me think about this, Opal. I need to confer with the members of the board. Off you go now. And don't take it into your head to do anything else revolutionary for a couple of days. I don't think we could stand any further upsets.'

'So you're not cross with me now, Mrs Roberts?'

'I'm cross with you for not being more tactful with Miss Lily, certainly, but I'm pleased with your initiative. Will that do?'

'Yes, I think so. We are still friends, aren't we? I know we have to be very formal here and you are my employer, but can I still see you at meetings?'

'Of course. And I dare say there will be more picnic luncheons too,' said Mrs Roberts, smiling at me properly at last.

I walked back to the design room in a daze. The other girls all looked at me, waiting for me to pack up my things and creep off in disgrace. They shook their heads in astonishment when I calmly started on a meadow design, planning in my head where the fairies would go. One would be paddling in a stream, another gliding along it on a lily leaf, and perhaps a third would be riding on a rabbit.

'What are you up to now, Opal?' asked Alice.

'You'll see,' I said airily.

'Didn't Mrs Roberts give you the push?'

'On the contrary. She *likes* my fairy designs. She thinks they're a brilliant new idea. She says I can carry on doing them,' I said. 'Well, perhaps. She has to discuss it with the board first.'

'They'll never agree. We've always done it this way. What will Miss Lily say?' said Alice.

'Oh, bother Miss Lily,' I said, though I felt hot and horrified when I remembered how she'd trembled.

Alice looked at me as if I'd blasphemed. 'Pride comes before a fall, Opal Plumstead,' she said. 'You think you're the bee's knees just because Mrs Roberts has taken a shine to you for some unknown reason. You think you can shove your way in here and lord it over us when you're just a chit of a girl. We've all been working in design for years. You mark my words, you'll get your comeuppance soon enough. I feel it in my bones.'

'You sound like a gypsy fortune-teller, Alice,' I said, 'and I never believe a word of that superstitious nonsense.'

I was secretly unsettled all the same. What if she

were right? I had showed off abominably, but Mrs Roberts hadn't actually said I could continue with my fairy designs. Perhaps the members of the board would all be traditional old fogeys, contemporaries of Miss Lily. Mrs Roberts owned Fairy Glen, but it sounded as if they had a say in factory policy too.

I'd just have to convince them with my work. I painted my meadow at lightning speed and inserted my fairies. I didn't break for lunch: I worked straight through the hour, having sips of water and nibbles of bun as I painted. I moved straight on to the butterfly design. The butterflies were always painted large, one Red Admiral, one cabbage white and one cobalt blue. This gave me the chance to make my fairies large too, with detailed faces. I gave them little outfits, seemingly fashioned out of flower petals, and wings in matching butterfly designs. They were all three flying together, holding hands, a girl pointing her toes gracefully, a boy running in the air, and a baby kicking his chubby little legs.

'Such nonsense,' said Alice, peering over my shoulder. 'You wait till Miss Lily comes back.'

'Miss Lily isn't my employer,' I said. 'I'm taking these straight to Mrs Roberts.'

I picked up my two box lids and went along the corridor to Mrs Roberts. I knocked on the door.

'Come in,' she called, sounding a little impatient.

When I put my head round the door, I saw that she

was poring over figures in a big accounts book. She frowned when she saw it was me.

'Not you again, Opal.'

'I'm sorry to disturb you, Mrs Roberts. I just thought I'd prepare you two other examples of my fairy designs for when you have your board meeting,' I said. 'Would you care to glance at them?'

'Later – I'm in the middle of totting up these figures,' she said.

I put them down carefully on the edge of the desk. She gave them a quick glance and then picked them up.

'My goodness, Opal,' she said, standing.

'Do you like them?'

'They're fantastic,' she said. She sounded almost as excited as me. 'They work. They work brilliantly.'

'I'll be able to do different fairies on each and every box. I'm practically brimming over with ideas.'

'They could be an entirely new deluxe range, our Fairy Glen speciality,' said Mrs Roberts.

'So you'll try to persuade the board?'

'They won't need persuading, believe you me.' Mrs Roberts reached for my hand and clasped it. 'Well done, Opal. You have real talent – and persistence too. Well done indeed!'

22

The board were equally enthusiastic about my designs. It was decided that the other girls would work on the three classic designs while I simply painted my fairies on top for the special deluxe range. Mrs Roberts suggested my wages needed revising and paid me an astonishing twenty-one shillings a week.

'Don't you dare tell any of the other ladies in design, though.'

'My lips are sealed,' I declared.

'And try to be extremely meek and tactful with poor Miss Lily.'

I did my level best, but no matter how I behaved, it was clear that Miss Lily could hardly bear the sight of me now. She actually shuddered when she caught glimpses of my fairies. After a month or so she handed in her notice.

I felt terrible. 'It's because of me, isn't it?' I said to Mrs Roberts.

'Well, you haven't helped, certainly. But Miss Lily is well past retirement age. She would have needed to stop work soon anyway. We're giving her a very good pension in recognition of her long time here. There's no need to look so stricken, Opal.'

I felt very guilty all the same and worried about poor Miss Lily, but I'm afraid I was not downcast for long. I gloried in my new senior position in the design room. I loved going to work now. I stopped wishing I could go back to school and complete my education.

It was wonderful to have the extra money too.

'You don't have to mind those wretched babies any more, Mother. *I'll* take care of the housekeeping from now on,' I said loftily.

'It's very good of you, dear, but I rather like having my babies around me,' said Mother. 'And perhaps this fairy stuff is just a flash in the pan. You'll run out of ideas, or they'll get tired of you and put you back on your basic wage.'

'No they won't, Mother!' said Cassie. 'Our Opal's done wonderfully.'

Mother didn't seem to think much of my fairy designs when I brought them home to show her. She said, 'Very nice, dear,' but it was plain she wasn't impressed.

However, Cassie thought them marvellous. 'You clever old thing! I'm so happy for you, Opie,' she said, hugging me.

On Sunday she told Mr Evandale all about my success. 'He seems very tickled, especially as you're so young. I rather think he'd like to meet you, Opal. Would you like to meet him?'

'Yes – yes I would,' I said, though I felt uncertain. I'd imagined him in so many Gothic guises, preying on my poor sister, that he'd become a fairy-tale ogre in my head. Yet I felt I *should* meet him, for Cassie's sake. I was also pleased he was taking an interest in me now.

'Then I'll fix it,' said Cassie. 'Perhaps we can go on a little outing together? Up to London, perhaps?' She paused, looking thoughtful. 'It seems such ages since we had that wonderful weekend with Father, doesn't it?'

'Oh dear, yes. But we'll be able to go on other outings with him when he comes back,' I said, though I wasn't sure I believed this now.

Father still wrote his monthly letter, but it was a

thin, flavourless document, politely asking after our health and wishing us well. He didn't engage with any of us on a personal level and still told us nothing about himself. I could hardly bear to imagine how he was coping.

I was sure he would be desperately worrying about us too, so I wrote him a long letter telling him about my triumph at Fairy Glen, my new status in the design room, and my magnificent new salary. I hoped that this would reassure him, but reading through it again, I realized I sounded as if I were bragging. It might make Father feel worse rather than better, more diminished if his own daughter had suddenly become successful. I tore up the letter and ended up writing almost as uninformatively as Father himself.

Dearest Father,

A day doesn't go by when we don't think of you. We are so concerned about you. But please don't worry about us. We're all flourishing and I have had a promotion at work – though we can't be truly happy until you are back home.

I remain your devoted loving daughter,

Opal

I drew him a few little fairies in the margins as whimsical decoration, but then felt they looked rather too frivolous. I tore up that letter as well and wrote out a plain version. Cassie wrote a line too, telling Father she loved him. I hoped Mother would do the same, but she shook her head. She no longer seemed to have any love left in her – for Father, for me, even for Cassie. The only ones she made a fuss of were the wretched babies.

That Sunday Cassie came back from seeing Mr Evandale even later than usual, but managed to lie smoothly enough about a long evening of card playing at the Alouettes'.

'With Philip?' Mother asked eagerly.

'Of course,' said Cassie.

'There must surely be an understanding between the two of you now?' said Mother.

'I think so,' Cassie replied.

'But he hasn't formally asked for your hand?'

'Oh, Mother! Patience,' said Cassie.

'How on earth are you going to sort this out?' I asked her. Mother had gone to bed and we were alone together at last.

'Oh, you're such a worry-pot, Opie. I can string Mother along for ages yet. I am good at it, aren't I?'

'But at some stage she really *is* going to expect you to come home with a diamond ring on your finger.'

'I *have* a ring,' said Cassie, reaching into her chemise and fondling Mr Evandale's signet ring on the ribbon around her neck.

'Yes, but it's plain that's not an engagement ring.

And Mother will want to meet Philip eventually.'

'Then I shall tell her we've had a sudden disagreement. I'll say I've suddenly realized he's a pathetic fool. No, Mother would think me the fool for turning him down. So I shall say I've discovered him canoodling with some other lady and I am now heart-broken. She will make an extra fuss of me.'

'Does Mr Evandale know how extremely duplicitous you are?'

'I'm not sure what "duplicitous" means. The words you come out with, Opie! But he knows I'm a little minx. I've told him all the tales I spin to Mother and he thinks it's a hoot.'

'Then he can't be a very nice man himself.'

'Nice men are generally very, very boring, Opie,' said Cassie in a worldly-wise way. 'Anyway, nice or not, he's still keen to meet you. He's suggesting next Saturday.'

'Saturday?'

I often attended meetings at the local WSPU now, and sometimes went back to lunch with Mrs Roberts, but I knew she was spending this weekend visiting her son, Morgan, at school. So I *could* be free on Saturday . . .

'But you're at Madame Alouette's on Saturdays.'

'He wants to take you to the National Gallery, and it's not open on Sundays.'

'Oh my goodness,' I said. I didn't think I wanted to

meet Mr Evandale at all, but I longed to go to the National Gallery. 'But then I'll be seeing him on my own!'

'Yes,' said Cassie. She didn't sound too happy about it, either.

'I'm not sure I want to do that,' I said.

'Well, tell you what – I'll come too.'

'You'll ask for a day off work? Will Madame Alouette let you?'

'Probably not, especially on our busiest day. But I'll invent a bad toothache on Friday, and then she'll believe I've gone to a dentist in desperation.'

'You're such a liar, Cassie! Your heart will be covered in black spots by now.'

'As long as my chest stays white as snow I don't care,' she said.

'You keep that snowy chest hidden away from Mr Evandale,' I told her. 'I'm glad you'll be there too. I should feel so awkward otherwise. But you've always said you find the idea of art galleries boring.'

'I haven't really changed my mind. I can't see the point of peering at a whole load of old paintings, unless they're Daniel's portraits of me! But I'm not sure I want you trotting around with him half the day. You know a lot about art and you use long words and show off. He might decide to swap sisters,' said Cassie.

'Don't be ridiculous,' I said. 'You know perfectly

well that no man would ever give me a second look while you're around.'

'Maybe that was true once, but you're looking a little different now,' said Cassie.

When we went up to bed, I stared hard in the looking glass. I'd had a mad hope that I'd suddenly transformed into a beauty. That hope was dashed immediately. I was as small and sharp and bespectacled as always. But when I smoothed my nightgown, I acknowledged that I was at last getting a little curvier, though on a very modest scale, and even properly clothed I had a different stance. I didn't slouch like a schoolgirl any more. Although my face hadn't changed shape, I wasn't quite as pale and my eyes had a different look in them, even though they were covered by my glasses. I had all the same depressing features, but now they assumed a different expression. I just wasn't quite sure what it was.

It was late and I only had a stump of candle that gave off very poor light, but I tried to sketch a quick portrait of myself. I managed a reasonable likeness in about fifteen minutes, and then stared at it intensely. I didn't have a portrait from before to compare it with. I'd always hated the idea of drawing myself and had only ever achieved a miserable caricature, which I'd always torn up. I realized I used to tilt my chin in a rather aggressive manner and often had a pinched line between my eyebrows. This was smoothed out now, which made a lot of difference. My face was still thin but not so taut. It seemed less cocksure, more confident.

However, I felt anything but confident the next Saturday at the prospect of meeting Mr Evandale with Cassie. She'd wailed all Friday at Alouette's, and Madame herself had told her to attend an emergency dentist on Saturday instead of coming to work. Cassie didn't try the same tale with Mother, who might well have bound Cassie's jaw up and marched her off to a dentist herself. She simply told Mother that Philip had begged his aunt to allow him to take Cassie up to London on Saturday morning, to make the most of the shops and the sights, and Madame Alouette was so fond of Cassie that she had agreed just this once.

So Mother understood when, after breakfast, Cassie got herself up in all her green finery. But she frowned at me when she saw that I was wearing Cassie's grey costume and white blouse.

'And where are you off to, missy? Mixing with those dreadful suffragettes again? You're going to get yourself into terrible trouble. All decent folk think those women want horse-whipping. The destruction they've caused! All the shop windows broken, policemen and politicians assaulted. Someone's going to get killed soon, you mark my words.'

'Someone already *has* been killed – Emily Davison

was trampled to death at Epsom under the King's horse,' I declared. 'And pretty soon some of the poor brave women stuck in prison and tortured with force feeding will die soon too. People say Mrs Pankhurst herself is in danger.'

'They bring it on themselves with their silly hysterics.'

'They're hysterical on *our behalf*, Mother. They want better rights for women. Once we have the vote, then everything will change.'

'I wouldn't vote if you paid me. Women have no business in the polling booths. We know nothing about politics or running the wretched country.'

'So we need to educate ourselves until we do,' I insisted passionately yet again. I felt boiling hot in my flannel costume and throttled by the high neck of my blouse.

'Oh, do stop getting so het up, both of you,' said Cassie.

'*You'd* vote if you had the opportunity, wouldn't you, Cass?' I appealed to her.

'Oh, of course I would. I'd vote for any candidate who was handsome. It seems to be a rule that all politicians are ugly. And then I'd want all the laws changed. I'd have everyone only working one hour a day, and I'd give all women a very generous dress allowance, but all millinery will be extremely expensive so Alouette's makes five times the profit.'

'But how could that possibly be economically viable?' I asked.

'Oh, you're such a pain, Opie. I'm not serious. Now do stop getting so agitated. I have to be off now to meet Philip, and you don't want to be late for your boring old meeting, so let's say goodbye to Mother now and be on our way.'

I let Cassie hustle me out of the house.

'Dear goodness!' she said as we were hurrying down the street. 'If you start all this suffragette nonsense with Daniel, he'll tease you unmercifully, I warn you.'

'It's not nonsense,' I said crossly, and proceeded to tell her *why* women needed the vote until she actually put her hands over her ears as we walked along. But the nearer we got to the railway station where we were to meet Mr Evandale, the less assertive I became.

I didn't need Cassie to point him out when we got there. He stood idly reading a newspaper, taller and broader than most men, a large soft trilby on his dark unruly hair. He was wearing a greatcoat left unbuttoned and a long purple scarf draped round and round his neck, contrasting vividly with the cherry red of his velvet waistcoat. His clothes were made of soft materials in girlish colours, but he still looked the most masculine man I'd ever seen.

'Oh my, isn't he wonderful?' Cassie breathed proudly.

She went rushing forward and peeped round his newspaper to surprise him. He laughed and took her hand. There was nothing especially intimate about their greeting, and yet somehow it seemed as if they were embracing. I felt myself going pink.

'Daniel, dear, this is my sister, Opal,' said Cassie. 'Opie, this is my Daniel.'

I quivered a little that she should call this man 'my Daniel'. It was clear that they were far more than friends.

'I'm delighted to meet you, Opal. The child wonder who has set the whole of Fairy Glen a-twittering with the wonder of her fairy designs,' said Mr Evandale.

I couldn't decide if he was being serious or sarcastic. I felt even more gauche than usual, stuck out my hand stiffly, and then recoiled at the warmth and vigour of his grasp as we shook hands.

'Cassie has told me so much about her brilliant little sister,' he said.

'I am hardly brilliant,' I said gruffly.

'Yes you are,' said Cassie. 'My Lord, you should have heard her this morning, Daniel, sounding off about women's suffrage and all sorts of dreary political stuff until I thought I should scream.'

'Really, Opal? Perhaps you'd care to enlighten me too while we journey up to London,' he suggested.

'Perhaps not,' I said, because even I could see that this would not be sensible.

The journey took less than an hour, but it seemed interminable. Mr Evandale was determined to draw me out, asking me all sorts of questions, seeming to flatter me – but I became more and more awkwardly monosyllabic.

'Don't be shy, Opie,' Cassie said, trying to encourage me. She was certainly the opposite of shy. Now that we were in an enclosed carriage, just the three of us, she snuggled up close to Daniel Evandale, tucking her hand under his arm and gazing up at him adoringly. He smiled at her every now and then, sometimes patting her absentmindedly, as if she were a little lapdog. I would have found such an attitude deeply offensive, but Cassie was clearly in seventh heaven.

I was starting to wish I had never agreed to come. I even hatched a wild plan to push off by myself when we reached Waterloo, but Mr Evandale swept Cassie and me into a cab. This was a novelty I didn't want to miss. It felt so grand to be swooping along through the busy traffic to Trafalgar Square. I'd never been there before, though I'd seen pictures of the huge Landseer lions and Nelson on his column. Little urchins were swarming all over the lions. It looked such fun that I longed to lift up my hobbling skirts and join them, but of course I refrained.

There were vast flocks of pigeons hopping and fluttering about the square. An old man was selling bags of birdseed to the children at a penny a time. Mr Evandale saw me looking at them and laughed. He handed me a penny from his trouser pocket.

'You don't want to feed those nasty flappy things, do you?' said Cassie. 'Aren't you afraid of getting pecked?'

'They're not *eagles*, Cassie,' I said.

I took great delight in feeding the birds. I didn't have to encourage them at all. They positively mobbed me the moment they saw the bag in my hand. It was wonderful when their little claws fastened confidently on my shoulders and their soft wings brushed my face. One even perched on top of my head, artistically posing on my hat, a living decoration to my grey outfit.

'Mind it doesn't mess on that hat!' said Cassie, shuddering. 'It's mine, remember.'

'Anyone would think you didn't like birds, Cassie,' said Mr Evandale.

'I don't mind pretty coloured ones in cages,' she replied.

We looked at each other, remembering poor lost Billy and *Happy Days*. My eyes filled with tears, and Cassie's did too.

'Come, girls – the birds are full to bursting now,' Mr Evandale said gently, and he steered us towards the gallery. We hadn't said a word. I was surprised by his sensitivity. Perhaps he wasn't quite such a bad man after all. We went up the steps. The gallery was extraordinarily crowded, which was a surprise. I had imagined us drifting through empty rooms.

'Shall we work our way through the paintings chronologically from the beginning, or shall we dart about at random, picking out favourites?' said Mr Evandale.

'Chronologically,' I said.

'Dart about,' Cassie said simultaneously. 'And not *too* many favourites.'

'It's Opal's treat,' Mr Evandale pointed out. 'I think we shall begin at the beginning. But after an hour or so I shall take you off for a cup of tea and a bun, Cassie. How about that?'

'I've got to look at paintings for a whole *hour*?' Cassie complained. She sighed as we entered the north vestibule to start with the early Italian paintings.

I stared in wonder at the glowing pinks and golds and scarlets and the brilliant lapis blue. I had a well-thumbed book about the paintings in the National Gallery, with over seven hundred reproductions, but they were all in black and white.

I wanted to stand and marvel at each one. But everyone strolled past at a measured pace. I tried to do the same, but when I came across the Duccio Madonna in the second room, I stood rooted to the spot. I wouldn't budge even when Cassie poked and pulled at me.

'Do you like her?' asked Mr Evandale.

I nodded, for once speechless.

'She is beautiful, isn't she,' he agreed.

'No she's not!' said Cassie impatiently. 'Her face is all greeny and isn't pretty at all. And she's far too big. That baby's out of proportion and the people are the wrong size. It doesn't look real.'

'It's not trying to look real. The early Italian painters wanted to show Heaven in all its golden glory,' said Mr Evandale. Right then I could have kissed him.

'She *is* beautiful, Cassie. The baby is Christ, so He's very magical. He's a tiny baby and yet He's already all-powerful. I love the way He's lifting her veil so tenderly and reaching up to stroke her face,' I said.

'I don't know why you're going so googly over the baby. You won't go near any of Mother's,' said Cassie. She flounced off, and Mr Evandale raised his eyebrows at me.

'I'll have to find paintings more to Cassie's taste or she'll make our visit very difficult,' he said.

None of the early Italians pleased her, though she conceded that the Crivelli Madonnas were 'more like it', but she took issue with their long delicate hands. I marvelled at Crivelli's enormous altarpiece, embellished here and there with real jewels. I wondered if this might be a good idea for Fairy Glen gift boxes, maybe at Christmas. A new design entirely – a dark night with a fairy Father Christmas flying through the air with sacks of toys in his sled and silvery enamel stars glittering in the sky.

'That Virgin's fingers are too long too,' Cassie said dismissively. 'And who are all the people?'

'Let me introduce you,' said Mr Evandale, as if we were at a party. 'St Peter, with his key, St John the Baptist, St Catherine of Alexandria, St Dominic, St Andrew, St Stephen with the stones of his martyrdom embedded in his head, and St Thomas Aquinas. And up on the top tier I see St Jerome, the Archangel Michael stamping on a dragon, St Peter the martyr, and there's dear little St Lucy carrying her plate.'

'What are those weird things on the plate?' Cassie asked.

'Her eyes, my dear.'

'Her *eyes*?'

'She plucked them out with her own hands and sent them to a love-struck youth,' I said, proud that I'd read about her in my art book.

'How truly disgusting. These fanatical religious paintings are too bizarre for me. Don't they ever paint anything else?'

'Come, Cassie, we'll find you some mythological goddesses. They might be more to your taste,' said Mr Evandale.

We both blinked at Bronzino's *Allegory with Venus*

and Cupid. I was determined to be sophisticated when it came to nudes, but this painting had an extraordinary amount of pearly white flesh. Venus and Cupid and Folly seemed to be flaunting it for all they were worth. Titian's *Bacchus and Ariadne* was equally compelling, with Bacchus seemingly leaping straight out of the painting, his pink robe flying out behind and practically exposing him.

'Look what you can see!' Cassie whispered.

I glared at her, lost in the poetry of the picture, but I couldn't stop myself peering. It wasn't very instructive.

Mr Evandale took Cassie off for her bun, as promised. I was hungry too, but I couldn't bear to waste a minute away from the paintings. I wandered around by myself in a daze, my eyes blurring now, colours whirling in my brain like a child's kaleidoscope. I noted every line and variation of angel's wing so that I could appropriate them for my fairies. I took comfort from the Early Flemish paintings because their women were as thin and pale and serious as me.

'Which is your favourite?' Mr Evandale asked, when they found me eventually.

'I can't say. I love so many,' I said helplessly.

'I'll show you mine,' he said. 'It's a Venus like no other.'

'We've seen enough Venuses already,' Cassie

moaned. 'I'm tired of all these painted ladies.'

'This one's like real flesh and blood,' said Mr Evandale. 'She's a beauty.'

Cassie pouted a little. 'Is she more beautiful than *my* portrait?' she asked him coyly.

'Oh, Cass, I'm a fine jobbing painter but I'm no match for Velázquez,' he said. 'Come and see.'

He led us to the Spanish paintings, and there she was, with a little crowd gathered in awe – mostly gentlemen. Mr Evandale was right. It seemed as if there were a real young woman lying there on her blue-grey silk sheet. She was calmly admiring herself in the mirror, showing us her smooth white back, her tiny waist, and her sensuous curves.

'I suppose she is beautiful,' Cassie said grudgingly. 'But don't you prefer a slightly fuller figure, Daniel?'

He laughed. 'Possibly. I daren't reply otherwise.'

'The painting's very fine, but I prefer your portrait of me,' Cassie told him.

'Then perhaps some dolt will pay forty-five thousand pounds for *my* painting,' he said. 'That's what the nation paid to buy the Rokeby Venus.'

'Forty-five *thousand*?'

'And worth every penny. What do you say, Opal?'

I nodded, scarcely able to breathe. I couldn't stop gazing at the painting, taking in all the sweeps and curves. It seemed astonishing that a man could paint a picture of a young girl more than two hundred and fifty years ago, a girl long since crumbled into dust, yet here she was, young and fresh and glowing, still able to attract the full attention of everyone in the room.

'It's just a *painting*,' said Cassie. She paused. 'Will your portraits be worth that much one day, Daniel?'

'Oh, Cassie, how I wish it were so,' he said.

'Is it lunch time yet?' she asked hopefully.

'We've only recently fed you two enormous currant buns. You'll burgeon into a Rubens if you're not careful!'

I was rather hoping that Mr Evandale would take us to a hotel. I was very keen to sample oysters and champagne. He took us to a chophouse instead, a much more prosaic choice, but I enjoyed my two pork chops with apple sauce, and then we all had golden syrup steamed pudding. I couldn't manage more than a mouthful of mine as I was so full of chops.

I'd hoped that we would return, refreshed, to the National Gallery, but Cassie objected fiercely.

'Let us go to all the department stores in Oxford Street,' she suggested, but this made Mr Evandale groan.

'I have a better idea,' he said, and he hailed a cab.

He took us to the Zoological Gardens. This proved to be an utterly splendid choice. We were all enchanted by the antics of the monkeys and the comical black and white penguins. We thrilled at the roar of the lions and tigers, though Cassie fanned herself ostentatiously, saying she couldn't bear the smell. Mr Evandale stumped up the money for Cassie and me to have a ride on Jumbo the elephant, though this was really designed for children. We certainly shrieked like little girls as the great beast lumbered to his feet and started plodding along while we perched precariously on a little seat on his back.

It was not properly spring, but the sun was warm and we sat in deckchairs in Regent's Park to ease our aching feet. Mr Evandale took out his sketchbook and started doing a quick pencil portrait of both of us. Cassie immediately struck a pose, throwing up her arm and smiling enigmatically. I felt stiff and self-conscious beside her and couldn't stop fidgeting.

'Here, Opal, you draw too,' he said, tearing out several pages of his sketchbook for me.

I tried to draw my sister too, but it was inhibiting after seeing so many masterpieces. I took inspiration from the Zoological Gardens instead and drew Cassie as a sleepy lioness, her hair a magnificent mane, her great paws emerging incongruously from the cuffs of her dress. She was smiling, as if she'd just dined on an antelope and several impala.

Cassie was irritated when she saw what I'd done, but Mr Evandale roared with laughter.

'Yours is far better than my conventional scribble. It's Cassie, right down to the last whisker.'

'I don't have whiskers! Honestly, how you do plague a girl,' said Cassie, pretending to be cross, but she couldn't help simpering at him even so.

We had another train carriage to ourselves on the way home. Cassie fell asleep, snuggled against Mr Evandale's shoulder. He offered to get us a cab from the station, but we decided to walk instead. I shook his hand and thanked him fervently. Cassie gave him a bold kiss on the lips right in front of me. Then we walked off arm in arm.

23

'So what did you think of him? Isn't he just the most wonderful man ever? He's got such style, hasn't he? And he knows so much, and he has such a wicked sense of humour. He knows exactly how to please a girl, don't you think? And he's so youthful, for all that he's so old. Don't you think so yourself? Do you think he really, really cares for me? Opie, do say!' said Cassie in a rush.

'For goodness' sake, give me a chance to speak! Yes. Yes, yes, yes!'

'Yes, you like him? And you think he likes me?'

'Yes to everything. I can see why you're so charmed.'

'Oh, Opie, I'm so happy. I wish he had a younger brother just for you, and then you could be happy too.'

'I'm happy as I am,' I said, not quite truthfully. 'And I'd never ever be able to fib to Mother so fluently. I don't know how you do it. Have you got today's story all prepared?'

'Oh, that's easy enough. I just open my mouth and a great long story tumbles out,' said Cassie. 'You wait and see.'

'Had we better separate? Mother will wonder why we're together,' I suggested.

'No, no, we'll say we simply met up by chance on the way home,' said Cassie.

We got to the front door and let ourselves in.

'Hello, Mother,' Cassie called cheerily. There was no reply, just a strange silence. Yet we could hear a series of thumps in the kitchen. We went in, and there was Mother ironing, her face as hard and steely as the iron itself.

'Hello, Mother,' Cassie repeated. 'Have all the shop girls' babies gone home? Oh dear, you do look tired. Sit down, and we'll finish the ironing off for you, won't we, Opie.'

'Where have you been?' said Mother, ironing hard.

'Why, you know where we've been. I've been at

Madame Alouette's and Opie's been to one of those boring old meetings,' Cassie said. 'Here, Mother.' She took off her hat and coat and went to take the iron, but Mother clung onto it.

'Get away from me,' she said.

'Mother, whatever's the matter?' I asked.

'I've got a liar for a daughter, that's what's the matter.' She thumped the table so hard it actually shook.

'Do calm down, Mother, you're getting in such a state. What's upset you?' Cassie was trying to sound casual, but she looked frightened now. I clutched her hand.

'I had a visitor this afternoon,' said Mother. 'Madame Alouette.'

I felt Cassie's hand tighten on mine.

'She came round specially, because she was worried about you, Cassie. It seems you had a bad toothache. She brought you a bottle of oil of cloves to soothe it. Wasn't that kind, taking time away from the shop specially? I thanked her for all her past kindness, the many days you've spent at her house with her nephew Philip. It turns out that she can't remember any visits whatsoever – and Philip himself is back in Paris continuing his studies.'

'Oh Lord,' Cassie murmured.

'So would you mind telling me exactly where you've been, madam? And you're clearly in on this whole deception too, Opal. How could you two girls let me down so badly?'

'Opal hasn't deceived you. She's just been going to her suffragette meetings – until today. It's all me. But I told you all those tales because I didn't want to worry you, Mother. I'll tell you the truth now. I have been seeing a wonderful gentleman called Mr Daniel Evandale.'

'Why didn't you tell me? Why did you make up this nonsense about Madame Alouette's nephew? What's wrong with this gentleman that you had to keep him such a deadly secret?'

'I didn't, Mother. I told you all about him the very day I met him. He came into the shop and ordered a fancy hat and I modelled all our latest designs for him. Don't you remember my telling you?'

'But that was a much older man!'

'He's not a callow youth. He is a cultured gentleman in his prime.'

'What does he do for a living?'

'He's an artist,' Cassie said proudly.

'An artist!' Mother exclaimed, thumping the iron down fiercely, as if she wished to brand Cassie's gentleman with it. 'An *artist*. Oh, Cassie, when will you learn? Of all the disreputable professions! He'll have you modelling for him next.' She saw Cassie's face and gave an anguished moan. 'How could you sink so low? I suppose you took your clothes off too!'

'Yes I did,' said Cassie. 'Daniel's painted several portraits of me, and they're all beautiful and may well be displayed in the Royal Academy. I'm so proud, Mother. Daniel is a fine artist. I know he'll be truly famous one day and I shall be too, as his muse.'

'As his *muse*!' Mother spat, as if it were a filthy word. 'Now listen to me, Cassie Plumstead. You are never to see that man again. I'm not going to let you out of my sight on Sundays. You'll stay home with me and help with the chores. And on Monday you'll go to Madame Alouette's and beg her forgiveness for all the ludicrous stories you've been telling, though I'm not sure she'll keep you on at the shop. She's truly shocked by your deception.'

'I don't care if she doesn't want me to stay on. I'm tired of working there anyway. Why should I waste my time sitting with a lot of silly girls making hats for other women all day long? I don't even earn anything yet. Daniel's painter friends are all keen for me to model for them and they'll pay handsomely!' Cassie shouted. 'You can't stop me seeing Daniel, Mother. I *love* him.'

'What do you know about love?'

'I think I know more about love than you do,' said Cassie, her head held high. 'Who are you to preach at me anyway? You ran off with Father when you were my age, or near enough.'

'And look at me now. Look what it's reduced me to,'

said Mother bitterly. 'Shame and penury.'

'Well, I hope to avoid both. Because Daniel is wealthy and I am proud to be seen with him.'

'I'm warning you, if you see him even one more time, you'll not set foot in this house again,' said Mother.

'Very well. I shall pack my belongings now,' said Cassie, and she picked up her skirts and walked upstairs.

Mother clasped the handle of the iron, suddenly helpless. She looked at me. 'Can't you stop her, Opal?'

I ran up the stairs after Cassie. I thought she might be bluffing, but she was calmly and methodically going through her chest of drawers, selecting her best nightgown, her set of underwear embroidered with little violets, her new stockings, her velvet bag of hair ribbons, packing them all into the big carpet bag. We never went away so we'd always used it as a storage bag. Cassie and I had kept our dressing-up clothes in it when we were little. I saw a discarded heap of tattered costumes on the floor – the 'princess' rose-pink dress we'd always fought over, the white 'ghost' gown that had once been Mother's wedding veil, the dark green velvet skirt that had been our mermaid outfit.

'You're not really packing your things, are you, Cassie?' I asked stupidly, because it was plain she was doing just that.

'I don't have any option, do I?' Cassie went to her wardrobe and rifled through her clothes. 'You can have most of these, Opie. I haven't got room to take them, and I'm tired of them anyway. I've got my green dress and I'll take my black costume with the pink blouse. I'll leave my cream one for you – and you can certainly keep the old elephant.'

'Mother isn't serious, I'm sure she isn't. She can't stop you seeing Mr Evandale. You could pretend you were somewhere else anyway.'

'I'm tired of pretending. I'm going to live with Daniel.'

'But – but what will *he* say?'

'He'll be jolly pleased,' said Cassie, but she suddenly stopped looking so frighteningly grown up. She sat down on her bed and started biting her thumbnail. 'He *will* be pleased,' she insisted, as if I were arguing with her. 'You see how he is with me. He's wild about me.'

'Do you think he'll marry you?'

Cassie nibbled at her thumb. 'I think he's still married to his first wife, though he left her long ago.'

'Oh, Cassie! What if he leaves *you*?'

'He won't. But if he does, I shall just have to fend for myself. His friends really do want me to model for them, you know. And when I get too old and fat for modelling, I shall start up my own hat shop. I bet I make a better go of it than Madame Alouette.'

'Yes, of course you would. You could do anything. But can't you still stay here, just for me? I'll miss you so.'

'I'll miss you too, Opie.' Cassie stopped her packing and put her arms round me. 'But you could come and visit me. Number 100 Hurst Avenue. There! It's easy to remember. Just don't tell Mother.'

'This is happening much too *quickly*. Mother doesn't really want you to go. She sent me up here to stop you.' I clung to Cassie. 'I won't let you go.'

'Opie! Don't be silly. Don't make it worse for me,' said Cassie.

'You're really choosing Mr Evandale over Mother and me?'

'Yes, I have to. I love him.'

'You're just trying to be like one the heroines in your romantic novels.'

'I'm the heroine in my own life and I've got to live it the way I want,' said Cassie. She gently pushed me away, grabbed a handful of trinkets from her dressing table (hairbrush, powder, necklaces, a little cherub ornament), thrust them in the top of her carpet bag and then pulled it shut. She picked it up and staggered under the weight.

'Oh Lord, I'm not going to able to walk far with this. I'll have to get a cab. You couldn't lend me some money, could you, Opie?'

I gave her all the change from my savings box.

'I'll pay you back, I promise,' she said.

She staggered downstairs with the carpet bag. I ran round her into the kitchen.

'Mother, Cassie's really going. Oh, do make it up with her quickly. She won't change her mind.'

Mother's face crumpled but she stayed where she was. 'I won't change my mind, either. If Cassie wants to live in sin with an older man, then she's no daughter of mine,' she said.

'Won't you even say goodbye to her?'

'I have nothing to say to her any more,' said Mother.

I left her and found Cassie at the front door, ready in her coat and hat.

'Promise you'll come back home if it doesn't work out,' I begged her.

'It *will* work out.' Cassie gave me a kiss and then set off determinedly.

I watched her lugging her carpet bag, walking lopsided to manage the weight. I couldn't bear to see her struggle. I went running up the road after her.

'Here, Cassie, give me one of the handles,' I said.

'I can manage,' she said. 'Go back, Opie. Look, you'll freeze without your coat.'

'I'll help you to the main road and then we'll find you a cab.'

'Mother will think you've left home too,' said Cassie.

'Oh Lord, are you really, really sure this is what you want to do?'

'Yes. No. I don't know!'

'I still can't believe it's happening. Too many things have happened in our family. We just jogged along in the same old way for years and years, and then poor Father made his mistake, and since then everything's changed.'

'Father's gone to the bad, and now it seems I'm bad too. But you're doing splendidly, Opie, with all your funny old fairies. I'm very proud of you, sis.'

'Oh, Cass, I'm proud of you too,' I said, and we had to put the carpet bag down so we could have another hug.

We got to the main road at last and Cassie found a cab immediately. The cabbie rushed to help her with her bag and handed her into the cab as if she were a queen. Perhaps I didn't need to worry about her quite so much. She did seem to have the knack of making every man fall at her feet.

I was clammy with the effort of lifting that bag, but I started shivering on the way home. I didn't have my key and had to bang on the door. Mother was a long time answering. I started to wonder if she'd locked me out. When she opened it at last, I saw the hope in her eyes and then the crushing disappointment as she saw that I was alone.

'So she's really gone,' she mumbled.

'Yes. I had to help her with her bag. Oh, Mother, don't look like that. It's not as bad as you think. Mr Evandale seems very fond of Cassie and he *is* a gentleman, even though he's an artist.'

'I don't care if he's a prince. If Cassie lives with any man, she's ruined. I had such high hopes for her. She could have made a brilliant match if she'd only set her mind to it. She's a wicked, wilful girl and I'll have no more to do with her.'

'Oh, Mother, don't talk like that. You love Cassie, you know you do. And you still have me. *I'm* never going off with any man, I promise you that,' I said earnestly, but Mother wouldn't be comforted.

It was a long, lonely evening with just the two of us. I felt despairing, wondering if all our evenings were going to be similar. Mother and I had so little in common. We didn't even really know what to say to each other without Cassie there. I ached to escape to my room, but I felt it was my duty to keep Mother company. I fetched a sketchbook and tried to invent new fairy designs, but for once I had no inspiration whatsoever.

Sunday was even worse. There were no babies to distract Mother. She sat in her armchair staring into space, brooding darkly. I roamed the house in a turmoil. I was starting to worry terribly about Cassie. What if Mr Evandale had turned her away when she arrived on his doorstep? What if he were entertaining another lady friend? I could see that he liked Cassie, but perhaps he was the type of man who liked many ladies. What if he tired of her quickly and simply discarded her? I had a taste for the paintings of the Pre-Raphaelites. I thought of all their anguished fallen women, and saw Cassie in a similar guise, her hair tumbling to her waist, her dress torn, a poor sad creature of the night.

I was so tormented I couldn't stand it any longer. After a meagre meal of fish paste and bread (Mother said there was no point in attempting a proper cooked lunch for just the two of us) I said I needed some air and exercise and must go for a walk.

It was a bleak, grey day, raining steadily, but Mother didn't question me.

'Do what you want. I can't stop you,' she said dully.

I tried to kiss her goodbye but she moved her head away, as if she couldn't bear me to touch her.

I set off anxiously, planning to take a cab myself because I knew that Hurst Road was on the other side of town, but there were no cabs waiting. None came, though I stood by the main road for a good ten minutes.

I wasn't sure which bus to take. In the end I walked all the way. By the time I reached Hurst Road at last I was drenched to the skin, my hat ruined, my skirts spattered with mud and my boots squelching.

I trudged along, counting the long way to number

100. The houses were imposing, tall three-storey dwellings with scrubbed steps leading up to important front doors with brass knockers and bell pulls. There were humbler doors for trade and servants to the side. I agonized over which door I should approach. I wasn't trade, though I felt like it nowadays. I was going to visit the lady of the house – even though Cassie wasn't really a lady.

Number 100 seemed especially splendid, if a little dilapidated. Stone lions crouched on each side of the steps, the spreading moss making it look as if they were growing green fur. The many windows were in need of a wash, but they were intricately leaded, and the downstairs ones had an elaborate stained-glass design. The front door had an ornate tarnished silver unicorn for a knocker. I grasped its horn and knocked timidly, feeling as if I were part of a fairy tale. I waited for quite a while and then knocked again, more boldly. I looked upwards, craning my neck, and saw a heavy curtain twitching at a top-floor window. Someone was there, but still no one came to open the door.

I started panicking. I forgot genial Mr Evandale of yesterday. In my imagination he had changed into Bluebeard, keeping my sister behind locked doors.

'Mr Evandale!' I called. I swallowed, summoning up courage. *'Mr Evandale!'* I repeated, shouting now. 'It's me, Opal Plumstead, come to see my sister. Please let me in immediately.'

This did the trick. I heard footsteps behind the door, and then it opened a few inches. Mr Evandale put his head round. He was wearing a voluminous artist's smock, heavily smeared with paint. He had a long streak of blue on one cheek, which gave him the unfortunate appearance of a Red Indian in war paint.

'Hello, Opal. Why are you shouting on my doorstep on this drizzly Sunday afternoon?' he asked.

'I've come to see my sister,' I said.

'Yes indeed, of course you have. But I'm afraid Cassie's rather busy just now. Perhaps you could come back a little later? Maybe you'd like to come for tea?'

Alarm bells were going off inside my head. What did he mean, Cassie was 'busy'? Could he really have her locked up somewhere? Was she helpless, powerless, while he had his evil way with her . . . whatever that meant.

'I demand to see my sister now!' I said, and pushed rudely past him, stepping into the hallway. 'Cassie? Cassie, where are you,' I cried.

'Opie?' Cassie called from a long way upstairs. I started climbing the staircase, running breathlessly in case Mr Evandale seized hold of me. I staggered to the top floor and burst through the first door I saw.

I jerked to a standstill, my mouth open. I was in an enormous room with a huge skylight. There was hardly any furniture to speak of, just a large artist's easel, a table littered with oil paints, and an old sofa losing its horsehair stuffing. It was spread with a deep blue satin sheet, and my sister Cassie sprawled on top of it, stark naked. Her hair was piled into a decorative topknot, and her back was to me, showing the smooth curves of her waist and hips. She was peering into a mirror propped against a plaster cupid. She was posing as a modern Rokeby Venus, and the effect was startling.

'Cassie!' I gasped.

'Don't move, Cassie,' said Mr Evandale, coming into the room. He groaned as she wriggled on the sofa and wrapped herself in the blue sheet, laughing.

'What do you think of the pose, Opie? Won't it look wonderful? Daniel's getting quite carried away,' she said.

'It took *ages* to get her into that exact pose,' said Mr Evandale. 'Oh well, let's have a tea break.'

I knew I was crimson in the face with embarrassment, but Cassie was totally relaxed.

'Have you come to check up on me, Opie?'

'I just wanted to make sure you were all right,' I said.

'Ah, what a dear sweet sister you are,' said Mr Evandale, lighting a little spirit stove and putting a kettle on top. 'Utterly unlike this bad girl.' He cupped Cassie's chin and shook his head at her. 'Is your mother still very upset, Opal?'

'Yes she is.'

'Oh dear. Well, I've tried to send Cassie back home, but she clings to me like a little limpet.'

'Oh go on, Daniel, you know you like to have me here. Didn't you enjoy the lovely steak I cooked for you last night? And I'm going to clean up this old house and buy some new furniture and make it into a proper home for you,' said Cassie.

'Don't you dare. I don't want to live in a little bourgeois nest, tripping over a lot of useless bits and bobs whenever I move,' said Mr Evandale. 'I don't trust your taste at all, Cassie Plumstead. You're a frills-and-satin-bows kind of girl. You'd dress *me* in a frilly shirt with a satin tie around my neck if I was fool enough to let you.'

'It would be a vast improvement, I tell you,' said Cassie, laughing.

They carried on with this banter non-stop. I wasn't exactly excluded from the conversation, but neither of them seemed at all interested in my contribution. I felt very lonely and foolish – and also extremely damp in my sodden clothes.

'Here's your tea, dear,' said Mr Evandale, and then he exclaimed when he put his hand on my shoulder. 'Dear Lord, you're absolutely soaking! You poor child. Take off that coat before you catch your death. Your dress is soaked through too. Cassie, give your sister something dry to wear.'

'No, no, I'm fine,' I insisted, terrified they'd pull my clothes off me. Cassie might be happy to cavort about naked, but I wasn't.

Mr Evandale seized my coat and hat all the same, and took them down to the basement kitchen to dry in front of the range.

'Oh, Cassie, are you really all right?' I whispered when he was gone.

'I couldn't be happier,' she replied.

'Aren't you worried about upsetting Mother so?'

'There's no point my worrying about it. I expect she'll come round eventually,' said Cassie.

I think I was looking very forlorn, because she suddenly put her arms around me.

'Goodness, you *are* damp. I hope you don't get a chill. There, I *am* worried about you, Opie. I will miss you dreadfully, but it can't be helped. I hope you will visit me lots of times.'

'How did Mr Evandale react when you turned up on his doorstep?'

'Oh, he was a little alarmed at first. He thought Mother might rush to the police and try to have him arrested. He *did* try to send me packing, but I wasn't having it. I soon won him round,' said Cassie, dimpling. 'And now he thinks it's a very jolly wheeze, especially as he's got this new idea for a Venus portrait. Look, Opie, it's going to be so grand.'

She sauntered over to the easel, her sheet trailing, exposing far too much of her.

The portrait was only lightly sketched out, but already I could see that it was working well. Daniel Evandale was no Velázquez, but he'd set off Cassie's pearly skin and soft curves against the deep blue satin in a manner that was truly breath-taking.

'Maybe *I'll* be hanging in a big gallery in hundreds of years' time,' said Cassie.

'I don't know how you can bear the thought of people staring at you,' I said, shivering. 'Cassie, do you think Mr Evandale will ever marry you?'

'I shall work on it, don't worry. But he'll have to get divorced first. I don't want to nag at him too much. He doesn't like it.'

'Oh, Cass. What would Father say if he knew you were living with a married man?'

'Well, he's in no position to judge, is he?' said Cassie sharply.

Mr Evandale came back upstairs with a bottle of fortified wine and three glasses. 'Here, have a tot. It'll warm you better than tea,' he said.

I took a wary sip. It didn't taste anywhere near as pleasant as champagne, but I found after a few sips that it really did stop me feeling so chilled. I drank a little more and the knots in my stomach started loosening. It felt astonishingly good to be sitting here with Cassie and Daniel Evandale. It no longer seemed extraordinary that my sister was modelling so brazenly and living with a married man. Deep down I was still very shocked and upset, but on the surface I could be calm and accepting. I enjoyed being part of this amazing bohemian world where all the rules were so easily broken.

The wine made us hungry, so Cassie tied her sheet around her like a Roman toga and went to forage for food in the kitchen. I still felt immensely shy of Mr Evandale, but the wine gave me courage. I took a deep breath.

'Mr Evandale—'

'My goodness, you're very formal, Miss Plumstead.'

'Daniel, you will . . . you will be kind to my sister, won't you?'

'Cassie doesn't respond to kindness. She needs firm handling, that girl. A thorough talking to every day, a diet of gruel and water, and I'll lock her up in a cupboard if she gives me any cheek.' He paused. 'I'm joking, Opal.'

'Yes, I know you are,' I said. 'But I can't help worrying all the same. Cassie really shouldn't be here.'

'It wasn't my idea. I didn't suggest she up sticks and set up home with me. It will cramp my style a little. When will I entertain all my other lady friends?'

'I do hope you're joking again,' I said shakily.

'Yes I am,' he said. 'Don't frown so. I dare say

Cassie and I will rub along very well together. I am truly fond of her. She's a dear girl. And you're a dear girl too, being so concerned about your sister.'

'We're dear girls?' said Cassie, coming back into the studio bearing a great tray of food. It was just cheese and bread and fruit, but such exotic sorts that I marvelled as I nibbled. I'd thought that cheese was cheese – hard, yellow, mousetrap Cheddar – but this cheese came in different shapes and colours and textures. There was a wheel of blue-veined Stilton that looked and smelled alarming but tasted surprisingly splendid, a soft creamy French cheese that melted on the tongue, and a bright orange Leicester that was truly delicious. The bread was a long crusty stick instead of a proper loaf, and there was plenty of best butter to spread on it. The fruit was amazing too – a huge bunch of purple hothouse grapes and crisp rosy polished apples.

'Where did you shop for all this wonderful food?' I asked in awe.

'Oh, Daniel gets Fortnum and Mason to deliver from London,' Cassie said airily.

I wondered just how much that would cost. It seemed ridiculous that Mother should have been thrilled by Cassie's 'match' with Philip Alouette, when Daniel Evandale was clearly a class above and his private income must be considerable.

I went home in my dried coat feeling that perhaps I could talk Mother round somehow. Mr Evandale had given me the taxi fare home, but I decided to walk. It had stopped raining and I wanted a long tramp to gather my thoughts. I also needed to sober up a little. I'd had two glasses of wine and felt delightfully swimmy. I didn't mind the discomfort of my still-damp boots. In fact I felt so light-hearted I skipped the length of several roads, and then played the childish game of not stepping on cracks in the pavement. I rehearsed a little speech to Mother in my head. I felt I could easily win her over with my warm persuasive homily.

I think I must have been drunker than I realized. When I got home, Mother would barely speak to me, her face a mask of misery.

'Oh, Mother, don't look like that,' I cried.

'I know where you've been,' she said. 'Don't take me for a fool. You've been to see your sister.' She practically spat the last word.

'Yes, to see Cassie. You mustn't worry, Mother. I promise you, Mr Evandale is a lovely gentleman and he's keeping Cassie in the lap of luxury.'

'She will be living in sin,' said Mother.

'I suppose so, but they seem very jolly and happy together. Mr Evandale's house is very grand, and he has fine food and wines.'

'And you've clearly been sampling them. Is that

creature trying to ruin *two* of my daughters? How dare he ply wine on a child!'

'I'm not a child, Mother, and it was simply to warm me. I got wet through. Oh, *please* try to be reasonable. I know just how much you love Cassie. You can't turn against her overnight.'

'I can and I will,' said Mother, with steely determination.

'Why must you always be so quick to make up your mind to condemn people?' I said, losing my temper. 'You were the same with poor Father when he first got arrested.'

'Hold your tongue,' snapped Mother. 'I won't have it! Oh dear Lord, what have I done to deserve a family like this? A husband who ends up in prison, a daughter who wilfully throws herself away on a married man, and another child who criticizes me endlessly and shows me no respect whatsoever.'

She put her hands to her head, clutching it desperately.

24

On Wednesday Mrs Roberts called me into her room at the factory. 'Look at this, Opal,' she said, thrusting a newspaper at me. She seemed unusually excited, her eyes bright, her cheeks flushed.

'Whatever's happened?' I asked anxiously.

Newspapers made me feel so nervous now. I thought for one mad moment that it might be further dreadful news to do with Father – a riot in his prison perhaps. I found myself staring at a large photograph of a woman, a naked woman. She was beautiful and very shapely, but she had terrifying weals all over her body, as if she'd been savagely attacked. I *knew* this woman – but she wasn't real.

'The Rokeby Venus!' I gasped.

'She's been slashed!' said Mrs Roberts.

'How terrible. What mad fiend could have done this to such a wonderful painting?' I said, my hands trembling as I held the newspaper.

'No, no, Opal. You don't understand. It was our Mary – Mary Richardson, one of our bravest and finest members. This is a triumph for the movement. We're on the front page of every newspaper.'

'But the painting's ruined! She's slashed it with a knife.'

'No, with an axe. Such courage, and the poor girl was attacked by the attendants. Members of the public hit her cruelly.'

'But why did she choose such a beautiful painting?'

'Read it and you'll see.' Mrs Roberts stood up and pointed at the account of Mary Richardson giving evidence at the Bow Street Police Court. 'She says she had to destroy the picture of the most beautiful woman in mythological history, to protest against a government which is destroying Mrs Pankhurst, the most beautiful character in modern history. There, isn't that wonderful! Mrs Pankhurst has been sent back to Holloway, and the poor brave soul will be on hunger strike, enduring that terrible force-feeding again. We are all so concerned for her health. And now bold, brave Mary is in Holloway too, with a six-month sentence.'

I stared at Mrs Roberts. 'So this is *Deeds, not words*,' I said.

'Exactly!'

'But it still seems so dreadful to attack a painting with an axe.'

'Would you sooner she attacked a real woman?'

'Of course not. I just think . . . Oh, I don't know what I think.' I so wanted to follow Mrs Roberts and believe that everything the suffragettes did was brave and wonderful. I understood that they needed to attract the nation's attention to the cause. I knew from the graphic accounts at Saturday meetings that suffragettes in prison suffered the most appalling violence. I struggled to feel as Mrs Roberts did – but I couldn't.

I went along to the WSPU meeting on Saturday and heard them all speaking jubilantly, especially as the National Gallery had been temporarily closed for fear of further attacks. I listened, I even nodded and pretended approval, but I couldn't completely agree.

It was a devastating blow. I had felt that these passionate, powerful women were like marvellous big sisters to me. I had felt part of a wonderful progressive movement. I was accepted and petted and praised as their youngest member. But now I was alone again. I didn't seem to feel at one with anyone at all now. I wasn't close friends with any of the girls in the design room, Freddy no longer gave me a second glance, Cassie had left me without a second thought, and Olivia wouldn't even meet up with me.

I couldn't bear to lose Mrs Roberts too, so I managed to hold my tongue and not argue any more about the slashing of the Rokeby Venus. I did not care for the WSPU meetings so much, but I still attended, because more often than not Mrs Roberts invited me home for lunch.

Those Saturdays at her house meant all the world to me, especially now that my own home was so starkly miserable, with Mother sunk in her own bitter gloom. One Saturday Mrs Roberts seemed particularly animated, and more elaborately dressed than usual in a pearl-grey two-piece, a pale sage-green blouse, with a purple iris pinned to her jacket and a long string of white pearls around her neck. I wondered if Mrs Pankhurst were out of prison again. Maybe Mrs Roberts had invited her for lunch, but although Mrs Pankhurst had indeed been released, suffering from heart pain, she was being nursed by friends elsewhere.

There were several leading members of the

WSPU speaking at our meeting, but Mrs Roberts didn't linger to talk with them afterwards.

'Come along, Opal,' she said. 'We mustn't be late for lunch. I have a gentleman visitor.'

She said it with an unusually coquettish air. I was very surprised. Mrs Roberts rarely spoke of her husband, but when she did, it was generally an obliquely disparaging remark. I'd gathered that she did not care for the way he used to run Fairy Glen. She did not sound as if she cared for him, either. I'd assumed she was one of the new kind of independent ladies who had little time for men, like most of her sister suffragettes. Like myself, in fact.

But now, as we drove home, she was all of a jitter, checking her face in her hand mirror, tutting over an escaped lock of hair, barely talking to me. Whoever this gentleman was, she clearly thought the world of him. I was already certain I would dislike him.

She practically ran into her house. 'Darling, I'm back!' she called, the moment we were inside the front door.

Darling?

I usually liked to linger in the hall for a minute or so, admiring the paintings, but now I hurried after her into the drawing room to see how she'd embrace this 'darling'.

I saw a tall fair-haired young man lounging in a

chair, a book on his knee. He was only a few years older than me! He stood up, smiling.

'Hello, Mother.'

Oh my goodness, what a fool I was. This was Morgan, Mrs Roberts' only son, obviously home from school for the Easter holidays. I was so used to seeing the portrait of him above the mantelpiece that I'd thought of him as a little curly-haired boy, not a grown man.

Mrs Roberts gave him a fond kiss on the cheek. They had different colouring. She had smooth dark hair and he was still fair, his hair less curly now, and falling in loose waves. His eyes were a surprisingly deep brown, with long lashes that made them look very large and intense. He was paler than his mother, the rosiness of his boyhood completely gone, yet in spite of all the differences, when they stood together they were clearly mother and son. They had the same willowy grace, the same ease of movement, the same elegance of stance and dress. Morgan's clothes certainly weren't school uniform. He wore a blue cable-patterned jersey, wine cord trousers and tan polished boots. An odd combination, yet somehow perfect on him.

I was suddenly horribly aware of my own pathetic home-spun appearance. I was wearing the elephant, more wrinkly than ever, the white blouse, which was also creased as I hadn't bothered to iron it properly, and my hair was scraped into its schoolgirl plait because I couldn't find enough hairpins that morning to keep it up tidily.

'Here's Opal, my little protégée from the factory,' said Mrs Roberts. 'Opal, this is Morgan, my son.'

I expected him to nod cursorily in my direction, but he smiled, reached out and shook my hand.

'Opal – plain-talking, fiery Opal, who fights her fellow workers, has taken over the entire design department and is now a mini-suffragette? I practically begged Mother to bring you home. You've clearly made a big impact on everyone.'

He was teasing me, of course, but in the most delightful way. I felt myself growing so hot my glasses started to steam up. His handshake was cool. I prayed that my own hand wasn't clammy. I couldn't think of a thing to say. I had to clench my toes to stop myself shuffling from foot to foot. I didn't know whether to sit or stay standing. They were both staring at me expectantly, waiting for me to say something amusing or interesting, and yet for once I was totally at a loss.

It was a relief when Mrs Evans announced that lunch was served. It wasn't our usual picnic affair. This was a formal luncheon in the dining room: game soup, then some kind of delicate white fish, with a potato dish that was all swirls as if it were cream, and then apple pancakes with cinnamon sugar.

'I'm so spoiled. I always get apple pancakes as soon

as I come home. They've been my favourites since I was a little boy,' said Morgan. 'What's your favourite pudding, Opal?'

So far I had been more or less holding my own during the lunch-time conversation. Morgan had asked me about school, and we had had a long and interesting discussion on English literature. He had seemed pleased to find that I had read a lot of the nineteenth-century novelists, though he was amused when I spoke of Elizabeth and Emma and Jane and Maggie and David and Pip as if they were intimate friends I'd known since childhood. He suggested I might care to read some French and Russian novelists too. I expressed enthusiasm, though privately I wasn't sure that I could tackle them, even in translation. Then we'd spoken of music. I could talk of Bach and Beethoven and Tchaikovsky because Mr Andrews had taught me well. I could offer a coherent opinion when the conversation turned to art, though I decided I had better not refer to the poor slashed Rokeby Venus. Morgan asked if I'd been to the National Gallery and I simply nodded.

'I was meaning to go there these hols, but Mother's sister suffragettes have made that impossible,' said Morgan, squeezing Mrs Roberts' hand. 'I do hope you don't decide to copy Slasher Mary, Mother. I shall have to examine your handbag every time you go out to make sure you're not hiding any little axes.'

I was astonished that he should talk about the suffragette cause so lightly. I wondered if Mrs Roberts would object, but she simply laughed at him. It was clear that Morgan could say or do anything and she'd still be charmed.

So the soup and the fish were consumed quite easily, but my apple pancake stuck in my throat when he asked his simple question about puddings. We didn't *have* puddings at home, apart from a plum pudding on Christmas Day. If we were still hungry and desperate for something sweet, we'd fill up on bread and jam, but that was hardly a pudding. I'd had puddings at school, but they were the institutional kind and bleak in the extreme, mostly sloppy milk concoctions of rice or semolina or tapioca, all disgusting.

'I don't think I'm particularly a pudding girl,' I said at last, 'though these apple pancakes are superb.'

Morgan expressed surprise and started talking about his favourite puddings, both at home and at school. I felt as if someone had gently loosened my corset. I had felt constrained discussing music and literature and art because Morgan knew so much more than me and had such intellectual, cultured views. But now that he was chattering away about treacle sponge and bread-and-butter pudding, he sounded as silly as any other boy. He even looked younger, a crumb or two of sugar gleaming on his lip before he remembered to check, wiping it quickly away with his napkin.

Mrs Roberts and I had fallen into a routine of a quick stroll around her beautiful garden before she called her chauffeur to drive me home mid-afternoon. But today she said gently, 'I think I am a little too tired for a garden walk today, Opal. You won't be too disappointed if I have a rest? I'll call Mitchell to drive you home.'

'That's right, Mother, you have a little snooze. *I'll* take Opal round the garden,' said Morgan.

Mrs Roberts flushed. I could see that this wasn't what she wanted at all. She had clearly planned to get rid of me in as polite a way as possible so that she could have Morgan all to herself.

'I think I'd better go home now,' I said quickly.

'Oh, please don't!' said Morgan. 'I shall enjoy telling you all the proper Latin names of the plants. It will give me a chance to show off like anything and feel splendid. Do say you'll stay.' He turned to Mrs Roberts. 'You don't mind, Mother, do you?'

'Of course I don't mind, darling. I think it's a very jolly idea. Perhaps I shall forgo my nap so that I can be impressed by your botanical knowledge too.'

'Oh no, you'll quibble and correct my pronunciation. You know you're more knowledgeable than me.' He kissed her on the cheek. 'You have your rest, Mother.'

She gave in gracefully and gathered up her bag. 'You'll see Mitchell for me, won't you, Morgan, so he can take Opal home? Goodbye, dears.'

She drifted off in a soft cloud of lilac scent. I felt a little uncomfortable and wondered if Morgan had deliberately out-manoeuvred her.

'Come, let's go into the garden,' he said. He reached out and took my hand. He kept hold of it as we went out through the French windows and onto the path. He behaved as if it were the most casual and ordinary of gestures. Did upper-class men hold hands with girls when they barely knew them? Or did he think of me as a *little* girl and himself as a kind uncle figure? I tried to relax, but it was impossible. I held my arm incredibly stiffly, while the hand at the end of it seemed to have tripled in nerve endings. They all tingled against Morgan's cool palm. It was a relief when he dropped my hand to pluck a strand of ivy from a flowerbed – yet I immediately wanted him to take hold of it again.

'You can't always pluck ivy right out. We should dig up the roots. When my parents first came here, the garden was a dense jungle of ivy, like the garden surrounding the Sleeping Beauty. Do you know that fairy story?'

'I love all the Fairy Books, especially the Blue,' I said.

'My mother's created a beautiful garden, but it's

hard to maintain. The ivy's always there, trying to creep back. The garden really comes into its own in May, when all the rhododendrons and azaleas are in full bloom. Wait till you see all the pinks and reds and purples.'

'It's beautiful now. I love all the soft spring colours,' I said, looking at the pale drooping hellebores, the pink and white tulips, the little yellow crocuses and tiny blue scillas dotted everywhere. 'Come on, then, tell me their Latin names.'

'I don't want to bore you. I'd certainly bore myself.' He breathed in deeply. 'Doesn't it smell marvellously fresh out here! Sometimes at school, stuck in that muggy atmosphere of chalk and lunch-time stew and stale boy, I close my eyes and try to remember exactly how this garden smells. Or I listen hard, blocking out the drone of masters and the crude whispers of all the chaps, and hear blackbirds and thrushes and the soft rustle of leaves.'

'You don't like school?'

'No, I hate it. The lessons are interesting sometimes, but I don't like being cooped up with all the others. You never get any time when you can be on your own, and yet it somehow feels lonely too, even though you're rushing around in great groups all the time and sleep surrounded by other chaps snoring. Did you like school?'

'Some of it. I liked learning, but I detested all the

silly rules. I felt lonely too. I had a friend, a very good friend in many ways, but I couldn't really talk to her – not about things that are really important.'

'Do you still see her now?'

'She's not allowed to see me,' I said. 'I suppose your mother's told you of my circumstances?'

'Yes, she has,' said Morgan, a little uncomfortably. 'I think you're jolly brave. I believe you were unhappy when you first came to work at Fairy Glen?'

'I was in the fondant room at first. It was so *boring* doing the same thing all the time and I couldn't get on with the other girls.'

'Those girls! Mother insists I come to the factory every now and then, as I suppose I'll be in charge some time in the future. They're so bold. They call all kinds of things after me. It's kindly meant, but I always go bright scarlet and then Mother laughs at me, which makes it worse. But you're happier now you're the chief designer?'

'I'm not really. I just do my fairies. They're not great art or anything – they're very whimsical.'

'Mother's shown me. I think they're brilliant, and so does she. She's shrewd enough to realize you're a tremendous asset to Fairy Glen – I can quite see why she's taken you under her wing.'

'She's been wonderful to me,' I said. 'I admire her tremendously.'

'Me too,' said Morgan. 'She's always been the most

terrific mother. I suppose she's spoiled me rotten. She didn't just read me *The Jungle Book*, or the King Arthur stories, or *Treasure Island* – she'd play the games with me too. She'd fashion me wonderful outfits. I was Mowgli in bathing drawers, or a medieval knight in knitted chain mail and a wooden sword, or a pirate with a kerchief round my head and a toy parrot on my shoulder.'

I was silent, trying to imagine my mother indulging me similarly.

'Then we'd make up our own imaginary games. They were the best. We played endlessly in the garden. It was our own fairyland, and we had to make our way from the house to the very end hedge without being spotted by the fire-breathing dragon who hid in the densest rhododendron bush, or the giant six-headed water snake who might rear up out of the stream and strike at us with six forked tongues.'

'Goodness, didn't this give you nightmares when you were little?'

'Yes, you're absolutely right. I never woke up my nanny, who slept in the room next to me. I always pattered downstairs and along the corridor to find Mother. Whenever I curled up with her I felt safe. That was all long ago, of course. I was sent away to school when I was seven. It came as a bit of a shock.'

'I don't think I could ever bear to send my child away to school – if I were a lady I mean, and rich enough to do so. Though I'm not going to have any children because I'm never getting married,' I declared. I blushed because it sounded so shrill and ridiculous.

'I thought all girls wanted to get married and have children,' said Morgan. 'Not that I really *know* any girls – just cousins, and sisters of chaps at school. They all seem like identical dolls, very pretty but rather terrifying, with blank china faces and staring glass eyes. But you're not like a doll at all, Opal. You're the most real girl I've ever met. We can talk properly, and you've got stuff to say too. You don't giggle or try to flirt.'

'I don't know how to, even though I've watched my sister Cassie at it long enough. She is a world expert.'

'And what does Cassie do? She doesn't work in the factory too, does she?'

I hesitated. 'No. She did have an apprenticeship at a milliner's. She's very good at sewing, but I'm not sure she's continuing.'

'Why, what is she going to do now?'

I knew Mother would die if I told anyone, but I wanted Morgan to know everything.

'I think she's an artist's model,' I admitted.

'Oh I say, how splendid,' said Morgan.

'Don't tell your mother, though. It's not very respectable. My own mother is horrified. She wants nothing more to do with Cassie, though she was always her favourite.'

'You weren't the favourite, then?'

'No, certainly not with Mother. Father used to be fond of me – he encouraged me with my book learning – but I think he secretly preferred Cassie too, because she's so pretty and beguiling. I've never been anyone's favourite.' I blushed again because now I sounded so pathetically self-pitying.

'Well, you're my favourite girl,' said Morgan, taking my hand again.

We meandered up and down the paths. I didn't learn a single Latin name for any plant, but Morgan pointed out various trees, including a quaintly named handkerchief tree and a monkey-puzzle. He showed me a nuthatch, a tiny wren, and a green woodpecker. The only bird I saw first with my short sight was a black-and-white magpie.

'Look for a second one,' said Morgan. 'Don't you know that old magpie rhyme – *One for sorrow, two for joy*?'

I peered until my eyes watered but couldn't spot another magpie. I didn't care. I felt as if I'd seen a whole flock of magpies because my heart was so full of joy.

We ended up in the little Japanese summerhouse. The wooden seat inside was cold and damp after days of rain, but the elephant was voluminous enough to cushion me, and I'd have sat on a bed of nails so long as I had Morgan beside me.

'Mother got carried away with this whole Japanese thing,' he told me. 'She used to conduct her own version of the tea ceremony, with little jade-green bowls decorated with fish. Blue carp are the Japanese symbol for boys, so I liked them well enough, but I can't say I ever enjoyed that traditional green tea. It's definitely an acquired taste. And I was always far too fidgety to kneel in the authentic way.'

'Your mother's so full of amazing ideas.'

'Yes, she is, but she tends to get almost too passionately absorbed – in me, in the garden, in the running of the factory, in the suffrage movement. That worries me particularly. You know she went to prison for demonstrating?'

'Twice. I think that's incredible,' I said.

'The second time nearly killed her. She went on hunger strike, and so they force-fed her. She still has deep scars inside her mouth from where those monstrous wardresses prised her lips open. She was desperately frail when she was released. She couldn't eat properly for weeks. You go to these meetings with her, Opal. Don't let her get carried away. If she goes to prison a third time, it will truly finish her.'

'I'll try, but I can't really tell her what to do.'

'I don't know about that. Mother says you're very opinionated and outspoken.'

'Oh dear, that makes me sound dreadful.'

'I think you're splendid. How old are you, Opal – only fourteen?'

'Nearly fifteen.'

'I think you're amazing for your age. I was absolutely hopeless when I was fourteen. I lounged about and mumbled at people because I didn't have a clue what to say. Still do, sometimes. But it's different with you.'

'It's different with you too.'

I couldn't quite believe this was actually happening. It was as if I were imagining Morgan, making him up in my head. It was all so easy, so extraordinary.

We sat in the little Japanese house for the rest of the afternoon, talking the whole time. When Morgan eventually summoned Mitchell to take me home in the car, he said he would come too, to keep me company.

'You don't have to. Please don't,' I said, suddenly worried that Morgan would be horrified by my ordinary, shabby terraced house. It was a whole world away from the charms of Fairy Glen. But he insisted on coming all the same.

When Mitchell drew up outside my house, Morgan just seemed calmly interested.

'So which one is your room, Opal?' he said, peering out at the lace-curtained windows.

'It's at the back. It's the little box room. It's not much more than a cupboard.'

'I bet it's full of books and paintings,' said Morgan.

'Yes, it is.'

Mitchell cleared his throat, indicating that it was time for me to go.

'I *have* enjoyed meeting you,' said Morgan. 'We can meet up again these holidays, can't we?'

'Yes, I'd like that. Very much.'

We smiled at each other. Morgan took my hand again and squeezed it. It was difficult to let go. We just sat there until Mitchell glanced round, clearly wondering why I was waiting.

I jumped out and walked to my front door. I heard the car revving up and departing as I fumbled for my key. When I looked back, it was already at the end of the street. I waved, even so. Then the car turned the corner and disappeared, and again I had that weird feeling that it had never been there at all. Had I made it all up? This couldn't really be happening to me, could it?

25

Mother certainly thought I was making it all up. I tried to tell her that I had spent the afternoon with Morgan Roberts and that he was the most extraordinary young man I'd ever met, but she actually put her hands over her ears.

'Don't you start this wicked nonsense too, Opal. I had enough lying from your sister to last me a lifetime,' she said.

'But it's true, Mother, really. We got on splendidly. He wants to see me again. I swear it's true.'

'You're telling me that Mrs Roberts' son, the one who will inherit the factory, is interested in *you*?' she said.

Her tone was so scathing that I gave up and rushed to my room. All right, I wouldn't say another word to Mother, not if she was going to insult me. I didn't want to talk about Morgan to her, anyway. She would somehow spoil it all even if she did begin to believe me.

I was desperate to confide in someone, though, so the next day I went to Hurst Road. Cassie was actually dressed this time, in a curious black satin smock patterned with big red poppies.

'Do you like it, Opie? Isn't it artistic? I embroidered all these poppies myself. I fashioned myself a smock because Daniel said he would give me painting lessons. Don't laugh – I know I'm not really good at art like you, but I thought it might be fun to try my hand at painting portraits. I have this idea of painting a nude of Daniel. After all, he's painted many of me now. But would you believe it, he utterly refuses to pose, even when I suggested a little loincloth to preserve his modesty. And this smock has turned out so prettily, perhaps it would be a shame to get it all covered in paint . . .

'Do come and see Daniel's Venus portrait of me. He's going to show it at the Academy. Just fancy, all of fashionable London peering at my nether regions!

Daniel's busy working up a portrait of some dull old duchess. He didn't really want the commission at all, but he says he needs the money to keep me in the style to which I've rapidly become accustomed! He's such a tease, but a dear, dear man. I couldn't be happier, Opie. I'm so in love.'

Cassie burbled on and on like that. It was quite a while before I could get a word in edgeways.

'I think it's happened to me too!' I blurted out eventually.

'What's happened to you, Opie? Oh, let me show you the hat I've made – a true Easter bonnet. I don't need to finish my boring old apprenticeship. I can make better hats than old Madame Alouette herself.' She showed me a mad concoction of tulle and straw covered in a veritable garden of silk flowers.

'Mmm, yes. It's lovely,' I said. 'But listen, Cassie. It's quite extraordinary – I never thought it would happen to me in a million years, but I think . . . I think I've fallen in love.'

'What?' I had Cassie's full attention at last. 'Not with Freddy?'

'No! Of course not. No, I think I've fallen in love with Morgan Roberts.' I said the name slowly and proudly, but Cassie looked blank.

'Who's he when he's at home?'

'Mrs Roberts' son. Mrs Roberts who owns the factory.'

'Oh goodness. So she has a boy?'

'He's not a boy. He's eighteen. He'll be going to Oxford this autumn.'

'Eighteen's far too old for you,' said Cassie.

'Cass! Daniel's much, much, much older than you,' I said.

'Yes, but I'm not still a little girl.'

'Meaning I am?' I said indignantly.

'Don't go all hoity-toity. You're ever so clever and talented, blah blah blah, but you're still terribly young and naïve when it comes to romance. What's actually happened with this Morgan boy? Do you just have a pash on him?'

'We had lunch and then spent the entire afternoon together,' I said.

'Where?'

'At Fairy Glen, Mrs Roberts' house.'

'Oh, I *see*. Don't you think he was just being sweet because his mother's taken such a shine to you?'

'No I don't. Why do you have to be so horrible? Don't you believe that anyone could ever be interested in me? You're just like Mother,' I said, fighting back tears.

'Oh, Opie, don't be so upset. I just don't want you to be hurt. You're so intense. And even if this Morgan is a bit interested in you, it's not going to go anywhere, is it?'

'Why not?'

'Because he's a gentleman who will own a huge great factory and have pots of money, and you're just a girl who *works* in the factory, and you've got a father who's in prison and a mother who's a babyminder and a sister who's an artist's model and living in sin,' said Cassie. 'I somehow think you're not Mrs Roberts' number-one choice for her son.'

I went flouncing off home in a huff. Perhaps I felt so upset because Cassie was probably right. I wished I'd kept my mouth shut now. Maybe I'd made a fool of myself. I tried to go over every nuance of the afternoon I'd spent with Morgan. Was he simply treating me like a bright child?

I spent Sunday night in turmoil, and had a splitting headache on Monday morning when I had to trudge to the factory. For the first time in weeks I had no inspiration whatsoever when it came to inventing new fairies for my deluxe specials. I sat sighing and stretching, stirring my paint water and fiddling with my brushes.

'You'd better not let Mr Morgan see you like that,' said Alice, the girl who had taken over from Miss Lily.

'Mr Morgan?' I said.

'The boss's son, dopey. He's come to work with his mother today and I dare say he'll be doing the rounds, peering here and there. Mrs R likes him to take an interest, seeing as it will all belong to him one day.'

'Oh my goodness, *that* Morgan!'

'Mister to you. He was Master Morgan until he was fifteen or so, but we have to call him Mister now, though he's not much more than a lad.'

It was a shock to think that Morgan might be only a few yards down the corridor. It gave a jolt to my inventive powers. I applied myself to the meadow design, inventing two magpie fairies joyously racing their birds through the air. I turned an ordinary bush into an azalea with its own flock of fairies flying above it, decked in the brightest pinks and purples. I was so absorbed that I jumped when Mrs Roberts suddenly came into the room, Morgan following.

'Good morning, ladies. Good to see you all hard at work,' said Mrs Roberts. She went across to Alice and started murmuring. Morgan looked around, saw me, and came straight over.

'Hello! Do let me see,' he said. He bent over my box lid. 'Ah, magpies. Two for joy! And azalea fairies. I wonder where you got that idea?'

I felt my face glow fiery red.

Morgan smiled. 'They're wonderful. Do you realize how popular your fairy range is?'

I shrugged, embarrassed.

'I've just been going over the books with Mother. Your boxes have done astronomically well. They're outselling the ordinary deluxe range by three to one, even though they're a shilling dearer.'

'Really?'

'Truly. And I can see why. Mother will have to get a full set of your box lids, frame them and put them up on the wall beside her own Anster Fitzgerald fairy paintings. I think you're better than him.'

Mrs Roberts came over to us. She smiled at me, but there was something a little chilly in her expression. 'Come and see the other girls' work, Morgan,' she said. 'They're all doing splendidly.'

Morgan raised his eyebrows at me, but said blandly enough, 'Of course, Mother.'

He wandered off obediently and murmured praise to everyone, but before he left he looked back at me and gave me a little wave.

'Oh, look at you, sucking up to the boss,' said Alice sourly.

I took no notice. I went on painting, but in my heart I was flying through the air with my fairies.

I hoped Morgan might come into the factory every day during his holidays, but he didn't put in another appearance that week. However, on Friday I received a card in the post. It was a comical picture of the Venus de Milo, with one onlooker saying to another, 'I suppose it was them suffragettes who hacked off her arms.' On the back it said, *Dear Opal, Don't get too carried away at your meeting. I'm looking forward to seeing you at lunch afterwards. Your friend, Morgan.*

'So who's this Morgan, then?' said Mother, frowning.

'Don't read my personal post, Mother! I told you all about Morgan. You simply chose not to believe me.'

'Is he *really* the factory owner's son?'

I didn't want to discuss him now. I wanted to keep the knowledge to myself. I read my postcard's little message twenty times. I even tried copying the fine italic handwriting, so much more stylish than my clerk's copperplate.

On Saturday morning I took immense trouble with my appearance, trying on and then discarding all my clothes. I couldn't wear my usual elephant, it was just too gross, yet my tartan was garish and made me look sallow. I wished Cassie were home to help me.

I went to her room and inspected the clothes still in her wardrobe. It looked as if she'd abandoned them for ever. I tried on a cream dress with a matching jacket. It had violets embroidered on the lapels to match a purple material belt. It had been Cassie's best summer outfit until she bought the green dress.

It was a cool spring day, not sunny at all, but I decided to wear the cream outfit because it was the prettiest. It would spoil the whole effect if I covered it up with my old coat. I decided I didn't mind if I shivered.

'Oh my Lord, you look as if you're going to a wedding and trying to outdo the bride,' said Mother.

I chose to ignore her, though all the way to the meeting I peered in shop windows, wondering if this were true. Certainly, most of the WSPU ladies were in business-like suits or plain white blouses worn with a purple and green striped tie. I told myself I didn't care.

Mrs Roberts was right at the front with the two guest speakers. She hadn't reserved a chair for me, but it didn't matter. I was happy enough sitting at the back. I would join her when the meeting was over.

It went on for a very long time. Both speakers praised Mary Richardson and her attack on the Rokeby Venus, glorying in the coverage it had received. I was alarmed to hear them suggesting further damage to art treasures. When one of the ladies suggested attacking every Venus painting in galleries all over England, there was a rousing cheer.

The meeting ended with a panel discussion with the two speakers, the president of our local WSPU, two ladies in very grand hats and Mrs Roberts – the latter three were clearly generous benefactors to the cause. Many women in the audience put up their hands to ask questions. Not all were one hundred per cent supportive of WSPU action. One lady seemed worried about the escalating violence, anxious that someone might get badly hurt or even killed during future demonstrations.

'How about our poor sister Emily Davison, who was trampled to death under the King's horse last year at Epsom? And think of all the desperately abused suffragettes in prison as we speak, tortured by force-feeding,' said the president. She went on to outline in grisly detail what this entailed. I felt great pity and sympathy, but surely this wasn't quite the point.

I listened and listened. None of the other ladies stood up to ask anything further, so I found my own hand waving in the air.

'Yes, right at the back? Oh, it's Opal, our youngest member,' said the president. 'Speak up, dear.'

'Of course I agree that the suffering of the suffragettes is terrible – but they are in a way self-imposed,' I said. 'And though I feel that all these women are incredibly courageous, their actions are surely ineffective.'

There was a huge surge of shock and horror at my words. All the ladies craned their heads round to stare at me.

'I don't think you can say they're not effective when these actions make newspaper headlines,' said the president, shaking her head at me.

'Yes, but they haven't achieved the goal of women's suffrage. A woman has given her *life*, but that's still not given us the vote. Our members are being tortured in prison, but that hasn't given us the vote, either. Miss Richardson has damaged one of the most beautiful masterpieces in the world, and that *still* hasn't given us the vote. The general public have been against women having the vote from the start of our campaign. That's terribly depressing and shows ignorance and indifference – but we haven't been able to change public opinion with our escalating campaign. Surely if we continue to destroy masterpieces, then history will look on us as we do the vandals in the past who destroyed all our medieval religious statues. Don't you see the inherent danger of our motto, *Deeds, not words*? Can't we achieve the vote by the persuasiveness of our tongues rather than the violence of our axes?'

Mrs Roberts stood up, her face flushed. 'I think it would be more sensible to hold your tongue, Opal, than expose your own ignorance of the cause,' she said. 'Now, do we have any more questions?'

I was left publicly snubbed, with no one taking up my points and debating them with me. The ladies on either side of me edged as far away as possible, as if scared I might contaminate them. I sat there trembling, going over my speech in my head, trying to understand why it had upset everyone so dreadfully. I had been rather forthright, perhaps too outspoken as a young newcomer to meetings. There were lots of points I didn't understand properly. I hadn't had to endure the horrors of force-feeding myself, but surely I could still offer a valid point of view . . .

At the end of the meeting the ladies gathered for their tea and biscuits, still giving me disapproving glances. Miss Mountbank came sweeping up, her hawk nose quivering.

'I see you haven't changed at all, Opal Plumstead,' she said witheringly. 'As full of yourself as ever, saying the most outrageous things simply to draw attention to yourself.'

I didn't want to waste my time arguing with Mounty. I pushed my way through the women until I reached Mrs Roberts, who was still at the front.

'Mrs Roberts,' I said, putting my hand on her sleeve. 'I'm so sorry. I didn't deliberately try to be controversial. You know what I'm like. I often say things out loud without thinking them through. I thought any opinion was valid during a discussion. I didn't mean to embarrass or upset you. I promise I won't open my mouth at meetings again.' I said it as humbly and sincerely as I could, but she still looked at me coldly.

'I think you'd better run along now, Opal. I am busy talking,' she said firmly.

'Shall I wait outside with Mitchell and the car?'

She stared at me. 'Why on earth would you do that?'

'Why, because . . . because we'll be taking the car to Fairy Glen for lunch,' I stammered.

'Not today.'

'But Mrs Roberts . . .' I didn't know how to continue. 'Surely this isn't because I asked that question? I didn't mean to offend you – you must know that.'

'This is nothing to do with your behaviour this morning. I simply have other plans for today. Remember, my son is home for the holidays.'

'But Morgan said he was looking forward to seeing me today,' I said.

She flinched. 'I'm sure *Mr* Morgan was simply being polite,' she said. 'Now run along.'

I trailed home, so burning with humiliation that I wasn't even chilly in my light cream dress. Had Mrs Roberts suddenly turned on me because I'd embarrassed her at the meeting? Or had she never planned to include me today? I'd got into the habit of going home with her after meetings – I'd taken it for granted. Perhaps it had been terribly forward of me to assume an automatic invitation. But Morgan himself had invited me by implication, surely. I couldn't have mistaken the message on his postcard. *Was* he simply being polite, sending a kind but meaningless message to an eager child? I was so wretched I nearly started sobbing in the street. It was worse when I got home because Mother wondered what I was doing there and asked all kinds of intrusive questions.

'Why aren't you off for lunch with your high and mighty friends? I thought Mrs Roberts always asked you home nowadays. And what's happening with this son of hers? I thought he was meant to be your special pal. Have they got tired of you already?' She went on and on until I wanted to scream.

I went up to my room, took off the cream dress and threw myself down on my bed in my petticoat. I wanted to cry, but I was burning too much. I couldn't let go and allow tears. I lay banging my head on the pillow. I tried to go over all my conversations with Morgan, starting to wish I had never met him. If this was love, I had been wise to be wary of it.

I lay there for a long time, and then I was dimly aware of a knocking at the front door. I thought it must be some young woman with yet another baby for Mother to mind, so I stayed on my bed. Then Mother herself came rushing into my room.

'For goodness' sake, Opal, what are you doing lying there? And in your petticoat! Get yourself dressed at once.'

'Why should I?' I said wearily.

'Because your Mr Morgan Roberts is downstairs, wanting to see you!'

'*What?*' I struggled up, wondering if Mother might be playing a cruel trick on me, but one glance at her flustered face told me she was telling the truth.

'Oh my Lord!'

'Do hurry! I can't leave him down there on his own. Well, there's Maudie's child rioting around, but he's hardly company. Be as quick as you can. I don't know what to say to him. Why didn't you tell me he might come?'

'I didn't think he would for one minute. Oh glory, all my hair's tumbling down, and where did I kick my boots to?'

'Hurry!' Mother hissed, and went back downstairs again.

'I am hurrying,' I said, pulling on my dress and trying to do it up. My hands were trembling, which made it difficult. Morgan here! But, oh my Lord, was he simply wanting to tell me off roundly for upsetting his beloved mother? At this thought I was all set to rip my dress off again and cast myself back on my bed, but I couldn't leave Mother in charge.

I tidied myself as best I could, tied my hair back in a childish plait with a cream ribbon because it kept sliding out of its topknot, and then pressed a cold flannel over my hot face.

I walked downstairs in a flurry of anxiety and went into the parlour. There was Morgan sitting on the sofa, giving the baby a ride on his knee. The child was in a paroxysm of delight, gurgling so much that a stream of saliva drooled onto Morgan's fine trousers – but he was still smiling. Smiling at *me*.

'Hello, Opal. My, that's a lovely dress. Are you ready for some lunch?'

'You're very welcome to have lunch here, sir,' said Mother, practically bobbing him a curtsy.

I prayed Morgan wouldn't accept out of politeness – all we had was a pot of vegetable barley soup, yesterday's bread and a morsel of mousetrap cheese.

'That's so kind of you, Mrs Plumstead, but I've made plans to take Opal to The Royal for lunch. If that's all right with you, of course?'

'Oh my, yes, certainly, sir,' said Mother. 'You lucky girl, Opal.'

I wished she would keep quiet and stop calling Morgan 'sir', but I couldn't possibly frown at her. I even found myself smiling at the dribbling baby.

'I'm ready, Morgan,' I said.

'Excellent,' he said, gently dislodging the child. 'Excuse me, my little man. Your horsey has to trot away to be fed.'

We said goodbye to Mother.

'Aren't you wearing a coat? It's a bit chilly today,' said Morgan.

'I'm very warm,' I said, truthfully enough. I was positively glowing.

'I'm afraid we'll have to walk into town. I didn't feel I could use Mitchell under the circumstances,' said Morgan as we went out of the front door.

'The circumstances . . .?' I said.

'Oh, Mother and I had a little dispute,' he said casually.

'Over . . .?'

'Over you, of course. There I was, waiting eagerly

at home, with all kinds of plans, but Mother comes back alone. I look around for you and she tells me that she didn't invite you, she thinks we will have a much cosier time just the two of us.'

'Oh dear. I think she's very angry with me because I said something untoward at the meeting and upset everyone.'

'So I hear. But I think Mother made up her mind not to invite you long before the meeting. Our dining table was only set for two people, Mother and me. She suggested we spend the afternoon going through a whole load of old photographs to stick in some tedious book. I thought, *What do I really* want *to do?* So I'm afraid Mother will be lunching alone and sticking her photographs in by herself.'

'Goodness. Oh, Morgan, I don't want to make trouble for you. Your mother will be very upset,' I said anxiously.

'She'll be fine,' he told me. 'I have to make a stand every now and then. She forgets that I'm not still a little boy. She wants to take me over and organize my life. I can't let her do that.'

'It's probably because you mean so much to her. I expect you became very close after your father died.'

'Mother has always felt particularly close to me – stiflingly so, if I'm honest,' said Morgan. 'As far as I remember, it was always Mother and me, with Father scarcely getting a look in.'

'You should be grateful that your mother is so very fond of you,' I said. 'And she's been exceptionally kind to me.'

'I dare say,' said Morgan, 'but I'm not sure she's feeling exceptionally kind towards you at the moment. She feels you might be trying to lure me away.'

'Oh, that's ridiculous,' I said, blushing.

'I hope you don't think it's too ridiculous,' said Morgan. 'I'm doing my level best to lure you. I say, you're shivering.'

'No I'm not,' I declared stoutly.

'We'll find a cab when we get to the main road. I took one to your house to get me there as quickly as possible. I should have hung onto it. You must be feeling desperately hungry too. Don't worry, Opal. In fifteen minutes we'll be sitting in a warm restaurant ordering a lovely lunch.'

Morgan was as good as his word. The Royal Hotel was every bit as delightful as I'd imagined. I was worried that I wouldn't know what to do or how to order, but he was wondrously tactful, whisking me past the supercilious head waiter, making sure I was comfortably seated, and talking me through the menu.

I became fixated on the word *honeydew*. It sounded heavenly, a meal suitable for my own fairies. I had no idea what honeydew would look or taste like, but I knew I wanted it desperately. There were all kinds of meat and fish to choose from, many that I'd never tasted before. I decided to ask for roast chicken, a tremendous treat.

'Perfect choice,' said Morgan. 'I'll have exactly the same.'

I was privately disappointed by my first glimpse of honeydew. It was a big watery fruit with a yellow rind. It tasted delicious, however, so I spooned it up hungrily. The chicken was even better, golden-skinned with succulent white flesh. We had chicken every Christmas (except this last one, when we'd had to make do with cheaper pork chops). But this chicken was served with bread sauce, roast potatoes, and a whole medley of vegetables.

When I'd finally cleared my plate, I was full and said I didn't want any pudding.

'Oh, you must have something! Don't worry, I'm not going to force you to have a large helping of roly-poly. I don't want you walking bent over all afternoon. How about something light? I know – raspberry meringues!'

They were quite marvellous: pale pink meringues with dark red cream. Each one disappeared in three mouthfuls.

'This has to be the best meal of my life,' I said.

'Me too,' said Morgan, though I was sure he'd eaten at any number of fine restaurants.

I caught a glimpse of the bill. It terrified me. There

hadn't been any prices on the menu. I'd known it would be expensive – at least twice the price of a Lyon's Cornerhouse meal – but this was astronomical.

'Oh my goodness! I didn't think it would be that much!' I gasped.

'Please don't worry, Opal. I've got more than enough on me, I promise,' said Morgan.

'Are you sure? I mean, you don't yet have a salary.'

'I have a generous allowance.' Morgan looked a little uncomfortable. 'Too generous. I should think it might make you despise me. You have to work so very hard and I just swan around in the holidays and do nothing very much. I don't even work that hard at school – not unless the lessons really interest me. Yet I shall waltz off to Oxford for three years, then stroll into the factory and take over. It's not at all fair, is it? Not fair on all the workers beavering away for very little.'

'You sound like one of those trade union people. They keep giving out leaflets outside Fairy Glen,' I said.

'Well, my heart's on their side but my head doesn't want them to have too much power, for obvious reasons. You don't want to join a trade union, do you, Opal?'

'I don't seem to be any good at joining anything. It looks as if I'll be drummed out of the WSPU unless I learn to keep my mouth shut. Oh dear, I'm still worried about your mother, Morgan. I think you'd better go back home straight away now we've had our lovely lunch.'

'I'm not going to do that. We're going to spend the rest of the day together. Where would you like to go? Why don't you show me all your favourite haunts? I want to find out about little-girl Opal.'

So we went for the strangest walk around the town together. Morgan carefully walked on my outside, offering me his arm. It was extraordinarily enjoyable to stroll along together. I was acutely aware that people were looking at us because Morgan cut such a fine figure and I didn't look too much of a disgrace in my cream lace. I *was* too cold, though, and when Morgan saw that I was shivering he took me straight to Beade and Chambers, the biggest department store in the town. I had sometimes wandered through with Cassie or Olivia, but I'd never actually bought anything.

'Why are we going in here?' I asked.

'I'm going to find you something to keep you warm,' said Morgan. 'The ladies' accessories are this way.'

'How do you know?'

'Oh goodness, I trotted around after Mother many a time when I was a little boy.'

The shop assistants clearly knew who Morgan was and bobbed their heads at him. It seemed so strange that I wouldn't be considered refined enough to work at Beade and Chambers, and yet here I was, shopping at my leisure with Mr Morgan Roberts.

I thought he might be considering buying me a muffler or maybe mittens, and I longed for this, even though I had a perfectly sensible muffler and mittens at home. But to my astonishment he smiled charmingly at the assistant behind the counter and said, 'We're looking for a cashmere shawl. It would be perfect if you had one in cream, to match the young lady's outfit.'

'Not a *shawl*, Morgan. And especially not cashmere. It'll be far too expensive,' I whispered in his ear.

But he insisted, choosing the finest they had, a wonderfully soft, luxuriously large shawl in a pale cream. It was a totally impractical garment because it would show the dirt dreadfully, but that made it even more glamorous. It was indeed dreadfully expensive, but Morgan still signed the cheque with a flourish. It made me feel very special. Of course, if I stopped to consider, it wasn't really Morgan's money because he wasn't earning yet. It was Mrs Roberts' money – which came from the factory. I worked for the factory. My fairy boxes were a big success, so I suppose a tiny percentage of the money came from *me*. It made it just a little easier to say yes. The assistant asked if we'd like the shawl wrapped or sent to a particular address.

'No, thank you. The lady is wearing it now – that's

the whole point,' said Morgan. He took the shawl and wrapped it very carefully and competently about my neck and shoulders.

Then we stepped back outside in style. We wandered around the town together. It seemed as if my own elfin creatures had sprinkled their fairy dust over the familiar dreary buildings. I told Morgan tales of trips to this shop and that. I even told him the story of poor Mother being ill in the butcher's shop and losing her job.

Morgan told me about his own excursions into town. He was kitted out at the saddler's when he got his first pony at the age of six. He used to delve into the sacks of dried apricots and figs at the grocer's when he accompanied the cook. He'd chosen *Treasure Island* and *The Swiss Family Robinson* and *King Solomon's Mines* from the bookshop near the park.

'My father used to take me to that bookshop to choose my birthday present,' I said. 'And then we'd go to the park and sit on a bench together and I'd read him the first chapter.'

Morgan and I went to that very park and walked down its small sandy paths and grassy slopes. The crocuses were out, cheerful clumps of colour in the green grass. We sat on a bench by the pond and watched two mothers help their children feed the ducks with bread scraps. We'd both loved to do that when we were little.

'I wonder if there was ever a day when I was six or so and a tiny Opal of two was standing beside me, flinging her bread to the wind,' said Morgan.

'Flinging herself in after the bread and being taken home dripping wet and in disgrace,' I said, laughing.

The only memory I did not share was the one of Father and me sitting on that bench together last autumn, when he was so late home from work. He hadn't told me what had happened, though I'd sensed something was very wrong. It seemed so long ago now. I still loved Father with all my heart and missed him dreadfully. I worried about him every day, but somehow I didn't feel quite so connected with him any more. So much had happened since he'd been sent to prison. So many sad and difficult things – yet today I was happier than I'd ever been in my life.

We walked right round the park and then out again.

'Show me where you went to school, Opal,' Morgan suggested.

'What about you? You must have gone to a little dame school before you were sent away to boarding school. Or did you have a governess?'

'Neither. Mother taught me,' said Morgan. 'Every morning. I would read and write and do simple sums. Mother thought I was a little genius, but it was simply that she'd drummed these lessons into me from the year dot. She bribed me dreadfully.

Whenever I managed a list of simple spellings or read a passage without stumbling, she'd slip me a candy kiss. It's a wonder I still have all my own teeth.'

I showed Morgan my own little dame school, where dear old Miss White had treasured her class of ten and taught us all the basics.

'Were you her little pet?' he asked.

'I *wanted* to be – but a ghastly boy called Cedric was her favourite. She made him a little paper crown and said he was king of the class. He had curly fair hair just like you. It's a wonder I didn't hate you on sight,' I said.

'Was Cedric brighter than you?'

'No, but Miss White thought he was. Still, I was the one who got a scholarship to St Margaret's,' I said proudly.

'I used to know some girls from St Margaret's – daughters of Mother's friends. Annabel and Antonia Mannering. Did you know them? Antonia was younger. Could she have been in your form?'

'Goodness, yes, Antonia was in my form. I'm afraid I didn't like her, either.'

'Because she had fair curly hair?'

'Yes, she was very pretty, but it was mostly because she called me "little swot" and yawned ostentatiously whenever I answered a question in class.'

'How horrible of her!'

'Oh, it wasn't just Antonia – they all did. They

didn't like me because I was poor and studious and a scholarship girl. I can't really blame them. I must've been very annoying.'

'I wouldn't have found you annoying. I'd have thought you endearing – and very brave. Let's walk past St Margaret's and sneer at Antonia and all that poisonous gang of girls,' said Morgan.

They weren't there, of course, because it was the Easter holidays, but their ghostly gym-slipped presence hung about the gaunt grey building. I clasped the iron railings and stared at my school. It was strange remembering how much it had meant to me not very long ago.

'Did you wander the playground all alone, clutching a book?' Morgan asked.

'I had one friend, a dear friend, Olivia,' I said, 'but I don't see her now my circumstances have changed.'

'Are you too proud to be in touch with her?'

'Her wretched mother forbade her to see me ever again!'

'Oh dear, that's mothers for you,' said Morgan with feeling. 'Still, it wasn't very spirited of Olivia not to try to stay friends with you.'

'She wasn't that kind of girl,' I said. 'But we did have fun together. When we walked home from school she always shared her sweets with me – usually Fairy Glen toffee chews!'

'Ah, at least she had good taste.'

'We used to hide from our strict teachers and eat our toffees in the graveyard,' I said. 'I love graveyards. Let's go there now, Morgan. It's beautiful in a strange sort of way.'

'I like graveyards too. They're generally wonderful for spotting wildlife,' he said.

'What about the *after*life? Have you ever seen a ghost?'

'No, but I'd rather like to.'

'I don't believe in ghosts, but I used to torment Olivia, making little keening noises so that she thought a ghost was oozing out from under a tombstone.'

'Perhaps it's no surprise that she didn't stay friends with you!'

'Will you stay friends with me, Morgan?' I said, before I could stop myself.

He looked me straight in the eye. 'I'll always be your friend,' he said seriously.

We wandered around the graveyard together. I admired the angels and read out quaint inscriptions on the tombstones. Morgan identified birdsong and wild flowers, and spotted a fox skulking in the shadows. Then he pointed in the same matter-of-fact way and said, 'There's my father.'

'What?' I said, startled.

'Over there – the big obelisk.'

It was the most ornate tomb in the whole cemetery,

new and stark and rather ugly, made of a mottled liver-coloured stone that didn't blend in with the white marble angels around it.

I went up to it and traced the engraving – JOHN JOSEPH ROBERTS, with his dates. It didn't say 'devoted husband' or 'beloved father', and there were no gentle messages like 'rest in peace', or 'sleep for ever'.

It seemed a strange choice for Mrs Roberts, who always had exquisite taste.

'My father chose it,' said Morgan, as if he could read my mind.

'Your father chose his own *tomb*?'

'My father had to be in charge at all times, even when he was dying. He had pleurisy and lingered a while. While he could still make decisions, he planned his entire funeral and designed his tomb.'

'He sounds an extraordinary man. Do you miss him very much?'

'Not at all, if I'm honest. I was rather afraid of him. I think it's obvious I was always a mother's boy. I don't think Mother grieved much for him, either. She'd always been very meek and under his thumb, but she certainly came into her own after his death. No one expected her to keep the factory, let alone run it, but she's done a grand job.'

'I admire her tremendously,' I said. I was very worried that she was displeased with me now. She would be downright angry that Morgan had chosen to be with me the entire afternoon. I shivered.

'Oh dear, we should've bought you two shawls,' said Morgan, tucking my cashmere more closely around me. 'Graveyards are always freezing cold. Let's go and find somewhere we can get warm.'

'You should go home. Your mother will be worried about you.'

'Opal, I'm eighteen. I can do as I wish. And you're the sort of girl who does as she wishes too. We are free spirits.'

'Free spirits,' I agreed.

We started running around the tombstones to get warm, laughing and shrieking. If there *were* any ghosts palely loitering, we must have frightened them away.

Morgan took me back to the Royal Hotel and ordered a glass of wine for me and a whisky for himself. We sat in a delightful little side room, almost like our own small parlour, with a velvet sofa and a roaring fire in the grate.

'This is splendid, Morgan,' I said, sipping cautiously.

I already felt light-headed. I didn't want to get completely drunk and make a fool of myself. Morgan ordered another whisky, but I still had half a glass of wine left and refused any more. After we had been there for an hour or so, Morgan suggested we have something to eat. I was still full from the delicious chicken lunch, but Morgan asked for cake and a pot of tea. A waiter brought us Madeira cake studded with red cherries, and strangely fragrant tea.

Morgan spotted a little cupboard and discovered that it was full of games – packs of cards, dominoes, even spillikins. So we played, sometimes inventing our own rules, but keeping strict count of who won each individual game. I won first, then Morgan, then Morgan again, and then *I* won.

It was getting late by this time – really late – but we decided to have one more game to choose the overall winner.

'And what will the prize be?' I wondered.

'A kiss,' said Morgan.

'Very well,' I said, as casually as I could, though I felt dizzy at the suggestion.

We played with a child's pack of Snap. The game went on for a long time, with much to-ing and fro-ing of cards, but I managed to win.

'Then you get the prize, Miss Plumstead,' said Morgan. He leaned towards me and kissed me. I thought he would simply brush my cheek, but he kissed me on the lips. It was a quick kiss, over in a second, but it was a real kiss. I knew I'd remember that moment for the rest of my life.

Morgan insisted on walking me home.

'But now you still have to get all the way back to your house, and it's miles away. Have you got enough money left for another cab?' I asked, aware that

Morgan had spent an enormous amount already.

'I have heaps of cash, don't worry,' he said, but I wasn't sure he was telling the truth now. He saw I was looking anxious. 'I shall probably run home.'

'*Run?*'

'I'm a good runner – honestly. I do five miles cross-country every week at school. I don't want to sound as if I'm boasting, but I generally come in the first three. And when we go on manoeuvres with the officer cadets, we often run ten miles, and that's lugging heavy equipment.'

'You're a soldier?'

'Not a real one. We all have to do army training at school. I hate it – all the barking orders and pointless discipline. I hate the whole idea of killing people too. I'd never fight in a real war.'

'Neither would I!'

'We have so much in common, Opal.'

We had very little in common. He was eighteen and looked like a man. I was now just fifteen and still looked like a little girl, in spite of all my efforts. He was very handsome and I was very homely-looking. He came from a wonderful artistic background and I was a factory girl with a disgraced family. He was very rich and I was very poor. Yet somehow Morgan was right. We were soul mates.

26

Morgan went back to school the following weekend. I didn't see him again until the summer, but I wrote to him and he wrote to me. We often wrote a letter a day, page after page. I kept his letters in my fondant fairy box. Quite soon I had to fetch another one home from work, and then another. I kept the letters in careful order, and went through Cassie's drawers for thin blue ribbon to tie them up neatly. I tied specially elaborate bows so that I would be able to tell if Mother had tried to read them. I would have died if she had. It wasn't that there was anything wicked or improper in those letters – they weren't even truly passionate love letters. They were letters in which Morgan bared his soul, telling me all his innermost thoughts and feelings, and I reciprocated one hundred-fold.

I didn't tell anyone at work. I certainly didn't tell Mrs Roberts that Morgan was writing me letters. She was very chilly towards me the first few weeks after he went back to school. She swept straight past me when she inspected the design room and didn't say a word – but she gradually thawed. I didn't go to WSPU meetings any more, so we didn't see each other at weekends, but Mrs Roberts started commenting on my artwork again. When I experimented with new backgrounds for my fairies, she became particularly enthusiastic.

I thought it might be a good idea to have season-specific novelty ranges: a blue and yellow summer seaside scene, with fairies riding tiny white horses on the crests of waves; an orange and brown autumn scene, with fairies and baby squirrels playing ball games with nuts; a red and green Christmas scene, with fairies decorating a great Christmas tree; a pastel spring scene with fairies playing kiss-chase amongst the primroses.

'You're a little marvel, Opal,' Mrs Roberts said. 'We'd better concentrate on the seaside scene for the summer. I'll suggest each girl paints one seaside background every day so that you can embellish them with your fairies.'

I worked extra hard, trying to be newly inventive with each box lid. As soon as the summer seaside scene hit the shops in June, there was an immense demand.

'Perhaps we might try several summer scenes,' said Mrs Roberts. 'We always go to Scotland in the summer. Perhaps you could try a Scottish scene, Opal – misty mountains and deer, and you could give your fairies little tartan dresses and wings.' She laughed at her idea. I wasn't sure if she were being serious or merely fanciful. I could only concentrate on one sentence: *We always go to Scotland in the summer*.

We? Did she mean Morgan too? Why hadn't he told me? Neither of us had specifically mentioned the summer, but I'd made so many plans in my head. I knew that Morgan would be finishing school and not going up to Oxford until October. I'd thought of all those Saturdays and Sundays we might spend together. I had a week's holiday due too. All day long, painting my fairies, I'd planned what we would do. Every night when I went to sleep, I pictured us walking hand in hand, going round art galleries, paddling in streams, picnicking beside a lake, walking along a cliff top . . .

My next letter to Morgan was terse and to the point.

Dear Morgan,

I was talking to your mother at the factory today and she said you always go to Scotland for the summer. Is this really true? Won't you be here at all? Why didn't you tell me?

I usually signed my letter *With great affection, your dear friend Opal*.

I signed this latest letter with just my name.

Morgan's reply was far more effusive, an[illegible] immensely apologetic.

Dearest Opal,

Oh dear, I'm such a coward. I know I should have told you about Scotland ages ago. We have a holiday house there, a converted farmhouse. We still have the farmland too, but this is managed for us. I've been wondering what on earth to do this year. I know Mother loves our Scottish summers – and yet of course I want to spend time with you.

I could simply not go with Mother, but I'm afraid this would upset her dreadfully, even though she has friends up in Scotland and wouldn't be too lonely, I'm sure. But then I'd have to find somewhere to stay. Mother shuts up Fairy Glen for the summer –

dustsheets everywhere – and Mrs Evans and Mitchell and the maids all come to Scotland with us. But this is certainly not insurmountable. Some of the chaps at school don't live too far away, so perhaps I could stay with their folks – or I could stay in a hotel – that would be quite jolly. I know, perhaps I'll stay at The Royal, and every evening you can come and dine with me – on honeydew and roast chicken and raspberry meringues, of course. Then we'll sit in our own little parlour and play games and have a truly splendid time.

I don't think I've ever had such a perfect day as that Saturday we spent together. Didn't we talk and talk and talk! I talk all day to the chaps here, but it's always in the most trivial boring way. We're mostly ragging each other or discussing cricket or telling stupid stories. We don't ever say anything meaningful. And as I told you already, my conversations with other girls have been such nonsense, silly flirtations to make one squirm. You are so different, Opal – closer than a sister.

I stopped reading then. I didn't want him to think of me as a sister! And for all his seeming joy that we could say what we really meant to each other, Morgan seemed artfully evasive in his letter. He indicated he *might* not go to Scotland with his mother, he *might* stay with friends, he *might* stay in a hotel. Why wasn't he more definite? Why couldn't he stay with me? Or indeed, why couldn't I be invited up to Scotland too?

I was being evasive myself. I knew why. Oh, it would be perfectly respectable for a young man to come and stay for the summer in my house. Cassie's room was empty, and Mother would be a vigilant chaperone. I could invite a young man like Freddy and no one would turn a hair. But Morgan was a gentleman. I couldn't imagine him in our house, going out to the privy in the back yard, making do with one bath a week in the old chipped tub, eating bread and dripping for breakfast.

It was even harder imagining Mrs Roberts saying, 'Do come and stay with us for the summer, Opal. Never mind work – you deserve a long holiday. You'll be such a delightful companion for Morgan. I'm so happy the two of you have such a close friendship.'

She clearly hated Morgan and me liking each other. She had been truly kind to me and I'd always be grateful that she'd taken me under her wing and given me my chance in the design room. She had looked after me at WSPU meetings (until I dared question their actions), and invited me for lunch. She'd been so charming and encouraging – until Morgan came home. Then she made it plain that though I might be good enough to be her little protégée, this didn't make me good enough to be friends with her precious son. She wanted me to know my place. I wasn't sure what my place was any more.

I went to see Cassie to ask her advice. She was actually fully dressed this time, in a splendid midnight-blue robe stitched with silver stars.

'My goodness, Cassie, you look amazing. Is this the latest fashion?'

'Of course not, you silly! I made it specially for Daniel's new portrait. I am the Queen of the Night – and look, here are my night jewels.' She lowered the neck of her velvet robe to show me a dazzling blue and white necklace around her beautiful white throat.

'Sapphires and diamonds!' I said.

'Hardly. Daniel's not *that* rich! They're glass. I threaded them myself. I've got glass bead bracelets and anklets to wear too, but I'm not bothering just now because Daniel's painting my top half first. It's a special commission – a thousand pounds, can you believe it! Maybe I'll get a real sapphire or diamond when it's paid for. And do you know why Daniel's got all this work? It's all because of your silly suffragettes. Did you not read about it in the newspaper? Some woman was inspired by the slashing of the Rokeby Venus and went along to the Royal Academy. She saw Daniel's portrait of me and went *hack, hack, hack* with her little axe!'

'Oh no! Was it ruined?'

'Not really. Her axe must have been very blunt. It barely made a mark. Daniel touched it up, and made it as good as new. But it was in the papers, so people flocked to see it – to see *me*, Opie. Daniel's been commissioned to do two more Venuses, which will be a bit of a bore, but he's willing enough. Then this old buffer, rich as Croesus, wants me being the Queen of the Night to hang in his bedroom right above his lordship's bed. He's a *real* lord, Opie – fancy that!'

'Eew! Don't you mind?'

'Of course not. I mean, it's not me in person. Come and have a peep at it. It's truly marvellous. Everyone says Daniel's never painted so well – and it's all because of me.' Cassie paused and flung her hair back dramatically. 'I am his muse,' she declared.

I sighed. I was truly pleased that things were working out well for Cassie, but she was pretty insufferable in this mood.

'Wait a minute, Cass. I want to ask you something. It's about Morgan, Mrs Roberts' son.'

I suddenly had Cassie's full attention.

'I thought you hadn't seen him since Easter . . .'

'I haven't, but we've been writing to each other every day.'

'My goodness, Opal! Every *day*?'

'He writes such wonderful letters.'

'Love letters?'

'Not exactly. They're full of his thoughts, his feelings, his ideas about the books he's reading, his nature observations.'

Cassie wrinkled her nose. 'No lovey-dovey bits at all?'

'He says I mean the whole world to him.'

'Ah, that's better. What does Mrs Roberts have to say about it?'

'She doesn't know.'

'Oh, you sly minx.'

'I don't want to be sly, but she doesn't seem to approve of Morgan and me.'

'I'm not surprised!'

'But the thing is, I'd so hoped to see Morgan this summer before he goes to university, and now I've found out that his mother goes up to Scotland for six whole weeks!'

'And he's going too?'

'Well, he says he'll try to stay here, but he doesn't sound very convincing. The thing is, Cassie, if he truly wished to see me, don't you think he would make a real effort? He says he doesn't want to upset his mother, but that sounds a little lame to me. I mean, we both upset *our* mother all the time, don't we!'

'I'll say. But our ma isn't as powerful as Mrs Roberts – she doesn't own a whole blooming factory that we'll inherit one day. I can see why your Morgan doesn't want to upset her. Can't he compromise a little? Go up to Scotland with Mama like a dutiful son, but make several day trips to see you at weekends?'

Cassie's grasp of geography was abysmal. She clearly thought that Scotland was only a short way from London.

'That's not physically feasible, you dunce. And I don't care for compromises anyway. I'm an all-or-nothing sort of girl,' I said.

'You don't have to tell me that,' said Cassie, pulling my plait.

It turned out that fate itself decided on compromise.

Dearest Opal, Morgan wrote.

Change of plan! Mother's been chin-wagging with various top men and she's a bit worried about leaving the factory to its own devices all summer. There's a possibility the trade union fellows will target some of our workers, so we're only going to Scotland for a month, hurray hurray! I will be back at the end of July and we'll have the whole of August and September. I hope you'll be able to wangle some time off work.

Didn't he know how his own factory was run? You were only entitled to a week, plus days off for Christmas and bank holidays. If I went to Mrs Roberts and said, 'Excuse me, I need to take weeks and weeks off so I can go around with your son,' I was one hundred per cent certain of her response.

But the rest of Morgan's letter was incredibly

endearing, telling me just how much he was missing me. He also wanted to make plans for the summer.

I think we should definitely make a special trip to the seaside. Which part of the coast do you care for most? Where did you used to go on holiday when you were small? Well, you're still small now, Opal – but where did you take your bucket and spade and go paddling when you were five or six or seven? I can just see you, dress hitched up, big sunhat, funny little plaits . . .

He went on for a page or two imagining me when I was a little girl. He got it all completely wrong. He clearly thought that our straitened circumstances had started when Father went to prison. In actual fact my earnings of twenty-one shillings a week as a design artist meant that our family was better off than we'd ever been. Father had earned piteously little as a clerk, and nothing at all from his writing. He'd had his own week off work every summer, but we didn't go anywhere because we couldn't afford to travel or stay in a boarding house.

We *did* manage a day trip to Brighton one summer. Cassie and I had been wildly excited for weeks beforehand, but the actual day was a sad disappointment. It was drizzling when we set off. The rain increased until, by midday, it was torrential. I still couldn't wait to see the sea, and skipped down the hill from the railway station, determinedly ignoring the rain. My first glimpse of it was baffling. I had seen coloured lithographs in my picturebook and thought it was always azure blue, and the sand custard-yellow. This Brighton sea was a steely grey, heaving itself against the railings – and what had happened to the golden sand? It was grey again, hard pebbles that hurt my feet when Father suggested we have a little run along the beach. There were bathing machines, but no one was foolish enough to go into such a turbulent sea. We ended up hunched in a fried fish parlour for a couple of hours. Even the fish didn't taste good because it had been doused in malt vinegar.

Dear Morgan,

I am so pleased we will be able to spend time together later in the summer. [I decided not to carp on about the whole month in Scotland because I knew it wouldn't get me anywhere.] *I would simply love to go to the seaside with you. I will even tuck my dress up and wear a big sunhat to amuse you. I do not mind where we go. I find most seasides delightful – though I think Brighton is perhaps a little overrated.*

So it was decided. I would see Morgan in August. I didn't know whether he had actually made this clear to Mrs Roberts. She seemed very excited when she made her last factory visit before Scotland.

'I can't wait to breathe in that wonderful air,' she told me, her cheeks flushed at the very thought. 'Morgan adores Scotland too. He joins in all the village fun. He even had a go at tossing the caber last year. We always hold a ceilidh too – that's a special dance, and it's such fun. The Dashing White Sergeant, the Gay Gordons, such wonderful dances. Morgan wears the kilt, of course, and looks splendid. All the little local lasses set their caps at him, but of course they have to understand that Morgan needs to marry a young lady from his own background.' She said it softly, smiling at me, but her beautiful eyes were steely.

I disliked her warning me off in this indirect manner, but I managed to smile back serenely. 'I'm sure you'll have a lovely time, Mrs Roberts,' I said evenly.

I did not have a lovely time in July. It seemed to go on for ever. I couldn't write to Morgan in Scotland. He had expressly asked me not to do so.

It will be dreadful not to be in touch with you, dearest Opal, but I fear it would upset Mother unduly. I will still write to you of course – as often as possible.

This wasn't as often as I'd have liked. He sent several wonderful long letters at the beginning of

July, telling me how much he was missing me. He said Penicraig simply didn't seem the same now and he was very bored. But then his letters became shorter and more sporadic. He resorted to postcards: a picture of lucky heather, a mountain glen, and a comical Scot blowing the bagpipes. I didn't need to hide the messages from Mother. They were terse and casual.

I lay awake at night imagining Morgan dancing with all those local lasses. I was so wrapped up in myself that I didn't look at any newspapers or listen to the talk on the factory floor. I wasn't aware of what had been going on since the assassination of the Archduke Franz Ferdinand and his wife in Sarajevo. I didn't even know where this was, for all that I felt myself so superior when it came to geography. I didn't realize that when Austria declared war on Serbia at the end of July, it meant everyone in England would be affected.

On Friday 31 July I was so happy because I knew that Morgan was packing up in Scotland, ready to come down south. He and his mother took the journey in stages, travelling to York on Saturday, staying overnight at a grand hotel, then returning home on Sunday. It seemed a long and cumbersome journey, but Morgan promised he would be up bright and early for our August bank holiday outing.

I didn't even think to worry about the news that

the London Stock Exchange had closed. Mother didn't seem fussed either.

'What do we care? We haven't any stocks or shares, have we?' she said bitterly.

I did get frightened that weekend when I saw all the newspaper placards in the town saying that Britain was on the brink of war. I longed for Father, because he had always explained any national crisis to me, and given me calm and measured assurances. That learned, knowledgeable father seemed to have been taken way for ever, not just a year. His monthly letters were alarming now. His handwriting had changed considerably, the words barely legible and the lines wavering up and down as if his hand were shaking uncontrollably. He wrote the same few sentences every time, practically word for word, as if he were a little child writing lines for a punishment. It seemed that his hard labour had affected his brain.

The thought of a war terrified me. What if Morgan had to go and fight?

27

On Monday morning I was up at dawn. I dressed carefully in my cream frock, taking my cashmere shawl in case the sea breezes were chilly. Morgan had suggested we meet at the railway station at seven thirty, so as to have as long a day as possible at the seaside. I skipped breakfast, too excited to eat, and set off for the station at twenty to seven. I knew I would be there half an hour early, but I was in such a fever of excitement I couldn't wait any longer.

It was a beautiful bright morning, still fresh, but it was clear that it was going to be a warm day. I found I was walking faster and faster. Even though I was so early, I still gathered speed. By the time I turned into Station Road I was running. The road was crowded. Some people were hurrying to the station like me, but others were going the other way, looking annoyed or upset – strange expressions for a bank holiday.

I got nearer and nearer the station. I knew that Morgan probably wouldn't appear for a full half-hour, but I kept thinking I saw him, although I was always mistaken. Then I started wondering if I would instantly recognize the real Morgan. It had been nearly four months since I'd seen him. I'd drawn his face two dozen times since then, but it had become harder and harder to get the line of his jaw, the exact curve of his mouth, the true wave of his hair. When I shut my eyes I could see him, but a little indistinctly, surrounded by a golden haze. Now, though, my eyes were wide open, and there he was, standing just outside the station entrance hall, the real Morgan, looking very tanned in his cream shirt and cricketing flannels, with a cream jersey slung casually around his shoulders. He wore a straw boater hat at a jaunty angle, his hair longer and wavier than ever.

'Morgan!' I cried and I ran to him.

'Opal!' He smiled and held out his arms. We embraced, hugging hard, both of us going pink with emotion. 'Oh, Opal, it's so good to see you at last.'

'I'm so glad you came. I was so scared you wouldn't,' I said.

'I wouldn't miss our day out for the world,' he said. 'But I'm afraid there has to be a little change of plan. Look!' He gestured inside the station. There was a big placard.

WE ARE SORRY TO ANNOUNCE THAT BECAUSE OF THE CURRENT SITUATION THERE WILL BE NO TRAIN SERVICE FROM SOUTHERN WESTERN. PLEASE ACCEPT OUR SINCERE APOLOGIES FOR THE DISRUPTION.
LET US PRAY FOR PEACE.

'Oh my goodness, there are no trains because of the war? We're not at war *now*, are we?'

'No, not yet, but it looks horribly likely. Don't let it spoil our day, though. By hook or by crook I'm going to get us to the seaside. I've been talking to a chappie who says that there are motorized coaches taking folks to the coast on day excursions. They stop outside the bus station. He thinks they leave at half past seven. Do you think you could run very fast? Then we might just catch one.'

'I'll run like the wind,' I said, hitching up my narrow skirts a little in preparation.

'Oh, you're such a good sport. How wonderful that you're as early as me! Come on, then, let's sprint.'

Morgan seized my hand and we ran hard, dodging through the gathering crowds, rounding the corner, down to the end of the road, and there was the omnibus station. There was a line of big shiny green and cream coaches.

Morgan raced ahead and started talking earnestly to the first driver. 'Not this one!' he said, when I caught up. 'It's going to Brighton. You don't care for Brighton, I know.'

'I don't mind. Brighton's fine,' I said hastily, but Morgan was already dashing to the coach behind.

'Where are you going, driver?' he asked.

'Hastings,' he said.

'Hastings?' Morgan said to me.

'Wonderful!' I replied.

'Then we'll have two return tickets, please,' said Morgan.

'No can do, sir,' said the driver. 'I'm fully booked, every seat. Just take a look.'

The coach was crowded with families, with children clashing their buckets and spades, shouting and laughing.

'What about asking some of the little ones to squeeze up together on one seat? I'm sure they wouldn't mind too much,' said Morgan. 'Then I could pay you for two extra adults. In fact, why don't I pay double for our tickets, just for your trouble?' He pressed money into the driver's hand.

'Right you are, sir. Jolly decent of you. How about you two sitting three seats down on the right? You kids budge up in the front with the others. You'll like that – you can make out you're driving the bus. If you're very good, I'll let you sit up in my driving cabin for a mo when we get to the seaside.'

In less than a minute both men had smoothed out the situation to everyone's satisfaction. We subsided onto the vacated seat. The driver started up his engine and we were off. There was a huge cheer from the passengers. The children kept whooping for a full five minutes.

'Oh dear,' said Morgan. 'I didn't realize it was going to be quite so rowdy. Do you mind terribly that it's a motor coach?'

'Of course I don't, silly. I think it was brilliant of you to get us on it.'

'I feel a bit of a fool not being able to drive. I could take us anywhere in a car. I'll get Mitchell to talk me through it, and then, later this summer, I'll take us out in true style. I'll *have* to learn to drive anyway. When Mitchell picked us up from the station yesterday, we were discussing the likelihood of war, and he said he was keen to join up. I think he'd like to drive an army truck.'

'Oh, Morgan, *you* won't join up, will you?' I said, squeezing his arm.

'Me? No, I hate the idea of killing anybody. I can't

even stand hunting. I haven't the stomach for it.'

'You promise you won't join up?'

'You're as bad as Mother, Opal. And this is all a bit premature. Maybe we'll be able to wangle some kind of peace treaty at the eleventh hour.'

'I do hope so.'

'But we won't think about it now. This is our day out. I do hope Hastings is jolly. I've never been there.'

'Neither have I, but I'm sure it will be lovely,' I said fervently.

It was truly lovely, though the sea still wasn't storybook blue and the beach wasn't as sandy as I'd hoped. But the sun was shining and we were together and, like most of the couples on their bank holiday outing, we walked hand in hand along the seafront.

It was crowded, with musicians and ice-cream sellers and fortune-tellers and tintype photographers clamouring for our custom. Morgan bought me an ice cream. I rather hoped we could have our photograph taken together, but he laughed at the idea.

We threaded our way through the crowds towards the quaint fishermen's huts at the end of the beach. They were very thin and tall, made of blackened wood. The fishermen in their tan smocks were busy selling cod and plaice to eager folk. There were whelk and cockle stalls too. Morgan offered me a penny pot, but I didn't fancy them at all.

'Let's find some *cooked* fish,' he suggested.

We went into a little blue and white fish restaurant. Their fried fish was truly delicious: golden batter, very crisp, with the whitest cod, still tasting salty from the sea. I ate every mouthful, with a big portion of fried potatoes, a plate of bread and butter and two cups of tea.

'And you're such a scrap of a girl! I don't know where you put it all,' said Morgan admiringly. 'This is such fun. I've always wanted to eat in a fried fish shop.'

We went for a walk around the old town, looking in all the strange curio shops. I'd brought a full purse with me, so I was able to buy Morgan a china shaving mug with an interesting mermaid design in blue and white. I liked the mermaid's unusual blue hair and shiny blue tail.

'It's lovely, Opal, but you mustn't spend your money on me,' he told me.

'You've spent much, much more on me,' I said. 'You've spoiled me utterly.'

'I don't have to work so hard for my money,' said Morgan. 'But very well, I shall accept my mug with enormous gratitude if you'll let me buy you a present in return.'

'You've already bought me my beautiful shawl.'

'I want to buy you something else,' said Morgan, pausing at a jewellery shop window. 'I tell you what! Do you own any opals?'

I didn't have any jewellery at all, certainly not opals. I saw the prices of the opal necklaces in the jewellery shop and grew frightened. 'No, Morgan. No, absolutely not,' I said.

But he spotted a slim silver chain hanging on a black velvet stand at the back of the display. It had a small opal pendant in the shape of a teardrop. 'That looks perfect,' he said.

It *was* perfect. I wanted it desperately, though I protested that I couldn't possibly let him buy it for me. He took no notice whatsoever. He went into the shop, had the little old jeweller take it out of the window, and told me to fasten the opal pendant around my neck.

'It could have been made just for you, madam,' said the jeweller happily.

'Absolutely,' said Morgan. 'I shall buy it.'

When we left the jeweller's, I looked to see if anyone was watching, and then I kissed Morgan very quickly on the cheek.

'It's the most beautiful present in the world. I shall never ever take it off,' I said.

We wandered further until we came to the bottom of the cliffs. There was a little queue waiting for the East Cliff funicular lift. It took passengers all the way up to the cliff top.

'Oh, we have to go up!' said Morgan.

We waited patiently, paid our two pennies, and

then ascended slowly and jerkily upwards. I was frightened we might come tumbling down and clung tightly to Morgan's arm, but we finished our journey without mishap and stepped out onto the tufty grass.

We stood there for a while, admiring the view of the sea before us and the tumble of rooftops below. Then we set off further along the cliff. The sun was very hot now, too hot to wear a shawl or a jersey. We took them off and knotted them together. We swung them between us like two cream-clad babies.

It was a great relief when we reached trees and started walking through a beautiful shady glen.

'Should we turn back now? We might get lost,' I said.

'I should rather like to get lost with you,' said Morgan.

So we walked on. When we were entirely alone in this lush green world, Morgan pulled me gently to him, tipped up my chin and kissed me on the lips. He kissed me, he kissed me, he kissed me . . .

Then we walked until the trees thinned. We were on the cliff top again, with steps leading down towards a little beach. Morgan helped me all the way down. There we were, on our very own stretch of beach with no one else around.

'Let's be terribly common and paddle,' he said, taking off his shoes and socks and rolling up his flannels.

I could take off my shoes easily enough, but I had to turn my back on him and lift my skirts furtively to undo my stockings. Still, I wasn't going to let a silly thing like modesty stop me from splashing in that sea with my sweetheart.

It was colder than I'd expected, but wonderfully refreshing. I hitched my skirts right up like a little girl and ran back and forth in the shallow waves, squealing with joy.

'Careful, you'll get your pretty dress soaked,' said Morgan.

'Who cares?' I said.

For two pins I'd have ripped off my dress too and gone swimming in my drawers, but when a bunch of little boys tumbled down the steps, threw off their clothes and dashed into the sea in nothing at all, I did turn my back again, feeling my face going pink.

'I shall have to protect you from such an alarming sight,' said Morgan. He put his hands over my eyes and led me further down the beach.

It was very strange not being able to see at all. I had to trust Morgan completely. He might lead me into the sea, he might make me stumble on the rocks, he might tip me over altogether – but he didn't, of course. He led me safely back to a sandy patch near the steps which was in the shade. He made me wait while he fashioned me a cushion from his jersey and then carefully helped me sit down.

'There now, open your eyes,' he said.

When I did, the beach and sky and sea seemed picturebook bright for one moment, and Morgan himself brighter than anything else, his dear face right before me.

He made me put on his straw boater to keep the sun off. There were daisies growing in the tufts of grass near the steps. He picked a handful. I thought he was going to present me with a little bouquet, but he selected individual daisies instead and carefully inserted them at each twist of my plait.

'There, now you look like a fairy-tale princess,' he said.

'Hardly,' I said, but I *felt* like a princess when I was with him. I was as dazzled as the Lady of Shalott.

I started murmuring the first verse, and Morgan joined in. We recited all our favourite poems, and then passages from Shakespeare. It had been so long since I'd read any poetry, but verse after verse came flooding back until I felt I might permanently talk in rhyming couplets.

Then Morgan looked at his watch. It was a quarter past five already! The motor coach left at six.

'Oh my Lord, we'll have to run for it. This is the day of championship sprints,' said Morgan, leaping to his feet and pulling me up with him. We hastily tugged our stockings and shoes back on, and made for the steps. It was a struggle going up them at top speed. I had to throw myself down on the cliff top and rest for a few seconds, my heart banging in my chest.

Then we had to set off again. It wasn't too bad running through the shady wood, but it was hard work when we emerged into the full glare of the sun. We decided to run down the windy cliff path instead of queuing for the lift. We got a little lost and had to ask people to point us the way to the coach station. They argued about the best route to take, which took up more time, but eventually we were on our way again. As six o'clock chimed, we turned the corner and saw a whole line of different-coloured coaches.

'Oh Lord, which one?' I gasped.

'It'll be green and cream. Don't worry, we'll find it,' Morgan said, running down the line. 'Here it is! Come on, Opal.' He held out his hand and helped me up the steps.

'Thank goodness!' I was so out of breath I could barely speak.

The coach driver laughed at us. 'Bit tight for timing, eh? Sit down and get your breath back, young lady.'

We collapsed on the seat while the whole coach smiled at us. The children were all pink in the face, their special-outing white clothes grubby now, or sodden from the sea. They were sucking great sticks of seaside rock or nibbling on disgusting cockles and whelks. The mothers and fathers were all eating out of greasy brown bags of fried food.

'Oh dear, we're the only ones without supper,' said Morgan.

'I'm still full of lunch,' I said, hand on my chest. 'My heart's thumping!'

'I don't know why we were in such a rush to catch the coach,' said Morgan. 'It would have been much more fun to miss it. We could have stayed overnight at one of those little hotels on the seafront.' He looked in his wallet. 'No, actually, we couldn't!'

'We could have walked the streets, watching the sun set. Then we could have found a fisherman's hut and curled up inside for the night,' I suggested.

'You could curl up inside. I'd have to sleep outside to protect your reputation.'

'Oh, bother my reputation. I wouldn't want you getting cold. Or possibly pecked to death by seagulls! You'll have to creep in beside me.'

'Then that will be very romantic, though I think there'll be a very strong smell of fish!'

'And if Britain goes to war, we'll never go back home. We'll stay in our fisherman's hut. I'll scrub it until it doesn't smell fishy any more, then I'll paint fairies all over the wall. No, hang on – mermaids like the one on your shaving mug.'

'Will you grow blue hair and a blue tail too?'

'Of course. I'll swim all night by the light of the moon. You'll swim too, but you won't be able to keep up with me because you're a mere human. Then I'll take pity on you and wait, flipping my beautiful blue tail until you catch up.'

'You'd better make yourself useful and catch us lots of fish while you're at it – or will that be my job? I could get my own fishing boat and cast my nets every night, while you're doing your moonlight swimming. Yes, I'd sooner be the one providing for you.'

'I shall provide for us too. During the day I'll decorate the pavement along the seafront with my coloured chalks. I'll draw mermaids and fishermen, and a converted fisherman's hut painted in soft sea blue and hung with multi-coloured lanterns. I'll chalk seagulls and shells and little children paddling, and small ships out at sea. I'll put your straw boater on the pavement beside me so that passing folk will throw pennies into it. When I've collected enough, I'll buy bread and potatoes to go with the fish you have caught. We won't mind eating this every day, but I shall work especially hard on Saturdays so that we can have our favourite meal on Sunday. I'll find a honeydew melon and roast a chicken, and whip up raspberries and sugar and cream to make meringues.'

We carried on spinning our elaborate fantasy until we got to the halfway house, where the coach driver took a break and we could stretch our legs and buy refreshments.

Morgan had used up all his money, so I spent the

last of mine on two bottles of ginger beer and a huge hot potato swimming in butter and sprinkled with salt. Morgan held it and we took alternate bites.

When we resumed our journey there was a singsong. Folk sang *The Boy I Love Is Up in the Gallery*, *It's a Long Way to Tipperary*, *My Old Man Said Follow the Van*, and others I can't remember. Morgan and I didn't know the words properly as we'd never been to a music hall, but the tunes were easy enough to pick up and we la-la-la'd in time. The children joined in too, but they soon fell asleep. After a while their parents started nodding off too.

Morgan and I were too tired to continue our imaginary games. He put his arm round me and I nestled close, my head on his shoulder. We slept for the rest of the way back to town.

We didn't have enough money left for a taxi. I begged Morgan to set out on his long journey to Fairy Glen straight away, but he insisted on walking me all the way home first. It was frighteningly late. I hoped Mother would have long ago gone to bed, but through a crack in the curtains I saw that the lamp was still lit.

'Oh dear,' I said.

'Shall I come in with you?' said Morgan.

'No, that might upset her more. You'd better go straight home now. I do hope *your* mother isn't waiting up.'

'I'm an adult now. I can stay out all night if I

wish,' said Morgan, but he sounded a little uneasy.

'Thank you for the most wonderful day I've ever had,' I said. I fingered my opal necklace. 'I meant what I said. I shall never ever take it off.'

'Well, I shall walk round with my mermaid shaving mug in my hand for ever too. It had better be my left, so I can still write and shake folks' hands with my right.'

'Go home, you silly man.'

'We must say goodbye properly first.' He pulled me closer and gave me another kiss. It lasted longer than the one in the green wood. I'd have happily stood there by the gate kissing him all night long, if it weren't for that ominous light indoors. At last we broke away from our embrace and I went in to face Mother.

She was sitting in Father's chair, as if she now had the authority of both parents. I think she had nodded off where she sat, as her head jerked when I came into the room. She looked at the carriage clock on the mantelpiece, her face grim.

'How dare you come home so late, Opal! What will people think?'

'Most folk will be fast asleep in their beds. And those who are out and about to see me won't think anything of it because they have stayed out too, so there's no need to fuss. Let's go to bed now,' I said.

I couldn't bear to let a row with Mother tarnish my wondrous golden day.

I ran upstairs, but Mother shouted and came after me into my bedroom.

'How dare you ignore me! Isn't it enough that your father and sister have both disgraced themselves? Why do you have to act like a little hussy too? You might have set your cap at that Morgan Roberts, but he's just using you – can't you see? He'll never respect you if you stay out half the night with him.'

'Mother, you don't know what you're talking about. I couldn't get home any sooner. I've been on a motor coach trip to Hastings. We didn't get back into town until half past eleven.'

'Don't tell me such wicked lies. A boy like Morgan Roberts would never go on a coach trip! Do you think I'm stupid?'

'Yes I do, because I'm telling you the honest truth. Now please go to bed, Mother. I'm very tired and I'm sure you are too.'

Mother started sobbing in rage and frustration. It was all I could do not to seize hold of her and push her out of the door. I made myself hold her and pat her back and mop her tears. I tried to reassure her, and eventually she crept away. I could take off my clothes and lie down in peace. I wore my opal necklace underneath my nightdress and fell asleep holding it tight in my hand.

28

I couldn't wake up the next morning. I was dimly aware of Mother shouting at me, but I buried my head under the pillow. I was dreaming of being in Hastings and wanted to stay there.

'Opal! What are you thinking of? It's twenty to eight!' Mother said, pulling the sheets off me.

I had to stagger up, wash my face, and struggle into my clothes. There was no time for breakfast. I grabbed a heel of bread with dripping and, once I was out of the house, started running. I knew I was going to be late for work even if I flew like the wind, so when I got a stitch in my side I started walking. By the time the factory was in sight I had slowed right down. I very much hoped Mrs Roberts wouldn't be at Fairy Glen today.

I had to slink in past Mr Beeston's office.

'Miss Opal Plumstead, a good fifteen minutes late!' he said.

'I'm very sorry, Mr Beeston,' I said humbly.

'So I should think. I'm afraid I shall have to write your name in my late book. If Mrs Roberts sees fit to dock you an hour's wages, I won't be able to stop her.'

'I'm not an hour late!'

'I don't make the rules, my dear. I simply implement them. Anyone arriving more than five minutes late forfeits an hour's wages. Anyone up to and including me.'

'Then these are ridiculously unfair rules,' I said, and I marched past him.

All the girls were hard at work in the design room.

'Ah, so you're deigning to grace us with your presence, are you?' said Alice. 'You're going to be for it, you know, even though you're such a favourite. Mrs Roberts has already had her head round the door looking for you.'

This totally unnerved me, though I tried to appear indifferent. I sat down and reached for a box lid, though I'd never in all my life felt less like inventing fairies. It was a struggle to keep my hand steady enough to control my paintbrush at first, but I gradually relaxed a little, and found myself painting a mermaid frolicking in the sea with a merry trio of green and blue fairies swooping down to speak to her.

'Opal Plumstead!' It was Mrs Roberts, her voice very stern. 'Please come to my office.'

Alice raised her eyebrows. 'Told you,' she whispered.

I took a deep breath, put down my brush and walked out of the room in a dignified manner, though my knees were shaking. Mrs Roberts didn't turn to acknowledge me. I followed her along the corridor into her room. She sat at the desk. I stood before her. She waited a good thirty seconds, staring at me coldly.

'I'm not surprised you were late this morning. You must have been very late home yesterday evening.'

'Yes, Mrs Roberts. Morgan and I—'

'I know, I know,' she interrupted. She'd winced when I said the word *Morgan*, as if she couldn't even bear me to say her son's name. 'I also know that you've been secretly writing to him for months. I found an entire cache of your letters hidden in Morgan's trunk.'

'You've been reading my private letters?' I said.

'Kindly don't use that tone to me. I have *not* read your childish outpourings. It was enough to simply see your signature at the end. How dare you bombard him with these letters?'

'He wrote just as many to me. He wrote *first*,' I said.

'My son is very kind and sympathetic. I'm sure he initially thought of you as a child, as I did myself. I had no idea you could be so scheming and underhand.'

'I am *not* scheming or underhand. I haven't done anything wrong. I don't know why you're being so horrible to me.' I was fighting hard not to burst into tears.

'I *thought* you'd set your cap at my son at Easter, though it was hard to believe your temerity. I decided to give you the benefit of the doubt. I never dreamed you were deceiving me all this time – even plotting to meet up with him the minute he returned from Scotland. Then you kept him out all day and half the night until I was nearly demented with worry.'

'We went on a coach trip to the seaside. We couldn't help getting back late.'

'A motor-coach trip! Of all the vulgar things to do on a bank holiday! I can scarcely believe my son went along with this.'

'We had a wonderful day too,' I said defiantly. I didn't know I was fingering my opal necklace until I saw Mrs Roberts staring at it.

'Did you wheedle that out of him too?' she asked.

'Morgan bought it for me, yes. I don't . . . wheedle,'

I said, tears starting to roll down my cheeks. 'Morgan *wanted* to buy it for me. He cares for me.'

'Now let us get one thing straight, Opal Plumstead. My son has befriended you and behaved in a very foolish fashion. I dare say he is partly at fault. But you must realize that there is no chance whatsoever for the two of you to continue this unseemly friendship.'

'Why is that?'

'My dear girl, do I have to spell it out? Morgan is my son. He will own Fairy Glen one day – the factory, and indeed the house, and various other properties and land. He is a gentleman and has been educated accordingly. He will be going up to Oxford at the end of the summer to complete his education. He will enjoy a pleasant social life there amongst people of his own sort. I'm sure he'll meet a suitable young lady and they'll start a romantic friendship. He won't dally any further with you, Opal. Surely you can see that.'

'What is so dreadful about me? You were happy enough to take me under your wing. You *liked* me. You invited me to meetings, you took me back to your home, you gave me the job in design, you think my fairies are really special. If I'm good enough for you, why aren't I good enough for your son?' I cried.

'I don't make society's rules, Opal,' said Mrs Roberts. 'You're simply not the right type of girl.'

'You've always clamoured to change rules. You

don't think it's fair that women are denied the vote, so you protested vehemently and even went to prison for your beliefs. But you're still bound by stupid rules of class. You say you want Morgan to meet people of his own sort. Well, *I'm* his sort, whether you like it or not. We are soul mates!'

'Stop shouting at me. I won't have it. I am your employer, please remember that.'

'Then I resign!'

'Don't be ridiculous. Where would you go? What would you do? No one else would give you such leeway. I've tried my best to give you the job you deserve. I'm not petty enough to take it away from you now, despite everything. You will carry on here, and I dare say we will resume our old friendship in time – but you are not to have any further communication with my son. He understands that now, and you must too. Now go away and wash your face, and then carry on with your work.'

He understands that now! Oh Lord, did Morgan really want nothing more to do with me? I *had* to see him! This was our summer month. I'd banked on seeing him every weekend. We didn't have to go on expensive outings. I didn't want any more presents. I simply wanted to be with him. I *would* be with him! Mrs Roberts couldn't lock us up. We would show her. Nothing could keep us apart.

I thought Morgan himself might be waiting on the

doorstep at home at the end of that terrible day, but he wasn't there. He hadn't sent a letter, though I quizzed Mother anxiously about it.

'There hasn't been any wretched letter,' she protested. 'I dare say the post office is shut. We're on the brink of war, you stupid girl. The banks are still closed and the shops have hardly any food left because folk are all hoarding. I don't know what we're going to do, how we're going to manage, and all you care about is a letter!'

It *was* all I cared about then. It wasn't even too terrible a shock to go to work on Wednesday and see all the newspaper placards, hear the folk chattering in the street. War had been declared against Germany late last night. I was too concerned with my own personal war.

I wrote to Morgan that night, a long passionate letter, page after page. I addressed it to him at his home and wrote *Personal and Private* at the top. I went to Father's desk and found a little stub of sealing wax. I melted it, and then carefully distributed it over the join of the envelope so it would be obvious if anyone had read it. Of course, Mrs Roberts might simply hide the letter from Morgan, or even tear it up, but she was an honourable woman and I didn't think she'd stoop so low.

There was no letter for me on Thursday. By Friday I was frantic, scared that Morgan wanted nothing more to do with me now. When I trailed into the factory, I found it was buzzing with rumours. There was a notice at the entrance.

There will be a meeting in the canteen for all workers at 11 o'clock.

Eliza Roberts

The girls in the design room were all of a twitter.

'Maybe she's shutting the factory down because of the war . . .'

'Perhaps she's going to have us making bullets or bombs, instead of sweets . . .'

'I think she's going to root out anyone suspicious, like that Geoff in the fondant room.'

'*Geoff?* Why on earth pick on Geoff?'

'Don't you know his surname? Geoffrey Rentzenbrink! It's German, clearly. He'll be recruited as a spy.'

'Don't be ridiculous! Geoff's as English as we are. And I think his father's *Dutch*, not German.'

'You can't be too careful, not with a war on.'

'My Michael's going to enlist – he thinks it's every man's duty.'

'Can't you talk him out of it? What if he gets injured – or worse?'

'What if we don't win this wretched war? My pa says the Germans have got a much bigger army than us.'

'We could beat the ruddy Germans even if their army was twice the size of ours.'

'Yes, our boys will be home by Christmas, just you wait and see.'

None of us knew any real facts, but everyone had a strong opinion. At eleven, the factory hooter went and we all stood up and filed off to the canteen. It felt very odd, all of us crowding in there in the middle of the morning. The long tables and benches were still stacked against the wall, so we all stood awkwardly, waiting.

I found myself standing next to Freddy. He nodded at me and then gave me a second glance.

'Hello, Opal,' he said, with some of his old eagerness. 'You're looking very well. There's something different about you. Maybe you're just growing up at last.'

'Oh, for goodness' sake,' I said, infuriated by his patronizing tone.

'Yes, quite the young lady,' he said, leering at me now.

'How's Edith?' I asked pointedly.

'Oh, she's very well too,' he said, though he didn't sound particularly enthusiastic. 'How are you getting on in design? I hear you're Mrs Roberts' favourite.'

'No I'm not,' I said with feeling. 'But she likes my fairy designs.'

'Fairies!' said Freddy. 'Still, the girls like them,

I know. My Edith's dotty about them fairies on the boxes. Maybe I'll get her the summer special box before I go.'

'Before you go where?'

'To enlist!' said Freddy, his eyes shining. 'I've had a word with Mr Beeston already.'

'You're going to join the army?' I said, staring at him. He looked more gangly than ever. I couldn't imagine him in soldier's khaki.

'It's my duty,' he said. 'Didn't you see the posters today? Like they say, it's for King and Country.'

'What does Edith say?'

'She's proud of me,' said Freddy.

'Isn't she worried?'

'She knows we'll see those Germans off and help the poor Belgians. There's no beating us British boys.' Freddy stood up straighter, as though he were already lining up for inspection.

I shook my head at him uneasily. Then the crowd started pushing forward and I realized that Mrs Roberts was threading her way through. Morgan was with her.

'Oh my goodness, Morgan!' I exclaimed.

'Yes, that's Mr Morgan,' said Freddy. 'I suppose he's come to put in his two pennyworth too, though he's nothing but a big schoolboy.'

'He's left school now. He's about to go off to Oxford University.'

'Yes, that place for big overgrown toffs,' said Freddy. 'Then he'll come back and lord it over all of us, making us work long hours and paying us nonsense for wages.'

'You've been listening to all those union men. You know nothing. Morgan will be a wonderful boss, truly fair, wanting justice for all,' I said fiercely.

'*Mister* Morgan to you. You keep saying Morgan this, Morgan that, just like you know him,' said Freddy.

'I *do* know him. He's my friend,' I said, before I could stop myself.

'You're having me on – you and Morgan Roberts are *friends*?'

'Dear friends,' I said.

Then Mrs Roberts clapped her hands and everyone was silent.

'My son and I are here today to try to give all of you at Fairy Glen hope and reassurance. We look on you as family and friends, not just our workers. We feel more united than ever now that we are at war. Of course we're all praying for peace. Let us hope the war will be over soon. We will continue to strive hard at Fairy Glen to produce the best confectionery money can buy.

'Now, I know that some of you brave, patriotic young men are considering enlisting already. Although we will be sorry to see you go, we are so very proud of you. I know that some of you are hesitating. You want to do your duty and fight for our glorious country, but you are also responsible hard-working men who appreciate your secure job here at Fairy Glen. Together with my son, who will one day be in charge himself, I want to reassure you that no matter what happens, there will always be a job kept open for you at this factory.'

'Excuse me, ma'am, but who will do all the heavy work if the lads go off to war?' someone shouted.

'Isn't the answer obvious?' said Mrs Roberts. 'Have I not been fighting for women's rights for years? We women will keep Fairy Glen going. We will build up our strength, develop our muscles, and toil away until our brave menfolk return home triumphant.'

'I can't quite see Mrs Roberts rolling up her dainty sleeves and handling a vat of boiling sugar,' Freddy murmured. He glanced at me for a reaction. 'Or her namby-pamby son.'

'Hold your tongue. You're just lowering yourself, Freddy,' I said witheringly. He flushed.

'Where do we go to enlist, then?' another lad called.

'Mr Beeston, step forward,' said Mrs Roberts.

'There's a recruitment office newly opened at the public library, only a step away,' said Mr Beeston. 'I'd go there like a shot myself if they were accepting gentlemen of fifty-two, and that's a fact. I'm proud of you boys, though my heart will ache to see you go.

Could you step to the front right now so we can see how many of you are truly serious about enlisting.'

There was a little jostling and pushing, and eighteen or twenty men stepped forward proudly, Freddy amongst them. Dear Geoff was there at the front too. I hoped those horrid girls in the design room felt ashamed.

'Well done, brave lads,' said Mrs Roberts. 'Let us give them a rousing cheer, ladies. They are an example to us all.'

There was a great cheer. I joined in, though I felt desperately sad. I knew that Geoff and many of the others had wives and children. How could they volunteer so recklessly when they might get badly injured, even killed?

'Just one moment, Mrs Roberts!' It was Freddy, standing right at the front, still bright red in the face. 'You're talking about examples. Well, what about Mr Morgan? Is he volunteering too?'

There was a little gasp. Someone shouted, 'For shame!' and another, 'Pipe down, Freddy' – but others muttered, 'Yes,' and 'Good point.' Morgan was very pale, but he held his head high. He cleared his throat, ready to speak, but Mrs Roberts clutched his arm to stop him.

'I'm sure my son feels just as strongly as you do. In due time perhaps he will volunteer too, when he's old enough. He has to finish his education first,' she said firmly.

'He doesn't look like a schoolboy to me,' said Freddy. 'And surely he'd be better off fighting the Germans with us lads than mincing around blooming Oxford.'

There were more gasps and also laughter. Mrs Roberts was white too. She started to say something, but Morgan stepped forward, stopping her this time.

'That's a fair point,' he said, loud and clear. 'It's a question I've been asking myself this week. You're absolutely right. I can't possibly swan off to Oxford and expect you to do the fighting for me. I shall enlist too.'

Mrs Roberts tried to say something again, but she couldn't make herself heard above the new cheer – for Morgan this time.

It rang in my ears and set me reeling. He couldn't really mean it, could he? Morgan hated the whole idea of fighting. He'd told me he'd be a pacifist. What was he doing, letting poor jealous Freddy goad him into fighting a war he didn't want?

Mrs Roberts saw that she had lost control of the crowd and waved her arm distractedly, dismissing us. Everyone trooped back to work, chattering excitedly. I watched Freddy being clapped on the back by many of the men. I felt terrible. If I'd held my tongue about Morgan, maybe he wouldn't have spoken out.

My stomach lurched and I had to push my way through the crowd, running for the ladies' cloakroom.

I was horribly ill, carrying on retching long after I had no food left inside me.

When I eventually crept back to the design room, I heard shouting coming from Mrs Roberts' study. I couldn't hear what she and Morgan were saying, but they both sounded in a terrible passion.

The girls in the design room were agog.

'Hark at them! Going at it hammer and tongs. She's nearly demented, and he's lost his rag too. Fancy, I've never even heard her raise her voice before.'

'She lives for that son of hers. She'd sooner fight herself than let him go.'

'Fancy young Freddy speaking like that! I'd never have thought he had it in him.'

'He's a cheeky young limb.'

'Yes, but he's got a point. He clearly hit home.'

'So even precious Mr Morgan is off to be a soldier now.'

'*Be quiet!*' I cried.

They stopped their silly gossip and stared at me. Then we heard hurried footsteps along the corridor. The door of the design room burst open. Mrs Roberts stood there, looking wild. She'd opened the neck of her dress to breathe more easily but she was still panting. She had tears rolling down her cheeks.

'Opal?' she called hoarsely.

'Yes, Mrs Roberts?' I said, jumping up.

'Come here.'

I ran to her while all the design girls gaped. She took hold of my wrist and tugged me out into the corridor.

'Please! You talk him out of it,' she said. 'I can't, though I've tried and tried. Morgan might listen to you.'

I saw just what it cost her to ask me. I felt a little glow of pride amidst my fear and sorrow and pity. I might be Opal Plumstead, the upstart protégée ordered not to have any further communication with her son, yet here she was, begging me to talk to him.

'I'll try,' I said.

We both ran along the corridor, past Mr Beeston's office and out into the yard. Mitchell was waiting in the car outside the gate, but there was no sign of Morgan.

'Where's Mr Morgan?' Mrs Roberts cried. 'Didn't you stop him?'

'I'm sorry, ma'am. He said he didn't want a lift. He's gone towards the town on foot. You've just missed him.'

'Then we must follow him. Quickly, get into the motor car, Opal.'

I did as I was told and we set off in pursuit. As soon as we turned the corner we saw Morgan loping along the pavement.

'Hurry, catch him up!'

Mitchell pulled the car up beside Morgan. Mrs Roberts hurled herself out before he'd stopped. She staggered, nearly falling.

'Mother!' Morgan clutched at her, holding her upright.

'Please, Morgan, get in the car. Opal's here. She wants to talk to you. I'm begging you. We can't brawl in the street. *Please*,' she cried.

'Oh, Mother,' he said helplessly. He handed her back into the car, while she clutched his arm with both hands. 'Very well, I'll go home with you. But I'm not changing my mind.' He looked at me. 'Oh, Opal, you too,' he said, seeing my expression.

He went to sit in the front.

'Are you wanting to enlist, sir?' Mitchell asked him. 'Quite right too. I'm going to do the same, though Mrs Mitchell's done her best to talk me out of it.'

'That will be enough, Mitchell. Drive us home,' said Mrs Roberts.

'Yes, ma'am. Don't worry, I'll stay until you get yourself a new chauffeur. I wouldn't want to let you down. But, please note, I'm going. You understand, don't you, Mr Morgan?'

Mrs Roberts sank back, covering her face with her hands. She was so distraught I wondered if I should try to put my arm round her, but I didn't quite dare. She sobbed into her lace handkerchief and I sat stiffly beside her, while Morgan and Mitchell exchanged banal patriotic clichés in the front of the car.

Mrs Roberts was in such a state that Mrs Evans had to help her upstairs to her room.

'You won't go, Morgan, will you?' she kept crying. 'You won't sneak away?'

'I won't go anywhere without telling you, Mother, I promise,' he said.

Then he turned to me. 'Let's go into the garden, Opal.'

We went out of the French windows. It was like stepping into a different world. There was a heady smell of honeysuckle and roses. Morgan took my hand and we walked along the path between the great rhododendron bushes, the little stream trickling beside us. We said nothing at all until we reached the Japanese house right at the end. Morgan sat down. I sat beside him, but he pulled me gently until I was sitting on his lap.

'Oh, Morgan,' I said.

'I'm sorry, Opal,' he said, his arms around me. 'I've written you dozens of letters this week and then torn them up. I've been so undecided.'

'About us?'

'About everything. It's so awful. All I want is peace, and yet it's war, war, war. Mother was in a terrible state when I got home on Monday. She was threatening, pleading, crying. I've never seen her like that before. She was hysterical, saying the most terrible things. She said I was all she had and now I was breaking her heart. She said so many things. She knows me so well. She knows exactly what to say to make me feel dreadful. I started to promise her anything just to make her stop.'

'Promise to stop seeing me?'

'Yes, but I didn't mean it. So then I went back on my word the next morning. Then we heard we were at war, and that changed everything again.'

'You really want to be a soldier and fight?'

'No! No, of course not. I meant everything I said in Hastings. I hate the very idea of war. It's not just the principle. I suppose I'm a rotten coward at heart. It's not just that I'm scared of dying. I'm scared of killing someone else, I'm scared of the squalor, the stench, the sheer misery of it all.'

'Then don't go! Please, please don't go. For your mother's sake – and for mine.'

'But I can't go on being a coward. I can't let other men fight for me.'

'Take no notice of that stupid boy who shouted at you. He was saying it to get at me. I told him that you and I were friends. He was just being spiteful, making trouble, because once upon a time he was sweet on me. Please believe me, Morgan.'

'All right, I do believe you, but it doesn't change

the truth of what he said. I've been in this terrible dilemma for days, wondering what I should do. I don't want to fight, but I'm already trained – all that wretched army cadet malarkey. I should know what I'm doing, much more than poor Freddy. Mother's spent a fortune on my education and now says I'm throwing it in her face, but the thing public school teaches you above all else is that you must do your duty as a gentleman.'

'Oh, that's such pompous nonsense,' I said. 'You can't truly believe that, Morgan.'

'I don't know what I believe any more. That's the trouble. I'm so weak and vacillating. I know what I *want*: I want to run away with you.'

'And live in our fisherman's hut.'

'Yes, of course, that's exactly what I want. If I were anyone else, maybe that's what I'd do.'

'Then let's!'

'Opal, we can't possibly. You're not old enough to marry me. You're still practically a child. And what would your mother say?'

'I don't care what Mother says.'

'I wish I could be as brave. I care dreadfully about my mother and her opinion, even though it's not very manly to feel that way.'

'Yes, but your mother is extraordinarily special. I used to love her a lot myself until she turned against me.'

'She hasn't exactly turned against *you* – she just can't bear it if I'm attached to anyone else.'

'Anyone socially inferior.'

'Stop it! You're the most superior girl I've ever met, in every single way. How I wish I was as honest and unafraid and implacable as you. And do you know something? I think that if you were a man you'd go and enlist.'

'No I wouldn't! I wouldn't go to fight a war and leave my poor sweetheart demented with worry. This is meant to be *our* summer, Morgan. Every weekend. You promised. And then you're going to Oxford. If it were me, I'd never give up a chance of going to Oxford.'

'Oxford will still be there when I come back from the war.'

'*If* you come back,' I said. Then I clapped my hand over my mouth. 'I didn't mean that. Oh, why did I say it? Morgan, you *can't* go, because I truly couldn't bear it if you didn't come back.'

'How can I stay when half the factory hands are going? They won't forget. When the war is over, when they've done fighting and I've graduated, how are we ever going to work together? They won't have a shred of respect for me. They'll think me a coward, and they'll be right. They won't listen to my orders. They'll rebel.'

'You can *make* them do what you say. You will be their boss. The power is all yours.'

'My father was that kind of boss. He ruled by fear. If folk broke his petty little rules, he sacked them without a second thought. My mother has worked hard to change things, to make Fairy Glen a decent place to work. Everyone respects her for it. If I'm taking over, I want them to respect me.'

'You *will* win them over.'

'I'm not sure I could. *You* can win anyone over, though, I grant you that.'

'Then let me win *you* over, Morgan. Please tell me you won't enlist. If I mean anything to you, you'll stay here,' I said, putting my hands on either side of his face and gazing at him imploringly.

'You already have my heart, Opal, but you cannot change my soul. I know deep within me that I have to go.'

I knew it too, though I spent hours more trying to persuade him. That very afternoon he went and enlisted in the East Surrey Regiment.

29

I hoped that we'd still have more time together, but the very next week he went away to train to be an officer.

I saw him the day before he left for France. He'd spent Saturday with his mother. I wasn't invited to Fairy Glen to spend it with them. But on Sunday he came calling for me. He was wearing his army uniform and looked so different. I scarcely recognized him in all that stiff, ugly khaki. He had even lost his beautiful long wavy hair. It was now clipped very short and straight. It made his ears look strangely prominent and his neck very bare. As if in compensation, he'd grown a little moustache over his top lip.

'Oh, Morgan,' I said, touching it. 'I'm not sure I like it.'

'Neither do I, but I've grown it to try to look older. I shall be giving orders to men much older and more experienced than me. It won't work if I look like a schoolboy.'

'Oh, Morgan,' I said again, at a loss for any other words.

Mother insisted on inviting him in and made us sit in the chilly parlour. She brewed us a pot of tea in the best china, with a plate of fancy biscuits that neither of us ate. She sat with us, telling Morgan several times that he looked a fine figure of a man in his uniform. He thanked her each time and sat awkwardly in Father's chair, fiddling with the shiny brass buttons on his jacket. It became harder and harder to think of anything to say.

At last Morgan said, 'Well, thank you so much for your hospitality, Mrs Plumstead. If you don't mind, I should like to take Opal out to lunch.'

'Certainly, certainly, though I'm sure I can do you a nice shepherd's pie here if you care to wait a while.'

'It's very kind of you, but I don't want to put you to any trouble. I think we'll go out.'

'As you wish, sir,' said Mother, just like a servant.

I went painfully red, but Morgan was impeccably polite. The contrast between our mothers was unbearable. I remained stiff and silent even when we were walking down the street. Morgan was very quiet too, striding out in his boots in a military fashion. Many people smiled and nodded to us. One old man even shuffled across the road to clap him on the back.

'Well done, young sir,' he said. 'You'll go and sort out those Germans. I wish to goodness I was young enough to join you.'

It made us more self-conscious than ever. Morgan took me to the Royal Hotel. There were other soldiers in the dining room, some with sweethearts, some with their whole family. The management served a free drink to every table with a soldier at it. Most called for many more drinks. The atmosphere was frenetic, people laughing and talking too loudly, like actors trying to project their voices in a vast theatre.

We ordered chicken again, but we were served much smaller portions. Food prices had doubled in less than a week, according to Mother. Somehow it didn't taste the same, either. Neither of us had much appetite. We didn't even bother with a pudding.

'Mother ordered apple pancakes for me last night, and wept when I only ate half of one,' said Morgan. 'And then it escalated into a ridiculous row, because she said if I had no appetite, it meant I was dreading going, so why *was* I going? She said I was risking my life unnecessarily, simply because of pride. She has this new scheme for me. She wants me to move to Scotland and manage the farm there. She's worked out that even if there is compulsory conscription and every man has to fight, I'd be exempt if I were producing food on the farm. What do you think, Opal?' he asked, looking at me.

'I think I agree with her,' I said. 'But it's not going to make any difference, is it?'

Morgan shook his head.

'Then I won't nag you further.' I reached across the table and held his hand. He had a row of callouses on his palm.

'Is this from handling guns?'

'Digging, mostly. Learning how to dig a trench. I should be able to show my men how to make an excellent latrine,' said Morgan.

'Well, I dare say it will be a handy skill when the war is over. I don't think our fisherman's hut will have any plumbing, so maybe you'll have to dig us a latrine in the sand,' I said.

Morgan held my hand tightly. 'When Mother's too old to work, I shall sell up Fairy Glen and with the proceeds I'll buy us a palace with top-notch plumbing on the cliff top, and we'll have the woods as our wild garden. Just once a year we'll spend a night in our fisherman's hut for old times' sake.'

This is how we coped the rest of that day. We wandered around the town again, making up an elaborate fantasy future. We wanted to be alone together, but everywhere was crowded. The park was full of soldiers and sweethearts. The only place we could find was the cemetery. The presence of all the people quietly mouldering underneath the earth made it terrifying now.

We walked in and out of the gravestones, the marble angels poised on tiptoe all around us, wings spread.

'You won't die, will you, Morgan!' I burst out.

'I won't die, not until I'm an old, old, old man,' he said.

'You promise me? You promise me you won't get killed in this awful war? You will come back safe and sound, not even wounded?'

'I promise you,' said Morgan, but when he pulled me close in an embrace, I could feel him trembling.

'Have you ever broken a promise?' I asked.

'Never,' he said, but I knew he was lying.

'I don't believe in ghosts, I never have, but if you *did* die, you would come back and haunt me, wouldn't you?'

'Of course. I'll never lie still like my father under his hideous obelisk. I'll roam free, flying above you like these angels, and I'll be with you day and night,' Morgan whispered.

'That's so beautiful. But promise again you will come back safe, even so.'

'I promise promise promise,' said Morgan, and then he kissed me.

Don't turn the page. Believe in happy endings. Chirp like little Billy, '*Happy Days, happy days, happy days*.'

Morgan was killed by a sniper in 1915 when he was trying to drag one of his injured men back to safety. It was a pointless effort because that man later died of his injuries. It might even have been Freddy, because he died around that date, according to Edith. Ten men never returned to the factory to reclaim their jobs.

I wasn't told officially. I had no claim on Morgan, though he wrote to me as often as he could. He told me a little of the horrors he had to face, worse than either of us had ever imagined. He always finished each pencil-written letter with his love, and then he wrote in capitals: *I'M KEEPING MY PROMISE*.

But he couldn't. I didn't have a telegram. I didn't receive any of his possessions – his watch, his books, his pocket knife. They all went to Mrs Roberts as she was his next of kin.

She had to tell me. She hadn't come into the factory for weeks. She kept herself busy attending patriotic meetings to help the boys abroad, run by the suffragettes. Mrs Pankhurst had called a halt to demonstrating for the vote while we were at war.

Then, one day, Mrs Roberts appeared, deathly white beneath the veil of her hat, dressed entirely in black. We all knew then, though she held a meeting in the canteen to make an official announcement. She did call me into her office ten minutes before, to tell me privately.

'I have devastating news, Opal,' she said, her voice husky.

'Morgan is . . . dead?' I whispered, wondering if he might simply be missing in action so there could be a shred of hope.

There was none. She told me about the sniper, the injured man, Morgan's courage.

'They say he will be awarded a posthumous medal,' she said proudly. 'He was very brave.'

I had to hold onto the corner of her desk to stop myself falling down altogether. Mrs Roberts didn't try to put her arms around me. She didn't even touch me. But she did say, very quietly, 'I know what this means to you.'

She didn't, of course. She still thought I was an upstart chit of a girl who had an inappropriate association with her son. She didn't see that I loved him, body and soul, and always would.

I didn't cry at work. I painted my fairies, day after day, trying hard to escape into their bright fantasy world. I had time to elaborate and concentrate on exquisite detail because the deluxe fondant range wasn't in such demand now. Sugar was in short supply, so Fairy Glen confectionery grew more and more expensive.

My fairies elongated, grew large pearl-white wings, and frequently wore white gowns too. They no longer harnessed birds or played games with little creatures. They flew solemnly through the air, their faces grave and composed.

I cried at home, every single night. Father would sometimes hear me and come and sit on my bed and put his arms round me helplessly. His release from prison had been so painful. We had been in a fever for weeks, longing to have him home with us again. On the day he returned I hung a banner across the front of the house saying *WELCOME HOME, DEAREST FATHER!* Mother was appalled, worried what the neighbours would say, but I didn't care. I wanted Father to see just how much I loved him and wanted him home.

But the man who came stumbling to our front door didn't seem like my real father any more, more like an aged grandfather. He had shrunk in size and become very stooped. He couldn't seem to pick up his feet as he walked. He had a new way of looking, his head turning constantly from left to right, his eyes never seeming to focus. His suit didn't fit him because he'd lost so much weight. He didn't have a collar to his shirt, he wasn't wearing socks, and his shoes flopped off his feet.

'Oh my Lord, Ernest, what have they done to you?' said Mother, starting to cry.

Father's own face crumpled and he made a little wailing sound.

'Don't worry, Father!' I said, hugging him tightly.

'We'll have you better in no time. All that matters is that you're home at last.'

But even when we'd kitted Father out in his old Sunday best and given him a decent shave and haircut, he stayed the same poor bewildered old man. He was still kindly and he tried to comfort me as best he could, but it was clear he didn't know what to say.

Even his voice had changed. He used to speak like a gentleman in low, measured tones. Now he spoke in a rush, often getting his words mixed up. The only job he could find was as a newspaper seller on the street. He'd call, '*Star*, *News* and *Standard*!' over and over until he was hoarse, the words distorted so they sounded like a cry of pain. Sometimes he muttered the words under his breath at home, until Mother spoke to him sharply. She treated him like one of her babies, and he responded in kind, hanging his head if he felt he'd displeased her.

I'd sometimes look at his poor shabby head and wonder if all his wits had addled inside. I tried to interest him in his precious books. He'd stroke the covers and tell me how much he liked them. Sometimes he would even flick through the pages, but he never actually read them now.

He still wrote a little, using his old manuscript pages, scribbling at random in the margins or crisscrossing uneven lines over his old copperplate.

'What are you writing, Father?' I asked, fearing it was gibberish.

'I'm writing my memoirs, my dear,' he said.

'Your memoirs?'

'An account of my year in prison.'

'For pity's sake,' said Mother. 'Isn't it enough that the whole street knows where you've been? Why do you want to advertise the fact?'

'I feel the world needs to know what it's like to be a gentleman in such a dreadful institution,' said Father, with simple dignity.

I wondered if he might have a point. I even wondered if his memoir might be published at some stage. I saw it as a Dickensian exposé of our prison system and hoped it might be his salvation. But when I crept into his room and deciphered his latest scribbling, I lost heart.

Prison is very bad.
It is full of bad men.
The gaolers are bad too.
The work is very hard.

It was like a bizarre reading primer for five-year-olds. I lost all hope that it would be the saving of my poor dear father, but I think it kept him happy enough.

I tried to get him to talk about his accountancy at

the shipping firm, eager to bring the real culprit to justice, but Father couldn't bear to remember. He put his hands over his face and shook his head again and again. It seemed cruel to pursue it further. What would be the point? Father could never get his year back now. It had broken him for ever, though his nature was still sweet.

He didn't really know why I cried so every night. He clearly still thought of me as a little girl.

'Don't cry, don't cry, there there,' he'd croon, patting my back. 'Just a bad dream, poor girly, just a bad dream.'

He was particularly good with Mother's babies, tickling them and fussing them and giving them rides on his knee. Mother stayed devoted to all of them, taking on another whenever one got old enough for school, but the baby she adored the most was little Danny, Cassie's child.

Oh, Mother had been so horrified to hear that Cassie was going to have a baby.

'Well, you've disgraced yourself for ever now,' she'd said. 'He's still not marrying you? He'll up and leave you when the baby's born, you mark my words, Cassie Plumstead.'

Cassie had simply laughed at her. 'Oh, Mother, the voice of doom as always! Daniel's tickled pink about the baby, and so am I. He's painting the most incredible portrait of me. It's called *Motherhood*, and although I'm so enormous he's made me look superb. He's got a whole series of paintings in mind. He can't wait to do one of me with the baby at my breast.'

Mother gasped in horror – but when the baby was born she couldn't wait to see it. She came with me to Hurst Road for the first visit. She was dumbfounded by the house. I had told her many times that it was splendid, if a little shabby, but she had obstinately pictured Cassie living in squalor. She was taken aback by Daniel too.

'Mrs Plumstead! How delightful. Cassie will be so thrilled to see you. Wait till you see our little baby boy. He's such a stunner, an absolute cherub. He takes after his mother, of course – and indeed his grandmother,' he said, escorting her inside.

Mother was overcome by his gallant attention, and starting dimpling and smiling, though she'd told me on our journey over there that she'd take him to task and call him a cad and a rotter.

Daniel turned back to me as he was showing Mother upstairs and pulled such a funny face that I nearly burst out laughing.

Cassie and the baby were in the large bedroom at the front of the house. It was clear that she shared the double bed with Daniel, but she had managed to Cassie-fy the entire room. It was papered with a blue rose wallpaper. Matching blue silk roses adorned the dressing-table mirror and dangled decoratively from the white wardrobes. The silk coverlet on the bed was a deeper blue that set off the pale pink of Cassie's skin to perfection. She was wearing a soft white nightgown embroidered with tiny daisies and had threaded delicate artificial daisies in her long fair hair.

She held the baby in her arms. When we stooped to look, we saw that he really *was* a little cherub. I was usually indifferent to the charms of any baby, but this small nephew of mine was enchanting. He was pale pink with a rosebud mouth. He had large blue eyes with long lashes, and very soft downy hair of the palest gold. He was wide awake, but he didn't screw up his face and wail. He calmly gazed up at Cassie, and let himself be cuddled by Mother, and then me, without protest.

'The little lamb. The perfect pet! Oh, the darling boy!' Mother cooed. Then she sat herself down beside Cassie and cradled her too. 'Oh, Cass, I've missed you so. Look at you, prettier than ever! Are you all right, dearie? Your confinement wasn't too difficult?'

'Oh, I shrieked so loud the midwife threatened to give me a good slapping,' said Cassie. 'The pain! I'm never letting Daniel come near me again.' But it was obvious from the way she was looking at him that she didn't mean a word of it.

Cassie had Daniel and little Danny. Mother had Father and all the babies. But since that terrible spring day when Mrs Roberts told me that Morgan was dead, I had no one.

I stared at the incongruously beautiful blue sky as I walked to the factory day after day and wanted to scream with the pain of it.

'Never mind, Opal. You'll meet another young man soon enough,' Mother said, trying to give me some kind of clumsy comfort.

Even Cassie didn't understand.

'After all, you weren't really grown-up sweet-hearts, you and Morgan. You're still only fifteen, Opal. You must try not to mope so and have a little fun.'

There was only one person who understood – Mrs Roberts. On the rare occasions she came to the factory we recognized the anguished expression on each other's face, though we barely spoke now.

She was absent for two months and the folk at the factory murmured anxiously. Mr Beeston was summ-oned to her house with the accounts books. He was questioned determinedly on his return, but he wouldn't say a word about Mrs Roberts and her situation. The girls in the design room thought she must be seriously ill. Maybe she'd lost her mind with grief.

She reappeared in early June, very pale and noticeably thinner, but she looked composed and beautiful in her pale violet blouse and black silk skirt. She sent for me almost immediately.

I went to her, not really feeling anxious. I was so eaten up with sorrow that I couldn't care about anything else.

'Hello, Opal. Sit down,' Mrs Roberts said quietly. 'How are you feeling? You don't look very well.'

I shrugged listlessly. I'd lost weight too because I couldn't be bothered to eat properly. I'd lost my new figure so that my clothes all drooped on me now.

'I know you must be missing Morgan dreadfully,' said Mrs Roberts. 'I think it's affecting your work.' She picked up one of my recent box lids. 'They're not really fairies any more, they're more like little sorrowing angels.'

I knew she was right.

'I'm sorry. I can't seem to paint them any other way,' I mumbled.

'I understand. They're exquisite in their own way but just not appropriate. Still, it doesn't really matter now.' She sounded very ominous.

I stared at her. 'Are you – are you sacking me?'

'I'm sacking everyone, Opal, even me,' she said sadly.

'What do you mean?'

'I'm closing Fairy Glen.'

'You're closing the factory?' I was so shocked I could only echo her dumbly.

'I'm going to announce it today. It's been very hard to keep going with just women and the older men.

And the sugar supplies are so sporadic now, our situation isn't viable. Our profits are down dramatically. If I don't close, we will simply slide into bankruptcy.'

'But you promised that everyone would have their jobs back when they returned from the war,' I said.

'Opal, there will be precious few of our men returning from this war,' she said. 'I feel very sad about all my loyal workers now, but there's a big new munitions factory opening in Miledon, and many will find work there.'

'Couldn't you just close for the duration of the war?'

'Who knows when it will end? And to tell you the truth, Opal, I've simply lost heart. I can't see the point of struggling to keep the factory going when Morgan isn't here to take over. I don't care about it any more.'

I nodded dully, understanding.

'But I do still care about you,' she added.

'I don't think you do,' I said. 'You made it very plain that you didn't want me anywhere near Morgan.'

Mrs Roberts sighed. 'Yes, I did. I wouldn't have minded if you were simply friends, but it was more than that.'

'It was much more,' I said. I felt the tears welling up, though I had never cried at work.

'I know,' said Mrs Roberts. She took a deep breath.

'I know how much Morgan meant to you. And he thought the world of you too, he made that plain enough. If he'd come back, I'm sure the two of you would have been devoted, for all that you're still so young. I wouldn't have been able to stand in your way. So for that reason – and because I *am* fond of you, Opal – I want to help you.'

'How can you help me?' When I said it, I sounded sullen and bitter. I didn't mean it that way. I was just past caring about anything.

'What are you going to do with the rest of your life?' Mrs Roberts asked.

I shrugged again. 'I suppose I'll have to go and work in the munitions factory too, though obviously I won't be painting fairies on each bullet.'

'I think we both agree that you're not really suited to factory life. Wouldn't you like to finish your education?'

'You mean go back to school?'

'I could talk to your headmistress. Perhaps you could resume your scholarship.'

I thought about it. Father earned very little as a newspaper seller, but we could probably scrape by with his meagre wages and Mother's baby money. My old school uniform was still in the back of my wardrobe.

I tried to imagine putting it on, sitting in lessons, arguing with Miss Mountbank, listening to music with Mr Andrews, resuming my friendship with

Olivia. I thought of Miss Reed berating me for my artwork. I felt bereft when I had to leave to work at Fairy Glen, but now I couldn't picture myself back there. I had grown too old to turn myself back into a schoolgirl.

'I don't see myself fitting in any more,' I said. 'Not that I ever did, really. But too much has happened to me, and I've missed out on nearly two years' work. I don't think I could manage. I don't even want to try.'

'I understand,' said Mrs Roberts. 'I don't think it's a sensible idea, either, but I still think you might benefit enormously from further education. Have you ever thought about art school?'

'Art school?'

'You're very talented, and we've benefited from your innovative ideas, but I think your art needs developing. You don't want to confine yourself to fairies all your life, do you, Opal? I think you could go far as an artist if you had the proper training.'

'But aren't I too young for art school?'

'Not nowadays, when so many young men are away in France. All the main art schools are accepting younger students, so long as they are exceptionally talented and disciplined. I have taken the liberty of writing to Mr Augustus Spenser, the principal of the Royal College of Art, and sent him a couple of your box lids. He wants to interview you first, but will certainly consider you for a place starting in September.'

'But how will I pay the fees?'

'He will give you a scholarship. And I am going to give you a small annual bursary. I think it would be a good idea for you to leave home. We can find you a young ladies' hostel. I think it's time you made a completely fresh start, Opal.'

I couldn't stop the tears rolling down my cheeks.

'Would you like that?'

'Yes, I would. I would dreadfully. It's so very kind of you. But what about you, Mrs Roberts? Can you make a fresh start too?'

'It's a little late in the day for me, but I shall try. I'm planning to shut up my house and live on the farm in Scotland for a while. There are too many memories at home. So will you accept my offer?'

'Yes please,' I said.

I stood up, walked round her desk, hesitated for a second, and then hugged her hard. We clasped each other tightly, both crying now.

30

So I went to art school. It was a revelation. The tutors were so different from schoolteachers – relaxed and casual, but brilliant at guiding and suggesting. At first I drew and painted on a very small scale, stuck in fairyland, but they encouraged me to be bolder, and soon I was filling each canvas with confidence. I didn't care for my work at first. I had to unlearn many self-taught slick tricks. But I could see that I was gradually improving.

I was desperately shy initially. The other students

were all so bright and confident and colourful. I felt like a dull little sparrow amongst a flock of parakeets. They nearly all came from better families than mine. They might swear and tell shocking stories, but their accents were cut-glass. Most of them had money, though they affected poverty with their bright market-stall scarves and unravelling jerseys.

I kept myself to myself at first, but they were curious and friendly and repeatedly asked me to tea, to supper, to impromptu parties. I couldn't resist for more than a couple of weeks. By the end of the term I was firm friends with everyone.

I got to know the boys as well as the girls. There was one boy, Sam, who became my particular friend. He also came from a humble background. His father was a window cleaner. During the vacation Sam went out to help his father. He had to work one-handed because he had a withered arm, but he managed wonderfully, climbing up the tallest ladders and then locking his knees in the rungs while he washed the windows vigorously with his one good hand.

He had tried to enlist in spite of his bad arm, but had been turned down. Some of the other boys manufactured spurious ailments when conscription came in. I couldn't blame them – but I didn't respect them, either.

I found myself spending more and more time with Sam. He was always patiently friendly, even when I was going through a very dark time. I'd told him about Morgan and he understood.

'I like you very much, Sam, but you do realize I can only ever be friends,' I said. 'I can't ever love anyone but Morgan.'

'I understand,' he said. 'Though I'll stick around just in case you ever change your mind.'

We painted portraits of each other. I think he flattered me outrageously. My portrait of him was more exacting, catching the resolution in his face as well as his determined cheeriness.

I painted Morgan too, of course. I did quick pencil sketches, I worked in smudgy charcoals, I painted miniature watercolours, I spent weeks on elaborate oil portraits. I had no photograph for a likeness but I felt I didn't need one. All I had to do was close my eyes and I could see him now.

By the end of my final year at art college his image wasn't quite so clear. I could reproduce the portraits I'd already done, but when I strained for some new aspect, Morgan stayed vague and hazy in my mind's eye.

I was terrified he was fading away – though perhaps I secretly welcomed it. Sam and I and four of the other students planned to spend the summer in Cornwall, living off bread and cheese and beer, and painting all day long in the open air. I was looking forward to it tremendously. I knew what that summer might also entail. I was ready to start a proper relationship with Sam, but I felt so guilty, as if I were betraying Morgan.

I went back home the day before we were due to leave. I visited Mother and Father. Mother tutted over my red blouse and turquoise skirt and purple stockings. Father patted me absentmindedly, almost as if he didn't quite know who I was.

I went to Hurst Road and spent several hours with Cassie and Daniel and little Danny and new baby Viola. Cassie was larger and more luscious than ever. Daniel and I discussed painting with fervour. I built bricks with Danny and cradled tiny Viola, wondering if I'd ever want children myself.

Then I walked all the way to Fairy Glen house. The factory had never reopened and was now being pulled down. It had seemed so strange seeing the ripped open walls and crumbled brick.

The nearer I got to the house, the more anxious I became, afraid it might be demolished too. The gates at the start of the long driveway were locked, but I was so determined that I hitched up my skirts and climbed right over. I fell heavily and grazed my knees. I was almost running by the time the house came into view.

I peered in through the windows on the ground floor and saw white sheets over all the furniture. I wondered if Mrs Roberts had taken all the paintings up to Scotland with her.

I went round the side of the house, and stared at the garden in horror. The ivy had almost taken over. There were still flowers in the borders, but weeds rioted everywhere, choking all the blooms. The stream still trickled in spite of vast tangles of waterweed. I followed it to the end of the garden. The little Japanese house was lurid green with moss. I sat on the cold seat and shut my eyes tight.

I remembered the times I'd sat there with Morgan. I thought of him now in some dreadful muddy grave in France.

'I'll try to believe in ghosts, Morgan,' I whispered. 'Come to me now. Haunt me for ever. Please. I'm waiting. I still love you so.'

I waited for hours, but all I heard was the whisper of the leaves, all I saw was the ivy-strewn wreck of the garden.